Third Strand of the Cord

A Novel of Love in Liberty

Catherine Richmond

 Formatted with Vellum

For all the students, families, teachers, paraprofessionals, and therapists I was privileged to work with - you inspire me!

Prologue

The motor rumbled beneath the floor of the Brookline townhouse, opening the garage door and doubling Caroline's heart rate.

"Daddy's home!" A quaver tainted her forced cheerfulness. She crossed the living room floor and knelt beside her baby. Her hair fell in a dark brown curtain around him. *If only I could hide you with my body, keep you safe like those first nine months.* She dried his chin with a corner of the quilt. "Ready? Time to do your stuff."

The purr of the engine filled the garage for a moment, then cut off. The car door shut with a solid thunk. An electric prickle laced Caroline's skin. She kissed the baby, then rolled him onto his round belly, facing him toward the stairs. "Show time!"

Orienting to the echo of footsteps, the baby alerted. His head rolled from cheek to chin, and bobbed up once. Eyebrows leading, his face raised an inch off the blanket.

"You can do it," Caroline whispered. Palms damp, she sat back on her heels.

The baby lifted his arms, then corrected himself, pushing his forearms beneath his shoulders. His head bobbed up to the grand elevation of two inches.

The door at the top of the stairs opened. Despite the two hour flight from Chicago, Bryan Ashcroft remained impeccably dressed, his navy blue Armani suit unwrinkled, every dark hair molded in place. Ice blue eyes narrowed at his son. "Caroline, that rug was a gift to my family from the Shah of Iran. I do not want it ruined."

Tears will only make it worse. "Bryan, look! He can hold his head up."

"No doubt that qualifies him for Harvard." Bryan set his leather suitcase on the hardwood floor. "I was looking forward to a quiet evening, just the two of us. You've disappointed me. Again." Frowning, he circled her. "I see you missed your salon appointment."

Caroline ran her fingers through her hair. When they were dating, she found Bryan's attention to her appearance flattering. Now his observations seemed petty. "Did you read the articles I printed out?"

"I'm busy." He crossed to the liquor cabinet. He lifted the Waterford decanter, measuring the level of Glenlivet, then poured two fingers of Scotch whiskey into a crystal shot glass. "Nothing you read is going to change him. His chromosomes are defective; he's defective. You need to take him up to that school and leave him, so we can get on with our lives. You haven't even asked about the deal I closed."

The baby's head dropped back to the blanket, but his eyes continued to follow the man.

"I'm not ready to leave him with a sitter, and I'm certainly not ready to leave him at some boarding school way up in New Hampshire. I'm still breast feeding."

"So stop."

"It's the best way to feed a baby. With good care, he can be healthy, attend a regular school with special help, even hold down a job."

"Job? What sort of job could a retard do?"

Caroline flinched. "Assembly, restaurant work, clean up." She bit her tongue. No Ashcroft ever cleaned his own house, much less did janitor work. "There's even an actor with Down syndrome on TV."

"Television is full of idiots." Bryan drained the glass with a silent swallow. The wind shifted over Boston Harbor. Sleet ticked on the mullioned windows. "If good care's so important, then I fail to see your objection to this boarding school. They're the experts."

"He's only two months old." She cupped the silky head in her palm.

"Caroline, stop being sentimental. He doesn't know you. He won't miss you."

"I'd rather raise him at home." She couldn't keep her words steady. "Look how much progress he's made."

"Call your obstetrician and get something for this postpartum depression. Pull yourself together. Mother's flying in from Belgium Tuesday, and I want this settled."

"Won't she want to see her grandson?"

"Her grandson?" Bryan thumped the glass on the marble-topped cabinet. "No one in my family, and I have seen portraits of six generations, looks like that." He dismissed the drooling baby with a wave of his hand.

Patience... "The geneticist in the hospital explained all people with Down syndrome have eyes like this."

"That quack? Where did he go to school? Wisconsin? Probably trained on cattle."

"Mayo Clinic, Rochester, Minnesota."

"I called a real genetics specialist over at Harvard." Bryan loomed over her and the baby. "It didn't come from my side of the family. Much as I'd like to continue the Ashcroft family line, I'm willing to overlook your problem on the basis of our past relationship." His fingertips touched the crown of her head. His voice dropped to a whisper. "He will be better off at school. This house wasn't designed for a sickly child. He might fall down the stairs." Bryan's cold hand moved to her neck.

"Bryan!" Caroline tried to move away, but his hand encircled her throat. "You're scaring me."

He continued in the same low tone of voice, as if he hadn't heard. "His heart might give out. He might quit breathing. Sudden Infant Death."

7

Caroline pulled his wrist. His grip tightened, cutting off her air. Her vision dimmed. Consciousness slipped.

The door to the study slammed.

Caroline gasped and slumped to the floor. Gathering the baby in her arms, she let her tears overflow. *I will keep you safe.*

Chapter One

Another IEP from hell. The first rule of Individual Educational Plan conferences should be bring chocolate. And Diet Coke. Caroline fidgeted on the hard first grade chair, positioned under the vent of the fire-breathing furnace. Its blast pummeled the construction paper hearts suspended overhead. The heat amplified her hot paint and solvent odor, announcing that she'd only had time for a quick scrub with a baby wipe on the drive from the plant to school.

Caroline wondered if anyone would notice if she snuck a couple aspirin from her purse. Why sneak? The rest of the team looked equally pained. The special education teacher and regular first grade teacher rearranged their stacks of papers showing how they adapted the curriculum to accommodate Trent. The speech therapist fiddled with her Harley-Davidson earrings. The occupational therapist picked white glue off her fingers. The physical therapist froze in a listening posture, leaning forward, head tilted slightly. Only her drooping eyes gave away the fact she had fallen asleep.

The school psychologist began her formal report. "I evaluated Bryan..."

"Trent," Caroline interrupted. "He goes by his middle name."

The psychologist made a note in her folder, probably "mother retains anger against ex-husband." She droned through her recitation of Trent's stubbornness, passive behavior, aggressive behavior, passive-aggressive behavior, social immaturity, and three year lag in cognitive development.

I know he's behind. Caroline had read countless notes about off-task behavior, poor seat tolerance, lack of cooperation. In conferences and phone calls the teacher had informed her of fights, destructiveness, refusal to follow directions. *Don't pound it in with a hammer.*

The meeting ground to a close with the decision to discontinue mainstreaming and return Trent to the Special Ed room until his behavior improved. Numb with failure, Caroline scrawled her name on the forms. Times like this she wished she were part of a two parent household, having someone to sit with in the parent corner. Sharon Buffum, her sitter, would be the appropriate person to ask, but then who would watch Trent?

"Mrs. Jameson." The O.T. held out a scrap of paper. "I'm a single mom too, and I know how difficult it is to find time and energy for after-school activities. Karate's only one hour a week. Now that the new Community Center has opened, it's close to home for you."

Karate? So Trent can act out his aggression more efficiently?

The P.T. came to life. "Karate would be a great way to work on Trent's balance, strength, kicking skills..."

"Motor planning, coordination, body scheme," the O.T. continued.

"And self control and attention span." The psychologist snapped her briefcase closed. "The small group atmosphere would promote social skill development. In the absence of a father in the home, a strong male role model can have a positive effect on a boy's self-esteem."

The O.T. flashed her colleague a dirty look. "Lee has a lot of experience with kids, with and without handicaps. My boys dropped softball and soccer, thank God, but stuck with karate because he's such a great teacher. Here's the number of the Community Center."

Caroline took the offered square of paper and crumpled it into her pocket, feeling under the dry cleaning ticket and last week's grocery receipt in hopes of a stray M&M. No such luck, just like the rest of her life.

"LITTLE BOXES ON THE HILLSIDE," Caroline hummed the Malvena Reynolds song as she turned into her subdivision. Plopped onto a field on the Kansas City side of Liberty, Missouri, the development wasn't ugly, just too new for charm. Last spring several neighbors, the optimists, had begun gardening. Make that landscaping. Only her sitter planted anything as practical as vegetables. Caroline parked her pickup in her garage and trudged across the street.

Sharon met her at the door with Trent's backpack. "How'd the meeting go?"

"Excedrin headache number IEP."

The sitter gave her a sympathetic nod. "Wish I could say it's been better here. A bunch of kids came over after school to shoot baskets. Trent ended up with a knot on his head. Half of the guys called it a fight. The rest said no, Trent walked into the boy's elbow."

Caroline sank against the foyer wall. Her energy level downshifted into low gear. "After everything the school just told me, I'd be inclined to believe Trent was the aggressor. Know what they want me to do about it? Enroll him in a karate class."

"Karate?" Sharon tapped her chin, her grim expression melting into a smile. "I bet Lee is teaching at the new Community Center."

"You know this Lee?"

She nodded. "He taught the home school group for their PE credit. Luke and Paul are crazy about him. Find out what time the class is. Maybe I can take Trent when the boys swim."

"Ma! Ma!" A three-foot-high whirling dervish tackled his mother in the knees. "Ma! 'lo!"

Caroline captured him by his round cheeks. His eye socket had already taken on a purplish black sheen. "Ow, Trent. What happened?"

"Pay bah, Ma!" With a proud grin, the boy slipped out of his mother's arms. He dashed out the door and across the street.

"Trent!" Caroline raced after him, nabbing him at the locked door of their split-level. "You could get run over. You need to wait for Mom to cross the street with you." She shook him. "Hold Mom's hand. Do you understand?" *No, he doesn't understand.*

Caroline unlocked the door. Trent dashed into the playroom, dumping boxes of toys onto the carpet. Lego blocks, little cars, play-sets. "No, no, Trent. One box at a time, remember?" *No, he doesn't remember.*

She plodded out of the rec room to the kitchen. After the rough day at work and the even rougher IEP, Caroline wanted nothing more than to collapse on the sofa with a bag of M&M's. She started dinner.

"No, Trent, not so loud," she called several times. Head pounding from Disney's *Cinderella*, Caroline waded through the toys and adjusted the volume on the DVD player. "That's too loud. You're hurting Mom's ears." The boy waved her out of his way.

Back in the kitchen, she dialed the number the school had given her for the behavioral specialist. Office hours are nine to three, the recorded message informed. Nine to three? Caroline slammed the phone down. She couldn't afford to miss work, even if her health insurance would pay part of the fee. And Trent would have to be pulled out of school. Wouldn't that reward him for his misbehavior?

Sports weren't in her plans, but never let it be said she'd passed up an opportunity to help her child. She retrieved the Community Center's number from her pocket. A real person answered. One point for karate, Caroline thought. She jotted down the class day and time.

The water boiled in the pot. Caroline added macaroni and frozen broccoli cuts. Out of the corner of her eye, she saw a naked boy sneak past the kitchen. "Trent?"

He took off for the upstairs bathroom at full speed.

Swearing under her breath, Caroline filled a bucket with soapy water. A search of the rec room revealed the wet spot on the carpet. Scrubbing on her hands and knees, Caroline continued to growl. "School thinks he's a terror there, they should see him at home." *He just gets too busy playing to remember to use the toilet.* She threw his wet sweatpants and underwear into the washer.

Upstairs, the pasta and vegetables had boiled to the consistency of oatmeal. Caroline drained the mess and added the cheese powder. She called Trent. No response. She dragged him out of the bathroom, dressed him in his pajamas, and hauled his limp body to the kitchen. Trent took a bite of congealed cheese and macaroni, and spit it in her face.

Caroline slammed her hand on the table. "No spitting!"

Trent flopped to the floor, sobbing. Maybe this is what the speech therapist meant: he can't verbally express his feelings about dinner, so he acts out. What a terrible mother.

"I'm sorry." Caroline crawled under the table. "Show me what you want for dinner." She carried him to the cupboards.

"No, no, no." He shook his head until they came to the freezer. He pointed to the ice cream.

"That's dessert. After dinner. How about a sandwich? Hot dog?"

Trent wriggled out of her grasp and ran to his room. His door slammed.

Caroline flinched. She shoveled the ruined dinner down the disposal. Her tired body traipsed up to her bedroom. She decided to shower, then go straight into her pajamas. Sitting on the bed to remove her shoes, the temptation grew too strong. Caroline flopped back onto the comforter. She still had to go through Trent's backpack, run a load of laundry so he'd have clean clothes for school, pack her own lunch for tomorrow, get the daily pile of bills from the mailbox. If she could find the energy.

Why? she asked the ceiling. *Why does he have to be handicapped? How am I ever going to survive this child? Help!*

God had helped her. She had an engineering degree, a job with generous pay and benefits, and a wonderful sitter. What more did she need?

A chair scraped across the kitchen floor.

Caroline shoved her feet into her slippers and raced down to the kitchen. She closed the freezer door and returned the chair to its place at the table. One of the more annoying *Barney* songs sounded from the rec room.

"Trent?" Caroline found him on the sofa, picking marshmallows out of the Rocky Road. Dark brown hand prints muddied the patterned upholstery. "Trent, you know you have to eat dinner before dessert." *Does he know?* "We eat in the kitchen." She snatched the soggy carton from him. A small, sticky middle finger flashed in her face. Caroline grabbed the offending hand and jerked her son off the sofa. *You're going to dislocate his shoulder.* "No! Don't. Where did you learn that? Pointing with your long finger is a very bad thing to do, very rude. No, no." She scrubbed Trent hard enough to peel off a layer of skin and dumped him in bed. His snuffling cries followed her through the house and out the door.

She dragged to the end of the driveway and leaned on the mailbox. If she wasn't so tired, she'd run away. Far away. Down the street and into the night. Perhaps Bryan had been right, Trent would be better off in a special school, with experts.

No!

She could do this. All she needed now was… a fairy godmother. White hair, huggable, and a magic wand to make everything right. Bibbidi-bobbidi-boo.

Pray for a fairy godmother? Get real. Caroline gathered the mail and returned to the now quiet house. Electric bill? Top of the fridge. Lingerie catalog? Trash. Pizza coupons? Under the phone. Valentine's card from Marnie? Oh yeah. The front showed a well-muscled man wearing only cowboy hat. He held a strategically placed heart-shaped candy box. Inside, her friend wrote: "Wishing you one of these. Bring his brother the next time you come to Boston. -Marnie."

Even more improbable than a fairy godmother.

Caroline zipped open her son's Tyrannosaurus Rex backpack. A wad of papers stuck together. She peeled the notice for softball sign-up and Trent's daily behavior chart off a sheet of red construction paper. A white heart-shaped doily had received a generous glob of glue. The words *Happy Valentine's Day* were printed neatly in marker across the top. Across the bottom, crayon traced over pencil lines: *to Mom, love Trent.*

Chapter Two

Lee rooted through the trunk of the ancient Volkswagen parked by the Liberty Community Center and Performing Arts Theater. Gotta clean up. Next time he visited his sister, he'd use her vacuum, maybe the window cleaner, too. If his students saw this mess-

Regardez donc! A little boy dashed across the front parking lot. Lee scanned the area for traffic. Nothing yet. A woman called to the boy. She shut the door of an emerald green late-model pickup. Bet her husband owns one of those construction companies throwing subdivisions all over the county. Short navy blue coat and dress slacks. Junior league type. At least she's wearing loafers, not spiked heels. Lee flexed his bare toes on the cold pavement. As long as the kid was safe, he'd let her do the chasing.

The boy headed for the street. Slamming the hatch of the compact, Lee tensed his body to sprint. The woman put on a spurt of speed and caught the boy by the hood of his windbreaker. The kid wriggled out of the jacket and bolted toward Lee. His small, round face lit up with an open-mouthed grin. He flopped his arms instead of pumping. His feet slapped the ground as if his shoes were too large. Down syndrome. *My student.*

Lee stuck his thumbs in the belt of his *gi*. The woman yelled. A few steps later she snagged the child. The evening air carried her shaking voice delivering a lecture. Mom's no brighter than the kid, Lee decided. The boy said something, one syllable. The woman bent over to hug him, still talking. She took the kid's hand and headed for the door of the Community Center, making the sidewalk before two minivans pulled into the parking lot. Just outside the door, the kid flopped onto the cement. Lee jerked on the ends of the white *obi* he wore for teaching. He expected this foolish woman to wring her hands helplessly. Instead she tucked the kid under her arm like a shopping bag and pushed through the double doors.

Lee shook his head. Ought to charge her double.

CAROLINE WEDGED Trent between her body and the Community Center information desk. Catching her breath, she asked an elderly lady in a warm-up suit for the karate class.

"Ya!" Trent kicked the counter.

"No, we don't kick! Very bad!" Caroline dragged him out of range. Good thing brick red doesn't show sneaker marks. She apologized to the woman.

"Lee's in the gym. Downstairs, end of the hall." Her nylon sleeve rustled as she pointed.

A second mother-son pair passed them as Trent marked time down the stairs. The boy, a child with Down syndrome, a couple years older than Trent, held the door open for them. Well-behaved and neatly groomed. Bet his mother doesn't work outside the home.

"You've come to the right place." His mom smiled.

She followed them into the gym, its new paint smell noticeable even to a nose accustomed to the odor.

"Kurt, bring your buddy over here and show him where to put his socks and shoes." A man motioned to them from the mat. He seemed lumpy, a karate uniform belted around a bean bag chair. His accent carried a little thicker Southern drawl than usually heard in Kansas City.

"We planned to observe tonight," Caroline informed him. "Trent's not enrolled."

"That's OK." The instructor's focus remained on the group of kids collecting on the mat. Sandy hair, nearly white, curled to his shoulders. "Shoes off," he signed and spoke at the same time.

Caroline bent to help her son.

"Hi, Trent. I'm Lee. Who's taking karate, you or Mom?"

Trent giggled and patted his chest.

"Then you take off your shoes, and Mom have a seat."

Caroline sent him a dirty look that said she was just trying to help, but the instructor had moved on to another student. She joined the other parents on the folding chairs, sitting on their far side so they wouldn't see her sneak Hershey Kisses from her pocket.

"Where are you going, sprout?" Lee grabbed a wobbly girl, pulling her into his lap.

"Chicken?" she asked, holding up her shoe.

Lee shook his head. "Shoe. And you've got one on the other foot, too."

Kurt, the older boy, showed Trent how to stow his socks in his shoes and leave them next to the wall. They sat next to an overweight girl. A boy Caroline recognized from Trent's school stomped in.

"Hey, Marco, you're late," Lee noted. "What did your P.T. say about wearing your AFO's during karate?"

"She say OK."

"OK, what? OK to wear them, or OK to take them off?"

"OK off." The boy unfastened the Velcro holding the translucent plastic braces to his ankles.

"Cool." Lee consulted a notebook. "Patrick, where he's at?"

Kurt shook his hand in front of his stomach.

"Good signing, Kurt, but the rule is you talk, too."

He tried again. "Sick."

"Then, let's get started. *Cha-ryot!*" Lee led the group through a series of warm up exercises and stretches. He introduced two stances: rest and attention.

Caroline held her breath as Trent followed instructions without tantruming. He wiggled constantly, doing a bump and grind to a song only he could hear. Lee reprimanded him with a word. Her son gazed up at the big man with his mouth open. A line of saliva dripped from the child's bottom lip. Without commenting, Lee held out a tissue box. After a long moment, Trent took a tissue and wiped his chin. Caroline sighed—she'd been working on "dry chin" all his life. The wobbly girl giggled. Lee playfully tapped her on the head with the tissue box.

"Well, guys and girls, I promised you I'd break a board this week, but I left the wood in my car."

"Ma!" Trent even raised his hand.

"Your mom, she would go get the board for us?" Lee dug a key out of his duffel bag and pointed to the side door. "It's a Volkswagen, light blue with chicken pox."

"Chicken!"

The Volkswagen's chicken pox turned out to be severe corrosion. Caroline raised the hatch, showering herself with rust. What a mess! Did the instructor live in his car? She rooted under grocery sacks of clothes, a sleeping bag, and a box of kitchen utensils until she came up with a one by four plank.

The students applauded her return.

Lee tapped the wood with his knuckle. "Your mom picked a good one, Trent." Her son bounced with pleasure. The instructor positioned Eva, the older girl, with the board between her outstretched arms. "How am I going to hold my hand?"

The class curled their hands into fists, thumbs tight across the fingers. Inspecting each one, Lee indicated his approval. He adjusted Eva's grip on the board. "Nervous?"

She nodded shyly.

"Not as nervous as me." He stepped back and raised his right arm. The entire class yelled "hai-yah!" with him. His bean bag body solidified just for the second it took for his arm to flash through the air. The board snapped in two. The kids cheered.

Lee bowed to them. "A few weeks from now, you're going to break your own board. Say 'yes, sir'."

Kurt managed a weak "Yes, sir". The rest giggled.

The instructor stood at attention. "Loud and proud."

"Yes, sir!"

"See you next week." Lee pointed to Trent. "Except you. Front and center, Mr. Trent." The karate instructor grew a couple feet as he loomed over the boy. Trent tried a smile. Lee remained grim—one bushy eyebrow raised, his mouth a fierce line under his droopy mustache, arms crossed over his chest.

"No running in the parking lot. You want to run? You run here." His finger traced a circle around the room. "Four laps around the gym. Run. Now."

Trent took off jogging. Caroline reluctantly approached the instructor. He towered over her by at least six inches. "Trent seems to understand you."

"You should have seen his face when he got away from you. He knows exactly what he's doing."

Caroline's mother bear instinct kicked in. "Basically he's a good kid."

"*Mais*, no, he's not. Basically he's a stinker." Dark brown eyes flashed in her direction. "We all are. We all need some authority—police, boss, parent—to keep us on the straight and narrow." He glowered at Trent. The boy picked up his speed. "Some day he's going to outweigh you, he's not going to look so cute, he's going to work for someone who won't tolerate his acting up. You've got to get him under control now."

A hot fudge sundae would taste real good...

Caroline leaned against the cinder block wall next to her son's shoes. Did this guy think she wanted Trent to misbehave? Mothering was a lot harder than it looked, a lot harder than repairing machines. At the plant she had senior engineers, vendors, maintenance to call on. At home, no one. She had read dozens of research articles on Down syndrome and spent as much time with her son as her job allowed. Social events and hobbies had been abandoned at his birth. Despite all her efforts, all her hard work, Trent grew more difficult every day. She sure didn't need some arrogant jock telling her what a bad job she was doing.

"And your child psychology degree is from...?" The second she said it, she wished she could take it back. It sounded like something Bryan would say.

A muscle twitched under Lee's eye. "Sorry, ma'am, my only diploma is from Jeff Davis High." His voice lowered and took on a fierce edge. "Give me six weeks. If you're not happy with the class, you can have your money back."

He called "done" to Trent. A subdued boy plopped down next to her and put on his socks.

Lee stayed another minute to make sure Trent stayed on task. This was his favorite kind of kid, energetic, feisty. Lethargic students seemed to spiral into obesity no matter what he did. He always worried some undiscovered medical problem made them sluggish. Overly compliant students reminded him of kids he'd seen at the shelter, all the spirit beaten out of them. This boy, Trent, had enough smarts to figure out his mom's number, and enough spunk to keep her running. Out of the corner of his eye, he studied the mother. Sure, he'd been hard on her, probably the first time in her life anyone talked straight to her. Long overdue. She had to get this kid under control. It wouldn't be easy. Up close, her even features and snowflake patterned sweater confirmed his impression of old money. Old money green colored her eyes. The hardest thing this lady had ever done was chair a garden club luncheon. Or find a parking spot on the Plaza. Lee hoped the kid's father did better in the discipline department. He grabbed a pair of blown out sneakers, size 13, and glared at Trent one more time. "No running in the parking lot."

"Ya, su!"

"Next week park beside me," he ordered over his shoulder. "Rust isn't contagious."

Caroline did a double-take. She could have sworn he winked at her.

Chapter Three

"Ma? Ma!" Trent patted his mother's cheek.

"Ssh, Trent. It's Saturday." Caroline squinted through the gray dawn at the clock radio. Five twenty. He never got up this early on weekdays. "Go back to sleep."

"Ma." The boy pulled her arm from under the comforter and placed her hand on his soggy pajama bottoms. "Weh."

Caroline groaned. "Put your wet clothes in the bathtub and go back to sleep."

A moment later the bed shook with the arrival of a forty-pound boy. Caroline opened one eye. A naked forty-pound boy. "Sleep." She patted his smooth back. He flipped and flopped. Just one more hour sleep. Please. The day will go better. She held her breath. From the other side of the bed she heard a nasal snuffle followed by a long whistle. She opened her eyes. Trent giggled.

"Ma." He pointed to his mouth. "Ee."

"All right." Caroline stumbled out of bed. Trent danced around like a sprite. Certainly no humans were this lively at o-dark-hundred. She opened the curtains in his room. No lights shone in the frosty darkness. Not even dog owners got up this early. "Let's get you dressed first." The occupational therapist had asked her to work on dressing skills. With Caroline's 6:30 clock-in time, weekends were the only time to practice. She set out a flannel shirt, jeans, and underpants. "Come on. If you're up, you need to be dressed."

Singing Tigger's song from his Winnie the Pooh video, Trent turned his bed into a trampoline. Caroline ended up tackling the boy and forcing him into his clothes. So much for self-care skills. Yelling "ee!" he escaped to the kitchen. 6:12. Rising this early, even before the paperboy, warrants a big breakfast. Caroline pulled a box of waffles from the freezer and popped two into the toaster oven. The sprite clambered into the chair and swung his legs. Caroline leaned over to dry his chin. He pushed her hand away.

"Dry it yourself, then." She held out the napkin. He patted his face with a delicacy worthy of tea-time with the Queen. Caroline felt a smile crack her mask of fatigue. The toaster oven chimed. She set the plate in front of him. By the time she found the Log Cabin, one waffle had hit the floor and the other lay in shreds on the plate.

Should I punish him for making a mess or praise him for trying to help himself?

Without saying anything, Caroline poured the syrup. For two seconds she considered buying a dog to eat all the food falling on the floor, but a pet would take more time she didn't have. She tossed the dirty waffle out the window for the early rising sparrows. Maybe she could buy a bird feeder. Trent might enjoy bird watching.

"Ee! Ee!"

She heated two more waffles.

After breakfast, Caroline started a load of laundry and hauled out the vacuum. All this piano does is collect dust, she thought, running the brush over its keys. Ought to give it to someone who would play it, but then the living room would be completely empty. She felt out a few chords before closing the lid. No time.

"Ma!" Trent yanked the vacuum cord out of the plug.

"Don't do that, honey. You might shock yourself or damage the cord." He dragged her down to the rec room where he had dumped his Legos, race cars, and set of wooden blocks. She built a model of the Michigan Speedway. Trent won every race.

They headed for the mall after lunch. In J.C. Penney's boys' department, Caroline picked out Trent's spring wardrobe, then towed him to the dressing room. At entrance a loud buzzer sounded. Trent dug in his heels.

"Come on, honey. Let's try on your new clothes."

"No!" the boy screamed. He bent over, looking for the source of the noise. His head broke the light beam, sounding the alarm again.

Caroline sighed. Smart women shop by catalog. "Let's go home." She set off the buzzer on her way to the cash register. Trent stayed in the doorway, making long honks and short, rhythmic beeps. The noise drew children from all over the second floor. With the flamboyant gestures of a magician, he set off the buzzer with his whole body, then just a hand, elbow, foot. He stepped over the beam, then crawled under it. Scientific method, Caroline realized with a flash of surprise and pride. The clerk slapped her Visa card on the counter. Harried parents dragged their children away. The adults' irritation hit her like heat from a welding torch. She grabbed the shopping bag and her son.

Chocolate. "Let's go get a cookie."

"Cookie!" Trent repeated in the voice of a Sesame Street regular.

The physical therapist had reminded her to work on stairs. Caroline took her son's hand and started, one step at a time, down the long flight in the center court of the mall. Making the 180 degree turn at the landing, she looked up and discovered a backup, a dozen people shuffling behind them. She lifted the boy to her hip. Trent took advantage of her height, waving and calling to his followers. Vocational training for a parade float rider, Caroline thought. Unable to stop him while holding the heavy shopping bag, she hurried to the bakery. Trent chose a frosted cookie and Caroline picked a brownie. After a bite, Trent raced around the carpeted steps of the atrium, calling instructions to the hot air balloon decorations, his version of up, down, come here. He paused to say hello to a toddler in a stroller. The family gathered their shopping bags and left.

They were leaving anyway.

They're nervous about Trent.

Caroline detoured through Penney's sportswear on their way to

Catherine Richmond

the parking lot. As she checked slacks for length, Trent slipped from her hand and crawled under the clothes rack. "Trent?" She bent to look for him. Gone. She eyeballed each rack. One would be shaking from a little boy crawling under it. "Trent!" Beginning to perspire, she looked behind her. Any second now he'd pop up. No need to cause another scene. "Trent, time to go home."

"May I help you?" The name tag said Mickie. Gelled bangs curled from her forehead like antennae.

Caroline bit her lip. The last thing she wanted was a major spectacle, but she couldn't let Trent run loose. "My son. He was just here. He's six. About this tall, dark hair, doesn't speak."

The sales clerk frowned. "He's six and he doesn't talk?"

"He has Down syndrome."

The young woman spun on her heels. "I'll call security."

"Well, I'm sure he's right around here. Trent?" Her heart hammered in her throat.

Mickie alerted another clerk at the register. The second woman raced toward the mall entrance. The clerk spoke into the phone, then motioned for Caroline. "Ma'am? It sounds like they've already found him, over in catalog."

"Thank you." She jogged through lingerie, past optical. Trent sat on the counter. A blue-haired sales clerk paged through last year's Christmas catalog with him.

"Ma!" The boy gave her a quick grin, then returned to the colorful pictures of toys. He seemed totally unconcerned about being lost.

Caroline hugged him. "Trent! You need to stay with me. Don't run away. I was so worried."

The clerk sniffed. "He left the store with another family. They counted heads, realized he wasn't theirs and brought him back."

What could she say? *Yes, I know this disqualifies me for "mom of the year".* Or *Have you read O. Henry's "Ransom of Red Chief"? They wouldn't have kept him long.* She squeaked out "thank you." Carrying Trent, she sped out to her truck and buckled the boy in. *Just forget it. Forget going to the mall ever again. Go home and lock the door.* Home to the laundry wrinkling in the drier, the vacuum

24

snaking across the living room, the mess of toys littering the rec room. Except there's no groceries at home. She leaned her forehead on the steering wheel.

"Ma!" Trent shoved the glossy book under her nose. "Set, go!"

Caroline glanced at the picture of the race track. "Yes, Trent. Ready, set, go."

LEE BACKED the VW up to the laundromat. Usually he washed while he house-sat, but after last weekend's vandalism, the pastor asked him to stay at the church, which didn't have laundry facilities. Tipping open the ashtray, he counted quarters. Enough for one load. No problem. All his jeans had faded past harming his *gi*. He started the washer, then returned to the car. Another disadvantage of the church - the food was limited to graham crackers in the nursery. His grocery cache had dwindled to half a loaf of whole wheat from the stale-bread store. Nothing to put between the slices. He opened his wallet. "Lonely?" he asked George Washington. "Time to join a few brothers over at Food Barn."

He headed for the grocery store, crossing the street and cutting through Winstead's parking lot. Last week Dale Underwood had dashed out and invited Lee to join his family for dinner. He looked hopefully at the restaurant. No such luck today. Hunching his shoulders against the brisk west wind, he continued on to the grocery store.

Tuna or lunch meat? Tuna was up to 89 cents a can. He wandered back to the meat department. He could swing a package of baloney or a little bag of thin sliced roast beef. Turning to check the dairy aisle for cheap cheese, a crash echoed from the front of the store. Three steps to the left gave him a clear shot down the cereal aisle to the ten items or less line. A fallen rack of knitted caps and mittens lay on the floor. Two red-smocked cashiers and a lady in a peacoat worked to set the metal frame upright. A small boy wiggled back under the shopping cart seat belt. Little Houdini. Wait a minute. Isn't that the new kid from his Tuesday night class. Brent? No, Trent. Shoot, he pegged the mom as the kind who never took her kid anywhere. He figured she'd leave him with the dad or do all the errands while he was at school. Now here she tried to grocery shop while the little stinker took apart the store.

Lee crossed his arms over his chest and glared at the kid. His short legs stopped swinging. The toothy grin faded into a closed-lips pout. He looked down and folded his hands in his lap.

Baloney it is.

MID-SEMESTER AT COLLEGE, *sometimes MIT, other times Wayne. Caroline checked her schedule. She didn't recognize one of the classes listed. Wait a minute. She had attended the first day. Here's the syllabus. She should have read three books by now. She had missed two tests. The deadline for the research paper was yesterday. Caroline's heart raced. She'd never catch up. Could she drop the class? No, that deadline had passed, too. She was already overwhelmed, but if she worked twice as hard, twice as fast, maybe she could keep from flunking.*

Caroline gasped and sat up in bed. The nightmare, again. 3:18. She fanned herself with her perspiration-damp nightshirt. Try to sleep. Stop worrying.

I forgot to take the laundry out of the dryer.

CAROLINE UNLOCKED HER OFFICE DOOR. Something fast and silent flashed toward her feet. She stepped close to the door and let the roll of tape race by. A face leered from the shadows near the tutone base coat booth.

"Get back to work!" she told the Behr operator, knowing he couldn't hear her over the roar of the fans and rhythmic clunking of the assembly line.

Entering the office, she stepped around the night engineer's desk, admiring the new photo of his wife and baby. Her picture of Trent was almost that cute, according to her totally objective judgment. With a wry smile, she clicked into her computer for the night shift letter.

A siren howled. A yellow strobe flashed on the office's glass walls. Lights on the marquee indicated the number one robot faulted. Caroline hurried out of the office. A second siren went off. The clear coat hood. She thumbed the microphone switch at her collar and radioed maintenance for a ladder.

The superintendent yelled a cussword-studded question.

Caroline pulled a padlock from her belt and shut off the power. She stepped onto the gridded floor of the booth. Paint drips, melded into a pale lavender, pulled at her rubber overshoes.

Al Tully pushed past her, swearing and pointing at the unit up the line. The cab shone a bright white, but the box glowed a shade of pink reminiscent of Trent's last antibiotic prescription.

A second engineer stuck his head in. "Whoa. Looks like Caroline's painting a truck for her Mary Kay Cosmetics lady. Call the paint kitchen, ask what they're mixing up down there."

"No, the cab's fine. Must be a problem with this robot," she yelled over the sludge water flowing beneath her feet. "What's the problem with clear coat?"

"The hood's dripping on both booths."

Al started tinkering with the pushout. A splat of vermilion red hit Caroline in the leg.

"Hey!" In seconds the paint soaked through her coveralls and her slacks to her skin.

"Sorry," he grunted without looking up.

The maintenance guy arrived with the ladder.

"Set it up by the clipper stack," she directed. "One of the cat track lines must have an air leak."

He started to argue that possibility with her.

Taz dashed up. "Hey, what's going on? The line says we're getting pink boxes whenever a white unit follows a vermilion."

"I'd better see if we've got carryover with other combinations." The superintendent stormed off.

Now we'll get some work done.

"Jameson. You got a phone call."

"Take a message." Caroline grabbed her flashlight and put her foot on the first rung.

"It's your kid's school."

She groaned and ran to her office. "This is Ms. Jameson."

"Good afternoon," a woman's voice drawled. "I'm so sorry to have to bother you at work. This is Almeda Fisk, the playground supervisor at Liberty Elementary School. Now, you're Trent's mother, right?"

"Could I call you back?" Caroline shifted from one foot to the other.

"This will only take a moment." On the floor, the line supervisor repeated the shutdown's per-minute cost. "Today at recess, most of the kids were playing dodge ball, well some were shooting baskets, but your son Trent joined the dodge ball game. Somehow, well I didn't exactly see it happen, but it was reported to me immediately afterwards. We have several reliable witnesses. Trent evidently bit one of the other... "

"Was there blood?"

Behind Caroline the supervisor bellowed, "Sixteen hundred dollars, people! Get it fixed!"

"Well, no, but... "

"I'll call you later." Caroline hung up without waiting for the woman to say goodbye, and dashed back to the floor. *What a bad mother...*

As ORDERED, Caroline parked behind the Community Center, next to the instructor's VW. All week she promised herself she wouldn't put up with the aggravation of karate class. But after yesterday's biting incident... Sharon said Trent must have enjoyed karate; Trent had showed off his moves and talked about Lee all week. Caroline decided to give it another chance. She cut the engine. The gym door opened.

"Ya, su, Lee!" Trent waved to him from the car.

The big man leaned out the door, spearing Trent with his dead-serious gaze. No smile appeared under his scraggly mustache. Wasn't he glad they'd come back?

Trent clambered out of the truck and marched straight into the gym.

"Way to go." Lee held out his hand for a high five. His mustache twitched with a smile.

The gym door slammed in Caroline's face. "Don't mind me," she mumbled. "I'm just the mother."

As if he'd heard her, Lee opened the door. "The wind. Uh, you need to, uh, register at the front desk." His face turned a bright shade of red.

This man blushes?

Caroline raised an eyebrow at him, considering his candidacy as a male role model for her son.

At the desk the same athletic senior citizen greeted her, her sweatsuit of rainbow stripes making her look like a hot air balloon. While Caroline completed the registration form and wrote the tuition check, the lady sang the praises of Lee: decades of karate, black belt to the umpteenth dan, years of teaching experience, body guard for some 'name' that rang no bell. Caroline didn't realize karate had cheerleaders. Either this woman was on Lee's payroll or she was his mother.

Down in the gym, the kids finished warm-up exercises. Lee motioned to the boy who had been sick last week. "Patrick, come here."

The child's large eyes blinked. He took a step forward.

"Come here. You're not in trouble, but it looks like you grew last night." Kneeling in front of the trembling boy, Lee unfastened the top button of his polo shirt. "Better?"

The boy took a big breath and nodded. "Thank you."

Lee taught a fighting stance, left foot forward, right foot back. Good luck, Caroline thought, my kid doesn't know his left from his right. School says he still switches hands for writing and cutting. She pulled a Hershey kiss and a two months old *Car and Driver* from her purse.

If I had a wife like the other guys at the plant, I could keep up with my reading.

29

Lee ran the class through the maneuver several times until Trent was the only one not getting it.

"Look at the other kids, Trent. Do the same."

The boy checked out his fellow students, but his body stuck in the wrong position. Lee threw him several more clues. Nothing connected. Caroline squirmed on the bleachers. It's bad enough he's in a class for handicapped kids. Does he have to be at the bottom of the pile?

Finally the instructor lifted him under his armpits and rotated him into the correct position. Trent compared his body to the rest of the class. He gave a big goofy grin.

"You got it." Lee grinned back at him.

Towards the end of the hour, Lee brought the class to sit around him in a semi-circle. "Why are you in karate class?" he asked each student.

"Mom said." The big girl pointed to the gray haired woman next to Caroline.

"Chicken!" The little girl seemed to know only one word.

"Ninja Turtles," answered Kurt, the other boy with Down's.

Trent pantomimed fighting.

"Okay. So you take karate because your mom brings you, you want to learn some cool moves like the Ninja Turtles, and you want to learn to fight. I'll tell you why you really learn karate—for yourself. I've been doing martial arts a long time, before you were born. In all these years I've only had to defend myself, fight, three times. I kept doing karate after my mom wasn't around to tell me. I do it to take care of my body. Use your body for good things. Do a good deed for your mom and dad. See you next week."

Trent put his socks and shoes on by himself. Caroline felt she should say something to the instructor, but she couldn't organize her thoughts. He grabbed a nylon gym bag and headed for the men's locker room.

Sodium vapor lamps cast yellow circles around the building. Lee's VW seemed to be leaning toward her truck. A flat tire. Caroline reached for the gym door to warn the instructor. Locked. May as well get the flat off before it gets any colder. His car doors were locked, too. The slope of the driveway held the VW against the curb. She set up the jack from her truck and directed Trent in raising it while she loosened the lug nuts.

"Whoa, far enough, Trent." She slid the tire off the bolts. Bald. It's a wonder he didn't have a blowout. A silver circle smaller than a dime flashed in the glow of the truck's dome light. A roofing nail.

The gym door squeaked open. "Hey, you trying to steal my tires?" Lee's voice harshened with a threatening tone never heard in class.

"Sure. I didn't have enough danger in my life, so I'm swapping my new Goodyear steel belted radial 75R15's for your no-tread doughnuts." Expecting to be karate chopped in two, she turned to glare at him. The gym's light profiled the impressive contour of the man in his civilian clothes. Her employer's slogan flashed through her mind: *Built Ford tough*.

"Flah." Trent filled the gap.

"Flat?" Lee squeezed the tire. The tread collapsed onto the rim beneath his hand. He could flatten her easily.

Caroline took a deep, shaky breath. "If you would get your spare, please."

Lee unlocked the hatch and began tossing clothes from the luggage compartment into the backseat. "Thanks for changing my tire. Trent, you're doing a good deed for your *sensai*."

The boy scampered to his instructor's side, his mouth open with hero worship.

"Swallow." Lee chucked him under his chin. "Now here's a lesson for you: don't keep all your junk in your car. Makes it hard to find the spare... if I've got one. Yeah, here it is." He retrieved the tire from the narrow confines of its well. It dropped to the pavement with a mushy sound. Its sidewalls bulged under the weight of the rim.

"Out of air. I'll run you up to the gas station. Do you live far from here?"

"I'm staying out by Excelsior Springs."

Caroline rolled the punctured tire to the back of the truck.

"Better have this one patched. The others are in no better shape than the flat. All four should be replaced. Trent, hop in."

Lee hefted the tires into the truck bed, then joined the boy on the passenger seat. The man filled up the cab. He propped his elbow on the back of the seat, his hand inches from Caroline's shoulder. His other hand rested on his knee, way over by the glove compartment. "Buckle up," he signed to Trent, his arms forming a circle around the boy.

Caroline pulled out of the parking lot. "Why do you sign to him? He's not deaf."

"Forty percent of people with Down's have some hearing loss."

The plant was full of people who recite statistics, but ignore the obvious. Scorn dragged at her words. "His ears are fine."

"When I sign, I speak slower, enunciate clearly, use a limited vocabulary, give him a visual cue. He may understand more. That's the receptive pay-off. He may use sign when he speaks, improving the chances I'll understand him. The expressive benefit. Sign is a bridge to speech. When he learns to talk, he'll drop the signs. The community college has classes if you're interested."

When he learns to talk? "I'm interested, but I don't have time. What garage do you use?"

"There's a Total station and a Quik-Trip by the shopping center."

"Neither of which have service bays. Let's hope Firestone is still open."

His large hand smoothed Trent's hair. "Has he had an atlanto-axial x-ray?"

Caroline nodded. The pediatrician had explained some kids with Down's have a weakness in their neck vertebrae. Even a simple somersault can cause a broken neck.

The man leaned forward, propping an elbow on his knee. "And?"

"And what?"

"What did the x-ray show?"

"Normal." Caroline turned onto the residential street, the cut-through to the main drag.

"This is a radar trap."

Gritting her teeth, Caroline forced her foot off the accelerator. Her low beams reflected off the blue and white police cruiser parked on the left. They slid by just under the speed limit.

"Has he had any heart trouble?"

"No, not even a false alarm on the apnea monitor when he was a baby. How do you know all this medical information?"

"I read a lot, talk to people. Who's his doctor?"

"Armonk." The shopping center's lights glowed at the end of the street.

"He's all right. Just be sure, if you ever take him to a hospital, go to Children's Mercy. Liberty's okay for you, but Trent needs specialists."

"I'm just the mother."

The big man made a grinding gear noise in the back of his throat. "Sorry. I get so attached to these kids. Trent, stay with me. Don't touch anything."

"Ya, su!"

The boy panting at his heels, Lee took the punctured tire into the service bay. Caroline filled the spare at the air pump.

Lee took the spare from her. "Oh, good, you've got a tire gauge. It'll be ten or fifteen minutes. If you need to get home, I can walk back to the Community Center."

"Carrying two tires, one point four miles?" With a flip of her wrist, Caroline indicated he should stow the spare back in her truck.

"Do you need to call home, let your husband know you'll be late?" He wiped his hands on his *Missouri Special Olympics, Fort Leonard Wood* sweatshirt.

"No. And you?"

Lee shook his head. "We'll go over to McDonald's. Trent can use their playground while we wait." The boy slipped one hand into his instructor's, the other into Caroline's. They headed across the dark parking lot. A hot rod packed with teenage boys squealed around the corner into the drive-thru lane. *Just try something. I've got the bodyguard to the unknown with me tonight.*

"Kids with Down's should be kept five percent underweight

33

because of their tendency toward obesity as adults," Lee continued to lecture. "Keep him as active as possible."

Trent pulled on their arms, lifting his feet to clear the curb. "Whee!"

He's plenty active, thank you.

Blinking in the restaurant's fluorescent glare, Caroline stepped to the counter. "What would you like?" she asked Trent, but he and the instructor headed for the play area. Caroline ordered a Diet Coke and chose a booth to watch. The boy climbed to the top of the ladder. Reaching to steady the child, Lee's sweatshirt lifted, revealing two inches of trim waist. Amazing what a karate uniform concealed. He squatted at the end of the slide, his faded jeans upholstering muscular thighs and— *Get a grip. You're too old to ogle.*

"Lee!" One of the uniformed workers stepped from behind the counter.

"Let's see, it's Deana, right?" He pumped her hand, although Caroline had the impression the young woman wanted to hug him. "How're you doing?"

"Terrific. Passed the GED, so now I'm taking classes at Maple Woods. Been working here three months. Got my own apartment."

"Glad to hear it. Any more trouble?"

"Not from my boyfriend. But one night at closing, I used some of the techniques you taught us. Threw out a drunk who was getting too friendly."

"Way to go."

"Is this your family?"

Lee motioned Trent down the slide. "One of my karate students. Deana, this is Trent. Put out your hand, look her in the eye, and say hello."

"Ya, su! Hi!"

The woman looked skeptical. "He's..."

"Don't say it. He knows he's cute, and it goes right to his head if you mention it."

Caroline could tell "cute" wasn't the word on the tip of the woman's tongue.

The clerk backed away. "I've got to get back to work. Just wanted to say thanks."

"You took the first step," Lee called after her. He noticed Caroline in the booth and slid in across from her.

"Girlfriend?" she asked, rolling the icy cup between her palms.

"Confidential."

"CIA or KGB?"

Finally got a smile out of the man. "I teach self-defense at the women's shelter."

"At the shelter? Since when do they let a man know its location? When we had our clothing drive at work, they insisted only a woman could deliver the donations."

Shrugging, Lee turned to watch Trent swimming through the ball pool. The restaurant's lighting revealed a scattering of brown hairs through the man's sandy mane, like the chocolate in fudge ripple ice cream. A name like fudge ripple raises high expectations. But the carton contains only vanilla with microscopic threads of chocolate, enough to ruin it as a topping for pie, but not enough for a decent chocolate fix. It needs massive infusions of hot fudge—

"How often does he see his dad?"

"He doesn't." Caroline shivered. Diet Coke always made her cold.

Lee looked at her from under his eyebrows, the stern look he gave students to get them in line. "He needs his dad."

"Maybe you need to walk back to the Community Center carrying two tires." She stood.

Lee's leg shot out, blocking her exit from the booth. He locked onto her right wrist. "What are you mad about?"

"What? You've done nothing but criticize my parenting from the moment we met."

"But we haven't met." Still holding her wrist, he enclosed her fingers with his other hand. The strength and calluses in his palm didn't surprise her, but the rush of heat through her body did. "Hi, I'm Lee Marivaux. I'd like to help you with your son, but I learned manners from starving gators."

No wonder Trent paid attention when those brown eyes bored

into him. "I'm Caroline Jameson. If you've really spent any time at the women's shelter, you'd know there are some fathers who do not want to see, do not deserve to see their children. Some fathers who've done things..." Rats. All these years, she couldn't mention Bryan without choking up. The pressure on her hand increased.

"Where is he?" The inner corners of Lee's eyebrows lowered and the outer edges raised. Perhaps he had descended in some bizarre way from an ancient Ninja warrior.

"Boston. We haven't seen him since Trent was two months old."

The Ninja warrior retreated. "The tires made a mess of your hands."

He reached for a napkin. Caroline broke free of his grip and stepped over his leg. "Trent, let's go see if the patch is done."

The karate instructor focused on his student on the ride back to the Community Center.

"I can take it from here," Lee said.

Caroline backed the F-150 up onto the curb so the headlights targeted the empty wheel drum. "See that jack? It's mine and I'm not leaving without it."

While Lee replaced the tire, Caroline popped the VW's hood. Two can play this advice game. "You're a quart low; not a good idea for an engine this small. When's the last time you changed this oil? It looks like coffee sludge. You're out of windshield washer fluid. The belts are worn, but the hoses are firm. The brake fluid looks good. These engines can outlast the body with proper mainte-nance." After he removed the jack, she latched the hood. "Wind-shield wipers need replacing. Wheel wells free of rust. Door panels look good. You could get another hatch from a junk yard, maybe even one with a wiper." She came around the rear of the car just as he tightened the last nut.

"You want your wrench back." Lee held out the tool, but wouldn't let go, making her play tug-of-war with him. "Mrs. Jame-son, where do you work?"

"I'm an engineer at the Ford plant."

The lug wrench dropped out of his hand. He tilted back his head and laughed.

. . .

LEE BUMPED along the dark two lane county road. Starting from his first karate competition, he made a game out of studying people. Sure, some folks kept their *gi* cleaner than others, but the karate uniform acted as a great equalizer. He used other clues from his guard work, like body language and the way a person talked, to figure out who they were. He'd honed the skill to the point he could tell a state trooper from a city cop, a college professor from a high school teacher. He even played the game at the shelter, guessing how much schooling his students had and what their husbands did when they weren't beating on them.

Lee shifted the VW into low gear for a hill. Caroline Jameson. He'd never been so wrong since... well, he'd never been this far off. Why? Straight teeth. Where he came from, people couldn't afford dentists, much less orthodontists. Good complexion. She hadn't done time over a grill at a greasy spoon. Doesn't use slang. Clothes that said high class, good taste. He might have guessed teacher if she had better control of her kid. He'd have guessed calling AAA would be her response to a flat tire.

He turned onto the gravel lane. Two small reflections flashed in his high beams. Deer. He slammed on the brakes, stalling the Volkswagen. A red brown body vaulted across the road.

"Should get you ladies a crossing guard." Three more does bounded out of the bush. Lee waited another minute before restarting the car. The oil light took its sweet time turning off, reminding him Mrs. Jameson thought he was a quart low. Thought? She's an engineer - she knows how to read a dipstick. What had he missed? The truck. He assumed it belonged to her husband, but she didn't wear a ring. Duh. He took his hand off the gear shift long enough to thump his forehead. She works with machinery. She doesn't wear a ring, or any jewelry for that matter. She hauled her kid around, not his favorite behavioral technique, but not an option for your basic lady of leisure.

His headlights caught a battered mailbox on the left. Lee turned into the driveway, opened and shut the rusty gate. Two hounds barked their welcome from the front porch of the old white farm-house. Mr. and Mrs. Reggie Tyler had flown to San Diego for some event in the life of their son, an officer in the US Navy. Couple years back, when the boy graduated from Annapolis, Lee had been hired to milk Reggie's six fussy cows. Mrs. Tyler or the market conditions finally convinced the farmer to give up the dairy business, hallelu-jah. Lee liked the dogs. They didn't need much care, and they made the place a little less lonely. He sat on the porch step. The border collie laid its head in his lap. The Brittany came around his other side for a scratch. Reggie had installed a street light between his back porch and the barn, but here in the front yard the fireflies were in charge.

Lee rested his eyes on the night sky, sprinkled with stars.

An engineer.

I suppose You think that's funny.

Chapter Four

"The kids have a few minutes left on their video," her sitter greeted Caroline at the door Wednesday afternoon. "Come on in. I've got chocolate chip cookies hot from the oven."

Caroline draped her raincoat on the newel post and joined Sharon in the warm kitchen. Sleet ticked on the window, accompanying the cartoon music from the basement. Children's arts and crafts projects decorated not only the refrigerator, but most of the wall space. Caroline closed her eyes and breathed in the distinctive brown sugar and chocolate fragrance. "Smells heavenly."

"It's covering up the moldy smell of broken dishwasher." Sharon moved the mop and bucket into the corner.

"No dishwasher? With all these kids?" Caroline opened the appliance's door and frowned at the pool of murky water in the tub. "Do you want me to look at it?"

"Thanks, but Pete says he knows what's wrong and he's got the parts on order." Sharon cleared schoolbooks off a chair. "I've heard all about karate from Trent. You haven't said what you think."

The warm cookie slipped over her tongue. "No miracles, yet."

The sitter nodded her curly auburn head. "I'd say his behavior is status quo. What do you think about Lee?"

Caroline hated to ruin the chocolate experience thinking about him at all. "He's the most intrusive..." She hunted for the right word, limited by Sharon's rules about profanity. "I helped him change a flat last night. He took the opportunity to interrogate me about Trent— what doctor I take him to, his medical history, his father."

Sharon passed her another cookie. "Ah. I wondered what happened last night. Trent kept making circles with three fingers."

"Sign language. Lee thinks I should sign to him. Like I have time to learn."

"Caroline." Sharon trotted out her mother voice. "When it comes to Trent, you have a hard time accepting advice. You bit off my head the few times I've made suggestions. You turn every school conference into an ordeal. And now, Lee. Trent is your child, but he's also shaped by the environment he's in—the day care at your college in Michigan, the kids here and at school, his teachers. He's got a heritage from your family, his father, his father's family. He's got a genetic whammy from Down syndrome. There's a lot about Trent you have no control over. Don't get defensive; we're not blaming you. We're trying to help."

The children thundered up from the rec room.

Caroline slouched in the chair, too far into a chocolate haze to feel anything more than mildly annoyed. "That's what Lee said."

LEE PARKED the VW next to the only other car in the parking lot, the Buffum's Chevrolet. He unlocked church door and called "hello."

"Down here!" Sharon hollered. Lee followed the scraping and bumping sounds to the toddler nursery. He found the woman wrestling with one of the long tables they used for potlucks.

"Wait, let me give you a hand with that." Dropping his grocery sack and sleeping bag, he helped her flip the table onto its legs. "What are you doing?"

"Wallpapering." Sharon filled a plastic trough with water.

"Pastor didn't tell me you'd be here."

"I left him a note." She carried a chair over to the corner and slammed it into place.

Lee retreated to the doorway. "He has me staying here weekends, on account of the vandalism awhile back."

"I know." Stomping around the room, she snatched up a plumb line, stabbed the tack into the wall, snapped the string, and yanked down the tack. Curls trembling, she unrolled, measured, and marked a sheet of the Noah's Ark patterned paper. With fast and furious slashes, she severed the paper from its roll.

"I'd ask if you needed help, but the way you're using those scissors..."

She whipped the paper into a tube, glue-side out, and drowned it in the trough. "I've got a razor blade, too. You'd best stand back."

"I'm real sorry and I promise never to do it again. If you tell me what I did."

Expression grim, she slapped the paper into the corner and beat it into place with a foot-long brush. Thirty years from now Sharon would make a perfect Granny Clampitt on a "Beverly Hillbillies" revival. "It's not you."

"Whew. Had me worried."

She stabbed the razor blade into the corner between the ceiling and the wall. "It's Pete."

Ah, now we're getting somewhere. Lee unrolled the next section, then stepped back while she cut. "What's he done now?"

"It's what he's not done." More chair slamming and paper slashing. "He hasn't fixed the dishwasher. I've got our three kids around the house all the time, another before and after school, a half-dozen other kids here and there. It adds up to a sink full of dishes, all day long."

"Have you tried..."

"Paper plates?" She slit the plastic off a new roll. "Too expensive. Kids eat too messy for paper anyway."

"Is he waiting for..."

"Nope, he ordered the parts and they've come in."

"Does he need help..."

"No, I pulled the dishwasher out before I left."

Lee stared down at the slightly-built woman. "You pulled the dishwasher out..."

"And left it sitting in the middle of the kitchen floor. He can't miss it." A quick nod sent her curls bobbing.

"Why did Wonder Woman marry an ordinary mortal like Pete? You've been married..."

"Seventeen years." Sharon started the next wall.

"And I've known you three..."

"Four years. Luke started karate four years ago."

"And I'm still trying to figure out this opposites attract thing." Lee lowered himself onto the floor - the Sunday school chairs wouldn't support his weight. "Like my sister and brother-in-law. Bernadette's idea of decorating is stealing a neon beer sign from the nearest roadhouse. Louis won't shop anywhere but the Plaza. Has his underwear monogrammed. And you and Pete! He's slow and steady, one thing at a time. But you race around like some of my hyperactive students. If you were in my class, Miss Sharon, I'd have to sit on you. You know he'll get that dishwasher running again, but you're going crazy waiting."

"That's the way it has to be." Sharon sighed and smoothed the new strip. "Two of me would make a chaotic home. Pete helps me stop and smell the roses. Two of him wouldn't get a darn thing done. Someone has to plant those roses." She pointed to herself.

"So, if a guy like me were looking for a wife, he should get an atheist terrorist vegetarian."

Sharon flicked a wet washcloth at him. "No, no, no. You're talking apples and oranges. Pete and I differ in the way we do things, but we agree on standards, values, what's important. God, family, community service, that sort of thing."

"Marriage?" Lee asked, her quick nod telling him Sharon wouldn't be completely happy until the dishwasher was fixed. Apples and oranges? His stomach growled.

"I don't know if you can help who you fall in love with." She stepped back to check her work.

"Sure you can. It's not like bourrée game, where you got to play what you're dealt. You can pick through the deck until you find the right one, like you choosing Pete."

"You may have to eat those words, Lee Marivaux." Raising an

eyebrow in his direction, she caught him putting together a cheese and bread sandwich. "Is that all you're having for dinner? Run down to the kitchen and see if day care has any leftovers."

Mouth full, he shook his head.

"I mean it. Their cook goes to all the trouble of saving extra food and then lets it go bad. Probably ravioli or fruit cocktail. Go on, now. You never got paid for building their playground."

"Because I never have enough money to tithe."

"Lee Marivaux," Sharon pointed the razor blade at him. "Get down there and clean out that refrigerator, or I won't tell you about that new student of yours, Trent Jameson."

He was back in two minutes with a bowl of chicken noodle casserole and a carton of chocolate milk. The kid he could figure out. It was the woman who had him puzzled. "His ma is an engineer. So she's smart, yeah?"

Sharon tipped her head side-to-side. "Book smart. Caroline reads all those fancy-pants medical journals—neurology, psychology, genetics—about Down syndrome. And understands them, too."

"Doesn't seem to help her much." This casserole could use some hot sauce. "The boy hasn't seen his father since he was a baby."

"I'd known Caroline two years before she told me that." Sharon glanced up from the wallpaper. "Did she say what happened?"

"Not in words."

Sharon winced. She knew about Lee's work at the women's shelter. "Whatever happened in Boston, she and Trent hightailed it out of there and moved in with her parents in Michigan. She transferred her credits from MIT, finished her engineering degree at Wayne State, then took a job at the Ford plant here."

"I'd pegged her as Mrs. Gotbucks, lady of leisure."

"Compared to you, everyone's got bucks." Sharon cut another length of paper.

"*Mais*, yeah."

"And no one has less leisure than Caroline. Her shifts run ten to twelve hours a day, most Saturdays, some Sundays. Paying off her student loans, providing for her son. Honestly she doesn't have time to take sign language or join a support group. Karate's the only class that's ever fit into her schedule."

Caroline didn't deserve all the grief he'd given her. Lee crumpled the empty milk carton in his fist. "Then karate will have to be enough."

LEE WRENCHED the steering wheel to the left to avoid a juicy, Volkswagen-sized sinkhole in the night-shadowed gravel road. Bare Osage orange branches scraped the sides of the car with a teeth-aching squeal. See the advantage of driving a junker? Doesn't even raise the old blood pressure. Not like it would if he drove newer wheels, say a late model, dark green Ford pickup. The VW lurched into another pothole, bottoming out on the center of the roadbed. Of course, there's a lot to be said for ground clearance.

The headlights flicked over a scattering of aluminum cans. Lee groaned. Oh well, Eldon wouldn't let him stay at his hunting camp if the place didn't attract the underage drinking crowd. Hoping they hadn't broken anything this time, Lee parked in front of the tar paper shack.

He found the key on top of the door frame as usual. Guess those partiers were too drunk to find it. The door opened to a scurrying, scratching sound and a recognizable odor. Better bring mousetraps on the next trip. He lit the Coleman lantern. A rusty kerosene heater lurked in the corner. One of these days the beast would explode and burn all his skin off. Or leak deadly gas and he'd never wake up. Not tonight. He brought in a second sweatshirt with his grocery sack. Eldon didn't cache much food, and Lee was running low. With apologies to his stomach, he downed a dry tuna sandwich.

Before climbing into his sleeping bag for the night, Lee opened his wallet. Food, tires, or oil change? He rubbed his mustache. The Community Center money had come and gone. The college didn't pay until the first of the month. He blew out the lantern. God will provide. He always does.

. . .

CAROLINE WATCHED the dark spot on Trent's pants spread into a puddle on the mat. If it had to happen, she tried to console herself, at least it happened at the end of class.

"Trent!" A deep voice echoed in the gym. Lee jerked his thumb toward the bathroom. The boy scampered into the men's.

"I've got spare clothes in the truck."

"If it wasn't so cold out, I'd send him home wet." Lee handed her one of his dilapidated sneakers. "Prop the door open so you don't lock yourself out."

"Yes, sir," Caroline muttered. The instructor missed her sarcasm. By the time she returned with clean slacks and underwear, the rest of the class and their parents had gone. "Trent?"

"In here," Lee called from the men's locker room.

Caroline hesitated. He couldn't expect her to dress Trent in the men's. "If you'll send him out, I'll help him change."

"Pass his clothes in." A well muscled arm shot out around the tiled privacy wall, giving Caroline a glimpse of light brown chest hair curled over a magnificent— *Stop it.* Caroline dropped the clothes into the hand.

Across the gym, the puddle accused her, evidence of her inadequacy in toilet training her son. Kneeling on the mat, Caroline attacked the spot with paper towels from the women's locker room.

"Mrs. Jameson!"

Caroline jumped.

The barefoot instructor towered over her, dressed in his civvies. "Trent will never stop wetting his pants if you don't allow him to learn from the consequences." The gym lights lit his hair like a halo. An avenging angel.

Squirming under the instructor's scowl, Caroline watched her son don his socks and shoes. "He just gets busy doing other things and has accidents."

"Accident? Do you get busy at the plant and forget to go to the bathroom? Do I get busy teaching and forget? Of course not. If Trent cleans up after himself; he'll learn." He knelt to tie the child's shoes. "At least you don't blame it on low muscle tone."

"Low tone?" She hadn't considered the effect of muscle tone on bladder control. Trent began running laps around the room.

"Also, if you expect him to get himself dressed, you can't deck him out like Little Lord Fauntleroy. Buy him sweatpants, pullover shirts, and Velcro shoes. He'll be independent and more comfortable."

"Lord Fauntleroy? That's J.C. Penney's." How could he dress himself? He's handicapped.

Lee held out his hand to help her up. Caroline shook her head, indicating the wad of soggy paper towels. Lee slid his hand down the inside of her forearm and cupped her elbow. The back of his wrist brushed her breast. She jumped to her feet.

Trying to hide her jumbled feelings, Caroline stomped across the gym. "I see you're still riding on bald tires."

"I wanted to ask you about that, yeah." Lee's voice lost its command edge. "I bought the oil and the belts, but I don't have tools or a garage. I was thinking, I could swap sign language lessons for your help. The problem is I'm only free Saturday after four. If you've got a date..."

"A date?" She slammed the towels into the trash can. "Even if I did, where would I get a sitter?"

"I'll bring you a brochure for respite care." Lee grabbed his sneakers and disappeared into the locker room.

Wait... had she just been railroaded into fixing this man's junker?

Chapter Five

"It's due for a good cleaning." Caroline flipped up the sofa cushions, and ran the vacuum through popcorn kernels and candy wrappers from Halloween and Christmas. "Overdue, really. Nothing to do with having company. Not company. My son's karate instructor is coming over to work on his car. No big deal."

Trent didn't hide his excitement. He kept a vigil at the living room window all afternoon. At three o'clock, Caroline showered. No reason, just felt like a shower. Every five or ten minutes she found herself raiding the coffee canister for M&M's. She organized the candies by color. First the yellows, then the reds. When the primary colors were gone, she could eat the secondaries. Trent's shriek at 4:07 announced Lee's arrival. Heart rate irrationally accelerating, Caroline pushed the button for the garage door opener. The Volkswagen squeaked to a stop beside her truck.

"Hey, little buddy." Lee swung the dancing boy into the air. Apparently the idea of a shower had occurred to him, too. He smelled soapy clean. Damp hair clung to his head, curling around his ears and down the collar of his faded denim shirt. "Hi, Mrs. Jameson."

"What's with the formality?" Caroline stepped into her coveralls. "Shall I address you as *sensei*?"

"It's a karate thing, respect. I always call the parents by their last name. What would you prefer?"

"Ma!" Trent suggested.

She smiled. "Then I'd really feel old. First name is fine."

"Caroline." Lee test-drove her name. "Fan belt..." He disappeared into the backseat of the compact, giving far too good a view of his rear end.

"Pop the hood while you're in there." To avoid gawking at the fit of his well-worn jeans, Caroline checked his car. "Lee, someone sold you four different tires."

He emerged with the fan belt and oil filter. "Three. One's the spare. They're all radials."

"They're used."

He shrugged. "The price was right."

Caroline focused on swiveling her tool chest into position. "How fast do you drive? Maybe I should take out life insurance on you."

He chuckled. "My sister says the same thing."

Lee turned out to be a fine assistant. He opened the Idiots' Manual to the correct page, strong-armed the wrench, passed tools upon request, and, best of all, kept Trent out of trouble. He started to help clean up, but the boy pulled him inside for the "grand tour". She heard them wander through the family room, up to the main level with its eat-in kitchen and living room, then above her head to the three bedrooms. He'd find plenty to criticize. Too many toys, not enough furniture, builder-white walls without artwork, ready-made drapes hung on off-the-shelf rods. Bryan had taken one look at her furniture arrangement in their townhouse and called an interior decorator. Steeling herself, she slipped into the kitchen.

"What a house!" Lee ran his hand along the kitchen peninsula. "All this counter space."

"Thank you." Caroline scooped the hand cleaner into her palm, working it under the fingernails of the other hand. Trent dragged his instructor into the living room. Empty except for her piano, the room served as a play space. Lee reappeared with the boy slung like a rag doll over his shoulder. He peeked into the freezer, the refrigerator, then the cupboards.

"Checking to see if I feed him right?" Caroline leaned against the sink, arms crossed.

"I've got another horse-trade for you, ma'am." John Wayne accent this time. "If you can play that there pianner, I'll swap you a feed."

"What?"

"Oh, classical, rag-time, jazz, oldies. Do you play or is this just for looks?" With a large hand on her back, Lee steered her to piano bench. "Come on, little buddy, let's cook."

Water rattled into a saucepan. Cupboard doors banged. It's dinner time. She should have planned on him staying. "Do you need a cookbook? I defrosted chicken."

"Tell Mom - play!"

Giggling, Trent raced into the living room. He shook his hands at her and dashed out.

Rusty from infrequent practice, Caroline felt out the notes of Simon and Garfunkel's "Bridge over Troubled Waters." By the first *forte* passage, her fingers warmed to the task. She lost herself in the challenging chords. When the music pounded to an end, the applause from the next room surprised her. Trent peeked in, tapped his fingertips together, then left.

"More!" Lee called.

Ah ha, Caroline nodded, the sign language lesson. She launched into one of Bach's piano *etudes*. Bach always felt so good to the fingers, like the composer considered the pianist's comfort as important as the sound of the piece. She segued into "Maple Leaf Rag," then her own arrangement of "Birdland," a jazz piece. After a few bars, Lee and Trent danced into the room. The big man provided the counterpoint with chanting, howling, and hooting. At the grand finale, he plopped next to her on the piano seat.

Caroline glanced at him from the corner of her eye, uncomfortable with his shoulder pressed against hers. "You know jazz."

A mischievous grin erupted from beneath his mustache. "We don't learn much in the bayou, but we do know jazz."

"Where are you from?"

"Lou'siana. Let's eat." He led the way into the kitchen, a foreign land of exotic aromas. "You jazz quite well for a Yankee."

Slipping into her seat, Caroline frowned at the Corning Ware. She used these as her everyday dishes because replacements were as close as Walmart. Too late now to get out the china. "It's obvious, that I'm not from Kansas City?"

"The way you carry yourself, how you talk..." His cheeks pinked, perhaps from the steam of the dinner. He raised his iced tea glass. "I poured you a cup of milk. Cajun food is too spicy for most people."

Caroline took a small bite. Eye watering, but palatable when mixed with enough rice. Trent seemed immune to the heat, in fact, he didn't drool through the entire meal. Lee entertained them with Cajun cooking stories of crawfish by the barrel, roasted varmint, peppers so hot they're assigned their own fire department.

The instructor leaned close to his student. "We made a pretty good mess cooking dinner," he nodded at the pan soaking in the sink. "Do you think Mom can clean it up faster than you can take your bath?"

The boy launched himself up the stairs. Water pounded into the tub before Caroline could load her plate into the dishwasher.

Now that they were alone, she kept her eyes away from the man sprawled at her kitchen table. "If I'm going to clean up, are you going to give him his bath?"

"No." He gave her a look that asked if she'd like to rephrase her question. "He's old enough to give himself a bath. I'm going to play the piano."

Caroline moved into the corner of the kitchen to let him pass. Several seconds later, "Chopsticks" plunked from the living room. Goofball, she thought, scrubbing the rice pan. He played "Heart and Soul," the high part, then the low part. Drying her hands, Caroline wandered to the piano. Lee slid over on the bench. Careful not to touch him, she sat down and made it a duet. Midway through the piece, a drippy boy wearing cowboy pajamas plopped in her lap, pushing her shoulder into Lee's.

"Smells clean. How's the bathroom look?" Lee moved another inch down the bench.

Trent swept his hands horizontally.

"Done," Lee interpreted. "Is Mom done in the kitchen?"

The little body wiggled with delight. "No!"

"Then I get to read you a bedtime story while she gets her job done."

"No fair," Caroline protested. "I was distracted."

"It's a conspiracy." He gave her a sly wink before Trent towed him down to the rec room.

Cleaning finished, Caroline popped a Hershey's kiss and joined the two. Her son snuggled under Lee's left arm. The man patted the sofa on his right. "Come on, Mom, we're going to need some narration with this story." He held up a photo album.

Caroline perched on the corner of the sofa. "I'm sure you can find something more interesting..."

Lee gave a quick intake of breath. "*Regardez donc.*" He pointed to the first picture. Her friend, Marnie, had brought a Polaroid camera to the hospital. Caroline had instinctively tilted her head, drawing a protective curtain of hair around the newborn. In the second picture, she posed with her hair drawn back, facing Trent toward the camera. The empire style robe embarrassed Caroline, revealing too much. She supposed her "Dolly Parton" figure attracted Lee's attention. His finger traced the edge of the first picture. "Your hair... looks really good long. Why did you cut it?"

She tugged at the bob, precision cut to the nape of her neck. "Working around machinery, it's dangerous."

He cleared his throat. "That's true, yeah."

Embarrassed by his scrutiny, Caroline redirected him to the album. "Here's Trent holding his head up." Just before Bryan returned from a business trip and ended their marriage. They paged through snapshots of the boy at the Detroit Zoo, the wading pool at a Metro Park, the stroller in front of their townhouse, first steps, birthdays, the move to Kansas City, the Penguin Park slides, the first day of kindergarten.

I am a good mom; I've got pictures to prove it.

But these pictures only tell half the story. What would this man think if he knew the rest? What if he'd seen me grocery shopping at midnight with the baby? He wouldn't understand about odd sleep schedules. And the morning I took a sick toddler to day care because I had a final exam. The many times I left him alone in the playpen while I ran down to the laundry room. Or moving in, when Trent fell out of his bedroom window while I unpacked the kitchen. That Christmas when he bounced on the bed, crashed into the wall, ending up with a goose egg and two black eyes. No, this man wouldn't understand.

"Looks like he chopped his own bangs." Lee pointed to a shot of Trent blowing out four candles on a birthday cake.

"It happened at preschool. I never let him have scissors."

"Then how's he supposed to learn cutting?" Brown eyes inspected her. "Something all kids do, me, my nephews, my sister. Normal, nothing to worry about." He flipped back to the beginning. "Only these two of your mom, Trent."

"Until he learns to take pictures."

"Do you have a camera? I'll take one of you both."

Trent scampered upstairs and returned with Caroline's cellphone. Before she could say no, he aimed it at the adults on the sofa and clicked the button.

"He learned to take pictures," Lee observed, his voice heavy with irony. He stood and grabbed the phone from the boy. "Sit with your mom, smarty."

Ever the gleeful ham, Trent posed on the back of the sofa, his chin on his mother's head.

"Really, I should take one of you guys, Trent and his karate teacher."

"Smile, Mom."

After one snap, Caroline grabbed the phone.

Lee kicked off his sneakers. "*Cha-ryot!*" The child snapped to attention. Caroline took a dozen shots of their karate demonstration.

"If you get prints..."

"I could email or text them to you."

"No phone, no computer."

No phone? How does he manage?

The instructor bowed to his student. "Bedtime."

The boy returned the bow, then marched up the stairs. Caroline put her phone back on the charger. She found Lee kneeling next to Trent's bed, his hand stretched across the boy's back.

"I'll listen to your prayers."

"Uh, we've never done that." Moving silently across the wall-to-wall carpet, Caroline pulled the Kansas City Royals curtains closed.

"I'll teach you. Say: God bless Mom." He paused for the boy to repeat his words. "God bless everyone at school. God bless Sharon and her family. Who else? Me? God bless Lee. Amen."

Caroline didn't know much about praying, but it seemed more peaceful than their usual bedtime battle of wills. When the man stepped away from the bed, she gave her son his good-night hug and kiss.

"Lee!" Trent called. He held a hand out, thumb, index and pinkie straight, middle and ring fingers bent. A hubcap-sized hand shot over her shoulder, the same sign.

Caroline followed him down the stairs. "Do you have any kids of your own?"

His head gave a shake.

"You'd be a good father."

"Easier to be a surrogate. All the fun stuff without the hard work." He tried to joke, but his voice sounded hollow. "Time for your sign language lesson."

Usually when her son fell asleep, the house echoed with silence. Tonight, Lee's bare feet creaked on the steps. The door to the garage opened. The Volkswagen hatch screeched, then thudded closed. Lee returned to the family room, settling into the sofa with a sigh. Now that Trent's asleep, he really didn't want to be here. He's just discharging his obligation. Iced tea glasses tinkling, Caroline descended the stairs. Lee sat cross-legged, a hardback book in his lap. He glanced up long enough to pass her a pamphlet.

"Here's the information on respite care. I'm one of their providers, if you're more comfortable leaving Trent with someone

53

he knows." His voice sounded gruff. "Now you can say 'yes' to all those guys who keep asking you out."

Caroline set the glasses on the toy chest that served as a coffee table and sat in the recliner. Her hands shook as she opened the brochure. *It's the cold. I'm not nervous.* "All what guys?"

Lee drummed his fingers on *The Joy of Sign.* "All the bachelors at the plant..."

"Where I have a picture of my son, a handicapped child, on my desk."

His mustache twitched. A long minute passed while he studied her. "I think it's a measure of a man, how he treats those who are weaker than him. That doesn't say much for the men you work with."

Caroline set the pamphlet down. "It's been years since I went on a date. I wouldn't know where to begin. How's the—" Her fingers made quote marks in the air. "—singles scene in Kansas City?"

His wide shoulders lifted. "You're asking the karate monk."

"You don't date because of some Japanese religion?"

"No." He smiled at his hands. "Teaching karate full time pays so poorly, I can't afford to date. It's like a monk's vow of poverty, chastity, obedience."

Now it was Caroline's turn to stare. "You teach full time? I assumed you had a day job."

"Sort of. Days I teach at Maple Woods Community College, the women's shelter, the home school group, hospitals..."

"You teach karate at hospitals? To patients?"

"No, to staff. How to handle violent patients, usually someone with psych or substance abuse problems, without hurting the patient or getting hurt yourself. Nights I teach karate at the community centers."

"Wouldn't you do better opening your own school?"

"*Dojo.* Then I'd have to sign kids up on contracts and double the price of the *gi,* the karate uniform, and worry about rent and insurance. I'm no businessman. My sister says I can't count past twenty because I run out of fingers and toes. No, the rec centers work fine, less driving for the parents."

"How do you manage?"

He shrugged. "Like the old song says: 'with a little help from my friends'. I house-sit in exchange for places to live. I swap sign language lessons for auto maintenance. You're getting shorted."

"I'm sorry. I didn't mean to pry."

"You have a right to know who's working with your child." Lee propped the book open on his ankles. "I'll leave this here, so you can look up the things you say most often. And you can download a sign language app for your phone. You'll need to memorize the alphabet because many signs are based on the first letter of the word." He put his thumb between the first two fingers of his fist. "Shake T for toilet, or tap your forehead with T for Trent."

"That's how his name is signed? How do you know?"

"I asked what he's called at school. He knows a fair number of signs. Have his speech therapist send home a list." Lee bookmarked the fingerspelling alphabet page with the respite brochure. "Don't worry about full sentences. Try for one word commands: go, stop, no. You talk way too much when you discipline him."

"Wait a minute, I thought you were teaching sign language, not parenting."

"Can't pull a fast one on you." He raised his bushy eyebrows. "Communication's a key to discipline, yeah. What signs do you know already?"

"Done. More. Play."

Lee demonstrated the precise movements.

"What was the last one Trent signed to you?"

"This one?" Lee signed toward the wall. "I love you."

Is it hot in here! Caroline reached for her iced tea.

"That's kind of shorthand, pardon the pun," Lee stood and paced the room, reminding her how tall he was. "You can sign each word separately or just use the one sign. You don't need a big vocabulary to communicate with Trent at this age. Each sign can say a lot." He gestured with dramatic motions, coming close to hitting the ceiling. "I could sign each word 'please, take a seat', or just one sign: 'sit', and let my body language and facial expression show the rest. I could sign 'get your butt in that chair,' or—" Eyebrows drawn together in a frown, he slapped his fingers together and lunged toward her. He paused, his expression melting into open-mouthed surprise. He stepped back, crumpling to the carpet at her feet. "I'm sorry."

"For what?"

"I scared you. It's just, you seem so together... but you're like the women at the shelter."

"No, I'm not. You didn't scare me," she lied. She had flinched, a barely perceptible pushing back into the recliner. The fact he noticed rattled her more than his feint. "I'm fine." She set the iced tea down with a thud.

"You don't trust men. That's why you don't date."

"No, it's not!"

"Have you ever considered taking a self-defense class? The sense of empowerment..."

"I don't have time."

His thumb stroked down his mustache. "Maybe when I need help with the car again."

Caroline pulled in a shaky breath, wondering why she would offer to help the most impudent, insolent, irritating man she'd ever known. *It's a safety issue.* "That would be real soon. You down shifted to turn into my driveway, and yanked the emergency brake to keep from crashing into the back wall of the garage. You need a brake job."

A slow grin lit up his face. The brown eyes twinkled. "Next Saturday?"

Chapter Six

Lee let himself in through the side entrance of Arthur and Margaret Hays' house. He slipped his sneakers off, leaving them to puddle on the tile floor, then reset the alarm system. Large wet snowflakes splattered floor to ceiling windows along the back of the house, hiding the view of Riss Lake. These docs sure picked the right week for a conference in Hawaii.

Lee found the clipboard of instructions on the kitchen counter. The first page listed the usual stuff about trash pickup and their number at the resort on Maui. The second and third pages detailed care of their fish. He squinted at the handwriting, a collection of marks resembling Chinese. Last time he house-sat, he had to run the instructions by the docs' office for translation. "Let's see: b.i.d. is two times a day, p.r.n. means as needed..."

The occupants of the living room's hundred gallon tank rose to the top to attack the sprinkle of dried food. "Fish should be caught and eaten," Lee told the flashing silver school. He wandered upstairs, matching special diets to the aquariums in the master bedroom, guest room, and study. "Ridiculous," he told the bubbling group on the landing. "None of you's big enough to make a decent snack." A foil-wrapped packet of tiny frozen shrimp went to the tank in the dining room. "What a waste."

Lee penciled a date and time next to each instruction. A fancy goldfish in a small bowl on the kitchen counter got a dose of antibiotic fish food. Out of the corner of his eye, he watched the fish snap up a red flake, then swim to his side of the bowl. "Keeping an eye on me?" He consulted the list. Samantha had a swim bladder infection. If she started swimming sideways, her water must be exchanged for the salt water in the jug under the sink. If she dies... "I don't do dead fish, Samantha." Her bronze tail flashed at him.

Lee rummaged through the refrigerator. The Hays kept a well-stocked pantry. He stir-fried beef tenderloin and boiled a pot of rice to the sound of gurgling and humming aquariums. Eating at the table, his left hand tapped out a rhythm, a ten note phrase. Samantha faced him, opening and closing her mouth as if asking a question.

"Dunno," he told the fish. "Just some old rock and roll song." He hummed the bars out loud. "'Green Eyed Lady.' Naw, don't remember the words or what it's about. Meatloaf, no, Sugarloaf sung it." The fish circled. Lee propped his elbows on the table, contemplating the shiitake mushroom at the end of his fork. "Yeah, there is this green eyed lady. Now, I've spent plenty of time hanging around garages, but I never met a grease monkey who knew, all the time, what tool to use and where to find it. I mean, she's got one of those seventeen drawer Craftsman tool chests." He swung his fork overhead. "Red thing, about this tall. She doesn't have to dig around in it. Everything's all lined up, neat and clean. That's the way she works, no mess, no fumbling around. All business." He chewed on a strip of steak. "Except when she tested the radiator juice. Told this story about a friend in Michigan who dropped the tester thing down into the radiator. Most mechanics I know snicker real good, especially when you ask for credit. But this one giggles." He scraped his plate clean and loaded it in the dishwasher. Samantha snapped at the bubbles on the surface of the water. "Hungry? No stir fry for you. Maybe a little more fish food." He crumpled a yellow flake into the bowl. The little mouth gulped the floating pieces.

Bracing on the cold marble counter, Lee stretched his hamstrings and calf muscles. Can't ask the students to touch their toes, if their instructor can only reach his knees. He dialed his sister's number. Her husband answered.

"Lee! Where might you be calling from this fine evening?" Louis asked, his accent the unique blend of French and African found in the Caribbean.

"Riss Lake. I'm baby-sitting some fish." He ran his thumb around the bowl. Samantha chased it.

"Oh, mon. I read about those houses. You're living it up, eh?"

"I guess." Lee shot a glance at the cherry kitchen cabinets, built-in refrigerator, and double ovens. He liked Caroline and Trent's house better: plain white walls not cluttered with paintings and wallpaper. "The biggest fish tanks I've ever seen."

"Impossible to impress, as usual. Let me call your sister to the phone."

The line stayed quiet for only a second. "Hey, Bear."

"Hey, Bernie. When are you having me down for dinner? I've got the envie for your pistolettes." Even after a healthy serving of stir-fry, mention of the buttery rolls with sausage, crawfish, and shrimp stuffing, made him hungry.

"Sorry, not my year to cook. What are you up to?"

"I was hoping you'd know. Anyone call for me?"

"Dale Underwood. Said he's short-handed and could use some help next week. Hope it's not outside work in this weather."

"In and out. It's a lumberyard. I'll give him a call." He switched legs. "Awful quiet there. My nephews have laryngitis?"

"Naw, they went over to the school, play some basketball."

"You should have a couple more kids, make a whole team."

Bernadette laughed, a low ha from the back of her throat. "I've done my part. Your turn, Bear. The dryer's buzzing. Gotta run."

Lee disconnected.

Samantha stared at him with one eye, then the other. "Lonely? Soon as you're better the docs will put you back in the study with the other goldfish."

She swam a figure-eight.

"I'll tell you what's lonely." Lee touched a finger to the water, sending the fish diving for the bottom. "Lonely is lots of pictures of a little kid all by himself: no dad, no cousins, no friends." He could recall only a half-dozen photos of himself as a kid and none were alone. His baby picture was taken on his grandpa's lap, rocking on the porch. He must have been almost a year old, mosquito bait, wearing nothing but a diaper.

When he was six or seven, Trent's age, the family had gone to the docks for the blessing of the shrimp boats. He'd grumbled about getting dressed up, wearing his buttoned-down white shirt and long pants on a warm day. But when the picture came out in the newspaper, he'd been standing proud with the other cousins in the front row by Uncle Norman's lugger.

Then Uncle Alex, flush from an oil rig job, had given Bernie a camera for her high school graduation. In the photo of the whole clan, Lee hid his gawky thirteen-year-old self in the shade of the porch. But Uncle Isaac caught him dancing with Aunt Jeanette. Somehow, the way the photo came out, it looked like Lee's eyes were bulging at the woman's ample bosom. When his sister was particularly steamed with him, she threatened to show that picture to his nephews.

The grandfather clock in the front hall solemnly announced the hour. Lee wandered into the living room, looking for the remote to the sound system. He planned to wade through the docs' library, find out about this disease one of his students had, juvenile diabetes. But first he had to get that song out of his head.

Green-eyed lady.

CAROLINE THREW dinner in the oven, a cartoon in the DVD player, and the sign language book on the kitchen table.

"Look at all this!" She flipped through the pages. "It's like starting college all over again!" College. How did they teach French? Through dialogues.

Madame, voulez-vous le vin rouge ou le vin blanc avec votre dîner?

Je voudrais le vin blanc, si vous plaît.

Ridiculous. What did Lee say? Start with short, one word

commands. He has the most beautiful hands. Large, but graceful. Long fingers. There's something musical, rhythmic about his signing. Like he's conducting a symphony.

The wind hit the west side of the house with a squelching, ticking mix of snow and sleet. No decent snow all winter, and now this mess. Caroline enjoyed winter. Before Trent, she skied downhill and cross-country, and, when she couldn't get out of the city, she went sledding, tobogganing, and even enjoyed walking in the snow. But not in this sloppy mess, no good for anything but wrecking a car.

She should have known. She had called Bryan from the body shop to explain why she was late. Why must she be so slow? he had fumed. And when she told him the Mustang was totaled, he became livid. He berated her for her carelessness, then hung up without asking if she was hurt. She had to call Marnie for a ride home. She should have known.

The theme music sounded from the rec room. Aargh! Had daydreaming wasted all her evening? That video must be half the time advertised.

Trent hopped upstairs. "So, Ma, so." He wiggled his fingers at the windows.

Caroline checked the book. *Snow.* "Yes, Trent, snow."

"Ee?"

"Yes, we'll eat soon," Caroline signed *eat*, then raced through the pages looking for the sign for *soon*. A sign language app on her phone would be faster, if she only had a spare minute to download it.

"Ee wuh?" The boy signed *eat*, then drew the index of one hand across the palm of the other. "Wuh?"

Sorry, she signed. "I don't know that word."

"Wuh? Wuh ee? Ee wuh?" He repeated the gestures.

"Okay, it begins with a 'w'. Let's see."

Trent flipped the oven light on and peered in through the window. "Ee fih," he said in a satisfied tone. He motioned as if he were brushing the table clear. "Fih." As if his hand were...

"Fish?" Caroline asked. The boy grinned. "Yes, we're having fish sticks and..." She looked up the sign. "And potatoes."

"No." Palm down, his thumb and index together, other fingers extended, he moved his hand in an arc. "Fie fie." He opened the cabinet, pointed to the five pound plastic bag of Idaho's finest, and made her sign. "Po." Back at the oven, he made the arc again. "Fie fie."

The book showed the sign for French fries just like Trent had made. She said each word with its gesture. "You are so smart!" she told her grinning son.

He scrambled onto her lap, and hugged her with all the power his short legs and arms could muster. "You too, Ma!"

Focus, Lee ordered himself. Usually he concentrated on his students and blocked out everyone else in the room. Hey, his karate class at the Antioch Rec Center shared the gym with beginning ballet. Anyone who could ignore that piano music chanky-chanking from a warped CD, could block out a certain lady perched on the last folding chair. He could block out when her hand slipped in the pocket of her navy blazer for a chocolate fix. He could block out when she crossed her legs to prop a magazine on her knee.

"*Cha-ryot!*" he called the class to attention, hoping the command would work on his own head.

The kids wiggled with excitement during warm-ups. Today they would split their boards. All the class, even Trent, managed to follow directions. Oh man, Trent. Just one day with that little stinker and he'd be toeing the line. How could his mom be so smart about cars and let her son run all over her? Lee wanted to rip that magazine out of her hands. *Watch me*, he'd tell her. *You're here to learn, too.*

Andie's mom leaned over and said something to Trent's mom. Good. Caroline needed to stop isolating herself like she's better than everyone else and— Marco tugged on the belt of his *gi*.

Focus.

"Your son's doing real fine."

Caroline turned to the woman next to her on the bleachers. "Thank you. Which child is yours?"

The cross-stitch needle pointed out the little girl who seemed to know only one word: chicken. She struggled to balance on one foot while straightening the other for a kick. "Andie, my foster daughter. She's a distant cousin on my mother's side."

"Has she been taking karate long?"

"Two years. She's the reason Lee started teaching handicapped kids. Our son was taking one of his classes and we brought Andie along to watch. Lee let her join the class, but she got so frustrated with her body. Somehow she remembers being able to run and jump."

"She remembers? You mean she used to..."

"Andie had a stroke."

"A stroke? I didn't know that could happen to children."

Carnation-pink embroidery floss tangled over the magenta jumper. "She was abused. Her mother let her seizure five hours."

"Andie was born normal? This could have been prevented?" Caroline's stomach fish-tailed out of control. Her hands clutched the *Road and Track* magazine, wrinkling it into unreadability. She blinked at the children arranging themselves on the mats for stretching. Lee paired up with Andie, easing the tightness from her left arm and leg. Adoration twinkled in her blue eyes. A dimple embellished one cheek. What kind of monster would hurt this beautiful child?

"Lee had Andie's therapists show him how to stretch her out. He's such a soft touch. Did you know he charges us the same tuition as his larger classes, kids without handicaps? Probably loses money on us every week."

Caroline studied the woman beside her. She carried a few extra pounds on her frame, just enough to make her huggable. Wisps of brown hair escaped from the clip at the nape of her neck. She wore a Nashua Elementary sweatshirt, faded jeans, and canvas sneakers. Her expression was calm, her tone matter of fact. Mother of the year. "I'm so glad you have Andie."

The children lined up to break boards. Marco cut in front of Andie. The little girl shoved him, sending him sprawling into Trent and Kurt. Lee put both kids in time out. Caroline thought he was a little harsh. With a one word vocabulary, how could she complain about Marco's crime? Andie crawled from time out and tried to bite the instructor on the leg. With a stern look, Lee sent her back into the corner.

A small sigh escaped the woman next to her. "Most of the time, we're glad to have Andie, too."

Lee made a great show of studying each child and sorting through his box to find a plank especially for them. He sighted down the length, held it to his ear and tapped it. Grabbing each end of the wood, he braced his elbows on his knees. The kids squirmed and giggled. Kurt split his on the first try. The parents applauded. With repositioning, Trent and Marco got it on the second try. Eva needed three tries. The instructor wrote each child's name and the date on the chunk of wood. Andie sniffled from the corner. Lee motioned for her to join them. She hop-skipped across the room and fell into his arms. He whispered into her ear. Holding onto Marco for balance, Andie positioned herself to kick the board.

"I saved this one just for you." Lee grabbed the ends.

The kick landed off-center, toes first. Caroline winced, expecting the little girl to burst into tears.

"Come on, Andie," Lee coaxed, his low voice fixing her attention. "A woman's strength is in her legs. You can do it."

Chin tucked into her chest, she glared at the board.

"Yell."

"Chicken!" The wood cracked. Andie raised her hands overhead in triumph, right arm straight, left arm gnarled with spasticity.

The instructor caught her in a bear hug. "You do me proud."

Lee dismissed the class and addressed the parents. "Some of you have asked about ordering the *gi*, the karate uniform. I've got the paperwork here. Ordering as a group, we can save on shipping. They're cotton and they shrink, so order a size large. They're fairly comfortable. Now, my sister got me a silk *gi* that's real comfortable..."
"

Silk draped over his shoulders, silk wrapped around his thighs... Caroline's magazine slipped between her knees, and slithered to the floor. Bending over, she rooted under the chair. An arm brushed her fingertips. Silk...

"I've got it." Lee placed the *Road and Track* on the seat in front of her. He had concluded his speech and the other parents left.

Caroline tried to stand up with as much dignity as possible. *If he could see my thoughts...* Her blush deepened.

"Are we still on for Saturday?"

She rolled the magazine in her palms, contemplating the colors at the edge of the pages. "Bring a light bulb; you've got a tail light out."

Ah, Romance, Caroline thought watching her birthday DVD from Marnie. Dennis Quaid and Ellen Barkin dance across the television screen at the end of *The Big Easy*. Yes, so easy. No sitter to pay. No discussion about where to go; it's always dinner and dancing at Tipitinas. No worry about what to wear since the actress always looks elegant, even when she's losing her dinner in the hero's toilet. Mindless; all the clever lines have been written and recited in an appropriately sexy tone. No date rape, sexually transmitted disease, wondering if he'll respect you in the morning. Easy.

Easy, but enough?

Absolutely, she told herself, ignoring the void in her heart.

Chapter Seven

"Pump. Hold." Sitting beside the Volkswagen's left front fender, Caroline watched the liquid level rise in the glass jar. "No air."

"Good job, Trent. Thanks for helping." Lee guided the boy out from beneath the steering wheel. Holding the man's foot onto the brake pedal wasn't necessary, but it kept Trent away from the corrosive brake fluid.

Caroline removed the plastic hose and tightly capped the former mayonnaise jar. Under the hood, she topped off the master cylinder reservoir level.

Lee rolled the tire to the hub. "I can finish this, if you change the light bulb."

Caroline returned her 7mm box end wrench to the tool chest. She opened the screwdriver drawer. No number two Phillips. She took off her safety goggles and looked again. Gone. "Have you seen my medium sized Phillips head screwdriver?"

"In your back pocket." Lee tightened the lug nuts. "So what's on your mind?"

Caroline ducked under the opened hatch. Perhaps he'd think she hadn't heard and drop the subject.

Trent careened around the front bumper, pushing the mechanic's creeper with one foot like a skateboard.

"Whoa, little buddy. Gonna get a big ow doing it that way." Lee caught the boy and flipped him onto his belly. "Pull with your arms, just like school."

"They use creepers at school?"

"Scooterboards. Kid-sized. To help build upper body strength, and give input to the vestibular system." Lee cranked down the jack and returned it to the spare tire well. He leaned over her shoulder, watching her fumble with the taillight assembly.

She held up the defective part, showing him the broken filaments. "Did you buy a replacement bulb?"

"Yeah." He cocked an eyebrow at her. "I gave it to you when I first got here, and you put it in a place I can't reach."

Blood surged to her face. Caroline retrieved the new light bulb from the chest pocket of her coveralls. "I'm sorry." Hurrying to finish the job, she mentioned one of her two preoccupations. "Ever since Tuesday, I've been thinking about Andie."

"Ah. You looked kinda flustered when you left. Should have figured Mrs. Holford would tell Andie's story. She used to do that to me when I went over to do respite care. Gave me nightmares. Seems like the only way of getting back at her cousin is telling the world all the bad things she did." Lee's hands tightened on the rim of the trunk. "Everyone gets upset about the mom, but what about the dad? Andie's got a younger sister, so he must have hung around. Why didn't he stop the abuse, make sure they got fed, take care of them? He never visits his girls, or calls to see how they're doing, or sends birthday cards even. Dads are supposed to..." Trent sideswiped Lee's sneakered foot. "Yeah, get off the soapbox. Andie's in good hands now. Don't worry."

Trent's father's no better than Andie's, Caroline realized with a jolt. She cleared her throat. "When you drive, go down about two houses at ten miles an hour, apply the brakes slowly..."

"Why don't you test drive it while I take Trent for a run around the block?" Lee closed the hatch.

Trent rocketed by on her creeper. With a full volume shriek he crashed into the garage wall. "Great idea." Caroline sent the boy inside for his coat. "Close the garage door after me." With thousands of dollars in tools, she didn't take any chances.

She turned the key in the VW's ignition, concentrating on the sound of the engine. No gauges, just idiot lights. Knobs missing from the right vent, left window, emergency brake handle. No air conditioning. How does he survive summer? Upholstery pins held the headliner to the roof. Fissures in the vinyl dash revealed the foam padding beneath. Caroline eased down the street, checking the brakes for pulling or fading. The lightweight car bounced over every seam in the concrete. This close to the road, ten miles an hour seemed like Mach one. Just for fun she continued through the intersection to an empty cul-de-sac. She twisted the steering wheel hard, doing a 180 in the middle of the street. Not a good idea on junk tires. Nice turning radius, though. She headed back to her house, feeling a vibration indicating the wheels needed balancing. The car braked to a smooth stop in front of the closed garage door. Should have taken the remote control. Caroline grabbed the knob of the front door. Locked. She rang the doorbell. No response. The sun had dropped behind the house. She turned her back to the brisk March wind, wishing she had thrown her coat on.

Lee and Trent rounded the corner. The man almost jogged in place so that the short-legged boy could keep up with him. Tucking her cold hands in her pockets, Caroline met them on the sidewalk.

"You didn't happen to take a key with you?"

"Stretch, Trent." Lee stepped forward into a deep lunge. "We're locked out."

Caroline frowned at the empty house across the street. "Until Sharon gets back."

He switched legs. "You have a sliding glass door."

"The builder said it's burglar proof."

"Maybe it's unlocked." Long strides took him around the house.

Locked out. *How could you be so stupid?* Bryan's words echoed from the time she'd left her keys in the house. Caroline shuddered.

The front door opened. "It's not burglar proof. You need a pipe or a broomstick..."

So critical, all the time. "You could karate chop a board for me."

"Maybe I will." One corner of his mustache lifted in an uncertain smile. "The answering machine on your landline was clicking when I came through."

Caroline hurried into the kitchen. She grabbed a handful of M&M's before pushing the flashing red button.

Her mother's voice announced, "I'm calling from University Hospital. Father and I are going to be fine. The number here is, uh, 813-555-9200, Room 618." The machine beeped into silence.

"Come on, Trent, let's play downstairs so your mom can make her phone call."

She punched the buttons so hard her fingers stung. "Mother? It's Caroline. Why are you at the hospital?"

"Thanks for calling back so promptly."

"Mother!"

"Well, we had a little problem at the house, just the Florida room. Your father said rainwater leaked in from the last storm and shorted out the TV. You'd know more about that than I."

"Why are you at the hospital?"

"Well, your father breathed in a little smoke. Well, more than a little. I don't want to worry you, but he did lose consciousness. The firemen gave him oxygen and he was fine. They just brought him to the hospital as a precaution. The doctor says he can probably go home tomorrow."

"The fireman? You had a fire? Is the doctor there now?"

"Well, no, dear. The doctor went on to his next patient."

Caroline pressed her fingers to her forehead. "He's fine, but they're keeping him in the hospital. Mother, how much of the house burned?"

"Well, I'm not sure. The firemen wouldn't let me back in. I think just the drapes in the Florida Room. I've been wanting to replace them anyway. Someone said something about turning off the electricity. I'm going to stay at the hotel across the street tonight."

"Mother, I'm coming down. I'll call the airlines and see how soon I can get a flight." Caroline brought up the airline's website on her cellphone.

"Oh, no, dear, you have work and Trent. I'm sure we'll be fine. I just wanted to let you know, in case you called the house and we didn't answer."

"Mother. How are you going to get home? What if the house needs a lot of repairs? What if Father needs special care? Are you going to call Chip, see if the Navy will let him swim home from the Persian Gulf? "

"Well, I haven't thought that far ahead. I suppose we could take a taxi."

"Stay right there in the hospital. I'll call you as soon as I have a flight."

Caroline called the senior engineer. He reluctantly agreed to let her take a week of her vacation. The Delta website informed her no planes ran Saturday night. Caroline booked two seats on the first flight out Sunday. So much to do. She pounded up the stairs and dumped the laundry on the landing. Whites, colors. Wash now, wash later.

"Caroline."

She'd forgotten Lee was in the house. He climbed three steps, just high enough so she could look him in the eye.

"Your folks all right?"

Some easily ignored part of her brain wondered if she should be embarrassed about sitting in a pile of dirty underwear. "My parents had a house fire—I'm not sure how extensive. Mother sounds rattled. Father's hospitalized, overnight at least. We're flying to Tampa tomorrow, so Trent will miss karate this week."

Lee followed her to the laundry room, handing her a sock of Trent's that escaped from the pile. "This is no vacation trip. You'll be busy taking care of your folks and their house. Extra work for you, taking Trent along."

Caroline stuffed the clothes into the washer. "What should I do with him? Suspended animation? Do you recommend Disney World or Cape Canaveral for that procedure?" She stomped back upstairs, calling over her shoulder, "I won't have time for a sign language lesson tonight, so you can go."

Lee tracked her to the bedroom. "I'm a respite care provider. I can stay with him. Then he won't miss school and you'll be able to concentrate on your folks."

Caroline gaped at the man filling her doorway. A crash and rattle echoed from the rec room; Trent dumping his race cars.

"I'll send him off in the morning, then go do my college and home school classes. Sharon has him afternoons. He can come with me to my evening classes. I don't have any house-sitting jobs this week, so it will work out good for me. I'll go start dinner."

She retrieved a Snickers bar from the nightstand and gnawed it down while staring blindly out the window. Would this work? All these years Trent had been solely her responsibility. She never admitted how much parenthood felt like a ball and chain. The day care or the sitter would call and she'd run. She declined over-time and double shifts to race home to Trent. Ford needed her in Dearborn, and she scrambled to patch together accommodations for Trent. Yes, the hotel provided child-care, until they found out the child is handicapped. Special fees for special needs. They sent a registered nurse. Ridiculous. And now Lee, his offer dropping in her lap. Too good to be true.

Caroline leaned her forehead against the cold glass. The last time they visited her parents, Trent had broken a Wedgwood vase, eaten half of a palmetto bug, and flooded the guest bathroom. He screeched at every seagull, generating a complaint call from a hard-of-hearing neighbor. This trip would be so much easier without him.

Lee's voice rumbled up from the kitchen, low and steady like well-tuned engine. Would Trent be all right with him? A pan rattled on the stove. At least the boy would eat well. Caroline considered the man, his remarks about fathers, the easy way he had with kids even when they disobeyed. Could she trust her child to someone she'd only known two months? She reached for the phone.

"Sharon. Thank God you're home." She briefed the sitter on the situation. "What do you think?" She hoped Sharon would offer to take Trent.

"Sounds like the perfect arrangement for all of you. Put Lee on, so he can tell me what time he'll stop by for Trent."

Caroline went down to the kitchen and handed her phone to

Lee. He had browned ground beef for tacos. A partially chopped onion lay on the cutting board. She set the table for three.

The man hung up the phone. "You called Sharon to check up on me." He lowered his head to scrutinize her with stern brown eyes.

"No, I..."

"I respect that. Don't ever leave him with someone you don't trust. He can't tell you if he's mistreated. I need your signature."

Caroline took the spiral bound notebook he shoved under her nose. Block printing read, "I give permission for Lee Marivaux to pick up Trent Jameson from school. I give permission for Lee Marivaux to seek emergency medical care for my son, Trent Jameson."

"I don't have the forms with me. I got the number of your folks' hospital off the message pad, but I'll need their home number, too. Write down your medical insurance carrier or leave the card. Is he allergic to anything?"

"No." Writing her name seemed to organize her thoughts. "I do not give you permission to take Trent in your car. Can you drive a truck?"

"I'll show you on the way to the airport." Lee tossed her his driver's license. "Clean. No points. My last ticket was for speeding on Interstate 10 between Baton Rouge and Lafayette. I was seventeen."

Caroline read the organ donor sticker, then flipped the license over. Five months younger than herself. Hard to tell. She said to the picture, "Ruskin Heights? Isn't that down past the zoo?"

He slid the plastic card from her fingers. "My sister's address. I'll throw your clothes in the dryer and check on Trent. Finish the onions."

Pulling the food processor from the appliance garage, Caroline ran the onions through in two seconds. She raced back upstairs to pack. Ten minutes later Lee announced dinner. He met her at the bottom of the stairs.

"Coveralls," he reminded her. "Doesn't bother me, but it might bother your fancy chairs."

When she popped the snaps open, he groaned and turned away. "What's the matter?" she asked his broad back.

His left palm circled above the counter before landing on the food processor. "Your dad's in the hospital, and maybe your mom should be, too. Their house burned down. You don't seem upset. You don't even cry when you cut onions." He waved the food processor in her face.

Caroline grabbed the appliance out of his hands. She shoved the bowl and blade into the dishwasher. The base returned to the appliance garage. "Now you're criticizing me for not crying? Mr. Marivaux, when you questioned what I feed Trent, how I dress him, what doctor I take him to, I put up with it. Your excuse was you cared about Trent. Well, where's the connection here?" Her nerves felt so frayed they might short out any minute.

"You traded me work on the car because you didn't have time for sign language lessons. Is there something else I can trade you, give you time to cry?" He leaned an elbow on the counter, bringing his face level with hers.

Caroline stared into his dark eyes. There was nothing she'd rather do than throw herself into his warm, strong arms and have a good bawl all over his stretched out gray sweatshirt. Lee's wrists rotated, his wide palms opened toward her. Caroline started shaking. She leaned toward him. That this man didn't even like her, that he was in her house only for his junk car, ceased to matter.

"Ma! Ma!" Trent smashed into her legs.

"Give your mom a hug, Trent. She needs it."

Chapter Eight

M orning sunlight bounced off the jet, freshly washed by last night's thunderstorm. *Airplane,* Lee signed to the little boy. Signing *go* required two hands and he didn't dare let loose of Trent after his mom's warnings. He signed *mom airplane,* and waved goodbye through the window. Keeping the tiny hand firmly encased in his large mitt, Lee steered the child outside and around the parking lot puddles. April wind shuffled his dark hair like a bourrée dealer, flipping it up, then laying it flat. So far, so good. No tears or tantrums. Yet. *Well, Marivaux, here's your chance to find out if any of your big ideas hold water. You asked for one day with this kid. What you gonna do in a week?* The back of his head echoed with an ominous lecture from a old karate instructor. Something about over-confidence.

"Well, let's see if I can teach you anything." He motioned the boy into the truck. "Can you buckle up by the time I get in?"

With a grin, Trent snatched up the ends of the belt. Lee jogged around to the driver's side.

"Yah!" Trent raised his arms, showing the fastened belt.

"All right! Give me five!" Lee held out his palm. Ten minutes of parenting. Still doing okay.

On the way back to the house, he stopped at the store. "Mom left us a ton of money. What do you want to eat this week?"

Trent signed *ice cream*.

"Use your words," he prompted.

"I key."

"I hope that's the only sign you know, not the only thing you eat." Lee directed the boy into the store. Trent held out his arms to be lifted into the grocery cart. "No. Today, you drive." He blew on each square palm and placed them on the handle. "Glued." Steering from the front, Lee headed for the produce aisle. "Apples, carrots, lettuce..." *Wham.* A cold metal bar slammed into both Achilles tendons, sending him sprawling into the cucumbers.

"*Mer*—" He cut short the French swear word. "Mercy!" He glared at Trent.

Bug-eyed, the boy shrank low, hanging by his hands. "Ow?"

"Big ow." Lee limped around the deadly vehicle. "You steer. I'll drive." Trent's body moved away, but his palms remained on the handle. Lee would have laughed, if his ankles hadn't been screaming with pain. "Stuck, eh?" He blew on the hands again, peeling them off.

Trent's fist circled his chest. *Sorry, sorry, sorry.*

"Apology accepted." Lee reglued one little boy hand to the front of the basket, the other into his pocket.

When they reached the back of the store, Trent's left hand shot up in the air, its thumb between the first and second fingers of the fist. *Toilet.*

"Where's the nearest men's room?" Lee asked a white-coated man stocking packages of ground beef.

"We don't have public facilities." The meat cutter glanced from Lee to the little boy fidgeting at the end of the shopping cart. He jerked his thumb at the double doors swinging in the back wall. "First door at the top of the stairs."

Lee tucked Trent under his arm and dove through a canyon walled by boxes. Ignoring his throbbing ankles, he took the stairs two at a time. He pushed open the first door, seeing the reason for the meat man's reluctance.

"Ugh. Hope you just have to pee."

Trent nodded. Lee stood him in front of the urinal. The boy held his palms up and shrugged in the universal *huh?*

"You've never used one of these before?" Wait a minute. The special ed bathroom at Trent's school has extra wide doors and grab bars, but no urinals. "Okay, can't blame Mom for not teaching you this." Lee reached for his fly.

Lesson completed, hands washed, Trent swaggered back down the stairs. His posture, shoulders back and chest out, seemed to say "real men pee standing up". He resumed his place. Except for a collision with a cardboard dehydrated soup display, saved from disaster by Lee's quick reflexes, they survived the shopping trip. His ankle pain tapered to a dull ache. An hour and fifty-two minutes. Slightly bruised, but teaching all sorts of interesting lessons.

Pulling up in front of the house, Lee tapped the remote control with his knuckle. The garage door slid open and the truck eased inside. "Here's George Jetson," he said to himself.

The theme song from the cartoon hummed from the passenger side. Little hands traced space ships in the air.

A chuckle rumbled through Lee's chest. "Okay, my little robot, get to work." Trent staggered in with the sack of potatoes. The man followed with the rest of the groceries.

"Now you learn to cook gumbo." Lee pulled a chair to the counter a safe distance from the stove. The boy climbed up, his face eager. Everything's an adventure for him: the airport, grocery shopping, cooking. That's the way to live, with eyes wide open and heart so happy.

"Lots of mess we make." Oil heated in a heavy pot for the roux. Water boiled in a saucepan for the okra. Celery, onion, and peppers sautéed in the Dutch oven. "Who's gonna clean up, now your ma's gone?" He pointed to Trent. "You."

The boy stabbed his pudgy finger into Lee's ribs. "You."

The big man looked down his nose at the child. "Me, I'm the cook. You clean up."

Trent giggled. "You!"

The oil sputtered. Lee stirred in the flour. "What say we let the dishwasher clean up?"

Trent pointed at the machine. "You!"

Lee shook the Worcestershire sauce over the vegetables. "Now a real gumbo, you make with fresh okra pulled out of your garden in the morning. Throw in everyt'ing you catch - de oysters, de crabs, de fishes, de crawfish. Now de crawfish, some call 'em mudbugs, jump around like this..." Lee wiggled his fingers and tickled Trent's belly. "You t'row dem in de water 'til dey red. Den you yank off dey heads, squeeze de tail until it crack, and *voila*, meat for gumbo."

Trent's gaze darted from the food to the man. Spit pooled on his hung-open lip. Lee tapped under his chin.

"No crawfish today. Just grocery store fish. Sometime we go fishing, eh? You and me, catch de crawfish?" He stirred the okra and roux into the vegetables. "And when you start talking Cajun, I'll catch it from your ma."

Trent watched his every move as he cooked rice, and added fish and tomatoes to the gumbo. The boy set the table without dropping any bowls. If he had a kid like this, they'd use plastic and not worry about breaking stuff. Guess high-class people don't think like that.

Lee ladled the gumbo onto a mound of rice in each bowl. "Now, you add your filé you collected from the sassafras tree during the last full moon of summer. You hung it up to dry, and ground it up, and saved in the refrigerator for this special gumbo. But if you didn't..." Lee saw a worried look pass over the boy's face. "If you didn't save your sassafras leaves, I'll give you some of mine." He added a sprinkle of olive green powder to each bowl, adding its wild parsley smell to the mix of aromas. "Now we eat!" Lee dug into the concoction. Not bad, considering all the substitutions he had to make.

Trent frowned at his bowl.

"Good. Try it."

The boy dipped out a puny spoonful, mostly rice. He touched his tongue to the corner of the spoon, gagged, and dropped it back into the bowl. Red sauce spattered the table.

"Hey. Why for you spit out good food?"

Trent's bones seemed to melt under Lee's glare. He slithered down the chair and under the table like some swamp varmint returning to its watery hole.

"What's wrong? Are you sick?"

"No."

"Well, come up and eat. We need to go to Gladstone soon."

"No."

"Aren't you hungry?"

"No."

"Then can I have your gumbo?"

A pause. "Yah."

Hah. Got you to say something besides no. Four or five bites later, Lee heard a sniffling noise under the table.

"Hey, you wanna cry, go to your room."

Trent crawled out. His bottom lip dragged low over his chin. *Want pizza please please please.*

"Today's lunch is gumbo."

No want that. Want hamburger.

"Today's lunch is gumbo."

Tears the size of wild onions dripped off his face. *Mom make good eat.*

Lee had some serious doubts about his mom's skill as a cook. Most of her cache consisted of canned spaghetti in cartoon shapes. Half her spices had never been opened. Lee shook his spoon at the boy. "Go to your room. When you're done crying, you come eat your gumbo."

Trent whimpered louder with each step. Reaching his bedroom, the boy went into a full-blown wail. Lee called to him to close his door. For a little kid, he slammed pretty hard. Ornery cuss. Lee fought back the urge to paddle his behind, against the rules for respite providers. The kid quieted down about the time Lee finished his second helping. Halfway through scouring the pot, he heard the clink of a spoon against a bowl. He turned just enough to see Trent shovel in a spoonful of gumbo. The boy polished off the bowl, then loaded it in the dishwasher.

Lee lifted him up, touching his big honker to the boy's stubby nose. "Was that so bad?"

Trent gave a big sniffly sigh with lots of looking at the ceiling, then the floor. He wobbled a flat hand. *So-so.* Such a critic.

Reaching for a tissue, Lee glimpsed the digital clock on the microwave.

"Oh, man! I've got to be in Gladstone in ten minutes. Trent! Shoes on! Let's go!" He raced through the house, checking the stove, grabbing the keys, shoving his bare feet into sneakers. Yelling for Trent, he dug his gym bag out of the VW and threw it in the truck. Still no kid. Running through the house, he searched the rec room, kitchen, and bedroom. He found the boy under his bed, eyes round and scared like the nutria pup he'd trapped under the porch when he was eight. "Time to go!"

Trent shook his head.

"Yes. Now." Lee lifted the bed and pulled the boy out. The problem was obvious: wet pants. "Pants off." He rooted through the drawers for dry clothes, then dressed Trent. Should make the boy do it himself and clean up whatever mess he had made. If the kid's mom saw him now... How does she ever get to work on time?

They pulled into the Gladstone church parking lot fifteen minutes late. Four hours and five minutes of parenting. Running behind.

LEE SAT on the edge of the twin bed, listening to Trent's prayers. This is what I'm here for, he thought, for this boy. "Good night, Trent." He smoothed the dark hair back from the low forehead. "I love you, too." He returned the sign. Beyond the bedroom window, a dog barked twice and was called inside. A car rolled past, its tires a low hum on the newly paved street. Leaving the door open an inch, he stepped into the hall.

Lee paused at the next room. Her room. The streetlight's beam fell across the king-sized bed, a clean set of sheets folded at its foot. She had said he could use her room, sleep in her bed. He closed his eyes, catching a whiff of her scent, something sophisticated and expensive, just like her. Caroline. Out of reach. Not an option. His fingers dug into the door frame. His toes curled into the carpet. Discipline. He shook himself, pushing away from temptation.

Lee opened the door of the third bedroom. No furniture, just cardboard boxes. He glanced into the nearest open carton. Textbooks stacked spine up. Lee scanned the titles: *Fundamentals of Manufacturing Processes, Design and Implementation of CAE Systems, Mechanical Engineering Tools.* Tools? Now, there's a word he recognized. He flipped through pages of fancy-schmancy numbers, gobbledygook diagrams, and drawings that looked nothing like any tool he knew. Naw, the word on the cover is the only familiar thing here. The book dropped back into the box with a crunch. Lee fished around underneath it, digging up a slightly crumpled wad of papers. The cover page read *Finite Element Methods for Calculating Machine Forces and Stress by Caroline Jameson.* He skimmed the first few paragraphs. Oh, man, she could have written this in Chinese and he'd get just as much out of it. Miss Caroline was way out of his league in every way possible. He headed to the car for his sleeping bag.

Passing through the rec room, Lee stopped to clean the popcorn mess. Trent had earned a showing of *Jonah: A VeggieTales Movie* through good behavior during karate class. Stretching out on the sofa with one arm around the boy felt so right, so good, he had indulged in a quick snooze. Until the little stinker spilled the bowl of old maids down his neck. Lee pulled up the cushions. Major mess. *Tomorrow's lesson is vacuuming.* What's this? A DVD, *The Big Easy.* The story of a Cajun and a Yankee who fall in love. Now why would Caroline watch this? Could she... Naw, that Cajun has a job.

Lightning streaked across the bare window of the third bedroom. Thunder rumbled over the house. *No dog to let in. All the windows are closed.* Lee rolled over, pulling a corner of the sleeping bag over his face.

"Ma!" Little boy feet padded in the hall. "Ma?"

Lee propped up on his elbows. "In here, Trent."

Another flash lit the boy, eyes dark and round in his white face.

He dove in beside Lee. His trembling body snuggled into the man's arms. He let out a big shaky sigh, then his breathing settled into a slow, even rhythm. Just that fast, he was asleep.

"I'll keep you safe." Lee adjusted the sleeping bag to cover the child. He rubbed his cheek against the silky crown of the small head. First night, twelve, fourteen hours maybe. All's well.

"Caroline, we've been so busy this visit, you haven't shown me any pictures of my grandson." Mrs. Jameson passed her daughter a drapery bracket.

She aligned the bit of the electric drill with the screw, then attached the bracket to the wall. "My phone's in my purse."

"Don't get down, dear, I'll get it." Mother disappeared into the guest room.

Caroline breathed in the gulf breeze, extra humid from drying paint. "Don't get down? Just move the ladder while standing on it?" She drilled the final two screws into the wall and snuck an M&M from the pocket of her shorts. She hoped Mother couldn't tell how much time she'd spent staring at those pictures, especially the one of herself and Lee. His relaxed sprawl in the middle of the sofa, his expression of delight at Trent's operation of the camera, contrasted too sharply with her edge-of-the-seat tension. She'd studied the other photos, memorizing the man's broad face, the deep smile lines framing his mustache, the dark eyes sparkling under low brows. His nose started narrow at the bridge, ran straight, then ended with a trio of interlocking spheres like a three dimensional Venn diagram. Waves of hair curled back from his face, covering all but the lobe of his ear, shining like the meringue on last night's Key lime pie.

"This must be the man staying with Trent. He sounds so nice on the phone."

"Did you see the ones from our last snowfall?" Caroline lugged the ladder to the other end of the Florida room.

"He's handsome, very handsome." The older woman would not be distracted from the pictures of Lee. "And over at your house."

"He takes a personal interest in all his students."

"Of course," she said, her tone implying she didn't believe that for a minute. "What are they doing here?"

Caroline paused on the first rung. The photo showed Trent flying through the air, the soles of Lee's feet supporting his stomach. "Working on balance and, I believe he said, extensor muscles."

"Muscles. I hope I can meet him sometime."

"You'd enjoy the class." She sorted through her memory file. "Lee works those kids like a maestro of karate. I can really see Trent improving. His posture, his coordination, even his behavior."

The sun glared on the arthritic knuckles handing her another bracket. "Caroline, you've done so much for us: driving your father to doctor's appointments, supervising the crew cleaning up the smoke damage, taking me shopping for drapes. Didn't you think that carpet installer, Jorge, had nice legs?"

"Mother, really."

"Anyway, you do so much for us and for Trent. Ford works you far too hard. And Caroline, I know men of your father's generation don't believe this, but women have needs. If you want to... well, if you practice safe sex..."

The drill slipped out of the screw and impaled the wall. "Mother! You've been watching talk-shows again." The woman had no idea how close she'd come to throwing herself at this man, behaving like a nymphomaniac. Caroline didn't need the guardrail of her mother's opinion dismantled. She lined up the drill for a second try.

Mrs. Jameson held up the picture of Trent on tiptoes, reaching for Lee's foot as the man executed a roundhouse kick over his head. "I'll visit you this summer. I've got to see this guy in shorts."

LEE PARKED the pickup in the driveway. Thanks to daylight savings time, the sun wouldn't set for another hour. The afternoon was warm enough, not much wind. He glanced over at the boy. Bath night anyway. "Let's wash Mom's truck."

Trent exploded off the seat into his arms. "Yah!"

As he expected, Caroline had organized a clean bucket, a large car washing sponge, a bottle of special soap, and a stack of chamois cloths on a shelf in the garage. Lee showed Trent how to connect the hose and the nozzle. While they sprayed the truck, the Buffum boys sped by on bicycles. Lee looked at Trent. The boy nodded as if reading his mind. The man crouched by the back tire and Trent peeked around the tailgate.

Come here now, he signed.

Lee jumped up and sprayed Paul and Luke. The afternoon deteriorated into a neighborhood water fight with a truck wash on the side.

When the sun went down, Lee passed out chamois to the kids and rolled up the hose. A couple left the house next door to walk their golden retriever. Lee introduced himself as they passed, mentioning his availability for dog sitting. Sharon called her boys in, ordering them to take a hot bath.

Lee glanced at his boy, all blue lipped and shivering. "You too. Hot bath."

Day seven of parenting. Don't want it to end.

CAROLINE STEPPED out of the the secure area at the Kansas City International terminal. Late afternoon sunlight through the clerestory windows gilded the wood paneled walls and lit the smile of a six year old boy on a tall man's shoulders.

"Ma! Ma!"

"There's my boy!"

Lee knelt so Caroline could lift the child off his neck. Her son felt different. It seemed he'd grown muscles, heavy muscles in the week of her absence.

"How was your trip?" Lee's hand brushed her elbow. For a second Caroline thought he intended to embrace her, too. She looked into his eyes. Her heart did an odd flip flop, like when the plane hit an air pocket in flight.

Chocolate deprivation.

"Fine," she managed to stutter.

The big man did an abrupt about-face. "I'll get the truck."

A mink-coated matron cornered Caroline and Trent by the baggage carousel. "Your husband is so good with the little boy."

"He's not my—"

"I was seeing my son off on a flight to Baltimore. He's in his final year at the Naval Academy, so I know discipline. Your husband has the discipline of a military officer and the patience of a saint. It's a rare combination in men," she flipped her wrist, "with normal children. It must be even more uncommon with special children. Why I can hardly believe how well behaved this little fellow..."

Caroline pulled Trent away from the conveyor belt. Her son, well behaved? Most people just ignored him, at best sending her a sympathetic glance. She had never been complimented on his behavior. The carousel spit up her maroon Samsonite. Caroline murmured "excuse me" and made her escape.

Lee met them at the revolving door. With a wave worthy of the hastiest chauffeur, he ushered them into the pickup, then jogged around to the driver's seat. His hands froze on the steering wheel. "This is your truck."

"Go ahead. I'm a little jet-lagged."

A smile twitched his mustache. He steered the vehicle onto Interstate 435. The Missouri farmland rolled by, a subtle mix of greens and yellows, soothing after Florida's glaring neons. "A guy could get used to this."

Lee's the kind of man we build trucks for, Caroline thought. He looks just right in the F-150, more comfortable than when he squeezes into his compact. There's enough head-room here for the tallest Stetson. "I'll be selling it when the new models come out, if you're interested."

"Even if I could afford the gas, 'fraid I've run out of things to trade you."

Trent pulled a crayoned paper from under the seat. "No-ah." He had scribbled over a line drawing of animals boarding a boat.

"Noah? You went to church?"

"Couldn't leave him home. Hope that's OK."

"How did he do?"

"They asked him back for next week. We went to the same place the Buffums go. Sharon leads the children's church."

Trent's first visit to a church and first compliment on his behavior, all in one day. She wrapped an arm around her son. Lee deserved credit, not just for the improvement in Trent's behavior, but for giving her the week to attend to her parents. She considered how to show her appreciation. Broke as he was, he probably wouldn't accept cash beyond the usual respite care fee. Not something for his home, since he was homeless. Were clothes too personal? "I could get you an application for the plant."

"Only if they need a karate instructor."

"You could still teach nights and weekends. It would give you health insurance, a regular paycheck, retirement benefits."

"So you think I should give up a job I love for... money." He slouched deep into the seat.

"What about going to college? I could see you teaching PE."

"Yeah. University of Missouri has a new Adaptive PE program, Phys Ed for kids with handicaps, that sounds good."

"Surely you'd qualify for financial aid."

Lee eased the truck onto the Liberty exit ramp. "Seems to bother you more than it bothers me."

Caroline stared at the limestone bordering the highway. So much for trying to help.

LEE SCOWLED at the rock outcropping on the north. Rich people had it easy. Daddy picks up the bill for college. All his little darling has to worry about is making it into a suitable sorority and meeting Mr. Right. He glanced at the lady leaning against the truck door, then reached behind her to push the lock down. She startled. "Sorry. Don't want you falling out."

Pretty lady, what makes you jump so? He focused on the road. Her Mr. Right had turned into Mr. Wrong. What had that jerk done? Was there any way to undo the damage? Monday morning when he taught at the women's shelter, he'd have a talk with the counselor.

. . .

RELEASED from an hour's car ride, Trent raced full speed, top volume through the house. Beef stew bubbled fragrantly from the crock pot. Lee corralled the boy into setting the table. Caroline had considered this chore beyond the child's ability, until she noticed plates and utensils had been outlined on construction paper placemats. Lee had made another change: every piece of furniture now sported an index card tag. "Why did you label everything?"

"It's not *Better Homes and Gardens*, yeah." One shoulder lifted. "I found an article about kids with Down's learning to sight read. Trent has a stack of flash cards. Ask him to make some sentences for you after dinner."

Reading? He can't even talk.

Caroline began sorting the week's collection of bills and ads.

Lee rested his elbows on the counter next to her, one leg stretched behind him. He flicked a business card between his fingers. "Remember I told you over the phone, my Thursday class gave a demonstration at Antioch Mall. Well, this photographer was there, working for the little shopping center newspaper. He got a good shot of Trent breaking a board. Most of this taking pictures of kids with handicaps, poster children, Jerry's Kids, doesn't sit well with me. But you may want to look over Phil's work. If you don't want Trent's photo published, just don't sign the release."

"All right." Caroline added the card to the "to do" pile. The next letter bore a Boston postmark and her friend Marnie's handwriting. She ripped into the envelope.

"Just in time for April fools," read the note. A newspaper clipping showed a classic pose, politician and wife waving at their supporters. Bryan had declared his candidacy for State House.

"'Real Estate Mogul Bryan Ashcroft.' Trent's father." Lee's eyebrows lowered and his face tightened with a clenched jaw. "Looks like a weasel. Why isn't he in jail?"

Caroline inched away from the big man. "Because he's smart enough not to leave any evidence."

"But not smart enough to keep his hands to himself." Lee

grabbed the clipping. "What's to stop him from abusing the new Mrs. Ashcroft?"

Her hands shook as she sipped her Diet Coke. "She probably won't produce defective children."

Lee speared her with one of his looks. The newspaper crumpled in his hand, then hit the wastebasket. "He's not good enough for Trent. Not good enough for you. And, in spite of being Yankees, I'm sure the people of Boston deserve better."

Caroline felt Lee holding his anger at idle throughout dinner. While Trent brushed his teeth, she found the man alone in the third bedroom. He sat on the floor next to her boxes of college textbooks, rolling up a green sleeping bag. "You could have used my bed."

"Don't matter." He jerked on the ties, snapping one off.

"What's this?" A Styrofoam block the size of an accelerator pedal hung from the ceiling, level with her head.

"For kicking practice." He pulled the tack from the ceiling and wound the string around the block.

"You can kick that high?"

"Not with jeans on."

With his jeans off... Put the brakes on that thought!

Caroline steadied herself on the door frame and cleared her throat. "Lee, you've been wonderful with Trent this week. And the house looks great." The toe of her pump traced the vacuum cleaner tracks on the carpet. "You're welcome to stay. That is, if you don't have another house-sitting job. If you do, well, please come back any time."

He tossed the sleeping bag over his shoulder. "No."

"I could buy you a bed. What kind of mattress do you like?" He pushed past her without answering. Caroline sighed, feeling the week's hectic pace catch up to her. "Okay. How much do I owe you?"

She went to the kitchen for her checkbook. The house vibrated with the garage door motor, then the sputter of a Volkswagen engine. She sprinted downstairs in time to see the tail lights of the VW turn the corner.

"Bad idea, anyway. I don't need you criticizing me every time I turn around."

LEE BRAKED at the entrance to the subdivision. His leg shook on the clutch pedal. All week he'd been telling himself not to get used to the good life - a home, plenty of food, a little boy. He'd long ago given up on the dream of a house in the suburbs, a wife and kids. An impossible dream for a swamp rat like him. Now Caroline, in asking him to stay, dangled this counterfeit in his face. She didn't know what it meant. It hurt so much to think about, he sure couldn't say it aloud. He'd apologize Tuesday at karate. "Su-wave and de-bone-er," he said to the face in the rear view mirror.

"LEE?" Trent climbed into bed.

"He's gone." Caroline smoothed the covers.

The bottom lip curled out. *No want go.*

"You'll see him Tuesday at karate."

The boy pondered this a moment, then shrugged his acceptance. From under his pillow, he presented a book with a construction paper cover. "Re?"

"Okay. Just one story." Caroline sat on the bed.

"No. Me re." Trent pointed to the words, his voice approximating the sounds. "Sunday Mom flew." Royal blue crayon covered the penciled drawing of an airplane. He turned the copier paper page. "Monday Trent vacuumed. Tuesday Trent made salad. Wednesday library." He pointed to a cardboard box by the bed. Dr. Seuss's *One Fish, Two Fish* topped the stack of books inside. An envelope glued to the outside held the boy's new library card. "Thursday Trent set the table. Friday we fed ducks at Winn Lake. Saturday we washed Mom's truck."

Is he reading or memorizing? Either way, it's amazing. "Sounds like you had a great week, Trent." Caroline set his book on the nightstand and listened to him pray for several hundred people. She added the amen when he yawned.

"Ma." Trent signed *I love you*.

Caroline arranged her fingers to mirror his. "I love you, too." She turned out his light.

Instead of the usual mess, she found the bathroom hotel clean. A construction paper grid posted on the wall showed why. Caroline translated the line drawings. Trent received stars for putting his clothes in the laundry, returning the cap to the toothpaste, hanging up his washcloth, and flushing. Finding a marker on top of the medicine cabinet, she added the stars for that night. Simple system. Break down the task into its components. Something an engineer should be able to figure out, given a demonstration by a karate instructor. Lee. Caroline smiled at her reflection in the mirror. Can't stay mad at anyone this innovative.

The phone rang while she polished off a slice of the devil's food cake Lee had baked.

Sharon's voice bubbled over the line. "Caroline. How was Florida?"

"Fine. My parents are healthy and back in their home. How did it go here?"

"Terrific. Lee's just what Trent needs."

"Well, that's what I thought, so I offered him the extra bedroom. He went tearing out of here like I'd promised him battery acid for breakfast." The sitter didn't say anything. "Sharon? You know him better than I do. Did I offend him somehow?"

"I think... he'd like to accept your offer, but it has to be on his own terms."

"Which are?"

"You're just going to have to wait for him to tell you."

Chapter Nine

L ee paused on the back porch of the shelter, watching an elderly woman work the flower bed. He knew what she was up to, trying to make the eight-foot privacy fence look less like a prison wall. The rhythm and sureness of her motions reminded him of Mama, the way she gardened. Except this refined lady didn't favor the chain-smoking earthy woman who'd raised him. And these formal arrangements of cultivars didn't look like Mrs. Marivaux's riotous mix of wildflowers and vegetables.

Miss Pearl Coverdell leaned back and waved. "Time for self-defense class already?" A trembling hand fumbled with the watch pinned to the yoke of her muumuu, its tropical flowers an inspiration for the spring buds.

"No ma'am. Just dropping off those seedlings Bernie promised you. Don't stop on account of me." Lee kicked off his sneakers and crossed the manicured lawn. Without waiting, she wobbled up onto her heron legs. He grabbed her bony elbow as she wove in the breeze. "Let's get you out of the sun."

"Dear boy," she murmured as he settled her into a porch chair, and again when he brought her a glass of orange juice from the kitchen. She took a dainty sip, then a generous swallow. "All this needs is a little champagne." She winked. The color returned to her face.

"Your doctor, what's he saying?"

Miss Pearl stirred the air with her wide-brimmed straw hat. Wisps of silver hair traced her skull. "Lee, two years ago, they gave me a month to live. Why ever would I listen again?" Violet eyes fixed on him. "You, dear, I will listen to. What's on your mind?"

Like a dog with an old tennis ball, he'd worried the subject to pieces. Now his thoughts wouldn't go back together. "These children here, how's it affect them?"

"Children who witness domestic violence," Pearl straightened in the rattan chair, slipping into her public speaking voice, "learn to use violence to solve their problems. The boys grow into men who perpetuate the abuse. The girls become passive women who accept beatings as the norm."

"*Mais*, yeah, but a boy who hasn't seen, well, he was a couple months old when his mom bailed out."

"So we're not talking about any of the children living here now."

Lee smoothed the bushy mustache he'd forgotten to trim. "No. One of my students. He's six years old." *Just now he's climbing onto the school bus. Did he show his mom he can dress himself?*

"Then, it depends on how his mother's adjusted." Pearl's statement asked the question.

"Seems okay. Makes a decent living, takes good care of the boy." He knew what she'd ask next. "They're safe."

"Would she come in to see me?"

Lee shook his head. "I asked. She doesn't have time."

"I can't say much..." The counselor tipped her chin up, squinting at the walled garden as if she might find Caroline out there. "Perhaps you've seen some difficulty with control issues, discipline."

"Spanking's out, yeah."

"As much as I paid to have this porch screened in! I will not abide spiders indoors." Clutching her hat to her chest, the woman stared at the tongue-and-groove ceiling. "Get the vacuum! Quick! The hall closet!"

"Miss Pearl?" Lee stepped closer, trying to remember if he should start CPR or call 911 first. "What's the matter?"

"If they're that big in April, they'll be tarantulas by August! Lee, the vacuum!"

He scooped up the spider.

"No! What if it's poisonous? A brown recluse or a black widow?"

"If it's a black widow, we'll keep it as house mascot." He tossed offending creature out into the garden.

"House mascot? Mr. Marivaux, however heinous the abuse, we do not advocate murder here."

"Except spider murder." His fingers pressed the inside of her wrist. Her pulse beat hummingbird fast, but regular.

"What if there are more spiders? Yet another reason for you to take one of our cellphones."

"Those were donated for victims of domestic violence, not me." Lee shook his head. "I get by."

Miss Pearl studied him over her glass. A nip of juice set her back in counselor mode. "A woman who leaves with her two-month-old baby and lives alone for six years, doesn't sound passive, dependent. Although in relationships, she may endure long periods of frustration, letting resentments build, rather than the healthy pattern of working through problems as they arise."

Lee sat cross-legged on the cement floor, avoiding the fragile wicker. "She doesn't date."

"Perhaps she equates intimacy with vulnerability, feeling unsafe."

"I think she's afraid of men, yeah. Couple times I've scared her. Six years. Will she ever get over it?"

"Once she knows you as well as I do..."

Lee picked dew-stuck grass clippings off his feet. "I'm just wondering, well, trying to figure out if this mom, her fear, might affect the boy somehow." He squirmed through one of those pauses counselors use to get people to say more. He'd dug this hole deep enough.

"Lee, with a teacher like you, I'm sure the boy will do just fine."

The tiny hand squeezed his shoulder with surprising strength. "As for the mother, remember what I taught you. Let her know you believe what she tells you. Reassure her the abuse wasn't her fault. Don't make decisions for her. With a friend like you, she'll learn to trust again."

Caroline scrolled through a week's worth of email she didn't have time to read: a message from headquarters about first quarter earnings, notes from personnel on benefits, and a query from Dearborn Truck about media barrier faulting on the 3.8 bell. Nothing that couldn't wait until this afternoon. She closed the mail file and printed the agenda for today's meeting. Al's voice crackled over the radio, "Jameson, we're waiting."

Ford Production System folder in hand, she raced down the paint line, glancing at the marquee and the Behrs. If everything continued to run this smoothly, she might have time for lunch today. She ran up the stairs, dropped her paint-sticky shoes on the landing, and hurried into the conference room full of engineers.

"So nice of you to join us," Al sneered.

Taz stepped to the white board. "Old Business. Labeling 2K pump assemblies inside the booth..."

Caroline felt her stomach growl. What's the deal? Usually she didn't notice hunger until she stopped to eat. Of course, all last week, Mother fed her like a visiting dignitary. Then there's the slice of devil's food cake in her lunch cooler. A man who can cook. What more could you ask for? Someone who'll stick around. Why—

"Caroline?" Taz interrupted.

"Left her brain in Florida," Al growled.

"At least she has one."

She sat up straighter. "I'm sorry. The question?"

"The prime overheads falling out of home."

"I'll work with maintenance. Find out why they're slipping." *Now if I could find out why my thoughts keep slipping back to a certain karate instructor.*

"Directional valves are on order. Item four..."

By taking detailed notes, Caroline stayed focused through the rest of the new business. She stood to report on the previous quarter's equipment malfunctions. "The problem with losing painting parameters on the Behrs seems confined to Monday mornings. It happened again yesterday when I came in. All operators were instructed to run a ghost and check their data when they first arrive in the morning."

The intercom beeped. "Jameson. Phone. The nurse at your son's school."

"Lee! You never come down here just to see me. Who is it this time?" Gemma, his favorite RN at Children's Mercy, popped out of the fourth floor nurses' station. She stood just about as high as his elbow.

He tightened his grip on the grocery sack to keep from patting her on the head. "Trent Jameson."

The Filipino woman motioned for him to follow. "The little boy with Down's. He's doing fine. Sleeping now, on oxygen. High white count. Antibiotics should have him home in a few days."

"Pneumonia?"

Gemma nodded, her long black braid rippling down the back of her peach colored scrubs.

"Oh, man. I got him wet Saturday, soaking wet, chilled. We got carried away washing his mom's truck."

Gemma punched him in the arm. "You're as silly as these parents. You know germs cause pneumonia, not cold water."

"Germs. Not my fault." Guilt let go of him so quickly, he nearly lost his balance.

Pausing before an open door, Gemma turned with a look of concern in her dark eyes. "If you stay, you can remove the restraints."

"Restraints? Isn't his mother with him?"

"It's the mother I'm worried about."

"Mrs. Jameson? Don't know if she'll want to see me. I got her mad Sunday night."

"Do you mean angry or catatonic?"

Lee bent to look the nurse in the eye. Gemma could pull a leg faster than a pair of too tight blue jeans. Nothing hurtful, just a way of putting people at ease in the tense hospital atmosphere. She looked dead serious tonight.

Taking a deep breath, Lee plunged into the shadowy room. Trent slept frog-legged in the hospital bed. He snored loudly with uneven grunts and wheezes. An oxygen line circled his colorless face, crossing under his nose. An IV dripped into his arm. The monitor showed normal heart rate and rhythm, near as Lee could tell. Setting the grocery sack by the door, the man untied one restraint, feeling the boy's hot, dry skin. He stepped around the end of the bed. Caroline hadn't moved, hadn't blinked, since he walked in.

"Hello." Lee worked at the knot. "Between the two of us, bet we can keep Trent from pulling out his IV." No response. The woman looked as pale as the child. "Caroline?" He touched the ice-cold hand holding Trent's.

She jerked back. "Lee? What are you doing here?"

Lee shifted back to the end of the bed. "You never miss class, so I called Sharon."

"Oh, yes. It's Tuesday."

"She told me Trent had been coughing and started running a temp. You did the right thing, bringing him here."

Wary green eyes stared back at him. "The right thing? That's a first. I was sure you'd chew me out for letting him get sick."

Lee shook his head slowly. Instead of being united by their concern for Trent, it seemed like they were on the verge of another argument. "You are doing a good job keeping him healthy. Kids this age usually catch something every six weeks or so. Despite all the germs he's exposed to in school, at Sharon's, in my class, Trent made it through the past three months without even an ear infection. No, I'm not blaming you for this pneumonia."

"Pneumonia? I thought it was his heart. They've got him hooked to this oscilloscope and it's making all these spikes."

"That's what it's supposed to do." Caroline looked so surprised,

Lee repeated the rest of the report Gemma had given him. The staff usually did an excellent job talking with parents. "When did you eat last?"

She glanced at her watch. "I missed lunch..."

"Go on down to the cafeteria. I'll stay with Trent."

Caroline pulled herself up by the bed rail. She swayed. Her pupils shrank to pinpoints.

Lee lunged for her, guiding her back to the chair. "Are you diabetic? No. Stress, maybe. I'll get the food." He retied Trent's restraints before leaving the room.

A raid on the vending machines yielded a turkey sandwich of unknown vintage and a pint of milk. Lee knew she preferred Diet Coke, but she needed calcium more than caffeine tonight. A little chocolate would be all right though. He added a Hershey bar to his haul.

Trent snored away when Lee returned. He set the food on the bedside table and wheeled it to Caroline. Her eyes glittered in the light from the hall. A dark smear streaked from the edge of one eye across her temple.

"Just now would be a good time to cry."

She shook her head. A shudder passed through her. She pressed her hands to her knees, trying to keep herself still.

He wanted to hold her, but instead brought her a hot soapy washcloth. "Can't have you getting sick, too."

"Ma..." Trent held up his fist, thumb tucked between the index and middle fingers.

"I'll take care of this. You eat." Lee grabbed the urinal. "Hi, little buddy. Guess what you get to do? Pee in this bottle."

CAROLINE STUDIED Lee's broad back as he encouraged Trent to "fill 'er up". Illness infuriated Bryan. He never got sick. She must be doing something wrong, have some weakness in her constitution that she succumbed to a cold or flu every couple years. He'd grill her: Did you use a public restroom? Did you buy food from a street vendor? Why didn't the doctor just fix her? He could have closed the Berwick deal if it hadn't been for her thoughtless disruption of his schedule. He wouldn't have had to share the commission from the Pennington sale if she'd followed his recommendation for a scheduled cesarean section, instead of this going into labor like a cave woman.

Tonight, instead of upset, Lee seemed helpful, friendly. She'd been falling, tumbling through some dark lost place in her mind. He pulled her back to reality, brought her food. She ate, peripherally aware of the limp lettuce and lukewarm milk. The nurse returned, the short one with the smile. She complimented Trent on his mastery of the urinal, noting his output in the computer. The boy gave her a sleepy smile and conked out again.

"You're looking much better, Mrs. Jameson." Gemma hung a new IV bag.

"Thank you." Caroline doubted she looked well at all. She hadn't had time to shower after work. The smell of paint and solvent clung to her skin. She felt gritty.

"You're staying, Caroline?" Lee returned from the bathroom. "Gemma, where can I find a cot for Mrs. Jameson?"

"I'll get it, Lee. One for you, too, or do you plan to share?"

Even in the dimly lit room, Caroline saw the big man blush to the roots of his light hair.

"Gemma, why they let someone with a mind like yours work with children."

"I'm too short to lift adults." She swatted him with the empty IV bag and scooted out the door.

"I didn't think you'd taken the time to pack." Lee handed Caroline a grocery sack without making eye contact. "Still have your house key. Hope you don't mind."

Caroline found her green and yellow Wayne State University sweats, a clean pair of socks, and her toothbrush. "Thank you."

"Can you make it to the bathroom?" Lee reached a hand to steady her. She wobbled and he supported her back with his other arm. Running water into the sink set her tears loose. He pulled her to his broad, warm chest. He smelled of laundry detergent.

Caroline whispered into his chest, "He couldn't catch his breath. He was coughing, struggling for air..."

He rubbed the sore spot between her shoulder blades. "He's going to be all right, *chère*, all right."

The squeaking of cot wheels grew louder in the hall.

Caroline stepped out of his arms. "I've gotten mascara on your shirt."

Lee glanced at the dark brown smudges on his T-shirt. "I'll say it's 10w-30. Isn't that what all the stylish engineers are wearing this season?"

"Well, for summer I wear 20w-50." She managed a smile.

"Get your sweats on. I'll fix the cot." He closed the bathroom door.

If that man shifts gears any faster, Caroline thought, her transmission would fall out. She traded her chinos and buttoned-down oxford shirt for the fleece, then stepped back into the room. Lee stood next to the bed, holding Trent's hand. The made-up cot stretched against the wall, out of the beam of the hall light.

"What time do you have to be at the plant tomorrow?"

Caroline let the sack slide to the floor. "You think I'm such a bad mother I'd leave my child alone in the hospital..."

Sit, Lee signed toward the cot. "I never said you were a bad mother. You've just gotten back from a week taking care of your folks. If you can't get more time off, I'll stay with Trent."

Caroline paced between the bed and the dark window, caged by the responsibilities of parents, child, work. "I already called in." Etiquette reared its habitual head. "Thank you for offering. Will you be staying long this evening?"

"Depends." Lee caught her arm when she passed and levered her toward the cot. "Rest, now."

"You're welcome to the house tonight." She sat in response to the steady pull on her wrist. "I seem to have offended you Sunday night. I've never... I hope you don't think... I mean, you're the first man I've let in the house since the piano tuner."

"Did you offer him your spare room?"

Caroline gritted her teeth. He thought she was that desperate, that promiscuous? Times like this she wished she could whip a smart remark out of thin air, like her friend Marnie's one-liners.

"I know you wouldn't. Lighten up." Lee laid his palm on her shoulder. "Loosen up. You'll never get to sleep like this. Lie down." He guided her down to the firm pillow. Sitting on the floor beside the cot, both hands worked at her muscles, kneading, rolling, soothing.

"Relax." He gave her a little shake. "Trent's going to be all right. Medicine's gonna wipe out those germs. He'll be running around in no time."

Caroline couldn't sleep with this man massaging her shoulders. He was so close she could hear him breathe over the oxygen's high speed bubble. She never knew anyone so exasperating, provoking. Provocative. Curse these adolescent hormone surges. Ah, but his fingers were strong and sure. She had been awake too many hours, stressed too many years.

Not just my shoulders...

"ALL RIGHT. He's gonna be all right," Lee kept a easy rhythm like paddling a pirogue downstream, matching his strokes to her slowed breathing. "Miss Pearl, what she say about you tonight, eh? You giving me the what for, not letting me boss you around." Moving slowly to keep from waking her, he leaned against the wall. "Miss Pearl say you doing real fine." His thumb rotated, catching a tendril of her hair. Fine as silk, he thought. She's gourmet food on fine china. He's Popeye's extra spicy fried chicken straight from the box. His fingers trailed down her shoulder, feeling the ridge of her scapula. Fine boned. It shows in her face: good breeding, old money. Can't hide it even when she wears sweats. Not like this white-trash lunk. Wouldn't look civilized in a suit if he owned one. Should have enlisted, college on the G.I. Bill. Or gone out for football, earned a scholarship, made something of himself. Ah, what's the use? This lady's just a distraction from my real job, who just now bobbed his fist over the bars of the hospital bed.

· · ·

99

CAROLINE SLEPT A HARD, dreamless sleep. She surfaced once when Trent coughed. Lee bent over the hospital bed, holding a cup to the boy's lips. She must have made some sound, because he looked up. A murmured French phrase came to her, low under the hum of the medical equipment, and exhaustion carried her back into the dark void.

"Caroline." A light touch on her shoulder. The curtains slid open to the sun rise. "Dr. DeGante, the pulmonary head honcho, is on the floor. Quick. She's on rounds. This is your chance." Lee hustled her into the bathroom. A wet washcloth served as beauty ritual and hairbrush. "Caroline, hurry, she's next door."

"You've been here all night? How's Trent?" She left the bathroom for her groggy son's bedside.

"That's what you're gonna find out."

A white coated swarm buzzed into the room. Lee slid around them to the doorway. A sharp-featured woman pulled a pinwheel from the pocket of her lab coat.

"Can you do this?" The doctor blew, sending sparks of light around the room. Trent puffed long enough for a quick listen to his lungs. Draping her stethoscope over her neck, the doctor turned to the dark-haired young man behind her. He delivered his report in staccato phrases of some unknown language. Nothing he said seemed to refer to her son. Dr. DeGante asked a question in a quiet tone. The student straightened his glasses. The others soundlessly inched away from him. He ventured an answer.

"Why the monitor?" Dr. DeGante's voice raised to include the entire group. "Anybody?"

"Because of the Down's syndrome." Shaking hands fumbled with the buttons of his short white coat.

"He's six years old, with no cardiac history. Think." The woman swerved around him, marching for the door, ordering removal of the cardiac monitor. She came to a screeching halt in front of Lee.

"Good morning, Doctor."

"Lee! Good to see you again." She held out her hand. "Ah, this little boy is one of your students."

"Sure is, and here's his mother." Lee used the handshake to steer the doctor toward Caroline. Over the woman's head he tapped the back of his wrist. *Time.* His index finger traced a half circle with a dot underneath. *Question.*

Dr. DeGante plowed back through the students to Caroline. Dark eyes speared with focused attention. "Your son is doing very well. His fever's down. He's responding to the antibiotics. His lungs sound good."

"When can he go home?"

"If he continues to progress, tomorrow."

"And back to school?"

"Probably next week. He shouldn't have any limitations or long-term affects from the pneumonia."

Caroline sagged with relief. The students milled in the space between their instructor and the formidable Lee. Standing tall with his arms crossed over his chest and a day's growth of stubble on his chin, she could see him as a bodyguard. He probably never used his karate skills, just intimidated everyone out of the way. He met her eye and gave her a fast wink.

"Thank you, Doctor."

Gliding like a regent with medical students-in-waiting, Dr. DeGante headed for the door. With a touch to Lee's throat, she moved the big man out of the way. He coughed and held up his hands in the universal sign of surrender.

"I remember the lesson well, *sensai.*"

"No kidding," Lee croaked out.

The entourage departed for the next room.

"Another student?"

He rubbed his throat. "Confidential."

Caroline stared at the hall. This doctor who could terrify medical students with a raised eyebrow, this woman who carried herself like a queen, had been abused? She blinked at Lee, now perched on Trent's bed.

"No kidding," he repeated. The hallway filled with the rattle of a dietary cart. "I asked them to send breakfast up for you. If the offer's still open, I'll run out to Liberty and get some sleep."

101

"Of course. Let me pay you for last night's dinner, and for the week of respite care."

Seeming not to hear her, Lee instructed Trent on the IV line and the oxygen.

At work, by listening carefully Caroline could troubleshoot equipment malfunctions. Yesterday she caught an unusual sound and knew the fans were off balance in the clear coat booth. Then Trent's wheezing precipitated the trip to the hospital. She heard something wrong now in Lee's voice, but she didn't know him well enough to identify the problem. She leaned across the hospital bed and rested her hand flat on his shoulder. Yes, the vibrations were irregular. "Thanks for everything."

He left without looking at her.

Chapter Ten

Three pages, single-spaced. *When is it due?* Caroline flipped through the instructions. *"Compare and contrast... List proofs of... Cite references... Analyze arguments for and against..."*

No due date. Caroline sat at her computer.

"Hey, Caroline! Let's hit the beach!" Ali snapped his towel into her dorm room.

"Sorry, I've got to write a paper. Do you know when this has to be turned in?"

The Egyptian student peered over her shoulder. "No, I'm not in that class. So sad. See you later."

McCormick Hall at MIT. A friend from Wayne. What's going on? She typed the heading.

Clad in moon boots and parka, Marnie stomped into the room. "Girlfriend, it's time you got away from that desk. Boyne Mountain's got five inches of new powder on a thirty inch base. Let's go, baby!"

"Can't. Research paper. Say, do you know, what's the deadline for this?"

Braids swinging, she shook her head. "Wouldn't catch me taking a class like that. Gotta go!"

Beach. Ski resort. This makes less sense all the time.

Bryan stormed in, wearing a tuxedo. "Caroline! My God! We

have to be at Rutledge's in half an hour. You haven't even started to dress!"

"Bryan, I'm sorry." *She kept her voice quiet, hoping to appease him before his shouting attracted the dorm's attention.* "I'm in the middle of..."

"Worthless." *He snatched the assignment from her hand.* "We're getting married. You don't need this. It's interfering with our relationship. You haven't even washed your hair today."

"No, I have to..."

"There's not even a due date on this. When is it due? When, Caroline? Do you even know?"

"April 15." Caroline sat up in bed. "Taxes are due by midnight April 15." She looked around the dark room, focusing on the clock. 2:50. A nice number for a pickup, but a terrible time to get up and work on taxes. Probably make some math error and end up owing the IRS a couple million dollars. She listened for coughing, and hearing none, flopped back onto the pillow. *Yes, but I could get it done while Trent's asleep.*

"Lee!" Trent shrieked. He dashed through the house and flung open the front door to the instructor and his classmate, Kurt.

"Little buddy! How're you feeling?"

Seated at the dining room table, Caroline shifted a file folder to cover the rows of her motivational M&M supply.

Kurt hung his jacket on the doorknob and waved to Caroline. Trent dragged the older boy down to the rec room.

Lee flopped into the chair by the window. The late afternoon sun gilded his sandy hair. In Caroline's experience, handsome men obsessed about themselves, checking the mirror, combing their hair, posing all the time. Lee never seemed concerned about his appearance. His attitude drifted between casual and indifferent. Of course by Bryan's GQ standards, Lee wouldn't be considered attractive. His skin was too thick, his features too large, his wardrobe untouched by fashion trends.

"Kurt's folks went out for their twentieth anniversary tonight. Thought we'd drop by and see how Trent's doing."

"He's fully recovered. No coughing at all. You can't tell he ever had pneumonia."

"Yeah, I could feel it when I hugged him. No more rattles in his chest." Lee picked a slip of paper from the stack. "Ford makes you bring your work home?"

Caroline grabbed her W-2 from his fingers. Nothing was more private than a person's salary. "Taxes. I know they're due Monday, but with everything that's happened... I suppose you've already filed and gotten your refund."

"I don't do taxes."

"Everybody does taxes, unless you want to get in trouble with the IRS."

"Aw, they only go after people that have money."

"It's says here," Caroline tapped a key on her laptop, switching from her tax return to the 1040 instructions, "everyone has to file, everyone with a gross income over..."

Lee leaned over her shoulder and studied the chart. "Not even close."

Embarrassed at having cornered him into admitting his income, Caroline rearranged her check registers.

"Can't say I'm sorry to miss this experience. It looks like those fill-in-the-dot tests that melted my brain in school." He settled into the chair. "Why don't you pay someone to do it for you?"

"It's not difficult." As much math as she'd taken, she ought to be able to manage the simple arithmetic necessary for tax forms. She flipped back to Schedule A. "I hate to be anti-social, but I've got to get this done. If I wait until Trent goes to bed, I'll be too tired to make any sense of it."

"Guess we shouldn't have dropped in on you."

"You could watch the movie with the boys. I rented *Chitty Chitty Bang Bang*."

"With Dick VanDyke? I remember seeing that when I was a little squirt." He disappeared down the stairs. While she was calculating Child and Dependent Care expenses, he returned to make popcorn in the microwave. He refilled her Diet Coke glass. He rooted under the potholders, found her M&M stash, and replenished her supply. Without a word, he returned to the rec room. She stared at the round candies. His hands had touched them. His bare fingers. Agile fingers on the snaps of jeans, strong fingers slipping under waistbands, warm and wide on bare- *Stop it!* She finished the Federal and started on the Missouri forms.

"How's it going?"

Caroline blinked up at Lee. Theme music heralded the movie's ending. Kurt followed Trent up to his bedroom.

"Good. I'm getting a little back on the Federal, and paying a little to Missouri." Best of all the job was finished, complete, ready to mail.

"You're done already? Guess you don't need to pay someone to do it."

"No. All I need is a couple hours without interruptions, but that's pretty rare around here."

"That's what respite care's for." He tied his tread-worn sneakers. "I'm going to take the boys for a walk. Why don't you come along, stretch your legs."

The sun slid behind a newly framed house on the next block. Almost dark. Caroline's gaze shifted to the Missouri Special Olympics sweatshirt stretched across a broad chest and shoulders. Safe. "Good idea." She grabbed her coat.

The boys raced to the corner stop sign. Lee stepped around Caroline, walking between her and the street. Southern gentleman, she thought, trying to remember the last time she'd felt so feminine, so protected.

"Saturday nights are supposed to be fun, relax, party."

Just when she started to unwind, Lee had to shatter her mood with his criticism. "So next year I should tell the IRS, sorry, I had to party?"

"Hey, easy there. I'm trying to say... That week you were in Florida was the hardest I ever worked. Trent's a lot of fun, but you can't let your guard down for a second. A job with no time off. What happens when you get sick?"

So, he recognized the stress she dealt with daily. "I don't get sick."

He chuckled, a low rumbly sound like a idling eighteen wheeler. "Yeah, keep moving faster than the germs." They caught up to the boys and Lee sent them walking backwards to the next stop sign. "No, really, I can picture you sick and Trent tearing up the house, eating nothing but ice cream..."

"Having accidents all over the place, staying up past midnight." Caroline shoved her hands in her pockets to keep from touching Lee. "Sharon got him off to school so I could rest, but she's so busy, I felt like a horrible imposition. Although her chicken noodle soup sure beats any cold medicine, prescription or over-the-counter."

"I'll have to remember that. Last time I got the creeping crud, I dragged down to my sister's. She fed me these pills that smelled like dog food, and orange juice with some sludgy stuff. Just the thought's enough to keep you healthy side up." Lee had the boys skip to the next corner. They startled a cottontail, sending it bounding into the weeds in the vacant lot. Trent's giggling filled the night. "Are you that cheerful in the morning?"

"He doesn't get that from me." She flinched as a memory hit her. "Or Bryan. Even as a baby, Trent always woke up singing and smiling, ready to greet the day."

"Yeah, and I was ready to take him down to Channel 7. Figure he can replace that sourpuss they got doing sunrise weather. Five a.m. Man."

She grinned. "Welcome to my world."

FOLKS in the bayou said all kinds of things about rich people. They were greedy, thought about money all the time. Despite never doing an honest day's work, they condemned poor people as lazy. They spent too much time on business, not enough with their kids. Rich women exercised for appearance, not health.

Lee peeked out the corner of his eye at Caroline. This lady strolling along next to him had the largest W-2 he'd ever seen, eight, nine times more than what he scraped together in a year. No makeup, au naturel. No jewelry, no mink coat. Just her usual peacoat, jeans, a turtleneck the dark red of cooked crawfish. Caroline blew his fondly held notions, ripened by years of bayou brainwashing, way out of the river. Now that he thought about it, he didn't know anyone fitting that mold. No, he knew a doctor who splinted a sprained finger in trade for hanging Christmas lights, a dentist who swapped a crown for a gazebo, a lumberman who threw work his way whenever possible.

"Lee." Caroline pulled him out of his lost swamp thinking. "I'd like to visit your church tomorrow, to thank all those people who stopped by the hospital to see Trent, and show them he's all right. Could you give me directions?"

He shoved his hands into his jeans' pockets to keep from brushing back the wisps of hair blowing across her face. "How 'bout I stop by in the morning and ride with you."

She smiled, sunrise after a storm. "Sure."

CAROLINE GLANCED over Trent's head at the man in the driver's seat. Lee steered her truck into the line exiting the church parking lot. How did he end up driving? This morning, she had handed him the keys so he wouldn't have to give directions. He pocketed them during the service. Afterwards he gallantly opened the door for her and Trent. It seemed natural. Maybe some women's rights activist somewhere would protest, but Caroline didn't believe letting this man drive meant giving up her independence. Besides he enjoyed the truck more than she did.

Lee waved to the kids in the conversion van ahead. "Thanks for coming to church."

"I think Trent knows more people in Kansas City than I do, almost as many as you."

Lee ruffled the boy's hair. "Hang out with me, little buddy, and you'll meet all million five." He glanced at Caroline. "You ever pray?"

She frowned at the developing pattern of rust on the van's wheel wells, hoping the corrosion hadn't eaten through the brake cables.

"Sometimes I ask for help, but I'm not sure if my request makes it past the ceiling."

"Straight through sheetrock, plywood, shingles, you name it." Lee pulled onto North Oak Trafficway. "Thinking of making church a habit?"

"It would give Trent experience with normal children. The school pulled him out of regular first grade, and put him full time in special ed."

As if on cue, the boy unfastened his seat belt. He wriggled down in the seat and kicked the dashboard.

"Trent, no." Caroline attempted to strap him back in. "It's the law. You must wear your seat belt all the time. It's not safe. Sit back. I didn't even know you were strong enough to..."

Lee whipped the truck into a bank parking lot and slammed on the brakes. Trent shot forward. He caught himself with his hands, bumping his nose on the dash between the radio and the heater control knobs. The boy blinked in open-mouth surprise first at his mother, then at the driver. Lee scowled at him. Trent scurried back onto the seat and refastened the belt. His fist circled his heart. *Sorry.*

Lee gave him a one arm hug. "If you keep your seat belt on, I'll take you out for a bike ride after lunch."

Caroline glared at him. Letting Lee drive was one thing, but he almost injured Trent with this stunt. Now he invites himself for lunch. Maybe she'd drive herself next week. Maybe they'd go to a different church, someplace closer.

Lee wheeled back onto the road. "You and I will have a talk when we get home." Yeah, he just bet they'd have a talk. From the way she was clenching her jaw, Lee figured she'd chew him up one side and down the other. Couldn't she see it was better to show the boy what would happen if he unbuckled? Her flood of words just went in one little ear and out the other. He pulled up to a stop light and tried to catch her eye. She seemed to be studying the Toyota next to them. Well, maybe that's what engineers do on Sundays, check out other cars. No one'd guess what she did for a living in that outfit. Caroline could be a model for Dillards' high-priced dress department. Good thing she wore slacks to work, with those legs.

The car behind them honked. The Toyota had pulled ahead two car lengths. He accelerated.

"Are you all right?" Caroline glanced at him.

"Just waiting for a better shade of green." He signed *sorry* before she could look away. "Do you still have those chicken legs in the freezer?"

"No." She gave him a puzzled look. "I put them in the refrigerator to defrost last night."

Chicken's not the only thing defrosting around here. Lee nodded. "Perfect."

THE SUN WARMED the dining area. Caroline tried to hide a yawn behind her napkin. Something about a big Sunday afternoon dinner...

"That's the fifth yawn in the past ten minutes. You'll have to miss the bike ride." Lee took his plate to the dishwasher. "Mom gets a time-out in her room for yawning," he told Trent.

Eyebrows wrinkled together, the boy shook a finger at his mother.

The phone rang.

"And put the answering machine on. No phone calls while you're in time-out."

Trent giggled.

She grabbed the phone.

"Caroline. Apparently you're sitting around waiting for the phone to ring."

Bryan. She shot a look at the two by the table. Lee sent Trent to the bathroom. "What do you want?" she asked.

"My, my, such hostility. You should consider therapy. The father of your child deserves at least a polite response."

"Since when do you acknowledge that relationship?"

"Since I saw his picture in the Boston Globe. Judo. Who would have guessed? I'll be in Kansas City Saturday. Bring my son to the airport. Unless you'd rather I come to your little house on the prairie."

I'd rather you dropped off the face of the earth. Caroline took a deep breath. "What time?"

"Good girl. I'd knew you'd catch on. Noon at the general aviation terminal. I'll even take you out to lunch, if you can find a restaurant that serves something besides barbecue."

Jerk. She slammed the phone down.

"Let go of the counter. Corian isn't built for that kind of pressure." A large, warm hand pressed down on her shoulder. "Who was that?"

"Bryan." Caroline glanced up the stairs. The bathroom door remained closed.

"I thought you said he never called." The fingers kneaded, pried at her knots.

"Trent's picture made the Boston newspaper. The photographer told me Associated Press bought it, but—"

A French swear word blew by her ear. The hand disappeared from the back of her neck. Caroline heard him jump down into the family room. Now what? She tiptoed down the stairs. The big man slumped on the sofa, face in hands.

"Lee?"

"Oh man, I'm sorry." His voice sounded hoarse. "Here I am worried about your sliding glass door, and I let this creep know where you are. I led him right to you. All these years working with the shelter, and I haven't learned a thing."

Even dropping the oil cap into the drain pan hadn't made him curse. Caroline perched on the recliner. "Lee, you didn't tell him anything. I mean, we don't exchange Christmas cards, but I've never kept my whereabouts a secret. He could call my parents or my lawyer for the number. Marnie, my friend who sends the newspaper clippings, belongs to the same club as Bryan. She makes a point to tell him all the good stuff, like first steps and holidays, that he misses."

Lee flopped against the back of the sofa. He opened his eyes warily, as if he expected her to punch him. "You're not in hiding."

She shook her head. "Never have been."

"Thank God." A deep breath seemed to bring him back to normal. "Is he here?"

"Not yet." A toilet flushed overhead. Caroline quickly recited the rest of Bryan's demands. "Guess I should have followed your suggestion to take a self-defense class."

His bottom lip formed a grim line under his mustache. "Next Saturday I've got back to back classes."

"He didn't ask to meet you."

"I don't like the idea of you alone with him. Maybe I can get another instructor to sub for me."

Trent barreled into the room, fists pedaling. "Bi?"

"Change of plans, little buddy. We're teaching your mom karate."

Trent went into demonstration mode. Kick, punch, kick, bow.

"He won't..."

"I've got twenty minutes to teach you three hours of material. No time to argue."

"This is hardly necessary."

"Caroline, when it comes to cars, you're the expert." Dark brown eyes stared her down. When she blinked, he stepped into lecture mode. "Keep to public places. An attacker's less likely to try something if there's witnesses, and you're more likely to get help. Shout 'fire', not 'help'. Stay alert. If he gives you a chance to escape you have to be calm enough to take advantage of it." He stood and paced the room. "Your gut reaction is to put some space between you and the attacker. If that's not possible, if he gets ahold of you, you may need to step toward him. It's like lifting a heavy fry pan." He held his arm out. "You don't pick it up with your fingertips. You step up to the stove, bend your elbow and lift. Get some muscle behind it."

"Leverage." Caroline nodded.

Lee studied her for a long moment. "Oh, man. You could explain this stuff to me. I never taught an engineer before." One thumb scratched his mustache with a sandpaper rasp. "We'll practice a few maneuvers. When you escape, shout and run. The garage door is your safe place."

"Should I..." Caroline gestured toward Trent who had pulled off his shoes and socks.

"No. You'll have shoes on Saturday. Stand up. Grab my wrist. The weak point is where the fingers come together. Twist out like this. Use your other hand if you need more power. Now, you try it." His fingers overlapped her wrist by a good inch and a half. "How big is he?" Lee whispered.

"Not as big as you." *This is ridiculous.*

While she yanked her arm in every direction, he continued the lesson. "We all have pressure points, places in our bodies where the nerves cross the bone. You can use these points to your advantage. There's one at the wrist. Make a fist, just like the kids do in class, thumb out. Punch down. Ow!"

"Did I hurt you?"

"Run and yell!" He pointed to the door. "Yes, you hurt me. That's the whole idea."

"Ya, Ma!" Trent held up two victory signs, looking entirely too much like Richard Nixon for his mother's taste.

He turned to Trent. "Maybe you shouldn't be watching escape techniques. Go out to my car and get my kicking pad."

Caroline strode to the middle of the room. "Teach me the one the doctor did."

"You remembered." He smiled. "With this technique, you can make the attacker back off with little effort. You may not be able to use it if his arms are a lot longer than yours, so step into his space. Twist your index and middle finger together for strength, and push on his throat." Lee demonstrated.

Whiskey. Cold hands at her throat. Need air. Dark. The baby. Protect the baby.

"Caroline, breathe," a quiet voice commanded.

She gasped. Her eyes focused, finding her sunlit home with its small boy smells.

And Lee, his dark gaze full of concern. "That guy strangled you."

Bryan had strangled her. She'd never told anyone and no one had ever guessed. Until Lee. She nodded.

His jaw tensed. "Do you have to meet him? What if you told him no?"

"He'd come here." To her home with unpainted walls and practical furniture. No heirlooms or antiques, nothing remotely resembling decorating. Bryan would contaminate everything with his criticism. His opinions would ooze through her head, tainting her present life the way he'd polluted her past. Ruining the safe haven she'd built for Trent. A shudder broke her paralysis. "Like this?" She pushed on Lee's throat.

He coughed and stepped back. "You got it." He demonstrated a few more pressure points, complimenting her on the use of fingernails, then rounded up Trent and the red pad from the garage. "Kicking may be your best bet. A woman's strength is in her legs. Aim for the knee."

Caroline tried a side kick.

"Your leg's gotta be straight when you hit." His thumb made another mustache circuit. "It's like you're the telephone pole and the attacker's the fender. At impact, you're straight and he crumples."

She practiced side and front kicks.

"I'll show you some standing throws after Trent's class, when we can use the mats. Let's try some floor work." Lee lined up the sofa cushions on the carpet. He lay on his back next to the cushions. "You're the attacker. Sit down here and grab my wrists."

There go the hormones again. Caroline wiped her palms on her jeans. Bryan's call had rewired her nerves, blown the circuit breakers of her overdrive protection system. She grabbed Lee's closest wrist, then reached across his broad chest for the other, bringing her face within inches of his. Her arms trembled. She licked her lips, inching closer. His warm breath rippled his mustache and stroked her cheek. She barely heard his voice over the blood rushing in her head.

"When the attacker lets go, reach up, grab the back of his shirt, and yank across your body. Flip him over with your hip. Run. Fire!" Lee jogged to the door.

Caroline lay on the sofa cushions staring at the ceiling. Too fast. Not fast enough.

He loomed over her. Bending one knee, then the other, he sat with his hip touching hers. His palm encircled her left wrist, then her right. She was having trouble breathing. Her mouth felt dry. He might kiss her and oh what would she do if he did. But what if he didn't—

"Caroline. Concentrate. I know this is hard, which is why I don't usually teach people in crisis. I just let go of your arm and you've got to react immediately. Don't give your attacker time, he won't use it for your good." Lee's head snapped right. A chair scraped across the kitchen vinyl. "Trent's into the brownies I made." The big man bolted up the stairs.

Caroline rolled upright. What a mess. Ought to see a counselor. *Here this guy is trying to teach me self-defense and all I can think about is how much fun this would be naked.*

"Trent's in time-out." Jingling his keys, Lee called down from the kitchen. "I've got to run. I'm teaching a junior high youth group in Gladstone in fifteen minutes."

Caroline studiously replaced the sofa cushions. His car door slammed. The engine started with a piercing whine. She ran out the door, yelling, "Pop the hood!" The latch released. Holding the hood open with one arm, she yanked the starter wire, killing the engine. "You need to replace your starter. Maybe your friend at the junk-yard can make you a deal on a rebuilt one." She peered around the hood, expecting to see a scowl of frustration. Instead he burst into a big smile.

"You signed *pop*, like soda pop." His open palm bounced off the end of his other fist. Then his warm hand clasped hers where it rested on the fender. "I'm not letting anything happen to you and Trent. You've got my promise on that."

Chapter Eleven

W ind pounded the house. Caroline peeked through the drapes. No lightning yet. She crawled into bed, pulling the comforter high to block the noise. Life in Kansas City seemed no different than Massachusetts or Michigan. Mostly the same fast food franchises, gas stations, brand names. Except for the wind. The wind called for an emergency: a hurricane, tornado, severe thunderstorm. Surely one ought to hide in the basement, listening to a portable radio by candlelight, waiting for a tree to crash through the roof. But here power lines ran underground, the only trees were innocuous saplings, and neighbors slept unconcerned in their beds.

The floor creaked in the hallway. A rapist? No, the ductwork expanding from the air conditioner cycling off. No more staying up late watching TV news magazines about women raped in their own homes.

The wind came at the house like a fleet of eighteen wheelers. Bang! The rapist! Her pulse hit red line. Squeak, squeak, squeak, bang! No, criminals don't make that much noise. It's the storm door. The pneumatic closer is out of adjustment. The latch needs a squirt of WD-40. Caroline listened to a few more cycles of the wind bashing the aluminum frame. Any possibility a gust would push it closed? Rough calculation: nil. Odds favored the next blast ripping

116

the thing off the house. No one else was going to close it. She untangled herself and staggered down to the living room.

Caroline paused, hand on the knob. What if the rapist jammed the latch and is waiting just outside, listening for the turn of the dead bolt? She put her eye to the peep hole. Night circled the feeble porch light. She didn't see anyone. He could be crouched in the corner. Maybe Bryan sent some thug to shoot Trent.

Stop this nonsense! You have to get up for work in six hours!

Paralyzed, she watched the flapping nuisance. If she had a gun... But no, she needed her right hand to snag the storm and her left hand on the wood door. The rapist would grab the gun out of her hand and shoot her. She needed a dog. Yes, a dog would know if someone was out there or not. She would open up... and the mutt would run out and she'd have to chase it down the street in her nightgown. No, she needed... more self-defense instruction. Next time she saw Lee she'd ask how to handle situations like this. Of course, if he were here, he'd take care of this crisis. A gust yanked the frame to the limits of its chain, shaking the house. Lee's not here, so, on the count of three. One, two... Caroline released the dead bolt. Her arm shot into the humid night. She grabbed the handle, yanked it closed, and locked it. The dead bolt twisted into place.

She dragged back upstairs, suddenly goose-bumped and shivering. There, now, was that so difficult? Honestly. What would Lee think about being grouped with guns and dogs? And the category is, tired brain, symbols of security. She crawled in bed and wadded the comforter around herself.

If Lee were here...

No. Don't start that. Go to sleep.

His warm arm, his broad chest, his hot...

U-turn. Think of something else, something a lot less exciting. The aerodynamics of storm doors.

WHERE IS EVERYBODY THIS MORNING? Stopping by her office, Caroline dropped off her lunch and retrieved her tool pouch.

Nothing new on the computer from her counterpart on the night shift. She returned to the dark corridor between the booths.

At the last paint shop meeting the engineers had discussed a memory problem with the MEBC booth. They had decided to run a ghost every Monday morning.

"Had a rough weekend?" she asked the Behr, the automation system for the paint sprayers. "At least you don't have an ex haunting your nights."

The lockout devices were in energized position. Caroline activated the bells, and waited for the green lights to stop flashing. The manual purge button cleaned the lines. The down button sent the overheads into home position. She reset the machine, then turned five keys: automatic, high voltage, conveyor, bypass, and ghost. Four lights: two green, one amber, one blue. Beyond the reinforced glass windows, the bells purged, loaded, and sprayed. Ready for the line of cabs and boxes from E-coat and prime.

An unidentified object shot by her feet. She shrieked and jumped, banging her knees on the metal cabinet.

"Hey, man." Diego grabbed the tape roll. "Running a ghost means testing the gizmos. Nothin' for you to be scared about."

Hoping he hadn't heard her shriek over the roar of the exhaust fans, Caroline concentrated on folding her coverall's sleeve back over her watch. "You're late."

"Taz just got a call from the hospital. His dad died. He's takin' it pretty hard."

"Oh, no. I'm so sorry. I'll send him home." She keyed her radio to call a relief worker.

Diego stepped up to the machine. "So, who died at your house?"

"No one."

"I'm supposed to buy that, the way you look? What is it? Boyfriend keeping you up all night? You let ole Diego show you how a woman's supposed to be..."

"Get back to work."

. . .

LEE CIRCLED the golden arched restaurant. Clear view of the parking lot from the highway. Clear view of the eating area from the parking lot. No place to hide. Halfway between Antioch, where he had to teach Saturday morning, and the airport, best he could guess. Couldn't tell exactly since the VW's milage measurer, odometer, was broken.

He rolled into a parking slot and shut off the engine. The sun popped over the shopping center east of the highway and flashed off the plate glass windows. Lee scratched his mustache, trying to ignore what the smell of frying pork did to his empty stomach. He must know someone who works here. Didn't he meet the manager at that Baptist church on down Barry Road? Naw, that guy worked at the Applebee's on the other side of the interstate. Someone... He pounded his palm on the steering wheel. Someone who could stop this jerk from showing up Saturday.

Come on. He'd bent the ears of the staff at the shelter, every cop he knew. Stayed up all night praying on it. Bryan was coming. Just gotta get ready. Best plan, Caroline could bring him here for lunch.

Lee uncurled out of the car and strolled into the restaurant. No familiar faces, no glimmers of recognition.

"May I help you?"

Lee returned the pimply-faced youngster's smile. "I'd like to speak to the manager. Please."

"You're looking at him."

He reached across the counter to shake the bony hand. "Lee Marivaux, karate instructor. Have you considered self-defense instruction for your employees?"

"Uh..." Confusion made the boy's eyes cross. Probably he could handle "hold the catsup", and "extra salt on my fries" requests. Lee's question just wasn't on the menu.

"You heard about that massacre in California, those robberies in Indiana?"

"We don't really... I mean, we haven't had any trouble."

"I can give you references. Satisfied Students. Police departments. Hospitals." He propped an elbow on the cash register and nailed the deal. "This week only, it's free."

. . .

"CAROLINE." Static crackled the phone line. Bryan. Maybe he called to cancel. "I'm calling from the jet. Change of plans. Be at Downtown Airport, Executive Beechcraft, at 11:30. I'm in a hurry, so lunch is being catered in. Is Trent looking forward to seeing his father?"

"Is that what you want me to tell him?"

"Careful, your hostility is showing." The connection went dead.

Caroline dropped the phone. Lee planned to meet them at the McDonald's by the International Airport. She had no way to let him know of the changed plans. He taught so many places; she couldn't begin to guess where he might be now. Grabbing a handful of M&M's, she glanced at the clock. Ten forty. Downtown Airport was about a thirty minute drive. Trent still splashed in his bath. She hurried into her bathroom and rummaged through the medicine cabinet. No antacid. The mirror showed dark circles under her eyes. She'd get her son ready, then put on makeup.

"Trent!" She raced to the other bathroom. "Time to go!"

He stood at the end of the tub, his hair still dry. Maybe Bryan won't notice. No, he'd be on a fault finding mission, as usual. Caroline grabbed the shampoo. With a ear-piercing whoop, the child belly flopped, sending a tidal wave over her.

"Trent! I don't have time to change clothes. We have to be at the airport in a few minutes."

"No Ma go bye-bye." He fought the hand shampooing him.

"Mom's not going bye-bye. Mom and Trent are going to see..." She didn't know the sign for 'dad'. The title certainly didn't fit Bryan. "We're going to see planes." She rinsed him and pulled the plug.

The boy grabbed his towel and stuffed it over the drain. *More,* he signed.

Done, Caroline signed back. She jerked him out of the tub. While she hung the soggy towel over the faucets, the drippy child scampered through the house making airplane noises. He'll dry, Caroline figured. She set underpants, a polo shirt, and twill slacks on his bed. "Time to get dressed," she called, then rushed to her own closet for dry clothes. Everything needed ironing. Into the bathroom. Grab the blow drier. Dry enough. Still need makeup. Better check on Trent.

The clothes lay untouched on his bed. Caroline found the child on the sofa with a carton of ice cream. Goose bumps made his skin look like a plucked chicken. She snatched the kid in one hand, and the brownie fudge ripple in the other, thankful it hadn't dripped. Too furious for words, she gave him a "Lee scowl". The boy hustled up to his bedroom. Caroline returned the carton to the freezer. The kitchen clock glowed 10:51. She raced to her room for knee-high stockings and flats, then to Trent's.

She fastened his pants and one button of his polo shirt. "Where are your new shoes?" Not hiding under the bed or in the closet. She checked the bathroom. His old ones were in the garage, but their worn out heels made his feet roll in. Bryan would have her head on a platter. When did Trent wear them last? Playing in the construction area. Caroline ran down to the front door. The sneakers sat on the front porch, encased in Missouri mud. Yessiree, we don't call this Clay County for nothing. She pounded the dirt loose, wishing the concrete steps were Bryan's head. Her watch showed the hour. Racing through the house, she grabbed Trent, her purse, and the keys. "Put your shoes on," she ordered as they pulled out of the driveway. *My kingdom for a Dove bar.* At the end of the block, a fisted hand waved in her face.

"Wait until we get to the airport." That will make a good impression on Bryan. Hi, Dad, gotta go. The boy signed toilet again. Caroline braked at the exit of the subdivision. Trent sat in a spreading puddle. The dark stain crept up his shirt, where it had been neatly tucked into his slacks. Rats. The spare clothes under the seat were last winter's, a size too small. No way around it. She had to go back. Seconds ticked by as she waited for the traffic to clear. She U-turned and headed to the house.

"Quickly, Trent. Leave your wet clothes in the bathroom." Caroline swabbed the upholstery with shop towels, then tucked a plastic Western Auto bag over the spot. Upstairs, she sorted through

T-shirts, discarding the one with the name of his elementary school. Bryan knows too much already. She selected a striped T-shirt and a pair of shorts. "Come on, Trent." He could dress in the car. Oops, forgot underpants. Back to the bedroom again, then bathroom, garage. Wonder what the penalty is for driving with an unbuckled, naked child. Probably double for handicapped kids. Eleven-seventeen. Bryan would be livid.

Caroline buckled the boy at the last stoplight before the highway. An ammonia tinged odor filled the cab. If the caterers didn't show, Bryan would have to sit in the puddle on the way to the restaurant. Fun... until he acted out his revenge. She turned up the vent fan.

Downtown Airport sat beside North Kansas City, but inaccessible from there because of the rail yards. One eye on her phone's map, Caroline navigated the spaghetti twists of roads and seemingly permanent construction zones. No signs announced this relic from the propeller era. Executive Beechcraft was the last building, almost tucked under the bridge to downtown. Caroline parked next to the road, hoping Bryan wouldn't see her out the window. Eleven forty-two. She smoothed Trent's hair, still damp in the humid June day. Glancing at the rearview mirror, she finger-combed her own mop. Rats. She'd forgotten makeup.

"Let's go see the airplane." Caroline held onto the boy, taking no chance on a parking lot chase scene in front of Bryan. She left the truck unlocked for a quick getaway.

Caroline blinked, nearly choking on the heavy coffee smell in the waiting area. Three people stood just inside the glass doors to the apron, silhouetted against the view of the runway.

"Ashcroft. Any relation to the Governor?" asked a man seated behind the counter.

The middle of the three stepped forward. "Hear that, Caroline? If you hadn't changed your name, people might think you were related to someone famous."

Bryan looked the same except for a distinguished touch of gray at his temples. Despite the long flight from Boston, his sharkskin suit showed no wrinkles. He hadn't even loosened his rep tie. He looked like a Saks Fifth Avenue mannequin: sophisticated, tailored, synthetic.

Two men in shirtsleeves flanked him. The one with the briefcase stepped forward, extending his hand, smothering her with his pungent aftershave. "Ms. Jameson, so nice of you to meet us here today. I'm Darrell Karanda, Mr. Ashcroft's campaign manager. This is Rico, publicity."

Rico, publicity, already had the video camera on his shoulder. "Man, Bryan, you should have kept this one. She photographs like Jackie Kennedy. The camera loves her."

Bryan backhanded the camera, pushing the viewfinder into the photographer's eye socket. "Not her, you dolt. The boy."

The campaign manager stepped between Bryan and Rico. "Campaigns are so stressful. Shall we retire to the conference room?"

Bryan ignored Karanda. "You're late, Caroline. Have to build yourself a truck to get here?"

Gritting her teeth, Caroline turned to the boy hiding behind her legs. "Trent, this is Bryan Ashcroft."

To her relief, Bryan didn't offer to shake hands. The thought of the man touching Trent made her skin crawl.

The boy pointed at the Learjet parked just outside the door. "Ah-ah."

"God, Caroline, why haven't you taught him to talk? He's how old now?"

The boy proudly held up seven fingers. Bryan spun on his heels and stomped down the hall.

Mr. Karanda bent eye level with the child. "Would you like to see the airplane? If you eat your lunch like a big boy, I bet your daddy will show you his jet. Follow Daddy." Guiding them down the hall, he said to Caroline, "I've got four little monsters of my own at home. None of them like this, of course, but..."

Trent turned to her, a puzzled look wrinkling his face. He made a sign similar to the sign for mom, only at the forehead instead of the chin. *Uh-oh, should have explained about "daddy".*

Inside the conference room, Rico directed Bryan and Trent to sit at the table facing the window. Mr. Karanda pointed Caroline to the other end of the room, out of camera range. She lifted the cover on her plate. Shrimp salad with angel hair pasta. Bryan couldn't pick something easy for a child to eat.

"Ms. Jameson, I ordered Trent a hot dog, in case he hasn't developed a taste for seafood."

Caroline thanked the campaign manager, then watched Bryan stiffly pour milk into a glass. "Half-way is enough." She shouldn't have said anything; Bryan should learn just like every other parent. She held her tongue as he spread mustard on the hot dog.

"Act natural, Bryan. A nice father-son reunion lunch. Smile, talk to him." Rico switched from the video to still photography.

"Hang on, Rico, the boy's getting lost in the chair." Mr. Karanda disappeared for a moment, then returned with two Kansas City yellow pages.

"Pretty thick phone books. List everybody twice?"

"Ease up, Bryan." Mr. Karanda helped Trent sit on the directories.

Bryan slouched in his chair, pouting. "Aw, she's not registered to vote in Massachusetts. She can't hurt me."

"We need her cooperation."

Caroline speared the nearest shrimp with her fork, but didn't bring it to her mouth. Queasiness tightened her stomach against any food, especially fish. "My cooperation?"

The manager served coffee to the adults. "Bryan's opponent is playing the family card hard and fast. Every ad, every photo op has him surrounded by his happy clan. Nails the Catholic vote. We'd like to level the field a bit, get some pictures of Bryan with his son."

She addressed her ex directly. "Why don't you order your wife to produce an heir?"

Bryan scowled and Caroline knew she'd hit a nerve.

"Unfortunately, Mrs. Ashcroft..."

"That's none of her business." Bryan hit the table. The silverware rattled. Trent scuttled off the phone books and crawled under the table to his mother's lap.

"My condolences." Caroline smiled over her son's shoulder. Bryan wouldn't meet her eye.

"Our polls indicate favorable voter reaction to the picture of Trent doing judo."

"Karate," she corrected, feeling better every minute.

"The Kennedys successfully play the handicapped card with this Special Olympics thing. A few pictures of Bryan with his son could go a long way toward building the voters' confidence."

"No. You will not exploit my son." Caroline stood, still holding her child. "I thought you came to see Trent."

"He did." Mr. Karanda opened his briefcase.

"Told you she wouldn't cooperate," Bryan sniffed.

He waved a legal file. "As a contingency, we're prepared to petition the court for custody."

Custody? Her blood turned to antifreeze. Caroline narrowed her gaze at the campaign manager. "You seemed like such a nice guy."

He didn't meet her gaze. "I'm paid to put Bryan Ashcroft into office, whatever it takes."

She perched on the chair. "What judge will agree to give custody to someone who's shown no interest for seven years? Or did you buy a judge in Missouri?"

"Shown no interest? He couldn't when the child's mother abducted him and disappeared. Then, when he discovers the boy's picture in the paper, he learns she's failed to provide a good moral home for him."

"What?"

"When you left, I said you'd never find another man. Not with an idiot in the house." Bryan leaned back and shook his head slowly. "An indigent. How very resourceful of you, Caroline."

"Your live-in lover." Mr. Karanda flashed a stack of eight by ten black and white photos of Lee at her house.

Trent snatched the pictures. "Lee! Ma, Lee!" His sticky fingers pointed to the man mowing her lawn, jogging with the boy, unlocking her front door.

"He can keep those," Mr. Karanda volunteered. "I have copies."

"I'll bet you do." She rose to her feet again. "First of all he's not my lover, and second of all, who cares?"

"Clueless Caroline, in case you haven't noticed, Missouri is part of the Bible Belt. There are several judges in town who believe in 'family values'. The boy would be much better off in a two parent family, than with a mother who dumps him with a neighbor while she builds trucks."

"If you had custody, he'd be back in that boarding school in New Hampshire in two seconds."

"It's not Phillips Andover, but maybe they could teach him how to talk."

"You can't afford a court case. The voters would remember you as the villain who ripped a child from his mother's arms."

"Ms. Jameson." Mr. Karanda stepped between her and Bryan. Caroline wondered if he'd refereed in a boxing ring. "All we want is to take some pictures. Nice, tasteful pictures. Trent won't mind. Let's just avoid this legal mess and take some pictures."

Caroline looked from Bryan to his manager. Slimier than axle grease. Slipperier than WD-40.

"I don't do exploitation," Rico volunteered from the end of the table. He'd eaten his own shrimp and started on Caroline's.

She frowned. "Let's get this over with." She set Trent back on his feet.

"Good girl." Mr. Karanda reached to pat her back. She side-stepped out of range.

"I've gotten some good interior shots. What say we try some outside?"

"Come on, boy, I've got a present for you in the Lear." Bryan snapped his fingers at the child.

Rico directed them around the apron. "Bryan climb off the plane. You spot Trent, your face lights up. Cut to Trent. You see your daddy and you smile. Bryan hold up the gift. There he goes. Run to Daddy, Trent. Pick him up, big hug."

My God, he could just throw Trent on the plane and leave. Caroline started across the ramp.

"Stay out of camera range, Ms. Jameson." Mr. Karanda grabbed her forearm.

Caroline yanked, freeing herself. Lee's technique worked. She ran behind Rico to the front of the jet. No one in the cockpit. Good.

"You're a suspicious one." Karanda tailed her.

Caroline glared at him. "You said it yourself. You'd do whatever it takes to get Bryan elected. But I wonder how well you really know your candidate."

The photographer took a couple still shots of Trent and Bryan. "It's a wrap."

"Ah-ah." The boy pointed at the jet.

"Caroline! He's still drooling!" Face contorted, Bryan dropped the child to the concrete and dabbed his lapel with a handkerchief. "I'm due in Brookline for a speech."

Karanda handed Trent a silver wrapped box with gold ribbon.

"Ma, ah-ah."

"You said he could see the plane." Caroline took Trent's hand before he could run.

"No time." Bryan stepped inside, rousting the pilot out of the big reclining seat. The other men joined him.

Howling, Trent threw the package at Bryan. It hit the steps and bounced to the concrete. Karanda pulled the door closed. The engines spooled to life. Legs shaking, Caroline picked up her tearful son and headed for the parking lot.

TURNING ONTO THEIR STREET, Caroline spotted the Volkswagen in her driveway. *He's going to be furious. I didn't show at McDonald's. I let Bryan use Trent for political gain. And these pictures.* She glanced at the photos clenched in Trent's sweaty hands. Lee rose from the front steps. Caroline slid the truck into the garage and turned off the ignition. The passenger door whipped open.

"Are you okay?" Lee filled the open space. His dark brown eyes inspected Trent, then turned to her.

Caroline gave a shaky nod. She closed the garage door. Lee unbuckled the boy and took him inside. Walking around the tailgate, she peeked through the window. Nothing out of the ordinary. Nothing to suggest Bryan still had her under surveillance.

"I'm sorry." Caroline stepped into the family room. "Bryan went to Downtown Airport..."

"I'm sorry I wasn't there for you." Still holding Trent, Lee tucked her under his other arm.

She leaned into his warm chest, reveling the softness of his well-worn T-shirt, the honest smell of detergent and perspiration. "He took pictures..."

"Ssh." His hand stroked her back. "You're safe. That's all I care about."

Lee released the emergency brake. The Volkswagen rolled down Caroline's driveway into the street. He hopped out, and, with one good shove, pushed the vehicle into the Buffum's driveway, then reset the brake. He strolled into the garage where Pete worked on his almost antique Chevrolet station wagon. Lee guessed Pete pulled a pretty decent salary at the post office. Spreading his check across a mortgage and three kids left his car budget almost as drained as Lee's. The overalled man had the fuel pump and injectors disconnected and his nose in the manual. Lee greeted Sharon, up to her elbows in potting soil, then joined her husband at the front bumper.

"Caroline has a nice set of tools." Lee braced his hands on the front fender and stretched his hamstrings.

"What happened with Caroline's ex?" Sharon asked.

"Yes, she does." A bead of sweat dripped off Pete's forehead onto the radiator. "Don't know if a clunker like this deserves tools like hers."

Sharon raised her voice. "Lee, is Caroline okay? She's got her drapes pulled."

"Might be easier to fix." Lee switched legs.

"Might." Pete studied the blackened bristles of the toothbrush. "She's got yours running all right."

Lee nodded. "Junkyard's probably wondering where I am."

"Lee?" Sharon smacked the dirt off her gardening gloves.

Lee knew she'd be smacking him next. He pushed out of his stretch. "I'm going for a run." Two houses down the block, he swerved to avoid a Big Wheel pile-up. His peripheral vision caught sight of Sharon halfway across the street. Lee circled a mailbox and intercepted the determined woman at Caroline's driveway. "No you don't." He linked arms with her and pivoted her back to her house.

"How am I supposed to find out what's going on?"

"Caroline's explaining the concept of 'dad' to her son." Lee moved his foot just in time to avoid getting it stomped. "After dinner, I promise."

Sharon gave him a gunfighters' squint. "Run fast, desperado. I'm fryin' chicken in five minutes."

Lee circled around the block behind Caroline's. He stopped at the house under construction. Yes, from this angle. The photos of him teaching Trent donkey kicks and handstands in the backyard were taken from here. He continued his run to the house for sale three south of Buffums'. From here he'd been caught unlocking Caroline's door, mowing her lawn, teaching Trent to bring in the mail. His rust-bucket had sat in her driveway, license plate wired front and center to the bumper for all the world to read.

He'd ask Pete if he ever had a car so junky it ruined the tools he used.

Chapter Twelve

Caroline opened the garage door, revealing Sharon Buffum standing in her driveway. "Good morning! Mind if I ride with you?" Sharon popped into the passenger seat next to Trent. "Lee wasn't sure if you'd remember the route to church."

"Sure, okay." Caroline backed out of the garage, seeing Buffum's van flash by. Lee must be really mad about yesterday if he wouldn't even ride with her. She wanted to figure out what to do about that man, but Sharon maintained a constant velocity of talk on the drive.

The women merged with the people flowing into the sanctuary. Sharon greeted most of them by name, but Caroline's brain misfired where names were concerned. One of the boys took Trent to Sunday school. Pete joined them and they found seats. A well-groomed lady in the next pew monopolized Sharon's attention, leaving Caroline adrift in the chatting congregation. She pretended to examine the bulletin, while a vague unease washed over her. A second visit to a church should be more comfortable. It was as if Lee had been a windbreak last time and without him she chilled. Were these people giving her a cold shoulder because Lee wasn't with her? Absurd. They weren't a couple, so what difference did it make if they were together? Turning from Sharon, the talkative lady asked about Trent, praising his behavior last Sunday. The service began.

Caroline looked up at the ceiling, searching for air conditioning vents. Some overdressed usher probably got hold of the thermostat.

"Where's Lee?" Caroline whispered.

Sharon put a finger over her lips. Several times during the service, Caroline glanced around. Can't hide a six foot tall man with hair like the foam on hot chocolate. Hot chocolate? It's not that cold in here.

Where was he?

LEE SLIPPED UP the back stairs into the choir loft. He knelt and closed his eyes. The organist finished the postlude and left without speaking. He inhaled deeply, breathing in the fragrance of bacon and blueberry muffins. "Anyone who cooks as good as you do, can't sneak up on a guy who like to eat as much as me." He opened an eye.

Sharon shifted from one knee to the other. "Guess I should use those perfume samples the Avon lady leaves."

"If it's all the same to Pete, I'd rather you didn't."

She flopped back onto the pew. "You go on. These old knees can't take my weight."

"All hundred pounds soaking wet." Lee sat next to her. "Shouldn't have to keep praying. God's already told you what I'm supposed to do."

She shrugged. "He uses messengers besides angels."

Lee tipped his head to examine the back of her shoulders. "Can't see your wings, but I have my suspicions. What's the scoop?"

"You said last night you can't protect Caroline with self-defense techniques."

His fingers dug into his legs, wrinkling his chinos. "*Mais*, yeah, even if I'd been there yesterday, I couldn't have stopped him."

"Not with karate, anyway, because Bryan's gone beyond physical attacks. The sermon text was: 'our struggle is not against flesh and blood, but against the powers of this dark world'."

"I heard."

Sharon frowned. "I didn't see you in church."

"Nursery duty." He endured her piercing look for a moment, then raised his hands in surrender. "Okay. I'll admit it. Something about rocking a baby puts the world in its place. Don't tell anyone. Please. I've got my tough guy reputation to consider."

"Tough as a marshmallow." Sharon poked him in the ribs. "I'll let you tell Caroline yourself."

"No. I can't. That miserable—" He hunted for a word he could say in church. "—louse used me to hurt her. I can't take a chance of that happening again."

"Even if you hadn't been taking care of Trent, Bryan would have found something to harass her about. The power of darkness. It's a struggle you can help her with. Don't desert her now, when she needs you so much."

Caroline needed him like a broken fan belt. "How..." He looked around the empty church. Late morning sunlight bathed the oak pews and crimson runner in white light. "How are we getting back to Liberty?"

Sharon dangled a Ford truck key from her index finger.

Lee snatched it from her and raced down the steps. "Yahoo!"

LEE GROANED AND STRETCHED, his feet sticking off the end of the mattress. He'd been worrying in his sleep, but now that the morning sun shot through the wavy plastic window of Eldon's camp shack, he couldn't think what had him tossing and turning. It'll come. Worries don't disappear on their own. Give it enough time and it'll come back. He waited, listening to the bird and insect song outside, the original country music. Close-by, the percussion section jumped in with a scratching sound. He looked up to a pair of black eyes and a whiskered nose peeking through a gnaw hole in the plywood underside of the top bunk.

"Boo!" Lee whispered and the mouse disappeared. Seconds later it scampered down the ladder by his feet.

He rolled upright, taking care not to bump his head, and reached for his sneakers. "*Regardez donc.*" Little rodents had eaten his laces. So much for the theory that his shoes smelled too bad for mice to bother.

He shoved the sneakers on and grabbed his sleeping bag. "You'll have it chewed down to the stuffing, you and your family." The shoes flopped on his feet, scuffing through the leaf mold to the car. He opened the hatch back, and gave the sleeping bag a good shake before wadding it into the back seat. Digging through the luggage compartment's junk unearthed a twist tie for one shoe, dental floss for the other. He sat on the bumper to do the repair. Sad thing was, all rigged up like this his sneaks didn't look any worse than usual. Have to stop by the thrift store on the way to Antioch. Get another pair. Laces at least.

He took a gulp from his water jug, then splashed his face, hoping to wash off the mouse smell until he showered at the gym. Deep blue sky showed between the cottonwoods. Nice day. Toss a little Spanish moss on the trees and it could be Louisiana. Except there'd be more bugs. And bigger rodents, nutria. And it'd be hot, even this early in the morning on the first week of June. Last week of school. School. Trent.

Lee tossed his shorts and T-shirt behind the passenger seat and threw on clean clothes from the laundry bag. Snatching up a blueberry muffin from Sharon's care package, he slammed the hatch, started the car and raced to town. Or would have if the starter hadn't screamed. He turned the key off. Still screaming. Pop the hood, he smiled in spite of the noise at the memory of Caroline signing soda pop. He hurried to the engine compartment and yanked the wire. Nonstop screaming. How could anyone think with this racket? Another wire. Any wire. Keep going. Pull the car apart if you have to. Stop the noise. Twist it loose. There. It stopped. Finally.

He glanced from his watch to the engine. The one morning he needed to be some place. Stop fussing and put it back together. He studied the connector. It would help if he remembered how it came apart.

After a trial and error session of car repair, resulting in no screaming, no nothing, he gave up. He squinted down the dusty road out of the camp. Whole darn state is one hill after another and

Eldon's camp has to be on the only flat land for miles. One hand on the steering wheel, the other on the door frame, he pushed. Be glad it's not uphill. A front tire dropped into a rut, smashing the car into his knee. Be glad it's not a tank.

An Osage orange bush stuck a branch out and slapped him a good one. He spit a leaf out of his mouth. Finally the VW got hopping fast enough. Lee dropped into the car and popped the clutch. Just then the road rose to meet him, as the Irish say, and he slowed to a stop.

He got out and pushed again. Sweat ran into the scratches on his face and stung. On the back side of the rise he found a downhill, got going good, and the car hiccuped to a start. He bounced down the dirt lane and onto the highway. Right behind a fully loaded hay wagon. Settling back in the seat, he downshifted into second and stuffed the muffin into his mouth.

Lee swung into the elementary school parking lot just after the school buses. So much for talking to Trent's teachers before school starts.

He parked and dashed through the incoming flock of minivans. "Which one's Trent Jameson's bus?" he asked a short lady wearing a striped dress. She clutched her clipboard to her chest and blinked. He ran his hands through his hair, wondering if he'd combed it this morning. Probably look like a pirate.

By the end of the row of buses, high pitched voices shouted, louder and more excited than the usual school yard bedlam. Lee waded upstream, knee deep in kids. "Trent!" he shouted, startling most of the students into silence. At the corner of his eye, he saw two more teachers hurrying toward the roiling ball of kids. Reaching the fight first, Lee grabbed a shirt he recognized and hauled Trent into the air. Limbs thrashing like an angry box turtle, the boy wrenched around to see who held him. His grimace changed abruptly to a smile, then an embarrassed pout. Blood dripped from his nose.

"Sho." Lee gave the command to rest. Trent went limp. The man pulled him to his chest.

"He attacked me!" A spike-haired kid pointed to Trent.

A teacher dragged off spike and a beet-faced boy who yelled, "I tried to stop them!"

"Sir?" The clipboard lady approached.

"I'm Lee Marivaux, Trent's..." The kid in his arms was no advertisement for karate. "Trent's respite care provider. Point us to the nurse's office, please."

The lady gestured without speaking. The stunned audience parted to let them through.

"No fighting," he said into the nearest small ear. "We don't use karate to hurt people."

The boy burrowed into him as if trying to hide inside Lee's heart. Just outside the building, a tall red haired girl stepped from the crowd.

"I'll take you to the nurse." She opened the heavy wooden door. "I know who you are. You're Ryan's karate teacher. I'm Ryan's sister. I'm in fourth grade." The girl chatted all the way to the office. Lee had to shoo her off so he could talk to the nurse. While Trent got cleaned up, the principal and the special ed teacher arrived. Detaching the boy with difficulty, Lee stepped into the hall. He filled them in on the reappearance of Trent's father and asked permission to stay in the classroom.

Mrs. Wenger glanced at the frowning principal. "We have permission from Mom to release Trent to Mr. Marivaux."

"I don't want to take him anywhere, just get him settled down."

"Any chance of the father showing up?" the principal asked, all business.

"He went back to Massachusetts."

"This is irregular, but I'll allow it as long as you don't interfere with the classroom routine." The woman returned to her office before Lee could thank her.

Mrs. Wenger gave a thumbs up.

"The bleeding's stopped," the nurse sent the boy out in the hall.

"Let's get you a clean shirt, Trent." The teacher led them back to the classroom. "Sorry I don't have anything in your size, Lee."

The man shrugged off the red-brown spatters dotting his T-shirt. "It'll wash."

She frowned and touched his jaw. "Did he scratch you?"

"No. Car trouble." At the teacher's confused expression, he added, "Long story."

The paraprofessional had already begun opening activities. Lee and Trent joined the circle of students on the floor. The boy crawled into his lap, collapsing against his chest. Lee felt the fatigue in the boy's limp body. If the he's this tired, he wondered, how's his mom holding up?

The rest of the class lined up for a bathroom break. Trent faced him. Blinking away tears, he signed *want dad you.* With sharp movements, he added *I want you my dad, please you dad me please.*

Lee wrapped both arms around the shaking boy. He'd dad the kid in a heartbeat. But his mom had the final say, and Lee couldn't do anything about her.

I friend, I teacher, he signed, unable to speak around the lump in his throat. *I love you.*

THE VOLKSWAGEN SQUEAKED to a stop next to the emerald green pickup. Must be late. Lee checked his watch. No, the Jamesons are early. Lee scanned the parking lot up the hill. Just the usual minivans. No nondescript private-eye sedans. Trent met him at the gym door with a hug.

Caroline joined them. "I understand you visited Trent at school yesterday."

"Today, too." He glanced up from his key ring. She didn't look the least bit pleased. "Did the school have a problem with that?"

"No." Shoulders stiff around her ears, she stomped through the door he held open.

"But, you have a problem with it." Lee sent the boy to the other side of the gym to turn on the lights.

"Why didn't you tell me? I'm his mother. You should have called, let me know ahead of time."

"I got up Monday morning, thought about Trent, and decided to go see how he was holding up. *Mais,* yeah, you'd be there if you could, but you'd already taken two weeks off on short notice." He grabbed a mat from the storage room. "If anything had happened, any strange guys with cameras lurking on the playground, I'd have called you. But I didn't think my visit ranked high enough to interrupt your work."

"If it concerns Trent, then it's important." Caroline lifted the other end of the mat. "You knew I talked to him Saturday. You think I messed it up. You think I couldn't explain about his..." Her fingers stiff, she stabbed her forehead with her thumb. *Father.* "So you had to step in with your own repair job."

"No, I'm sure you did a fine job talking to him. But I feel some responsibility here. Me, I taught him how to punch and kick, but the lessons about self-control don't come so easy." He dropped the mat into position and got in her face. Arms crossed, she scowled at the floor. "I get up early, drive to school, sit with Trent all morning, and you're ready to roast me on a spit. Caroline, I ask my students to look at me when I talk to them. Look at me. I'm not Bryan. You don't have any reason to be mad at me." Once more, real slow. "I'm not Bryan."

She flashed him a quick look, no longer than a second, but in that second he saw a hurricane of anger, fear, worry.

He kept his voice quiet, almost a whisper. "Maybe I should have stopped by Ford."

"That's hardly necessary."

In the proud tossing of her head, he saw Caroline wouldn't bean a coworker with a wrench, or slug back too many brews after work, or even cuss under her breath. Oh no, that was too blue-collar for Ms. High Class. And she was too good a mom to take it out on Trent. No, she just let the storm beat her up from the inside, until he crossed her path like some unlucky road kill. Lee grabbed his bag and marched to the locker room. If he were a betting man, he'd be willing to lay odds no one else had seen this Caroline. Not her coworkers, not her son, not her neighbors. Just him. He yanked his *gi* out, sending a black sparring glove flying. It ricocheted off the tiled wall and whacked him on the head. He grabbed it and dug his fingers into the foam. Just him, with all the brains of a tree roach.

Thank you, Jesus.

Caroline felt safe with him, the only person in her world who could handle her anger. Not unlucky at all. He dumped out the bag, found the other glove, and returned to the gym. Kurt's mother agreed to watch the boys for a minute. Approaching the pacing lady, Lee brought the gloves together with a noisy smack. She jumped and glared at him. Yeah, post a hurricane watch. Storm coming in.

"Follow me." He moved fast enough that she couldn't stomp.

She caught up with him at the end of the corridor. "What?"

"This is the weight room. They ran out of money before they could equip it, so you'll have the place to yourself." He unlocked the door and hit the light switch. A punching bag hung in the middle of the empty room. "There he is, Caroline. Go 'n' get him."

"Who?"

"Come on now, use your imagination." He laid a hand on the bag. "This is Bryan. Ow! Little weasel has sharp teeth. If you don't knock him out, I may just give it a go." He pinned her arm between his elbow and his side and forced on the glove. "I'll lock the door from the outside, so no one bothers you. Come back to the gym when you're done. This room is sound-proof; go ahead and tell him off."

She tried to slap him with her free hand, but he strapped on the other glove. "I should tell you off."

"Later. Got a class to teach." He left her standing in the middle of the room.

When she didn't follow him, he expected her to return sometime midway through the session. He checked the row of parents' chairs every few minutes. No Caroline. After class, he left Trent with Kurt's mom again. Didn't want the kid to hear his mom chew him out big time. He inched open the door. She wasn't where he'd left her. Women. He could never guess what one of them would do. In all his years of karate, the only times he'd been injured was teaching women.

"Caroline?"

Silence. He stepped inside. The click of the latch echoed off the cinder block walls. Caroline slumped in the corner to the right of the door. Her legs stretched out in front of her. Her arms hung at her sides. She looked like his sister's Raggedy Ann doll: limp, glassy-eyed, red-cheeked.

"Caroline, you okay?" Lee squatted next to her, out of range of her kick.

She blinked. Her eyes focused. "Yes. Thank you."

He gathered up the sparring gloves. "Trent's waiting for you."

"Thanks for checking on him this week."

Lee let out his breath slowly. The storm is over. "He's got three more days of first grade. If it's okay with you..."

"I'd appreciate it." She pulled herself together. A little shaky, but he didn't mind giving her an arm to lean on. Her skin felt different, the cool, dryness replaced by a warmth that made him stick to her. Dark strands of hair clung to her face just in front of her ear. The base of her throat shone in the fluorescent lights. She'd worked up a sweat. Naw, rich people don't sweat; they perspire. Dark smudges under her lashes melted into damp trails down her cheeks. *Oh, man. She's been crying.* He gave her hand a squeeze before releasing her to Trent.

Caroline said good night to Kurt's mom. "Lee, thank you." She nodded at the gloves he carried, then smiled up at him. He knew he'd never seen anyone so beautiful.

A CAR DOOR SLAMMED. "That's them now," Lee pushed up from Miss Pearl's flower bed. He squinted through the late afternoon sun at his sister's Hawaiian print shirt, Royals baseball cap, and cutoffs. He usually didn't let his family to drop by the places he house sat, especially a snob knob mansion like Coverdells'. Where could he hide her?

Bernie yanked off her construction-zone orange gardening gloves. "Great. I've been looking forward to meeting Miss Pearl." Leaving behind her flip-flops, she dashed down the moss and stone path.

Lee shut off the garden hose and followed his sister around the house to the circular driveway. "Miss Pearl!"

A rail-thin woman stepped away from the taxi. "Lee, dear boy." She gave him a hug and peck on the cheek.

Bernadette took the purple suitcase from the driver. She pushed past him. "I'm Bernie..."

"Lee's sister! How delightful!" Pearl folded his sister's hand between hers.

"Older sister," Lee sighed. "Doesn't trust little brother to water your plants."

"You were drowning them." Bernie glared at him. "Catananche Coerulea Major doesn't tolerated wet feet."

"My garden is honored by your expertise." Miss Pearl ascended the marble steps. "Let me change shoes, and you can show me how my babies are doing this week."

"Mr. Coverdell didn't come back with you?" What's more important than making sure his wife gets home safe? Lee kept one arm around Miss Pearl.

"Henry had an emergency in Washington." She paused, fingers tracing the pattern on the brass doorknob. "Mint juleps would taste good in this heat, don't you think?"

"Yes, ma'am." Lee winked back at her.

Once those two started talking plants they wouldn't be in until forced by dark. Lee had time to put away the wheelbarrow and set the table on the verandah. As he lit a citronella candle, Miss Pearl collapsed with an unladylike plop onto the glider.

"You're tired." Lee handed her the tall, cold glass. "Those Mayo doctors, they have any good news?"

"Bunch of sour-faced pessimists." She closed her eyes and sipped her julep.

"What's got you?" Bernie asked.

The eyes opened a fraction of an inch. "The file's on my desk in the library."

Bernie banged through the screen door.

"How are you—"

"How are things at the shelter?" she interrupted.

Lee blinked. Ladies, and Miss Pearl was the most ladylike of all, never interrupted. "Quiet. Same guests as when you left. Did the doctors—"

"And your friend?" she jumped in. "Any more trouble from her ex?"

Must be bad, her not wanting to talk about it. The cancer, it spread? How long did she have? Could they do anything for her? For tonight, he'd honor her wish to leave it alone. What had she asked? *Mais*, yeah, Caroline's ex. He shook his head. "The boy made it through the rest of first grade without any more fights."

"And his mother?"

Lee poked at his mint sprig. "She'll be all right, yeah."

"So why are you hanging out on a Friday with an old lady and your sister?"

Bernie stomped out. "The chemo you had last year disqualifies you for clinical trials, but I think we can get you adjunct TR486 on compassionate use. It's a derivative of a pine bark found only in southern Manchuria. Similar to Juniperus communis. We're trying to grow it on tree farms in Wisconsin."

"Miss Pearl's no lab rat." *Stop*, he signed at his interfering sister.

She slapped a thick manila folder on the glass-topped table. "Excellent preliminary results. Fifty percent reductions in tumor load. Minimal side effects: hair loss, nausea..." Bernie paused, catching sight of the older woman and touching her on the knee. "I'm sorry. Just now, you're not wanting to talk about this."

Pearl twisted a lace handkerchief in her lap. "I was asking your brother about his lady friend. I'm looking forward to meeting her."

Curiosity spread over the worry in Bernie's face. "Lee has a girlfriend?"

"Mother of a karate student," Lee protested, hoping the candle-light wouldn't show his red face.

"I'd like to meet her, too." Bernie gulped her drink. "Fourth of July. My place. Barbecue."

"Thank you, but I'm joining Henry in Washington." She looked genuinely regretful. Lee breathed a sigh of relief. Miss Pearl leaned toward Bernie. "I'll call you when I get back. You can tell me all about Lee's lady friend. And this new medication."

Lee squirmed on the wrought iron chair. "She's pretty busy. Probably has to work."

"He knows who butters his cornbread. He'll bring her." The two women clinked glasses.

"RETURN BOOKS TO LIBRARY," commanded the calendar in Lee's block printing. Obnoxious and overbearing, Caroline thought as she drove Trent and his haul across town in the early summer evening. Why can't he write "books due"? Finding his Volkswagen in the library's parking lot didn't improve her mood.

"Lee! Lee!" Trent squealed and bounced against the seat belt. Caroline took him in one restraining hand, the books in the other.

The big man sat with Kurt at a table. The boys' greetings earned a tolerant smile from the librarian and a firm "hush" from Lee.

"What is Mom carrying?" he asked Trent.

My books. The child's shoulders dropped. *Want books, Mom,* he signed, adding *please* with Lee's prompting. He took them to the circulation desk, then raced back to look at the dinosaur pictures Kurt had found.

Lee strolled to the glass front doors and scanned the parking lot. Pacing back, he focused on Caroline. "How's he doing?"

"Fine. I read to him every night." She crossed her arms, trying to capture her evaporating crankiness. "So, you're checking up on us, making sure we don't forget?"

He studied her for a long moment, long enough for his thumb to make a circuit of his mustache. "No. Kurt's folks went to Springfield to bring his sister home from college. We had an hour to kill before my intermediate class." He glanced at his watch. "Suppose you have to work Fourth of July."

"No, I'm off. And you?"

"My sister fixes Cajun food, too spicy for most people. Fireworks up the road, probably not a big show like Worlds of Fun."

"That sounds great."

"Nothing fancy." He tugged at the end of his mustache and scrutinized his sneakers. "You don't have to. No big deal."

"I'd like to meet your family. What should I bring?"

"Don't matter." He shrugged. "I'll call you. Give you a chance to change your mind."

"Lee..." Caroline squinted at him. Did she invite herself?

He lifted his chin in her direction. The autocrat was back. "Know your way around the library?"

"I didn't think Trent was ready."

Lee nodded at the children's section. "Beginning readers, mostly Dr. Seuss, over here. Picture books under the windows. What are you reading? Romance, mysteries, westerns? I bet those Tom Clancy techno-thrillers are mandatory for engineers."

"I don't have time."

"Not much in the way of car books at this branch, but I could show you how to order stuff on the computer." He thumped his forehead with his palm. "Sorry. Engineers know computers."

Caroline headed for Nonfiction, the 600's. "Anything new on Down's?"

"Have you read this one?" Lee pulled out a slim volume, *Count Us In*. "Written by two young men who have Down's. Pictures in the middle."

"Written by? Are you kidding?" The book opened to a middle section of photos. "He looks just like Trent in these baby pictures. Bar mitzvah, Special Olympics, girlfriend. What? Is he voting?"

"Yeah, one of the chapters is the two of them debating the presidential race. Much more civilized than my sister and brother-in-law."

"This boy actually voted? In a real election?"

"Mais, yeah, he's a high school graduate, passed the New York Regents exams and everything. What Mitchell and Jason say, about moving out on their own and what it means to be a man, makes more sense than the garbage most guys spout."

She leafed through the pages again. "I wonder if Trent..."

"Before you know it, yeah. Look how he's grown." Lee nodded at the child paging serenely through a picture book. The big man turned, blocking off the end of the aisle, and lowered his voice. "Any trouble this week? Phone calls?"

Caroline shook her head. "Bryan got what he wanted."

"Hmm." Lee pulled out a book with a dancing boy on the cover. In his usual loud voice, he said, "now this one, some of her ideas are okay, but that new age stuff is too California for me."

"Yes, but I liked reading about someone who's older than Trent and still not toilet trained. Guess I'm not the worst mom in the world."

"Never said you were."

"Then why do I feel like you've put me on the Lee Marivaux Parent Improvement Project?"

He grinned. "You got something against better parenting? Then why you bring your kid to my class?"

The kid in question raced over and peeked at the book his mom held. *Me same* he pointed to the picture of Mitchell. *Same him* he pointed to Kurt.

"Yes, you and Kurt and Mitchell are boys. Same."

"No." Trent tapped the picture. *Face same.*

"Want to show Kurt?" Caroline watched him take the book to his friend, then turned to Lee. "Does he know he has Down syndrome? Did you say something to him?"

"No, but you'd better." He signed *time go* to Kurt.

She'd been driving down a dark road and, without warning, the pavement ended. "Your parent improvement project doesn't cover how to tell a child he has Down syndrome?"

"*Mais*, that's a tough one. Almost as bad as telling him about Bryan." The man's face reddened. "Kurt's mom might have some ideas on that. I'll ask her to give you a call."

"Where is Andie when I need her?"

Heading for the exit, Lee flapped his bent arms. "Squawk!"

CAROLINE CLIMBED INTO BED, hoping she could finish a chapter before she fell asleep. She thumbed through the photos, stopping again to study the pride on Mitchell's face as he stepped out of the voting booth. Remarkable. From a remarkable family: the parents advocate for their sons, grandparents live nearby, they have the financial means to pay for weekly counseling sessions.

Trent padded in.

"Why aren't you asleep?" She lifted her head from the cocooning pillows, listening for thunderstorms.

The small square hands put his and Kurt's school pictures next to the picture of Mitchell. Caroline took a deep breath.

He signed *boy same.*

"Yes, you are all boys."

He trotted out of the room, returning with the Buffums' Christmas card photo. He pointed to Luke and Paul. *Boy same.*

"Yes, they're boys, the same as you."

"No, no, no!" He stomped his foot and glared. *Same mom dad. Boy same.* He pointed to Rebecca and signed *girl same.*

Awfully late at night for the gears to turn. Caroline grabbed Lee's *Joy of Sign* from her nightstand. The sign for brother was made by signing *boy*, then *same.* "Yes, Luke and Paul are brothers."

Trent's hands circled down from his shoulders and flopped on his legs, apparently the sign for exasperation. "Yeah, ma."

"But, no, Kurt is not Mitchell's brother. He's not your brother."

Look same.

Because you both have a nondisjunction of your twenty-first chromosome, Caroline thought. Now, how to explain that? How to tell someone he's mentally retarded? That life will be harder for him? That there are limits to what he can do, to what others will let him do? She took a shaky breath. "Yes, you all look the same because you all have Down syndrome."

"Oh, yeah. Okay." He gathered his pictures and stepped back from the bed. *Good night.*

That's it? That's all he wants to know? "I'll tuck you in again."

"No." He pulled the comforter up to her chin and patted it. *Time sleep. Brush teeth you?*

"Yes, I brushed my teeth."

He planted a wet kiss on her forehead and turned out her bedside lamp. Caroline heard the plastic rustle of his mattress cover.

She let out her breath. "And good night, Lee Marivaux, wherever you are."

"Zeus, Apollo. Heel, boys." Heel? Isn't that what you say to make them stop? These commands for dogs are more confusing than the ones for karate. Lee snapped leashes on the fidgeting Rottweilers. Marv said they'd stay with him; the leashes were just to keep the little old lady neighbors from 911ing. Lee stepped out onto the porch of the bungalow, locking the door behind him. He figured a poster of the boys stapled to each door would do more than any lock, but hey, if Marv wanted the house locked that's what he'd do. He squinted in the early morning sun, and, led by the dogs, began jogging down the sidewalk to the shady park.

Mais, yeah, ought to get a picture of the boys for Caroline's house. Have Zeus and Apollo on the welcoming committee next time the weasel shows his face around here.

Almost to the corner of the second block, the toe of his sneaker caught in the cracked concrete. Lee twisted, landing with an oof, shoulder first on a grassy lawn. He rolled onto his back and watched the blue sky spin until he caught his breath. This wouldn't happen if he kept his mind on his running and off a certain elegant lady.

"Zeus, Apollo!"

Several seconds later, two massive brown and black faces peered into his. Zeus lifted a whiskered eyebrow, then sat facing Marv's house, waiting for someone competent to take him on his run. Apollo gave him a thorough sniff, including a sneeze on his left knee and a lick of his ear.

"I'm okay." He rolled upright. The shoulder smarted, but moved in all the directions it was supposed to. Nothing broken. Better than wrenching his knees or skinning his palms.

"Are you hurt?" A young fellow in dark suit raced out of the house. The dogs wagged their tails and the man greeted them by name.

"Not bad enough that I need your service today." Lee nodded at the navy and gold Waggoner's Funeral Home sign.

"That was quite a spill. You know how to fall. Actor? Football player?"

"Karate teacher. Lee Marivaux." Raising his arm to shake hands sent a stabbing pain under his shoulder blade.

The man squatted, bringing his hand within a comfortable range. "Carter Waggoner. I believe you had a blowout."

Lee followed the man's gaze to his sneaker. The sole flapped, loose all the way to his heel. He'd used Sharon's hot glue gun on it last week. Or was it the other shoe? No way around it. He needed new sneakers. Maybe one of Bernie's boys had an old pair of Nikes he could have.

Carter scratched the nearest Rottweiler's ear. "So Marv decided to take up karate. Two big dogs aren't enough."

"No, I'm dog sitting." Lee pulled off the shoe. Have to finish the run barefoot. Risk stepping on glass. "Been trying to talk him into a few self-defense lessons, since he can't take the dogs on business trips. Might make him less nervous."

"When he finds out we elected him neighborhood watch block captain, he may take you up on that offer." Carter stood. "Stay right there. I'll get you some tape."

"Daddy! We're going to be late!" Two girls in matching ruffled dresses and hair bows passed him on his way inside. "The dogs are out! Hi, Zeus. Hi, Apollo."

The boys went wild. Apollo had a sneeze for each of them, blowing apart their carefully arranged blonde ringlets. Zeus picked up the end of his leash in his teeth and dropped it into one girl's hand.

"Zeus, you silly boy." She patted his wide head, level with hers. "I have to go to school." From her pink lunch box, she fed each dog half a sandwich. The triangle of bread and lunch meat disappeared in a gulp.

"Now what are you going to eat?"

Four bright blue eyes blinked innocently at Lee. The one with the empty lunch box put her finger over her lips. "Ssh. Daddy doesn't like tattletales."

"We'll share. We keep telling Daddy, they just don't give us hardly enough time to eat at school. Rush, rush, rush."

Lee smiled, imagining them flitting around the elementary cafeteria. "Are you old enough to take karate?"

"We're six. We'll be seven October 20th."

"Ballet keeps us quite busy."

"Did you know Zeus and Apollo are twins just like us?"

Carter returned with duct tape. "You can leave the roll by the side door. Okay, ladies, I'm ready." Shiny white patent leathers skipped back to a navy hearse.

"Thanks. I'll pay you back in few years. Self-defense lessons for your little heartbreakers."

Carter grinned. "Yeah, I'm keeping my shotgun oiled."

"Daddy! Hurry!"

The hearse sped away with the girls waving like parade princesses from the front seat. The dogs watched until the Cadillac turned the corner.

"Soon they'll be big enough to dog sit. You can bet their running shoes won't fall apart." He measured out a strip of tape, then lifted the roll to his teeth to start the tear. Pain shot through his shoulder. "I'm getting too darn old for this."

Chapter Thirteen

Ruskin Heights' fifteen minutes of fame arrived in 1957 in the form of a tornado that killed 44 people and left hundreds homeless. When the repairs were complete, the neighborhood faded back into dormancy: cookie cutter starter ranches, a good place to raise kids. Lee said his sister picked the area in the belief tornadoes never hit the same place twice. In the decades since, she'd been right.

Lee parked the truck in front of the one story house, distinguished from its neighbors by the riot of exotic flowers replacing the standard petunia and marigold garden. "Wait here," he told Caroline and Trent. "Looks like they're out."

He jogged to the front door, knocked, waited. From behind her sunglasses, Caroline admired the ripple of thigh muscles running from beneath the frayed edge of his cutoffs. Was he limping a little, favoring one shoulder?

Trent squeaked. Caroline turned just in time to catch her son's feet as he dove face first out the driver's side window.

"Hey, trying to earn another trip to the hospital?" Lee grabbed the boy. "They're out."

"Did they know we're coming?"

"Yeah. They'll be back in a minute." Still holding Trent, he slid onto the seat. "There's something I need to tell you about my sister and her husband."

Caroline expected him to say they were unreliable, or forgetful, or unfriendly to visitors.

Lee continued in a matter-of-fact tone. "One of them's a Democrat and the other's a Republican."

"So, don't bring up politics." A flash in the side mirror caught her attention. "Are either of them police officers?"

Lee anchored his hands high on the steering wheel. "No. Your license plate sticker up to date?"

The uniformed woman sauntered up to the driver's window. "Good afternoon, sir. May I see some... Lee! For the love of... Neighborhood watch called and I thought I'd caught the Ruskin Heights burglar. Didn't recognize you. You're usually driving tow-truck bait."

"Hi, Stephanie." He shook her hand. "This is my student, Trent." The boy offered his hand without prompting. "And his mother, Caroline, owner of this fine vehicle. Say, you haven't seen my sister around, have you?"

"Tennis courts, although I don't know why. She never gets a point off her husband. And he doesn't have the decency to break into a sweat." The officer propped her sunglasses on top of her head. "Say, I'm glad I ran into you. Independence's hiring, if you're interested. Free doughnuts. You'd look great in their uniform."

"I'll call and see if they need an instructor for their self defense class."

"Just as stubborn as... here she comes now."

A red minivan turned the corner at the end of the block.

"Steph," Lee lowered his voice, "do me a favor, will you? Keep an eye out for anyone sneaking through the bushes with a zoom lens."

The police officer glanced at Caroline and Trent, then back to Lee. "Be careful." She gave a casual salute.

The Chrysler squealed into the driveway. A blonde dynamo jumped out as soon as it stopped. Three lanky teenagers in various shades of brown popped from the sliding door. A black man in pristine tennis whites unfolded from the passenger seat.

Caroline turned to Lee. He'd been watching her reaction. "Who's the Democrat?"

"My sister." He grinned.

The woman in question stomped up to the police officer, hands on hips, ponytail swinging. "Well, Stephanie, did you catch... Lee? Where'd you steal this truck?"

The police officer laughed and returned to her car. "You boys stay away from illegal fireworks."

"Yes, ma'am." The teenagers chorused. The two younger ones raced over and climbed in the pickup bed. "Where'd you get the truck, Uncle Lee? Way cool. Can we ride with you to the fireworks?"

"Don't scratch the paint." Lee vaulted into the bed and proceeded to toss the boys back onto the lawn. He jumped down and opened the passenger door. "Caroline, Trent, this is my sister, Bernadette Marie, brother-in-law Louis, nephews Jacques, Guillaume, Etienne."

The boys shook hands, introducing themselves as Jim, Bill, and Steve.

"We've got the volleyball net up," said the middle one, squeaking between two octaves. "You can be on my team."

The youngest tackled the big man. "No, mine, Uncle Lee. Come on." The oldest hovered by his father, shifting his hands between his front and back pockets and keeping a hopeful eye on his uncle.

"The Bear's always on my side. Sister's rights." The lively woman leaped over her sons to pump Caroline's hand. Her brown eyes measured with a wariness reminiscent of Lee at Trent's first karate lesson. "Call me Bernie."

"We brought some food."

"Food!" The pile of boys rolled toward the truck. Caroline passed them a cooler of pop, a long loaf of French bread, and a pan of brownies. The brownie carrier pumped his arm in the air. "Yes! She likes me best!"

"What is it this year, Bernie?" Lee tugged on his sister's ponytail. "Alligator, crawfish, crab?"

She pinched her brother's nose. "Like you don't know crawfish are out of season."

"Squirrel, then? Rabbit?"

"To serve your Yankee friend?" She clicked her tongue against the roof of her mouth. "No, we have red snapper. Louis will start the grill. Let's go volley the boys into the ground."

"Come on, Trent." Lee lifted the boy to his shoulders. "You're on our team, so we won't be outnumbered. *Laissez le bon temps roulez!*"

The ruckus moved to the backyard. Louis stepped to the truck. "I'm afraid they're rather preoccupied with each other. Thank you so much for keeping me company."

Caroline blinked, startled at his French accent. "Thanks for inviting us." By the time the grill fired up and they settled on the patio with iced tea, Caroline's curiosity overwhelmed her. "You're not from Kansas City."

"Barbados." He poured sauce over the fish, then wrapped it in foil. "My grandmother is a herbalist. Marion Labs recruited me to research tropical plants used as medicine. Although I'm beginning to think grandmother's incantations and faith provides the cure, not the chemical compounds in the herbs." He closed the cover of the grill. "You also are not from Kansas City."

"Boston."

The red haired boy stepped to the service line. Lee shouted encouragement, calling him Etienne. Jacques was the lighter version of his father, and Guillaume was the one with his mother's sharp features and his father's dark complexion. She tipped her glass toward the volleyball court. "How did you meet your wife?"

"On a gathering trip to the Mississippi Delta. Her grandmother was also a healer, *une traiteuse.* I tell the boys, with this bloodline, they will all go to medical school, become fine doctors. I'm afraid their aspirations are more in an athletic direction."

"So you recruited Bernadette for Marion."

"And Lee followed her to Kansas City, to make sure I treated his sister well, but he would not join us at the Lab."

Caroline could barely imagine Bernadette in a white lab coat, much less Lee. The adults now had three points over the teens. Trent had found a role chasing out-of-bounds balls. He darted around the court wailing like a police siren.

"Yes, I offered to get him an application for Ford."

Louis sighed and stretched his long ebony legs. "People who grow up with little either become materialistic, greedy for possessions, or become like Bernadette and Lee. They know they can be happy without money, without owning anything. It gives them a freedom the rest of the world does not know."

"I disagree. There's no freedom driving a car that's always on the verge of breakdown."

"Point taken." Louis gave a Gallic shrug. "And if he should be involved in an accident, without health insurance. Catastrophe."

With an easy swing of his arm, Lee slammed the ball into the teen's court. Caroline bit her lip, imagining him confined to a hospital bed or wheelchair.

"Did your wife call him Bear?"

"Her name for him since childhood. Sometimes the boys call him Uncle Bear." He flipped the fish. "What do you do at Ford, Caroline?"

"Build trucks. I'm an engineer."

"Ah. I have something in the garage to show you."

The volleyball players didn't give them a glance as they left the patio. Caroline followed the regal man around a quartet of ten-speed bikes, past the lawn mower, to a small lump in the corner. Louis rolled the tarp away from a 1973 Porsche 914.

"You see, I am possessed by my possession. It takes up space in the garage. I cannot drive it in winter after the roads are salted. I don't dare leave it alone in a parking lot. And the insurance—*sacré bleu*—my agent sends postcards from his villa on the Mediterranean."

"It's beautiful." Caroline bent down to peer at the dashboard. Just a little over thirty-six thousand miles.

"You haven't seen the best part." He opened the hood.

Not a speck of grease marred its cast aluminum perfection. After the cavernous Ford engine compartment, the Porsche seemed a wonder of miniaturization, like an intricate doll house.

"Amazing."

"Louis." Bernadette stomped into the garage. "You're letting the fish burn and boring our guest with your toy car."

"Hey!" Lee stepped around his sister. "You never showed me this."

"In fear you'd ask to borrow it." Louis turned to his wife. "Caroline is an engineer at Ford."

Bernadette raised an eyebrow. "Even gearheads have to eat. We'd better get to the table before those gators inhale everything." She whirled back into the house.

"Where's Trent?" Caroline asked. She felt Lee's hand brush the small of her back as she passed him.

"Don't worry. The boys are teaching him to dunk."

Etienne had her son on his shoulders. Guillaume cowered on the other side of the net, yelling "don't hit me!" Jacques retrieved the balls he threw.

"They're so good with Trent." Caroline remarked as she helped set the table. "They must have a lot of experience with Lee's students."

"This is the first time he's brought anyone over." Bernadette plunked a pan of red beans and rice on the picnic table.

"By their very existence, they ask for a world free of prejudice." Louis peeled the foil off the red snapper and returned it to the fire for a final grilling.

Bernadette shook some spice onto the fish. "They're Southerners. Hospitality's in their blood."

"Like lynch mobs, the KKK." Louis pushed her away with the spatula.

Lee flashed a peace sign between his sister and brother-in-law. "Wash up, so we can eat," he called to his nephews.

They queued in the narrow hall outside the bathroom door. Caroline wandered into the living room. Framed photos of the boys covered the wall opposite the picture window. Older pictures hung over the TV. Bernadette in cap and gown. Louis on a sailboat. A barefoot group on the weathered porch of an unpainted cottage. Matching deep-set eyes under low brows identified them as family. Noses started as narrow triangles, then grew knobs with age.

"Wonder any of them has sense to get out of a hurricane, bunch of inbreds." Bernadette straightened the picture.

"You, also," Louis interjected from his place in the bathroom line. "I have Acadians in my family tree. They traveled from Nova Scotia to Louisiana via the Caribbean."

"Yeah, yeah. Next you'll be telling me you're Elvis's dead twin brother," Bernadette dismissed her husband's claim and returned to the photo. "Of all these people, my family, this is the only one still talking to me." She pointed to a toothpick-legged toddler in a sagging diaper.

"Lee?" Caroline asked.

His sister nodded. "Runt of the litter then. That's why he sides with the underdog now."

"Who is this?" Caroline indicated a portrait of an elderly couple, the man looking like Lee with a full beard.

"Our grandparents. Grandpa was a German from Robert's Cove. That's where we get our light hair. You can tell Lee won't get much uglier."

Caroline laughed. "Not ugly at all."

"I'd offer him my blonde-in-a-bottle, but I like looking younger than my baby brother. Now you want to see really ugly, this is when he got his black belt." Bernadette opened a photo album to a picture of Lee in his karate uniform. His hair was just a shade darker, not brown enough to be called brunet, not yellow enough for blond. She paged through stances, punches, kicks, blocks. The foreground showed a blur of fist or foot. The camera focused on his face, his concentration more frightening than an expression of anger.

"Where did you find a photographer brave enough to get this close?"

"She took them herself." Joining the women, Lee made a grab for the album.

"He won't hurt me." Bernadette shouldered her brother out of the way and turned to a picture of Lee chopping a stack of boards.

With a yank on her elbow, Lee snatched the book.

"Be fair," Caroline protested. "You got to look at my pictures."

"They weren't of you, they were of Trent, and he asked."

Bernadette looked Caroline up and down. "Wash up, before the fish burns." She stomped out of the room.

Caroline looked to Lee for an explanation, but he concentrated on putting the album back in the right place on the bookcase. "You heard the boss. Go wash."

When Caroline rejoined the party in the backyard, Bernadette had arranged them: Lee next to her, Trent on his other side, Caroline and the boys on the opposite bench. Louis pulled his lawn chair to the head of the table.

"Beer?" Bernadette asked, holding up a Coors Light can.

"No, thank you." Caroline distributed pop to the boys.

Lee cleared his throat.

"Keep it short," the blond woman warned her brother. He said a quick grace, then they dug in.

Bernadette passed around the French bread. "I want to hear how a lady like your friend here ended up with a dirty job like building trucks."

Caroline fidgeted on the bench, uncomfortable with the older woman's challenging manner. "My father had a car dealership."

"For which manufacturer?" Louis refilled her iced tea.

"Lincoln."

Bernadette whistled. "Money," she said to Lee.

"Talk about." He seemed preoccupied with cutting Trent's fish. A considerable amount of food had spilled in the gap between plate and mouth. Lee lifted the child onto his knee, wedging him between his chest and the table.

"He can be pretty messy." Caroline reached for her son. "Shall I..."

"Don' matter." Lee motioned with his fork for her to sit.

"Why not management or sales?"

"Father rotated my brother and me through all the departments,

156

on the premise the owner should understand all facets of the business. Chip didn't like any of it, so he enlisted in the Navy. I enjoy fixing things, so I went to engineering school."

"Where did you go to school?"

"Two years at MIT, finished up at Wayne State in Detroit."

"MIT," Bernadette whistled. "Money and brains."

"How did you end up at Ford?" Louis asked.

She grimaced. "Shortly before graduation, I got a call from a guy named Bill Edsel. With a name like that, I thought it was one of my classmates playing a prank. So I hung up. Fortunately, Mr. Edsel called back. I've been with Ford ever since."

"A guy named Edsel who works for Ford. I'd hang up, too." Bernadette splashed her fish with hot sauce. "Do you think you'll stick with them?"

She nodded. "They're a great employer. Good pay, good benefits. With the annual model changes, new technology, and staying ahead of Chevrolet, I can't see it ever getting boring."

"Yeah, you should see her riding down the highway, checking out all her trucks, looking so proud." Lee mopped his plate with a slice of bread.

Caroline sent him a fierce look, which he ignored.

"Now, pay attention, boys," Bernadette directed. "How important are high school grades?"

Ah, Caroline thought, that's what this interrogation's about. "All your grades are important, not just math and science. An engineer who can't communicate won't have much of a career."

Etienne didn't look too happy with the mention of grades. "Miss Caroline, wanna join the game after dinner?"

She glanced at the red-faced, sweaty volleyball players. "No thanks. It's too hot for me."

"Too hot!" Lee looked at her from under his bushy eyebrows. The boys chuckled, obviously familiar with this routine. He continued in an accent as New Orleans as pralines. "This is not'ing. Now Lou'siana is so hot..."

"How hot is it?" the two youngest chorused.

Bernadette groaned and shook her head.

"You see, Boudreaux had not led a good life. In fact, he'd been such a bad boy, you know where he ended up?"

"Hell!" the boys said in unison, even the oldest chiming in. Trent squirmed around on the big man's lap to watch him tell the story.

"And the Devil met him at the door: 'Boudreaux, you've been a vairy bad boy, so I've got a vairy hot place for you.'" Lee shook his index finger. Trent stage-whispered "uh-oh", sending the nephews into fits of giggles. "So, he locked Boudreaux away. After a time, the Devil came back to check on that bad boy. He wasn't even sweating. 'Boudreaux,' says he, 'is it hot enough for you?'

'It's fine,' came the answer. 'Like Lou'siana in the summer.'

So the Devil turned up the heat. Way up. When he came back, one trickle of sweat crossed Boudreaux's face. 'Now is it hot enough?'

'Like when I mow my lawn in Lou'siana in the summer.'

Well the Devil thought a moment, then he turned heat off completely. The next time he visited Boudreaux, icicles and frost covered everything. Boudreaux was dancing around, arms overhead, nevair looked happier." Lee waved his arms. Trent imitated him, knocking over a can of ginger ale. The big man caught it without interrupting the story.

'What now?' asked the Devil.

'The Saints won the Super Bowl! The Saints won the Super Bowl!'"

The boys burst out laughing. Etienne fell off the bench and rolled under the table. The little boy scrambled off Lee's lap to join him.

"That Boudreaux, his eyebrows connect in the middle," Bernadette explained.

"Speaking of trucks," Lee began. "Pete and Repeat were taking driving lessons..."

Bernadette snatched her brother's plate off the table. "Enough already. Let's go to the fireworks."

"Can we watch the fireworks from your truck, Miss Caroline?" Jacques asked from the curb.

"Sure." She grabbed a blanket from under the seat.

"Don't scratch the paint." Lee inspected their clothing for rivets.

The boys climbed over the side rails, whooping and hollering like they'd made the summit of Pike's Peak. The adults turned toward the grassy slope dotted with other 4th of July revelers.

"Miss Caroline?" Jacques again. "Could Trent stay with us?"

"Yeah!" the other boys chorused.

Caroline glanced at Lee. He swung the boy into the pickup bed. Before he left, he held Trent by the shoulders and looked him straight in the eye. "Stay with the boys."

"Yah, suh."

Lee squinted at each nephew.

"We'll keep a real good eye on him," they promised.

Caroline pointed at the brightly lit outdoor arena at the base of the hill. "What's all that?"

"Benjamin Ranch," Bernadette answered. "They have a rodeo, then put on the fireworks."

Louis spread out the blanket. "Perhaps you could go next year. Trent would enjoy the animals."

"Don't wait a year." Bernadette plopped down in the middle. "The American Royal Rodeo is in November. They have a parade, petting zoo, exhibits. Trent would have a blast."

Caroline bit her lip. "Have you ever been?" she asked Lee.

"Too expensive."

"It was easier when Trent was confined to a stroller." Caroline perched on the edge of the blanket. "He gets away from me so fast. And, he can't tell people who he is or my name."

"Pin a hunting license holder on the back of his shirt," Lee set down the cooler, then sprawled on the grass. "Stick in a card with his name, your name, address, phone number."

"Good idea." Caroline nodded, distracted by Lee's long legs stretched out beside her. She wanted to rest his head in her lap, run her fingers through his curls. What would Bernadette do if she knew? Probably give her a swift kick in the pants, send her flying back north of the river.

"Whatda we got here?" A teenage boy raised his beer can in

their direction. "A pimp taking his girls to the fireworks." The rest of the six-pack, a matched set of backwards baseball caps and baggy shorts, swaggered toward them for a better look.

"Hey, cutie, how 'bout some real fireworks?"

"I get the blond."

Caroline glanced to her left. Louis had frozen in place. Only a ripple across his cheek showed his tension. The Coors can crumpled in Bernadette's fist.

In one smooth motion, Lee rolled to his feet. "Gentlemen."

The leader stopped. His pimpled jaw dropped open. The kids behind him took a step backwards.

Lee circled his arm and tilted his head, a motion reminiscent of the fanciest restaurant's maitre-d'. "May I present the ambassador from Barbados, his economic liaison, and his social secretary." Behind his hand he continued to the boys, "don't worry. They don't speak English. Show them how friendly we are in Kansas City. Bow."

The leader whipped off his Royals hat and placed it over his heart. His knees bent in a clumsy plié.

"Mark," hissed one of his cohorts. "That's a curtsy."

The boy straightened and sent a worried glance at the sandy haired giant looming over him. Facing Louis again, he bent from the waist. The black man acknowledged him with a regal tilt of the head.

"Hey," yelled one of the boys. "Does he give autographs?"

"I'm sorry, but that's considered very bad karma in Barbados." Lee ushered the gang down the hill, away from the nephews. "The ambassador's police escort's up by the road. They may want to know who sold you the beer. Enjoy the fireworks." He waited until the boys were out of sight before flopping on the grass.

Caroline spoke first. "You were ready to fight those guys."

He stretched out, arms folded under his head. "Naw. They're just kids."

"Thank you, man." Louis wiped his face with a handkerchief.

"Karma in Barbados." Bernadette reached behind Caroline to

swat her brother. He handed her another Coors Light. "I want to know which of us is the social secretary."

"I suppose this is more excitement than your usual Fourth of July?" Louis asked Caroline with strained cheerfulness.

"If I don't have to work, we watch the Worlds of Fun's show from across the interstate. There's a parking lot where you can even see the Spirit Festival Fireworks, although not well at that distance."

"You like jazz. Why don't you go down for the Festival?" Lee passed her a Diet Coke.

"Trent..." She frowned.

Lee followed her gaze to the row of turquoise portable latrines behind the horse barns. "No reason he couldn't use those."

"I'm sure he could," Caroline squirmed, "but he wouldn't wait outside one."

"Have to give up the hard stuff." His large finger tapped her Diet Coke can.

"How did you manage, with three boys?" she asked Bernadette.

"I borrowed some iron from the state pen and shackled them into a chain gang."

"Hah. You never took them anywhere without me," Louis snorted. "Caroline, have Lee go with you. Solve your problem with Trent, and Lee's problem with..."

The big man rose up on one elbow. "She's not paying my way."

"Gigolo," Louis pronounced. "Nice work if you can get it."

Bernadette blocked the fist Lee tossed at her husband. "You didn't pay admission when you were doing body guard work."

Caroline glanced at the big man. His bottom lip stuck out under his mustache, his stern look. An awful lot like Trent's stubborn look.

"I don't know how you single parents do it." Bernie sipped her beer. "When we had that FDA trouble and Louis spent three months in D.C., I went berserk. Halloween just about killed me."

Caroline groaned. "I hate Halloween."

Lee propped on one elbow. "You hate Halloween?"

His sister set her can down to count off each problem on her fingers. "First off, kids eat all that junk at school."

"Trent got sick on his costume."

"*Mais*, yeah. You got to get that costume cleaned, and get him something to settle his stomach, and all the time the doorbell rings. Maybe you want to fix dinner, so they eat something besides candy."

"But the doorbell keeps ringing," Caroline interjected.

"And between all that answering the door, you got to get the little monsters into their costume, find the missing pitchfork, put on their makeup. And when you're all ready to go, you realize..."

"You have no one to pass out candy while you take him trick-or-treating."

"All this after a full day at work." Bernadette leaned back to eyeball her brother. "What are your doing October 31st?"

He shrugged. "I usually cancel classes. Kids have better things to do that night."

His sister jabbed a thumb in Caroline's direction. "You be at this lady's house, then. Help her out with that boy of hers."

"And if I don't?" The mustache twitched.

"You can kiss your corn *macque choux* goodbye."

"Caroline, whether you want it or not, you got my help come Halloween."

"Appreciate it."

With a red, white, and blue chrysanthemum blossom, the fireworks began.

TRENT'S HEAD bobbed as the truck bounced over the expansion joints of Interstate 435.

"Come here, Trent. *Do-do*." Taking one hand off the steering wheel, Lee pulled the boy toward him. His head settled on the man's leg. Caroline loosened her son's seat belt and adjusted his sneakered feet around her knees. The instrument panel lights glowed softly on the boy's closed eyes.

"Seemed to have a good time." Lee stroked the dark brown hair back from the small forehead.

Caroline released a deep sigh of relief. "He behaved all right in front of your family."

"You should be proud of him." Lee changed lanes to accommodate merging traffic from I-70. "Wish I could say the same for my family. You'd think they could take time off from arguing for the holiday."

"You mean your sister and her husband?" Caroline heard a groaning noise of affirmation from the driver's seat. "They feel free to disagree with each other. That's a sign of respect, commitment, love."

"Strange way to show love," he said slowly. "I wouldn't want to live like that."

"You wouldn't want to live at the opposite end of the spectrum either, where one person humiliates everyone who disagrees with him. Anything different, anyone different must be wrong. There's only one answer and it's his." Caroline pressed her fingers over her mouth. How did that slip out? She never talked about Bryan.

"Put up and shut up. Yeah, that'd be worse." He nodded. "How'd you get hooked up with someone like that anyway?"

"We were introduced at the Holly Ball. I don't know if you have those in Louisiana."

"Marriage-go-'round for the old money set. Yeah, I think that started in the Old South." Lee scratched his mustache. "So you were a debutante?"

"No, I was a guest of Marnie's. My brother Chip was her escort." She paused, remembering the rush of dances, golf outings, steeplechases, Boston Symphony performances. "I think Bryan married me for my pedigree, the Mayflower ancestors."

"And when Trent's genes weren't quite up to his standards..." Lee's right hand launched off the steering with an exploding rocket noise and landed softly on the boy's shoulder. "That doesn't answer the question: why'd you hitch up with him?"

"Bryan told me to marry him." Caroline studied the sleeping boy, surprised at the reflective turn of her thoughts. Life's hectic pace had allowed no time for analysis, and, until now, no interested listeners. "In the bad old days, I made contacts instead of friends, spent my leisure time networking, decorated the house instead of furnishing it. I thought children should be trophies, not individuals. Trent sure has rearranged my priorities."

Lee nodded slowly. "These kids show you what's important, yeah. I don't want to have the biggest classes in town, take the most students to regional competition. I just want each kid to do his best." The mustache twitched, rolled. "Did you love him?"

"Now there's a question. If I say no, you'll wonder why I married someone I didn't love. If I say yes, you'll question my judgment for falling in love with such a jerk." Wee-hours insomnia often cross-examined her on this point, but never gave her the answer. "I was so relieved to see Boston in the rearview mirror. I had two years of college to finish and a handicapped child to raise by myself, but the weight of the world had been lifted off my shoulders."

All day she'd felt like an engine on rebuild. First his sister and now him picking her life apart. Time for turnabout. "Have you heard anything from M.U.'s Adaptive P.E. program?" She held her breath. Confronted with the possibility of his leaving, panic rode the rear bumper of her mind.

Lights from an oncoming car showed his knuckles tense on the black steering wheel. "Guess what they're asking just to look at my application."

"How do they want the check made out?" Caroline reached for her purse.

"No." Lee's hand snapped onto her forearm. "What kind of man takes money from a woman? If I got accepted, you plan to whip out your checkbook for my tuition, books, all that stuff?" He gave her arm a little shake. She dropped her purse.

"I'm sorry." More relieved than afraid of his anger, Caroline touched the back of his hand. "It's ridiculous. With everything you know, they should be asking you to teach."

"Thanks for the vote of confidence." He caught her fingertips with his thumb and squeezed. "Don't know what I need a degree for; I've already got the job I want. *Mais*, yeah, it's not a good time to leave Kansas City. Trent's class is really making some progress. Kurt's ready to workout with non-handicapped kids. I'm starting a new group at Liberty's workshop, adults with disabilities. And the turnover at the women's shelter is keeping me hopping."

She looked down at the hand holding hers, wondering if it

meant a change in their relationship. "I... Trent and I would have missed you."

"And I'm going to sit for Trent every Saturday night while you date, soon as you're done with changing the plant to the new model year."

Caroline groaned.

"You both had a good time today. Think how much better it would be with a real family, not just a bunch of ragin' Cajuns."

"You're family isn't good enough for me?"

"What's that supposed to mean?"

She didn't know the answer, so she changed the subject. "So, I should start prowling the singles bars?"

"Naw, that's not safe." He squeezed her hand again. "Heck, I know just about everybody in town. Ought to know somebody you could argue with."

"Are you adding matchmaker to your list of professions?"

"Who knows? Maybe it will pay better than teaching karate."

Yesterday at the plant, a new-hire had noticed Trent's picture on her desk. The young man shook his head sadly and said a few words of condolence. The world mourns, Caroline thought, but I've moved on. "Good luck with that."

Chapter Fourteen

Lee sat on Sharon's deck, enjoying the comfortable morning breeze. This afternoon would be hot enough for the kids to hit the pool, if they finished their schoolwork. Trent perched on his lap, reading Dr. Seuss's *Hop on Pop*. Sharon's daughter leaned against his side. As he'd instructed, Rebecca pressed her hand over her four-year-old mouth to keep from bursting out with words the boy struggled over. On the other side of the sliding screen door, Sharon bent over the dining room table where Luke calculated a cost-benefits analysis of his phone book delivery job. Then she paced to the living room computer to check Paul's progress on a script about the signing of the Declaration of Independence.

"Play all day," Trent read, his words understandable even without the signs. He pointed to the next word and shrugged.

Lee gave the nod to Rebecca.

"Night. Fight."

Trent read the next twenty pages without help. He put all his energy into his reading, going at each word head down with a full breath of air. He held himself straight, not leaning back as he did when he was read to. His stubby feet curled, soles together, toes flexing and straightening as if trying to duplicate the fingers' signing.

A car turned onto the street. Lee listened to the quieting hush of slowing tires, the squeal of a garage door, the thump and slide-bang of people exiting a minivan. The Godards are home.

Seems quiet. Anyone else would let down his guard. *Mais*, yeah, Caroline might think Bryan was gone for good. At the shelter that attitude's known as denial.

The boy finished the book and put it inside. Lee rolled out Sharon's card table. He squirted three globs of shaving cream on its royal blue vinyl top. Artificial lime fragrance wafted through the air. No wonder this stuff was on sale.

"Write your name." Lee carved his three letters into the white foam, then helped Trent find his index finger. Rebecca finished her name, drew a picture of herself, and started on labeled family portraits. Trent worked through his five letters, and managed three stick figures.

"Who's this?"

The pudgy finger scrawled a wobbly MOM.

"And this?"

Large stick letters formed LEE. The round face burst into a gap-toothed grin.

"Hey, you wrote my name. Cool." Lee chucked him under the chin, leaving a white spot. "Swallow."

"You." Trent tickled the man's scratchy chin.

Sharon stepped into the sunlight. "Interesting. Trent counts you as a member of his family."

"He's just copying what I wrote." One swipe smoothed the shaving cream. Lee kept his head down so Sharon wouldn't see the pride and the wanting sparring in his eyes. "What other words do you know?"

Rebecca wrote and illustrated "House, mouse," from the book.

"I heard you reading, Trent. Good job." Sharon sat on a lawn chair.

"I won't be here the rest of the week. I'm helping Gene Shanks put a new fence around his paddock tomorrow, and Caroline's parents are coming into town."

Sharon frowned at him. "You should charge for tutoring, so you wouldn't have to take extra jobs."

"No." He probed the sore molar with his tongue. "Gene's a dentist. I got a tooth needing some work."

"If you're not going to shave, you may want to dry off your jaw." The woman passed him a tissue. "Lee, you have more patience with that boy, he's made more progress with you. Caroline can afford to pay."

"Lagniappe." He dismissed his services as a small gift.

"Does she have any idea how much time..."

"It's my time." The shaving cream dried in the hot sun. The children skipped off to the swing set. Lee held his breath while the boy climbed up on the swing. "Maybe Trent told her."

"Why are you doing this?"

He stood and stretched without looking at the eagle-eyed woman. "Thanks for breakfast."

JULY DOWNTIME WOULD BE FUN, Caroline decided, if the hours weren't so long. With a sigh of exhaustion, she squeezed her truck into the garage next to the Lincoln. Father always rented the biggest land yacht on the road, then griped about the car falling short of the ones he used to sell. Caroline could remind him of a hundred improvements, from gas mileage to climate control, but she knew better than to argue cars with her father. Despite her degree and years of experience, he always had the final word. She toed-off her shoes by the door and crossed the family room.

Stretched out in the recliner, Father snored under the Business section of the Kansas City Star. PBS's Nightly Business Review droned in the background. Shifting her lunch cooler to her left hand, Caroline patted her father's foot. "Hey."

"Hey, yourself." Mr. Jameson didn't look up. He turned the page, acting as if he hadn't been asleep. "How's work?"

"Making progress. Looks to be a good year."

"Hope you're doing more than changing the chrome. Stock price dropped a quarter today." He folded the paper. "We met Lee."

"Oh?" Caroline paused with one foot on the stair.

"Mother thought two old people couldn't handle Trent at

Worlds of Fun, so she dragged him along. No ambition, but does all right with the boy."

Caroline opened her mouth, but decided she didn't have enough energy left to defend Lee. Her mouth widened into a yawn. "Uh-huh." She dragged up the stairs.

Mother rose from the kitchen chair to take the cooler. "I found the prettiest nightgown for you. It's hanging in your bathroom, all washed and ready."

The shower pounded the grime out of her pores. Caroline attacked her fingers with a nail brush. The other problem with July downtime is it happens during the hottest two weeks of the summer. Grit soaks in as the sweat pours out. Her usual deodorant soap had been replaced with a Crabtree and Evelyn bar. Ah, Mother, still nurturing after thirty-two years. Couldn't make it through retooling without her. Caroline emerged from the shower smelling like an English garden. She slipped the sleeveless white gown over her head. Lace, gathers, ribbons, tucks. A little on the fussy side, but the sheer cambric skimmed light and silky over her body. A good change from her stiff, heavy work clothes.

Caroline returned to the kitchen. "Thanks. It fits perfectly."

Mrs. Jameson gave her a head to toe inspection. They had an unspoken agreement: don't look until after the shower. "Keeping your girlish figure, just like your mother."

"We're mistaken for sisters all the time. Hi, Trent." She hugged her son. "Tell me about Worlds of Fun."

While Caroline ate the chicken amandine her mother served, Trent reenacted their day. The doorbell rang.

"Don't get up," Mrs. Jameson told her. "Hello, Lee. Thank you for picking up the prints. Won't you come in? You can show them to Caroline."

"Mother!"

Mrs. Jameson swung the door open. Lee filled the entryway. Two steps toward the kitchen, he spotted Caroline slouched in a chair holding a napkin to the low neckline of her nightgown. He reddened and detoured into the living room.

"Why don't we sit here on the piano bench, Mrs. J.? Hi, Trent.

I'll show you how to hold pictures. By the corners, like this. Pass it to your grandma."

Caroline dashed to her room and changed into a T-shirt and shorts. She ran a comb through her wet hair and considered make-up for a moment. Why couldn't her father answer the door? He wouldn't let Lee in. Mother should have warned her. She tromped down the stairs.

Lee sat on the piano bench by himself. He wouldn't look at her. Still embarrassed. Well, so was she.

"Your mom took Trent for a walk."

"After walking around Worlds of Fun all day?" She slid next to him. "You must be beat."

"I didn't get up at four a.m." He handed her a stack of pictures. "Your dad wouldn't let me pay for anything."

"You wouldn't let me pay you for mowing the lawn." Caroline flipped through the photos. Trent's expressions ranged from wide-eyed amazement to open-mouthed gleeful grins. "Trent looks like he's having a good time.

"It's all real to him: 'I'm flying an airplane! I'm driving a motor-cycle! I'm floating in a canoe!'"

"Did you ride anything?"

He ran a hand through his hair. "Your mom took me on all the water rides. She's really..."

Caroline had a flash of the words Bryan used to describe her mother: insipid, irresponsible, ludicrous.

"She's a hoot. She flirts with your dad constantly. All those park workers were tired and cranky in the hot sun, but your mom had a kind word for each of them. And adventurous. We rode all the roller coasters. She's got to be in pain, with her arthritis, but... Here's a good one: Trent got to feed the dolphins."

"Did anyone say anything about him..."

"Naw. No problems. One person recognized him from the karate picture, but he handled his fifteen seconds of fame with good grace."

Caroline sifted through the pictures again. No one would complain about Trent with his body guard present. Then again, with his behavior under control, what would anyone have to complain about? She clenched her jaw to hold back a yawn.

"I'm keeping you up." He lifted his hand and reached for her knee. Caroline held her breath, waiting for his touch on her bare skin. His hand circled and ended up on his own leg. He pushed himself standing. "Sleep well."

Mrs. Jameson and Trent came in the back door as the Volkswagen pulled out of the driveway.

"You should have seen him in a wet T-shirt."

"Really, Mother."

"We're going to Oceans of Fun tomorrow and look what I've got." She showed off a disposable camera designed to take pictures underwater.

Caroline managed half a smile. Even if she hadn't been tired, she couldn't talk Mother out of her outrageousness. "Take sunscreen."

Trent's gleeful expression appeared on his grandmother's face. She rubbed her hands together. "Sunscreen. Oh, I can't wait!"

LEE MADE the rounds of the Hubble-Flahive Residence, checking the doors and windows, turning on a light here and there. Frank Lloyd Wright hadn't designed a security system into this place, so the purist owners refused to have one installed. They settled for what they called "the architecturally low-impact solution," a house sitter.

The building clung to the top of a bluff above the Missouri river. Lee paused at the floor to ceiling glass window, gazing out over the lights of the city. He wished he could bring Caroline here. She could tell him the engineering feats involved in its construction, like how Wright hung this concrete slab without supports. He would show her this breath-taking view. Yeah, her folks would be impressed with a Frank Lloyd Wright house. A job in one of those glass office buildings across the river. A three-piece suit.

Lee turned back to the earth-toned living room with its custom furniture. *Who am I kidding? I'll never be anything more than a bum, a leech sponging off their daughter.*

He stomped over to the corner kitchen and made himself a tuna sandwich, trying to drive the smell of Caroline from his memory. Now if he could erase the mental picture of her in that nightgown. Her shoulders, her neck, the sunset outlining her— Need water, cold water, lots of ice. Where do they hide the glasses? Lee banged his head on the cabinet door. Who'd want to live here, anyway? Pitiful excuse for a kitchen. Wright must have lived on carry-out.

"Hey, Jameson." A safety-booted foot reached under the conveyor to tap her shoe. "You asleep under there?"

"Almost." Sliding her tool pouch and radio ahead of her, Caroline crawled out. Her back and knees howled as she struggled to stand. She removed her lock from the power shut-off. "Let's see if I've got this hooked up right."

"Mañana." Al Tully scratched his bald head. "The guys are going across the street for a cold brew. Wanna come?"

Caroline blinked the perspiration from her eyes. She'd wipe her face on her sleeve if the left wasn't greasy and the right greasier. The radio said it hit 104 degrees today outside. Had to be hotter inside. "They won't let me in like this."

"Aw, hell, Jameson, you don't smell any worse than the rest of us. Come on. I heard you tell Diego at lunch your folks are watching the kid."

"Thanks, but I'm ready to fall asleep standing up."

"You only been at it fifteen hours. Another night, then. We'll let you know ahead of time, so you can stop by the beauty parlor on the way over."

"All I want is a shower." She stowed her tools and retrieved her lunch cooler. Sunset dropped the temperature outside to a sticky 92. A light breeze wafted across the parking lot. She pulled her shirt tails out of her waistband, trying to catch some coolness. Inside the truck, Caroline flipped the air conditioner on high and set the radio to a country station, full volume. She sang every song, even the ones she didn't know, to keep herself awake long enough to make it home.

"Something's missing." Caroline pulled the truck into the garage. Her clogged brain turned over several times before firing. *The Lincoln's gone. What are they doing out past Trent's bedtime? At least no one will have to smell me.* Muscles cramping in protest, she slid out of the truck. She pried her shoes off and opened the door.

"Man, I was afraid they were working you all night." Yanking the lever on the recliner, Lee pulled himself upright.

Caroline stepped back into the garage. She started to close the door, but Lee held it open.

"Your folks went out for dinner and dancing on the Missouri River Queen. Trent's already asleep."

Caroline turned out the garage light. She leaned on the wall, out of the glare from the family room. "You can go now."

"I have orders from a higher authority, your mother. You're to get a decent meal. Come on in, you're letting the air conditioning out."

Her voice cracked with exhaustion. "Go. I don't want you to see me like this. Please."

He leaned against the door frame. His words brushed her left ear. "You've seen me get all sweaty at work."

"But never this dirty." Impending tears tightened her throat.

With a firm grip on her elbow, Lee steered her inside.

"Don't. I'll get grease on you." She tripped on the threshold.

"I know where you keep the hand cleaner." He looked her over, from the clumped hair, to her appropriately named sweat socks, and back to her grease streaked face. His eyes softened. One side of his mouth tucked into the corner of his mustache. "I see a hard worker who deserves a good meal. I'll have your dinner on the table by the time you're washed up."

Caroline staggered through her shower. She gave a longing look at her bed. If Lee hadn't been rattling around in the kitchen, she would have dropped right in without another thought. Instead she pulled on shorts and a sweatshirt. She checked on Trent, then stumbled back down the stairs, holding onto the railing to keep from collapsing.

The light over the sink cast a restful glow on the table. Caroline slumped into the chair. She took a bite of a flour tortilla rolled up with cold roast beef and lettuce.

"This is good. What's the seasoning?"

"Horseradish." Lee joined her at the opposite end of the table. "Cajuns believe in hot food in hot weather. *Mais*, yeah, cold weather, too."

Caroline sorted through the day's accumulation of junk mail, unearthing a letter from Marnie. She'd seen Trent on one of Bryan's TV ads. The boy looked good. Bryan came across as less than photogenic. The enclosed clipping should have been labeled 'campaign ad', it was so obviously gleaned from a press release. It reported the tear-jerking story of Bryan's reunion with his son. The dastardly mother had abducted him shortly after his birth. Unending, costly investigation failed to locate this beloved child. Then Bryan noticed the boy's picture in the paper. Despite a life on the run, under an assumed name, the child appeared to be in good health. The candidate expressed concern about his son's speech deficit.

Caroline let out a deep sigh, too tired to hold onto her fury. "Is there a Pulitzer Prize for fiction in journalism?" She passed the article across the table.

Lee read it. His lower lip jutted further and further from beneath his mustache. "Reminds me of Nixon. If you can't dazzle them with brilliance, baffle them with bull." The wadded article swished into the wastebasket. He watched Caroline try to yawn and chew at the same time. "Do you have to work so hard? Can't you come home earlier?"

"July downtime. It's always like this. Next week, normal hours, if all goes well."

"Awful lot of food left in your lunch box."

"Too busy to eat today."

"They need to air condition your plant."

She shrugged. "My office is air conditioned."

"Sorry, but I don't believe you passed time in any office." He leaned on the table. "There's got to be an easier job."

"Golden handcuffs - pay and benefits I can't get anywhere else." She washed the sandwich down with milk. "It's really a good job. A machine breaks and I'm the one who gets it running. Or figures out how to keep it from breaking down again. And when the line workers come back and the trucks start rolling and showing up on the street, I feel proud. I did it. I helped to set it up, make it all run. And it runs well."

"Yeah, but it wears you out."

She recycled a line he used in reference to his job. "Sounds like it bothers you more than it bothers me."

He raised his iced tea glass in salute. "You make me feel lazy."

"You put in as many hours as I do. That weekend you took your older students to St. Louis for a competition, how much sleep did you get?"

He looked at the clock on the microwave. "Speaking of sleep..." He cleared the table.

"I'm going, I'm going." But she couldn't move. She repositioned her legs and pressed her palms to the table for leverage. She crumpled back into the chair. A groan escaped from her gritted teeth. Opening her eyes after the wave of pain passed, she found Lee standing over her. "It's nothing. I've just been under a conveyor all day."

"I'm going to touch your back. You've got a big mama muscle spasm and a mess of baby spasms. Don't move."

Like she had a choice, Caroline thought.

Lee returned with two pillows. "Put your head here." He set the pillows where her placemat had been.

"Lee, if I put my head down, I'll never pick it up."

"Just for a minute. You sleep with your back this tense, you'll curl into the cramp. You'll be the hunchback of Kansas City tomorrow."

Caroline submitted to the firm pressure on her shoulders. "Aah. Where did you learn this?"

Lee told her about one of his karate students, an athletic trainer in Excelsior Springs who also held a certificate in massage therapy. Jill had been a tomboy as a kid. She still remembered the day her mother took her aside and told her, from now on, no matter what, she had to be on the 'shirts' team.

Lee stopped. His hands rose and fell slowly along Caroline's ribs. He leaned down to peer in her face. Long brown lashes fringed the pale, translucent skin under her eyes. "Pretty boring story, eh, *chère?*" he whispered. For a few more minutes, he unknotted each muscle. Squatting beside the chair, he eased her head from the pillows to his shoulder. One arm around her back, his hand just above her elbow, other arm under her knees. He stood. Her head wobbled. He braced it with his cheek, getting a full dose of her some sort of spicy flowers. She didn't move as he carried her up the stairs and set her in bed. He tucked the comforter around her shoulders. His mouth came within an inch of her cheek before he caught himself. She'd given him trust, a trust he would not break. Three quick strides took him out of her room. He closed the door with a click. His shaking knees gave out on the first step. Head in hands, he gasped for air.

"I'm in... big... trouble."

Chapter Fifteen

Caroline joined the line at the Ford dealership's parts window. One hand held Trent and the other the bulb from the pickup's dome light. Tuesday night after karate she had noticed it was inop. Today, Saturday, she finally had time to replace it.

"Hey, how 'bout those Royals? Good to see you. How's it going?" A man wove through the crowd. Shirt and tie. Clean cut. The sales manager. Caroline remembered him from her truck purchase. He spotted the boy and did a double-take. She steeled herself for a sympathetic glance, but the man squatted down.

"Hello." He held out his hand. After a hesitation, the boy shook it. "My name is Jerry."

Her son made an approximation of his own name. The man glanced at Caroline for confirmation.

"Trent, I'd like my brother to meet you." The man stepped behind the counter and made a call on the intercom. Caroline ordered her part. While she paid for it, the brother arrived.

"Dusty, this is Trent."

"Hi, Trent. Oh, you Down syndrome, same as me."

Caroline almost dropped her light bulb. Dusty was built a little shorter and rounder than his brother. In fact he looked more like he could be related to Trent.

"Why don't we go to my office, if you have a minute?"

Caroline nodded her consent. Jerry led the group across the sales floor. Once again she pondered the enigma: how can new car showrooms smell so good, when car factories stink?

"I working, Jerry."

"I know, Dusty. We'll stay a few minutes late to make it up."

Entering a corner cubicle, Dusty and Trent sat under a wall of sales awards and plaques from Rotary and Special Olympics. The young man began talking about his job keeping the cars and the dealership clean. He pointed out his uniform, especially the name patch on his shirt.

Jerry poured a cup of coffee for Caroline, then refilled his mug. "This is good for him, show off a little, be a role model."

"It's good for Trent, too." She nodded listening with half an ear to Dusty talking about his apartment in the basement of his parent's house. "Dusty's speech is so intelligible. Did he ever have to use sign language?"

"Sure. No one outside the family could understand him until, oh, about when he was fourteen or fifteen."

Dusty began lecturing on physical fitness, Special Olympics, staying in shape. He swam and lifted weights three nights a week at William Jewel College's gym. Her son finally got a word in and it was "Lee". He demonstrated a perfect karate punch.

Jerry choked on his coffee.

"Are you all right?" Caroline handed him a napkin.

He turned beet red and hurried out of the office. Caroline followed, certain she would have to put her recently renewed CPR training to work.

"I'm fine." He leaned against the glass partition. "You're Caroline. I didn't think you'd... look so pretty."

Caroline stepped back from him, wondering how she could grab Trent and make her escape.

"Lee stopped by here Monday, asking all these funny questions - if I was seeing anyone, what I was doing Saturday night."

"Lee? Oh, no." His scheme to find her a date. Caroline pulled the damaged light bulb from the bag. "When I get my hands on him..."

"That would be tonight. He's sitting for us."

"Sitting?"

"He made reservations for us at the Peppercorn Duck Club."

"Oh, no." *Come here* she signed to Trent, but, chattering with Dusty, the boy missed her signal.

"Caroline, would you join me for dinner tonight?"

"This is absurd." She tucked the bag under her arm so she could sign with both hands. *Go now!*

"I know. I've never had a blind date work out before. Maybe this will be a first for both of us." Rotating a quarter turn, he propped his elbow on top of the glass partition. "You work at the plant. I remember, let's see, couple years ago, you came in to buy an F-150. I wanted to ask you out then, but I was afraid of blowing the sale. The reservation's for six, I know that's early, but Lee said you don't stay out late. Shall I pick you up a little after five?"

"Jerry."

"Lee said to tell you they have a chocolate dessert bar."

Chocolate? Finding no escape, she said, "All right, then. Five o'clock."

"CAROLINE? This is Bernie, Lee's sister."

The woman had called to warn her away from her brother. Caroline tightened her grip on the phone. "I wanted to thank you for having us over for 4th of July. Trent and I both had a great time."

"*Mais*, yeah, it's not every holiday you get mistaken for a street walker. If you don't mind being seen with us again, we'd like to do the Spirit Festival with you and Trent. I know it's not until Labor Day weekend, but sometimes it takes me that long to track Lee down."

"I'd love to. Say, I'm expecting Lee after four. Shall I have him call you?"

"That'd be great. He won't let me buy him a cell phone, so I have to track him down every time I want to talk to him."

"And he does need talking to." Caroline reported Lee's match-making effort.

Bernadette whistled. "Peppercorn Duck Club. Louis and I went there for our anniversary. Hope this guy is loaded."

"I need to dress up, then."

"Oh, man. The most expensive thing you've got. The tighter, shorter, and lower cut, the better. We're talking make-up, hair spray, jewelry, that perfume you're saving for a special occasion. Wish I had time to drive up there and get you all dolled up."

"But won't that... encourage Jerry?"

"Oh him I'm not worried about." She made a clicking sound. "It's what you got to do to stop my brother."

THE SUBDIVISION SIGN rose on the horizon. Here goes nothing, Lee thought. *Oh, come on now, should have fixed these two up months ago. They're perfect for each other. Once she's happy with someone else, the weasel'll leave her alone, I'll leave her alone, stop acting crazy. Mais, yeah, never been interested in married women, never stolen another guy's girl.* He downshifted into the subdivision. Jerry better treat her good. Stop worrying. He'd known Dusty and his family for years through Special Olympics. Jerry's okay. If not, Lee knew where he lived.

He cut the engine and rolled into the Jameson's driveway. Now, Caroline on the other hand. There's something to worry about. What if she's mad? If she's sitting around in her sweats, he'll know she's not going anywhere. Well, that wouldn't be so bad, would it? Not bad for him, but not good for Caroline, hanging out with a deadbeat.

Trent spotted him sneaking up the stairs and flung the door open.

"Hi, little buddy." He swept up the boy, then almost dropped him when he spotted Caroline. He went hot all over, like he'd bitten into a supercharged habanero pepper. The boy squirmed and escaped from his arms. "I'll wait outside 'til you're done getting dressed."

"I am dressed." Caroline glanced up from the kitchen table where she stroked blood-red polish onto her nails. "I ought to have you arrested for vandalizing my truck."

"Hey, I checked the dealership to make sure they had those light bulbs in stock." He approached cautiously, taking in her fluffed hair, face paint, and earrings that looked like gold buttons. The shiny material and narrow straps of her dress reminded him of a slip, only it was dark green, almost black, instead of white. He'd imagined her wearing something like she wore to church, not this. Oh man, not this.

"What if I hadn't gone Original Equipment Manufacturer? What if I'd gone to an auto parts store?" She dipped the brush into the bottle. "One F-150 key. On the table. Now."

Lee fumbled, dropping his key ring twice. Reluctant to go any closer, he set her key on the far end of the counter.

Glossy lips the same red puckered and blew on her fingertips. "Oops. I should have done my shoes first." She leaned forward.

"Oh man. Don't do that. Do not bend over." He sat on the floor with his back to her. Painted toenails peeked from under stockings that shimmered like her dress. He buckled the licorice strap sandals with all the care a bomb squad uses to disarm a ticking explosive. If even one fingertip touched, he'd never be able to stop himself. He'd run his palm right up that stockinged leg. "You should give this get-up to Sharon's little girl. Fit her Barbie doll."

Something cold touched his hand. Iced tea. He gulped the entire glassful in one swallow.

Deep red nails dangled a necklace at him. "Are you as good with clasps as you are with dome light covers?"

"If you weren't wearing enough perfume to blind a guy," he grumbled. His big fingers worked the clasp of the heavy gold chain. "You didn't get this from no cable TV huckster."

"Harry Winston," she volunteered.

"Like I know all your old boyfriends." Lee stood and came around behind her, trying to keep his eyes off her bare back. The women's underwear he knew about would show under a dress like this, meaning she must not be wearing any.

Feeling dizzy, he stomped back to the front door for air. A pristine Lincoln sailed into the driveway. "Your date is here. Is that his car or did he steal it from the dealership?"

"You ask him, while I make a last pit stop." Caroline dashed up the stairs, well-shaped calves rippling under her stockings.

"Slow down, Caroline. Those shoes aren't safe on stairs." Lee opened the door for Jerry. The sales manager wore a gray suit with a dark red tie just about the same color as Caroline's nail polish. He held out his hand. Lee considered flipping him off the porch or crushing his fingers, but settled for a stiff handshake.

"Lee. I couldn't believe it, I mean most of these set-up jobs are dogs, you know what I mean?"

"She's almost ready."

Jerry looked over his shoulder and his jaw dropped. "Knockout," he whispered.

Lee turned to see Caroline glide down the stairs. Late afternoon sun through the dining room windows glowed a halo around her. Miss America could take lessons. She held a thing that looked like a black velvet pencil case, certainly not big enough for the Smith and Wesson he thought she should pack. "Trent!" he barked down into the rec room. "Say goodbye to your mama. Caroline, you need a sweater, jacket, coat?" A full sized dress?

"It's a warm night; I'll be fine." Caroline blew a kiss to her son, then disappeared out the front door on Jerry's arm.

Lee chugged down another glass of iced tea. "Trent. Let's go running." The boy hurried into his sneakers. Leaving the house, he slammed the door hard enough to make the knocker bounce. Turning the corner, Lee noticed the kid panting four houses behind him. He dashed back, threw him over his shoulder, and continued around the block. His mind ignored warning messages about joint injuries and muscle strain, and Trent's cries of protest. He didn't see Sharon until he almost ran into her at the end of Caroline's driveway.

She pried the child off his back. "Lee, if you calm down a little, I'll let you split some firewood."

"Once more around," he gulped. "Maybe twice."

By the time nine o'clock rolled around, Lee had run two miles, split three cords of firewood, rototilled Sharon's garden, scoured Caroline's oven with a toothbrush, and done three loads of laundry. He glared at the clock. How long does it take to eat dinner? He put Trent to bed, took a shower, cold of course, then cleaned the bathroom. He considered vacuuming, but didn't want to wake the boy. 9:35. Even with dessert, they ought to be home by now. Channel surfing netted him a ball game. Unable to sit still, he made another jug of iced tea and a bowl of popcorn. 9:47 on the microwave. Where are they? Jerry's driving new wheels - he can't pull the car trouble trick. Not while there's an engineer sitting next to him. Oh, man, sitting next to him, no little boy in the middle- *Cha-ryot!* With the game as background noise, he ran through his *kata*. His breathing wouldn't slow down. He messed up the order of movements he'd practiced daily for fifteen years. He hung up his Styrofoam block to practice kicking, wishing he could give himself a good kick in the butt. He had only himself to blame. Jerry's the perfect guy for her, unfazed by Down syndrome, career in the auto industry. Get a grip.

Car doors slammed in the driveway. Lee took the stairs three at a time. No swapping spit on his watch. He flung open the door. "Hi! How was dinner?"

"Terrific!" Jerry pounded him on the back.

Lee saw the fatigue in Caroline's eyes. He studied her mouth, trying to see if the lipstick had rubbed off on her food or if Jerry had gotten a kiss off her.

"How's Trent?" she asked.

"Good. Went right to sleep after his bath."

"Hey, nice place you've got here, Caroline. How long have you been living here? Is that a ball game on?" Jerry drifted downstairs. "Hey, the Royals are playing. How 'bout that new pitcher?"

"How much do I owe you?" Caroline dug the wallet out of her real purse.

"Nothing. I ate all the food in your house, even your M&M's."

"That's SOP for sitters." Caroline held out a twenty dollar bill.

"No. I owe you for damaging your truck."

She pushed it into his shirt pocket.

"I saw the note you left, to call my sister. Did she put you up to this?" He looked her up and down, indicating her dress and heels.

"No, you put me up to this." A polished red fingernail pointed toward the rec room where Jerry had been absorbed by the game. "And you will get me out of it."

"You're mad at me."

"No, just tired. You're right about these shoes. Unsafe at any speed."

Lee tried not to watch her climb the stairs, but gave in. After all, he figured Jerry had been making goo-goo eyes at her the whole night. She closed the bedroom door. Lee joined the lucky guy in the rec room.

"Top of the eighth. Royals are back by three. Great TV, don't you think."

Over Jerry's play-by-play, Lee heard water run in Caroline's bathroom.

The bottom of the eighth inning or maybe the bottom of the popcorn bowl, roused Jerry from his trance. "Where's Caroline?"

"Sleeping."

"Guess I'd better be going. Royals are losing anyway."

"Yeah." Lee collected the iced tea glass and popcorn bowl. He started the dishwasher, then gathered his stack of clean laundry from the piano bench. Feeling a streak of meanness, he sorted through his keys in the porch light, and deliberately let Jerry watch him lock Caroline's dead bolt.

"Thanks, Lee." His skinny hand clapped him on the shoulder.

"Any time, old pal. You sure can pick 'em."

"Hey, Jameson, you're wanted in the parking lot." Al Tully slapped a message slip on her desk late Monday morning. "This guy's got nerve. I don't let nobody drive my pickup."

Caroline glanced at the paper. "Need your truck for a couple hours. Lee." She grabbed the key from her drawer and headed outside. After the cavernous passages of the paint shop, the summer sun washed all color from the outside world. When her eyes adjusted, she found the big man in the shadow of the gate, talking to a guard. She hadn't seen him since Saturday night, when he'd babysat. Shyness hit like a speed bump. She yanked off her hair net and stuffed it in her pocket of her paint-spattered navy blue coveralls, wishing she'd stopped by the bathroom to scrape off the sweat.

"Hey, you know this guy?" the guard asked. "We used to do security at Kemper Arena together. I tried to get him to come work with me. He said you'd already offered."

"He doesn't want to work here." She gave Lee a quick glance. "What's up?"

"Emergency. Confidential." He held out his hand for the key. "What time are you off?"

"Two-thirty."

"Be back by then." He jogged across the gravel. The dull blue roof of the old Volkswagen hunkered down, sore-thumb obvious, in the row of shiny late-model Fords. Lee motioned and called to someone inside the compact. A woman climbed out. Honey blonde hair curled down to her waist. A Little Bo-Peep dress rippled around shapely legs. She bent into the car, helping out a fair haired little girl. With a hand on her back, Lee ushered them to the truck. He lifted the girl in, helped the lady, then closed the door. He left the parking lot without looking back.

Pressure built in Caroline's chest. Heart attack. No, she'd stopped breathing. She gulped air, feeling the pain spread.

Stop it. Confidential, he'd said. Nothing to be upset about. Just a mission of mercy, someone in need of help. Just like he helped her. That's all she was, someone in need of his help. Nothing more. No promises, no commitments. Long hair, you know how he likes long hair. A dress.

Caroline jammed the net back on her head and dragged her stodgy, grubby self back into the plant.

Al Tully, Diego, and two line workers stood guard around her desk.

"Where is your truck, eh?" Even Diego's ponytail trembled with indignation.

Caroline frowned at Al. "Don't you have anything better to do than gossip?"

Al rubbed a grime-encrusted palm across the back of his neck. "Who is this guy? What do you really know about him?"

"Not that it's any of your business, but he's my son's karate instructor."

"What's a karate instructor need your truck for?" Lavon asked.

"He's helping someone move." Trying not to think about who he was moving, Caroline flipped through her appointment calendar. "Don't we have a vendor coming in this afternoon?"

"He's late." Diego crossed his arms, then shoved his hands in his pockets, but they whipped out when he started talking again, gesturing wildly with each word. "Caroline, you don' just give your truck to any pretty boy who asks. What you know about this guy, huh? Maybe he scratch it up. Maybe move drugs, not furniture. Maybe not bring truck back. You sure 'Lee' his real name, heh? Tell him, call U-Haul, Ryder, use his own truck."

"He drives a Volkswagen." She jammed her appointment book back in her pocket. "That week I was gone in April, Lee stayed with Trent. If I can trust him with my son, I can trust him with my truck." The guys looked skeptical, so she added, "He washed and waxed it."

"Washed and waxed? You even know what kinda soap?" Diego flung his arms in the air.

"Wait a minute, wait a minute!" Taz finally got a word in. "Karate instructor who drives a Volkswagen, right? Rusted hatch, four different tires?"

"They're all radials." Caroline rummaged in her purse for change for the vending machine. Let there be chocolate.

"I know this guy. He took care of my neighbor's Rottweilers while he was in Philly. He's all right."

"Would you let him borrow your truck?"

"No, but I'd let him date my sister."

Arguing whether he had a sister and how ugly she was, Lavon and Taz left her office.

Diego leaned over her desk. "This guy gives you any trouble..."

"You're the only guys who ever give me any trouble." She headed for the break room.

The afternoon stretched into a long session with a recalcitrant robot. Despite running a few minutes late, Caroline stopped at the restroom. She swabbed her face with a damp paper towel, spreading the grime in an even layer. She joined the flow of line workers out of the plant.

"Caroline!"

She turned, expecting Lee. Instead, the guard waved her down by the gate.

"Here's your key. Truck's back in the same place. He said to tell you thanks."

Numb, Caroline traipsed across the parking lot. She climbed into the cab with a deep sigh. Did it smell different in here? *She* probably wears perfume, not eau de auto paint. Caroline reached for the radio, changing the station to rock. No country "so lonesome, I could cry" songs.

The assembly line ran with fewer snags than usual for this time of year. She hadn't worked more than the regular shift. So why did she feel like she was chugging up a 20 percent grade in a wrung out Pinto? Time to switch to high octane. Add bittersweet chocolate to the shopping list.

"We're out back," Sharon called from the deck.

Caroline trudged through the house and out the sliding glass door. Down below in the backyard, the children drenched each other in a celebration of water. Trent waved to his mother, then raced after Luke with a gigantic yellow water pistol. She joined the sitter on the glider.

"I'll give you a fudge brownie if you'll tell me what's bugging you."

"You sure know how to twist a person's arm." Caroline accepted the napkin wrapped treasure from her. "This is ridiculous."

"Are you insulting my cooking?"

"Never." The gooey chocolate melted into ecstasy. "I'm ridiculous." She related that day's incident with Lee, the truck, and the princess.

Sharon passed her another brownie. "If he's getting you back for Saturday night, you'd better put a stop to this. I'm out of firewood and the garden has been rototilled to powder."

"Wait a minute. He did chores for you while he was supposed to be watching Trent?"

Sharon gave her a grim nod, as if she held Caroline responsible for Lee dumping the boy at her house.

"But, Saturday night was his idea," Caroline said, her protest rolling as far as a flat tire with her neighbor. She finished a second brownie. "My head knows Lee and I can never have a relationship, but my hormones... I know you'll disapprove, but maybe if I could get him in bed, you know, scratch the itch."

"You're darn right I disapprove. Scratching doesn't help mosquito bites and it won't help you with Lee. God has some good reasons for saving sex for marriage. Just imagine today's scene if you'd been intimate the night before."

Caroline winced. "Better stick with movies." Trent sloshed onto the deck. She snagged him. "Oh, no, you're not running through the Buffum's house like that. Thanks for everything, Sharon. You'll keep me from doing something stupid."

"It takes two. Lee wouldn't."

Not while he's got his mind on Rapunzel.

CAROLINE SQUIRMED on the folding chair, her thumbnail tracing the ridged edge of the Food Barn sack between her knees. She watched Lee position his students for dismissal. Almost in unison, the children returned his bow, then scattered. Patrick's mother asked the instructor about juvenile diabetes. With a few brief sentences, the man unraveled the relationship between blood sugar and activity. Despite attempts to pass himself off as a dumb jock, Lee not only understood a vast amount of medical information, but could explain it. Patrick's mother thanked him and left.

Carrying the sack, Caroline crossed the gym toward the big

man. He backed up and slid down the wall next to Trent, watching the boy don his socks and shoes with business-like efficiency.

"Lee."

His words came out from under the hand holding his mustache. "Thanks for letting me use the truck. Hope we didn't scratch it."

"If this happens often, maybe I should get a bed-liner."

"The shelter's looking for a panel van." He propped his elbows on his crossed legs. His *gi* folded open, revealing way too much chest. "Suppose Ford would be interested in making a donation?"

"I'll ask." The edge of the grocery bag curled and grew soggy under her hands. "Harvey called for you, from the thrift store on Vivion Road."

"Yeah. He said he'd keep an eye out for clothes in my size."

"If you're going down there anyway, could you take this for me?" She passed the bag to him. "A couple things I've grown out of."

He opened the bag with two fingers like he expected a snake to bite him. The gym lights reflected off a hunter green satin dress and black spike-heeled sandals. Lee wadded the bag closed. A line appeared at one side of his mustache, then his face crinkled into a big grin. "I'd be delighted."

Chapter Sixteen

Caroline watched from the folding chairs as Lee organized the children in a line, a feat of incredible patience. She had given up trying to read during class, and instead spent the hour enthralled by the marvelous, magical wonder of Lee's teaching. Alignment complete, he braced a red foam pad against his knee, waist high for the students. Kurt pivoted on his left foot, raised his right knee, and executed a perfect side kick to the target.

"Good. Again. Other foot."

Trent stood next in line, waiting without fidgeting. He ignored Andie's hand tugging the white belt of his *gi*. Patrick raised up on tiptoes to see over the other kids' heads. Eva lagged as usual, last in line. From her own grade school gym class, Caroline recognized the position: hoping the bell would ring before her turn. Lee never let any of his students get away with it.

"Nice work, Kurt. Okay, Trent, side kick."

An abrupt movement at the end of the line caught Caroline's attention. The girl's head snapped to the right. Her arms and legs stiffened.

"Eva!" Lee dropped the kicking pad and darted around the kids. He caught the girl as she tipped backwards and eased her to the floor. He glanced at the large wall clock, then back to the child. Her body jerked rhythmically. He rolled her onto her side, supporting her shoulder to keep her in position.

Caroline ran across the gym. "Shall I call 911?"

Lee shook his head, concentrating on the girl.

Andie leaned against Lee's back. "Chicken?"

"It's a seizure. It's not catching. Eva will be okay. It's like a lightening storm in her head. We're waiting for the storm to be over."

"Hurt?" Trent squatted by Eva. His round hand patted her forehead.

"No, it doesn't hurt. It's like when the lights go out at home."

A disheveled woman scuffed in from the hallway. Without looking up, Lee told her to put out her cigarette.

"Fits make me so freaking nervous." The butt dropped to the hardwood floor. A dirty pink slipper ground it out.

"Has she taken her medicine today?"

The woman fumbled with the catch on her lighter. "Yeah. And I don't keep it on the window sill no more, so don't give me no grief about that."

Lee glanced at the girl's hip. "Oh, man, she's wearing diapers," he groaned. "You've got her in diapers. This isn't the first time, then."

"Naw. Second one today." She paused for a hacking cough. "School says she's having a bunch there, too."

"When's the last time she saw a neurologist?"

"Well, I don't know. Took her down to Children's last winter when it was so damn cold thought I'd freeze to death."

"She's grown a lot. Maybe she's outgrown her dose."

"Makes sense. She's grown out of every other thing I buy her."

Eva took a deep, shuddery breath. The tension went out of her muscles. She seemed to be asleep.

Lee checked the clock. "Ninety-two seconds."

"Yeah, same thing all the time. First her head, then her body, then the shakes."

"Her seizures always look the same?"

"You seen one freaking fit, you seen 'em all."

"Caroline, do you have anything to write on?" Lee stroked

Eva's cheek with a big, gentle finger, calling her name. Kurt took up the job, rubbing the girl's hand. "Mrs. Powell, I want you to make an appointment with a neurologist and tell him about Eva's seizures. I've been reading about cryosurgery, where doctors freeze part of the brain to stop them. If it worked for Eva, she wouldn't have to take medicine any more. No more side effects like the problems she's been having with her teeth. I'll write it down."

"I could put an ice pack on her head."

Lee pressed his fist to his mouth for a few seconds. "No, I'm sorry, Mrs. Powell, it's a little more complicated than that." He wrote out the information for the woman, then bent over the girl. "Eva? Wake up. Time to go home."

She stretched and blinked.

"You had a seizure. Mom's going to call the doctor tomorrow. Will you help her remember?"

The girl nodded. "Mom call doctor." She wobbled out behind her mother.

Lee gathered the other students in a bear hug. "She's okay." He touched each on the chin, looking in their eyes and repeating the reassurance. "Class dismissed."

Andie's mother stomped over from the parents' corner. "That woman! I've half a mind to hotline her."

Lee rubbed his forehead with his palm, looking tired for the first time since Caroline met him. "You know it won't do any good. Social Services won't remove kids from the home unless their life's in danger."

"She'd be better off in foster care, away from that chain-smoking couch potato."

"You're preaching to the choir, Mrs. Holford."

Andie's mother turned to Caroline. "You know what really steams me? Lee waives Eva's tuition because that woman cries poor, but she always has plenty of money for cigarettes."

"It gets Eva off the sofa and breathing clean air once a week." His hand rubbed across his mustache, making his voice sound hollow. "It's not much..."

Caroline came to his defense. "He can monitor this medical problem."

Mrs. Holford blinked back angry tears. "She'll never remember to call the doctor."

"Eva's seizures are short. She's still on medication." He pushed himself upright to look Andie's mom in the eye. "I'll call her every day until she gets that appointment made. I'll drive her down to Children's if I have to. Eva is not going to stroke out."

Mrs. Holford lifted Andie to her hip, holding her close. "Thank you." She left with Kurt, Patrick, and their mothers.

Lee retrieved the pad and paper. He held them out to Caroline. "Thanks."

Maybe her imagination had gone on overdrive, but Lee seemed to make an extra effort not to touch her or even look at her. "Having a rough week?"

"It's nothing." He shrugged. "You?"

"Normal schedule."

"What time's my family getting to your place Saturday?"

"Five. We'll eat right away, since the play starts at 7:30."

He shuffled off to the locker room. "Okay. I'll come over after class, help you with the food. My nephews go for the grub like seagulls at a dock."

Caroline didn't have to touch him to know his engine sputtered and misfired. She could see it in his halting walk, in the way his gym bag hung from his hand. Was it Eva's seizure? Why is he so tired? His sister would know how to get him back in sync.

The roar of the shower sounded from the locker room. Trent tugged on her belt. "Ma, Lee..." *wants ice cream.*

She steered him out to the pickup. "You mean Trent wants ice cream." But when she reached the end of the road, she turned into the shopping center and parked at Baskin-Robbins. She ordered their largest banana split and two chocolate shakes. Hoping the police hadn't set up their speed trap, they raced back to the gym. Her headlights hit the side door just as it opened.

"Caroline? What's wrong?"

"Your ice cream's melting. Hop in."

Lee dropped his duffel bag on the hood of the VW and climbed in the passenger side. Trent handed him the dripping bowl. "Hey, how'd you know it's my birthday?"

"It's your birthday?" She should have remembered the date from his driver's license.

Trent hummed "Happy Birthday" around the straw of his milkshake.

"Well, if you didn't remember," Lee fingered the pink plastic spoon, "what's the occasion?"

"You seemed a little... I don't know. Are you all right?"

The utensil circled the dessert. "This is huge." He scooped the cherry and popped it in his mouth. Whipped cream caught on the underside of his mustache. The tip of his tongue cleaned it with a single swipe.

Concentrating on breathing, Caroline rolled the window down all the way.

"You didn't get ice cream?"

"No, just milkshakes. Remind me to talk to the design team about some sort of ice cream holder for the new models."

"*Mais*, yeah. With plastic seat covers, a squirt bottle of soapy water, and a roll of paper towels."

She passed him a wad of napkins. His fingertip caught a drip of hot fudge off the bowl, then slid between his lips. Caroline forced her gaze back to the sticker on her windshield. *He needs a friend, and all you can think about is dipping him in chocolate.*

She cleared her throat. "If my first five months are any indication, it's not so bad being thirty-five."

He looked up from sawing the banana with the plastic spoon. "You're older than me? Older and wiser. Yeah, guess it wouldn't be so bad, if I had more to show for it than just a junkyard reject." He nodded at the Volkswagen.

"Lee, don't run yourself down. What about all the people you help?"

The spoon snapped. "One of them got hurt this weekend." He leaned forward, holding the bowl between his knees with both hands. "Guest at the shelter. Went to see her so-called husband, a real whiz with a baseball bat. Compound fractures of her radius and ulna."

Bones in the forearm. "So you feel guilty that she left the shelter and her husband hit her. Or that, because of you, she knew how to block the shot and doesn't have a fractured skull."

Trent reached halfway around the man in a hug. Over the boy's head, Lee studied her, not saying anything. The rhythm in his breathing told her, he may not be completely tuned up, but at least he was firing on all cylinders.

"Let me hold your ice cream while you get another spoon."

He grabbed a metal spoon from his car. Taking the bowl back, he dug in. "This whole mess wouldn't happened if our director had been there. She was at St. Luke's. OD'd on chemo. She's the energy behind the shelter, the glue holding us together. This cancer, it's like turning off her lights."

"You're staying with her, taking care of her?" *Rubbing her back?*

"Naw, they have money. Her husband hires nurses, private duty, whenever she needs help." The tongue came out to meet the loaded spoon. His lips pulled at the ice cream. The mustache rippled out, in. Caroline pressed her hands, cold from the milkshake cup, to her cheeks.

A loud, long slurp announced the end of Trent's shake.

"Me, I'm talking when I should be eating. Help me finish this." Lee sent a chunk of banana into the boy's eager mouth, then scooped another for himself. "*Regardez donc.* All this chocolate on the bottom."

"Ma."

Caroline touched the icy cup to her face.

"Yeah, you right. For mom." He leaned over the boy. "Before it drips."

Please... The cold metal touched her bottom lip. She opened for him, letting the chocolate fill her, closing around the bowl.

His mouth dropped open, making a sound somewhere between ah and I. His hand froze a long moment, then slowly withdrew the spoon. "It's getting late," he whispered.

She licked her lips. "Do you need a place to stay?"

He hurried out of the truck. "No. House-sitting. Dog sitting. Rottweilers. They watch the house. I watch them." He dropped into the Volkswagen, then popped out again to grab his duffel bag off the hood. "Thanks for the ice cream." He roared off into the night.

Trent knelt on the seat, moving his hands inches from her face. "Back in your seat belt."

"Ma! Lee!" A small finger pointed at the retreating taillights. *No want him go. Want sleep my house. Want eat play my house.*

Caroline sighed, feeling the lateness of the night. "Me, too."

LEE FROWNED through the glass doors of the Antioch Rec Center. Enough water out there for a hurricane. Should have gone home with one of the kids. Except this class was all first year students, and he didn't know them or their parents well enough to ask for a place to stay the night. His mind ran through a list of friends in this part of Kansas City. Rick was just down the road. May as well head on over there.

The wipers skipped across the windshield. Lee guessed they were making a racket, but the rain pounding on the roof drowned out every other sound. The right front tire dropped into a pothole, sending water sloshing against the chassis of the Volkswagen. He reached behind the passenger seat, saving a wad of clothes from the fountain gushing through the floorboard's rust hole. The neon glow of Church's Fried Chicken lit up the dark stretch of road. "Hush," he told his growling stomach and turned onto a side street.

Hunched down in the seat, Lee peered through the night at the apartment buildings. "People who put up the signs should have talked to the people doing the streetlights. H, J, K. There it is." He swung into the closest parking spot. Headlights reflected off the red painted curb: Reserved 5222. He jammed the gear shift into reverse and backed out. The next empty slot, labeled guest, he spotted over by Building M. He parked, then hesitated a moment, debating whether to run for it or just slog along. If he wore his shoes, would they be dry by morning? If he stepped on glass...

Several gallons of cold water dumped down the waistband of his jeans as he grabbed his sleeping bag from the back seat. Sneakers on, he dashed across the lot. Not exactly like a hurricane, he thought. This rain goes down, hurricane goes across. Katrina sounded like a hundred fire hoses spraying the school they'd been evacuated to. Not enough tears for all the funerals, including his folks'. The house smelled of green army canvas and kerosene until just before Christmas when the roof got replaced and the power got hooked up again. Grandmere's garden had turned brown from the saltwater, forcing them to eat store-bought food all winter. Food. He hugged his sleeping bag tighter. Don't even think about food.

The reek of cat urine and fried onions in Building K's stairwell made him forget his hunger. His sneakers squished each step to the third floor. Lee knocked, then tried to shake some of the water out of his hair. He had almost decided no one was home when the door opened a crack. Three candles flickered on an end table, then a face blocked the view of the dark room.

"Lee," Rick whispered over Michael Bublé's latest love song. "Oh, man, I'm sorry. I know I said any time, but... I've got company."

Lee ran back down the stairs, his ringing footsteps on the metal treads almost covering Rick's "some other time". Back in the car, he headed east on Vivion Road. The windows fogged, even with the fan on high. Halfway through Claycomo, the left wiper came loose. The metal tab scraped the windshield, gouging a long arc across the glass. Lee pulled into the drive-up lane of a closed bank. He unearthed his roll of duct tape and a dirty T-shirt from the back seat before a maroon Crown Victoria pulled up in front of him. Taking advantage of the police car's spotlight, he dried the blade and taped it back to the wiper arm.

"This is private property. I'll have to ask you to move on," the officer shouted over the rain hammering on the metal overhang. Hands on hips he sauntered over to watch Lee work. His name tag read Symanski. "Gas station across the street probably sell you a new wiper."

Lee shrugged at his jerry-rigged repair. "It'll do."

"Going far tonight?"

"Depends. What are you hearing about the roads?"

"We got flooding up in Platte County from the river to Smithville Lake."

The road to Eldon's camp would be washed out.

The officer glanced toward the interstate. "Some talk of closing the bridges over the Missouri until the river crests."

Lee tossed the T-shirt and tape under the driver's seat. Getting kind of late to show up at his sister's, anyway. "Makes drought look good."

The officer cracked a smile. "Ought to tell those people who've been praying for rain, they can stop now." He climbed back into his cruiser.

Lee headed east again, leaning right to see through the area cleared by the remaining good wiper. Caroline told him in February to replace these things. Six months. Wasn't there a Neville Brothers song, something about how it seemed like he'd known her all his life?

The sign ahead said Liberty. If he'd said yes to her offer, he'd be home now. Not a chance. She'd have figured out real quick what he had on his mind. Then, bam, out on the street again. Probably pull Trent out of karate. Probably call the cops, have him arrested for being a lech and a leech. Lee, lech and leech. Has a certain ring to it.

The VW squished to a stop in front of the Buffums'. Lee shut off the headlights and wipers, thankful the duct tape held this far. All dark across the street. Caroline goes to bed early. She sleeps curled on her side, hands under her chin. Plenty of room in that bed for someone to curl up around her.

The Buffums' garage door screeched open and Pete waved him inside. Lee jumped over the flooded gutter, then raised his face to the deluge. *Gutter's full enough without my mind in it. Got the message.*

"Lee?"

"I was wondering..." He held up his soggy sleeping bag.

"Raining cats, dogs, and karate instructors." Sharon's curly head peaked down the stairwell. "Come on in. Throw that thing over the railing so it'll dry out."

Pete disappeared behind the hood of the Chevy.

"Mom?" A nightgown-clad five year old padded down the hall.

Before her mother could send her back to bed, Rebecca spotted Lee and launched herself into his arms. "You all wet."

"And I'm using you as a towel." He wiped his forehead on her sleeve. "Isn't it past your bedtime?"

"Way past," Sharon confirmed.

Lee carried the giggling girl down the hall. "You brushed your teeth? Said your prayers?"

"I could say them again."

"Good night, Rebecca." He tucked her under the hearts and flowers bedspread.

He followed the rattle of pans to the kitchen where Sharon filled a plate with pot roast. "Sit," she commanded, nodding at the table.

"Don't you know, you're not supposed to feed stray dogs? They hang around and you're never rid of them."

The woman pulled a mug of spiced tea from the microwave. "Don't you know, I find homes for all the strays around here. Just this week, I found an elderly man over by the courthouse to take that Siamese. Swing by there in the morning. You'll see the two of them sitting on the porch, just rocking the day away. And that litter of black and white kittens? Every single one of them has a new home, even the mama cat."

Lee palmed his fork and dug into the savory beef. "But old dogs with bad habits, they're hard to find homes for, yeah."

Sharon pulled the fork from his fist, rotated his forearm, and replaced the utensil in his fingers. "Don't worry, old dog. For the right home, I'm sure you can learn a few new tricks."

Lee stopped Caroline in the narthex. "Where are you going?"

"Home."

"No, you're not. We're staying for the potluck." He needed the watchful eyes of the congregation to beef-up his ebbing self-control.

She shook her head. "I didn't bring anything."

"Don't matter. Sharon cooked enough for the entire Chiefs football squad."

"But, Trent..." She motioned at the boy dancing at the end of Lee's hand.

"He's got an appetite on him. Come on, it'll be fun."

Caroline stared blankly at the cars shimmering in the August sun. "I didn't plan..."

"Plan?" Lee slapped his forehead. "I forgot, you're an engineer. How much time do you need to plan? Gotta get through the line before Mrs. Dana's double chocolate bundt cake is gone."

Caroline shot past him with a swirl of pleated skirt around her well toned calves. He caught up with her at the end of the line. "Thanks for staying."

"You have my truck keys," she said over her shoulder. She held herself stiffly—she must be annoyed.

"Do you ever do anything without planning, spontaneous?"

"Do you ever plan anything?"

"Naw, it's easier to take life as it comes." He herded Trent out of the way of a group of people carrying loaded plates. "Though I've got this gig mapped out. I'll do the food. Trent, you carry the silverware and napkins, and find three empty seats together."

"And my assignment, *sensai?*"

"Dessert."

Her shoulders dropped and she flashed her green eyes in his direction. Lee dragged his attention to the heavily laden table, spotting Dr. Shanks's turkey and sage casserole. He looked up again, catching her gaze. Sage green eyes.

Lee filled two plates, then followed the boy to the long table. He introduced Caroline and Trent to the man across from him, Jay Hannaberg. He's single. But he's a couple inches shorter than Caroline. So? Not talking ballroom dancing here.

He introduced them and asked, "Jay, when are we getting together for some karate?" Lee tucked a napkin into Trent's collar and wedged him tight against the table. "Good off-season training for hockey. Keep those reflexes sharp. Loosen you up so you can get through a season injury-free."

The musclebound man cleared his throat and shifted in his seat. "Well..."

"I promise to go easy on you." Lee moved Trent's milk cup out of elbow range.

"It's just..."

"Don't tell me a hockey player thinks karate is too violent."

Jay leaned on the table, and lowered his voice. "No, it's the connection with Eastern religions, Buddhism, Confucianism."

"*Mais,* yeah. Some instructors get into that." Lee bit into a chicken leg, taking the chew and swallow time to line up his arguments. "Karate's like any other tool. Use it in the practice of Zen, or as a way to keep in shape. Fire can cook food or burn your house down. Or a factory..." He realized the rudeness of shutting Caroline out, and the impossibility of keeping Jay's attention away from a pretty lady. "How long would it take to switch your plant to making weapons?"

She looked up from the roll she was buttering. "Conventional or nuclear?"

"Engineer," he murmured in a teasing tone before turning back to Jay. "I use karate for physical conditioning and self-defense."

The hockey player pressed the tines of his fork into the Styrofoam plate, making a pattern. "What about 'turning the other cheek'?"

"What about 'love your neighbor'? Jay, if you came across somone beating up your grandma—"

"I'd stop him."

"*Mais,* yeah. She's probably praying for her hockey player to stick him where it counts. I just don't think God wants his people, especially the kids, to be sitting ducks for muggers and rapists. Do you have something to write with?" Lee flattened his napkin on the table. Jay reached inside his suit coat and pulled out a hand-tooled leather folder. Flipping the memo pad to a blank page, he passed it to Lee. His pen was one of those fancy silver jobs people give high school graduates with college plans. "Check out what the Bible has to say about it. I'll give you a few verses on self-control, physical training..."

Caroline broke in with the story of their Fourth of July confrontation, making him sound like a hero. His face grew hot.

Trent started humming. Lee signed *no eat and sing same time.*

Jay paused over his apple pie. "Do some martial arts incorporate meditation?"

Lee nodded. "You see that sometimes with t'ai chi and aikido. Again, be careful who teaches you, watch what you're meditating on. Some verses on that..." He paused in his writing to bring Trent's fruit salad closer to his mouth. "I do use some of the breathing techniques, especially with these little guys, helps them open up their lungs."

Caroline added another comment about posture and balance.

"Okay!" Jay tossed his napkin on the table. "When can I start?" He scheduled a lesson, entering the time in his fancy phone, then got up to leave. "Nice to meet your family."

Oh man, Jay, you can't believe how that hurt. Lee gulped down his iced tea, then braced himself. Here come the questions. Yeah, Jay's single. And yeah, he has a good job, runs the accounting department for one of those trucking companies out on the interstate. Yeah, he does his own fancy leather work.

"You've studied this issue." Caroline tilted her head toward him.

"You've read your truck's owner's manual. The Bible is our owner's manual for life."

"I should read it, then." Caroline nodded. "I'm impressed with how many verses you've memorized."

"Not bad for a shiftless bum, eh?"

A little smile curved her lips. "You're not shiftless; you drive stick."

This time he couldn't stop himself. He reached over Trent and gave her shoulder a squeeze. "Engineers making jokes. Must be the end of the world."

Swimming. Caroline pushed through the water. *Twenty-third lap. Keep going. Stroke. Breath. Kick. Must be the Olympics, from the sounds of the crowd. Come on. Another lap. Doorbell.*

Doorbell?

"Uh-oh, we woke Mom up." Lee descended the stairs jiggling

Trent over his shoulder. He had on a white henley shirt and faded jeans shorts. It must be Saturday.

Caroline pushed up from the sofa. "I shouldn't be sleeping with him running around loose."

The television caught his attention. "Well, if NASCAR can't keep you awake, you must be pretty tired."

Trent pulled him down. "Lee, ray. Vroom, vroom."

"Cool set up." The big man sat cross-legged next to the blocks and Hot Wheels cars.

"It's supposed to be Watkins Glen." She rubbed her face, hoping the upholstery texture hadn't embedded onto her cheek. "Guess I should buy him a real race track."

Trent took a convertible around the course, sideswiping half a dozen race cars and a school bus.

"Naw, this is better. Gets him using his fingers. All those motor noises are great exercise for his mouth. Looks like the Mustang's got the lead."

"I used to have one just like it, baby blue."

"What happened? You have to sell it to pay for college?"

"No, I totaled it in one of those spring storms that's more ice than snow."

Lee sat up straight and blinked, wide-eyed, at her. "Were you hurt?"

You pass. "Just my pride. I could have kicked myself for not taking the T in weather like that."

Lee chose a monster truck and joined Trent's race. After a lap, the vehicle left the track and chugged up the boy's leg. Tickling and giggling led to demolition of half the race course. Lee glanced at Caroline, catching her in a yawn. "Not feeling well?"

"I'm fine."

Lee sent Trent upstairs for her Diet Coke. "Bryan call?"

"No, but the school tells me he's written for Trent's records." She watched the man turn pale. "Lee, what are you thinking?"

He flicked the dragster's tires. "It's probably nothing. He's just jerking your chain."

She snatched the tiny car from him. "Tell me. Please."

His fingers retreated to the mustache. "You know anything he gets his hands on he'll use against you. When I'm at the shelter tomorrow, I'll see about getting you some legal advice."

"Thanks, but I already have a call in to Wilson-deGrazia, my lawyer in Massachusetts." She pressed her fingers to the bridge of her nose. "It's bad, isn't it? He trying to..."

Lee jumped up to take the sloshing glass from the boy. "Hey, this guy I've been dog-sitting for, he gave me passes to that indoor playground off I-29. Wanna go?"

"Could Trent do that?"

"*Mais*, yeah, it'd be great fun for him. For you, too, blow off some steam. Put on some socks."

"We haven't had dinner."

"Neither have I." Lee bolted up the stairs. The refrigerator door squeaked open. "What you got defrosted? Hamburger. All right, I'm cooking, but I don't hear your piano playing."

Caroline rummaged through the music in the bench, deciding show tunes would wake her up. She started with *The Music Man*'s "Seventy-Six Trombones". Trent marched through the living room, pumping his arms. The *Godspell* overture elicited a rich baritone from the kitchen. Halfway through *Fiddler on the Roof*'s "Tradition", Trent called her for dinner.

Lee served the taco casserole. "Dinner's ready before my song."

"Your song? 'Matchmaker'?"

The corners of his mustache turned down. "Oh, no. Never again. You cured me of that. Mine is 'If I were a Rich Man'."

Caroline sipped her milk, washing down the world's spiciest casserole. "So what would you do if you were came into money?"

"Build stairs. Isn't that what the song recommends?" His fork stabbed a clump of ground beef. "The choir director will be glad to hear I found a piano player for when they put on *Godspell*."

"I can't do that. What about Trent?"

"Rehearsals are Sunday afternoons. I'll take him to my Gladstone class."

The boy bounced in his chair. "Yah!"

"I'll call your sister," she threatened.

"Hey, it's gonna be a good time." He grinned. "A good time, just like tonight, soon as you finish your dinner."

THE GIANT PLAY structure swarmed with kids.

"Like one of those gerbil cages." Lee held out the plastic bin. "Shoes, please."

Trent had his sneakers off in a millisecond. *Play go play,* he signed, bouncing up and down.

"Is it strong enough for adults?"

"Sure. It was tested by a couple hundred pounds of karate instructor and his class last year."

"Maybe I should just watch."

"No!" The boy tugged her hand.

"Moms need to have fun once in a while."

Caroline dropped her shoes into the bin, then joined the queue. A year ago at a neighborhood playground, Trent barreled to the front of the line, pushing and squeezing to be first. The rest of the children had started to object, but then, noticing his "differences," let him go. Today he waited behind the last boy, leaning sideways to check out the action. Chalk up another one for karate class.

Trent climbed onto the platform. Lee followed, lifting him to the trapeze. With a joyous whoop, the boy swung out and dropped into the pool of plastic balls.

"Swim to the other side and wait for us." Lee turned to Caroline. "Okay, Mom, you've seen how the expert does it." His warm hand circled her elbow.

Trent reached the far side and climbed out. "Go, Ma, go!"

"This is silly." Caroline squinted into the glare of the ceiling fixtures, trying to see the trapeze's attachment hardware.

"Okay, stop with the structural analysis. You're holding up the line." Lee slapped the bar into her hands. Four kids fidgeted on the steps behind him.

"Why don't you go first?"

Lee's bushy eyebrows lowered. "Go!" he yelled. Something hit the back of her knees and she swung out. Her hands let go and she flopped into the balls.

"Yea, Ma!" Trent did a victory dance.

"Lee!" Caroline grabbed the nearest ball and beaned him good.

Go, the red-faced man signed, laughing too hard to talk. Just as she reached the other end, he executed a graceful back flip, sending balls bouncing off the net partitions.

Caroline pointed to the next part of the maze. "From now on, you stay ahead of me."

"Okay." Lee grinned. "Right behind you, Trent."

The boy led them across water mattresses, up steep vinyl hills, through rooms with bouncy floors, and into a larger ball pool. Trent climbed the pyramid in the middle. Caroline retreated to a corner to catch her breath. Under the high-pitched squeals of the children, came the bass notes of the theme from *Jaws*. A hand grabbed her ankle and jerked her deep into the pool.

"Lee! You..." She came up throwing, hitting him several times before Trent tackled him from behind. The big man disappeared, surfacing behind Caroline.

"Stick 'em up. You're under arrest for trying to sneak balls from the playground." He patted her back. Several plastic spheres had worked under her loose T-shirt.

"It's a set-up, I tell you! I'm innocent!" Turning, she stuffed two green ones down Lee's shirt.

"Hey, quit making so much noise in there!" A dark-haired man leaned in the doorway. "You having fun or something?"

"Hey, Toshi. Thanks for the passes!" Lee pumped his hand. "This is my student Trent and his mother Caroline. Toshiro Kashawahara, head honcho of the playground. Come on in, the balls are fine."

"Can't. Vacation dumped a paper blizzard on my desk." He turned to Caroline. "Nice to meet you. Say, I think that guy's trying to take souvenirs home. Will you frisk him for me?"

"I'd be delighted." Caroline pushed two more balls under Lee's collar.

The big man turned engine-light red. "I'm getting out of here!"

Yanking his shirt out of his waistband, he waded to the far exit. Trent followed in hot pursuit.

Guess moms can have fun!

Caroline caught up with them in a tunnel. Trent's skinny knee had caught in the webbing. Lee untangled the boy and he scuttled off.

"Let's go try the roller slide!" Lee called, crawling along behind him.

Caroline followed the threadbare heels of the man's white athletic socks. He usually goes barefoot, takes off his shoes at the door. His soles are calloused. His toes are short and stubby, unexpected in a man so large all over. Beyond the cuff of the socks, calf muscles bulged, scrolled with light brown hair. Then thigh muscles, and the denim draped curve of his...

Lee sat on the object of her admiration. Over his shoulder he said, "I'll go down first to catch him at the bottom. Remind him to hold his hands up." He turned to see if she heard. "Caroline, are you okay? You're all red in the face."

"It is a little warm in here." Afraid to look at him, she wiped the back of her wrist across her forehead. "Maybe I'll get a drink. Would you like something?"

"Naw, Toshi charges too much for his pop. Water fountain's fine for me."

Which means he doesn't have any money.

Lee launched himself down the roller slide, rattling and whooping to the end.

"Hands up!"

Shrugging off her prompting, Trent shot himself into Lee's waiting arms.

"Ma!" The boy motioned for her.

"Come on, Mom. Hands up!" Lee added his encouragement.

Caroline pushed herself onto the rollers. So, this is what parts boxes feel like on the conveyor belt. She jiggled and bumped all the way to the end.

A large hand reached for her. "You're still flushed; go get your drink. I'll stay with Trent."

Caroline stumbled off to the refreshment stand and bought two pops. On the way back to the play area, a Ford truck commercial on the silent overhead TV screen caught her eye. She hoped the ad promoted the improvements in multiport electronic fuel injection, but it seemed to be touting the truck's value as a bikini magnet.

A strident New Jersey voice cut through the hubbub. "I'm telling you. When my ex took the kids and went back to Paramus, that was it. You know what I mean." The voice belonged to a fuzzy haired man seated on a bench next to Lee.

"Talk about," the big man murmured, the Cajun phrase rolling unnoticed past the preoccupied easterner.

"I mean, look at your kid. Sure he looks like his mudda, but he acts like his fadda. He's you all over again. He's got your walk, how he stands, moves his hands. He's your kid, all right."

"Think so?" Lee draped his arm on the back of the bench, watching the boy build a tower with large foam blocks.

"Absolutely." New Jersey chopped his hands in the air. "You got it made with that kid. I'm telling you. Now my kids. They look like their mudda, talk like their mudda, act like their mudda. Two weeks in the summer and every other vacation? It's nothing. Nothing, I tell you."

"*Mais*, yeah."

"Hey, you got a great kid there. Handicap or no handicap. Lots of fun. Really looks up to his dad. Nice fadda-son thing you got going. Great kid."

"Thanks to his mom."

"His mom, wow. Classy lady. Hey, you know what I mean? Sure you do." A frustrated hand slapped at the air. "Two weeks in the summer and every other vacation? Guess I better get back at it. Try to get some fadda in these two weeks."

"Maybe your transfer will come through."

"Yeah, I'm due for some good news." A frizzy-haired tot pulled the guy back into the ball bath.

Caroline tiptoed over to the bench and perched on the edge of the seat. She handed Lee his drink.

"Thanks. You didn't have to." The straw disappeared under a

fringe of mustache. Caroline dried her hands on her hot neck, feeling her pulse pound under her fingers. Lee motioned toward Trent. "He's quite the architect."

Trent set a cube atop a rectangle, then stepped back to study his creation. One thumb circled his mouth.

"That guy was right," Caroline whispered. "Look, he's imitating you."

The big man took his turn at being red faced. "You... I didn't, I mean he..."

"Bryan tried to get rid of him, did everything he could to deny Trent's existence." Caroline blinked. "And you sit here pretending to be his father."

"Guess that's not the most honest thing I've ever done, but I wasn't lying when I gave you the credit."

"Lee." She stared at him, wanting to grab him in a big hug, and, right here in front of everybody, find out exactly what he hid under that mustache.

"Well, seems like it's not any of his business, but if you want me to let him know you're available." He stood.

Caroline grabbed his arm before he could walk away. "You have got to be kidding. That voice..."

Lee plopped back onto the bench, sitting far enough away that she had to let go of him. "You could wake up to 'Gud mawning, Mudda,'" he whined.

"Stop, you'll give me nightmares." She feigned a shudder. *Ask me how I'd feel about a Cajun drawling in my ear every morning.*

"Cha-ryot." Trent commanded his stack of blocks. He bowed.

"Ready stance," Lee said, using the undertone of a commentator following the action at a golf tournament. "Rising punch to the head, center punch to the chest, power side kick to the knees. Well done."

The boy bowed to his vanquished opponent, then raced over to his applauding mother. *Drink, please,* he signed.

"Here, take mine." The man held out his cup. "Mom's carbonated caffeine will keep you up all night."

Is he hinting about staying? She checked her watch. "It's almost his bedtime." They retrieved their shoes and headed out into the starry night.

He's not turned off by Trent! Caroline cheered to herself. So, what is the problem?

Lee opened the passenger door and motioned them inside. "Trent. Mom."

There's the problem. He sees me as "Mom".

Trent fell asleep before they left the parking lot. Caroline rested her arm on the boy's shoulder. On the Fourth of July, Lee had squeezed her hand. Tonight she wouldn't stop with hand-holding. She would raise his arm, rub his wrist across her cheek, plant a kiss on the back of his hand, then another, wet this time, on his square palm. She'd slide her tongue into the sensitive places between his fingers. He wouldn't be able to leave.

His hands stayed glued to the steering wheel the entire ride.

Quick, Plan B! Lee lifted Trent from the truck seat. Caroline opened the door for them. The phone rang. As she reached the kitchen, the answering machine clicked on.

"Jameson. Rada here. Bad news. SOL on the body decking. Again. Almost sliced Nuñez."

A shiny new truck body swung down like a guillotine blade. Caroline picked up the phone. "Mike."

"Get over here."

"Sounds like a programming error. Call an electrical engineer to change the memory card."

"That'd be Haliburton. He's the one that fu...uh, screwed it up. My dachshund knows more about 'puters."

"Then have Gretchen fix it." She hung up. Plan C, anyone?

Lee came down the stairs. The streetlight through the living room window silvered the hair curling onto his broad shoulders.

She grabbed a Diet Coke from the refrigerator. "I have to go in."

The mustache rolled in and out. "Want me to stay?"

Caroline took a deep breath. "Yes, I want you to stay." *Yes.*

He brushed past her and turned the light on over the sink. "Make you a sandwich?"

"It won't take that long. I hope." She headed to the plant.

Around midnight she came home to an empty house and a note: "Took Trent to Buffums' so you could sleep in. Lee."

Abort, retry, ignore. She dragged up to bed. Shut down system.

Lee circled Caroline's block. No cars he didn't recognize. The neighborhood seemed quieter than the usual Saturday afternoon, most of the residents out of town for the Labor Day weekend. Parking in the Buffums' driveway, he caught a glimpse of himself in the rearview mirror. Should've done a better job shaving. He fished under the passenger seat for his comb, finding an empty plastic water bottle and a nickel. Aw, what's the difference? Louis, Bernadette, and the nephews would be arriving any minute to grill before the Spirit Fest. He better help Caroline get ready. Crossing the street, he waved to the boy jumping in the living room window. He'd seen him at karate Tuesday, but it felt like a year ago.

"Lee! Lee!" Trent bounced off the threshold into his arms.

He threw the boy up in the air. "Hey, little buddy!" How could anyone count it a bad day with a kid like this? *Joie de vive* in one little body.

Good boy, Trent signed between giggles. *Play?*

"Let's see if Mom needs help." He threw the boy over his shoulder. The kitchen was too clean, too quiet. "Caroline?"

"Down here."

Crouching to keep from bumping Trent, Lee went down to the rec room. Caroline lay in the recliner.

"You okay?" Lee tried not to look at the legs stretching out from khaki shorts.

"Your sister called. They won't be able to come. Stomach flu again."

"That's why you haven't started cooking." Lee nodded in relief. "I was afraid I had the wrong day."

"You don't seem surprised. Do they get sick often?"

"No. Don't worry about it." With all the spicy food his family ate, not a chance they were sick. No, this was all part of his sister's scheme. Where Caroline plans, Bernadette schemes. He lowered

Trent to the floor, then gave his mom another glance out of the corner of his eye. "You look worn out."

"And embarrassed." Her upturned palm indicated the sliding glass door. A bunch of little bushes, cone-shaped evergreens in plastic pots, sat on the patio. One tree had been planted at the northwest corner of the yard. A shovel, its long handle cracked in two, lay across a lawn chair. Caroline pulled the lever on the recliner, uprighting herself. "The problem with owning a truck is you haul off more than you can plant. Compact car drivers buy sensible things like mums, not windbreaks."

"No problem." Lee pulled his heavy key ring from the pocket of his cutoffs. "I'll get Pete's shovel."

She shook her head. "The first tree took three hours. There's eight more. That's twenty-four hours. It's not just digging the hole. This tobacco-smelling stuff has to be mixed into the clay to break it up."

"Yeah. It's like cutting lard and flour for pie crust. I helped one of the guys from church landscape a subdivision entrance. Trent, you mix it. Build up those arm muscles." Relieved at finding something to do with his hands, Lee borrowed a spade from the Buffums' garage. He squinted at the popsicle sticks evenly spaced along the north and west lot lines, about ten feet apart. Naw, knowing Caroline, they're exactly ten feet apart. Once they grew, the trees would be a nice wind break. Must mean she's planning to stay. He'd been worried that Ford moved people around, or that she might get a better offer from another company. If she and Trent left... He stabbed the blade into the ground.

"I thought I'd have all these trees planted by the time you arrived. Lee, you don't have to do this. It's too hot out here. I'll take the trees back."

"Just warm enough to get the blood flowing in a Cajun." *This Cajun's blood heats just seeing you.* "Trent's mixing the clay?"

"I think he's doing the witch scene from *Macbeth*, you know, 'Boil, boil, toil and trouble'."

Lee glanced up to see if she was kidding. He caught a glimpse of smooth shoulders and the curve of a collarbone above her tank top, then jerked his attention back to the dirt. "Your mom didn't happen to leave her sunscreen here?"

"Yes, she did. I'll get it for you."

The backside of those shorts? No. Don't look. Don't even dream about it. This isn't making out with Joanie at the drive-in or meeting Tanya under the bleachers. This is a real lady. Hands off would be a lot easier if she grouched or pouted or complained. Instead Caroline had to be the hardest working woman he'd ever met. Smart, practical, organized. Keeps her spices in alphabetical order, but she hardly ever uses them.

By sunset Lee had planted eight leyland cypresses. Digging didn't bother him, but he felt sore from not watching Caroline bend over to pick up the garden hose, and not drooling when she knelt to fill the hole around the tree, and not staring when she leaned forward to tamp the dirt. Good thing he had Trent around. "I've got to walk Bear, the neighbor's dog. I'll take Trent, give you a moment to rest."

But when they returned, Caroline had set the table and fired up the grill.

"Hey, I was gonna help you with dinner."

"After all the work you put in on those trees?" She shook her head.

She handed him the platter of flank steaks rolled with bacon. "We could use a Bear around our house."

Bernadette called him Bear, but Lee figured Caroline was talking about the neighbor's dog. Holding the meat so Trent could remove the toothpicks, Lee nodded. "Golden retrievers are good-natured. Smart."

"I'd like to have a dog."

"*Mais*, yeah, you wouldn't have time for obedience school, walking, all that." But if she had a husband, someone with a flexible schedule, someone who help her— *Lord, help me control my wild hope.* Trent reached for a long ear of corn, nearly knocking over his milk. *Thank you, Jesus, for reminding me why I'm here.*

"I'm changing jobs."

Lee choked on a bite of steak. "You're moving?"

"From the paint shop to the assembly line, Plant Vehicle Team."

He flopped back in the chair. "You better tell me this job is easier, cleaner."

"Well, no more coming home paint splattered." She passed him the salad. "The hours are better. Clock in at seven."

"Oh, man. You got promoted." How much more money would she make? No, it wouldn't make any difference. He'd never catch up to her.

"Peppercorn ranch?" She moved the dressing to his side of the table. "The downside is it may require occasional travel."

"Want me to stay with Trent?"

The boy bounced in his chair. *Play eat sleep my house. Good, good, good.*

He smiled at the boy. "Anytime. Let me know Tuesday, when you come to class. They'll give you a few days notice?"

"Two to four weeks, usually."

"No problem." His steak knife sliced the beef. "Hey, congratulations on your promotion. You worked hard for it."

"We'd better get going." She stood to clear the table.

Lee shook his head. "You're too tired to go to the Spirit Fest."

"But we planned..."

"Next year."

Go music? Trent signed.

"Well how about..." *How about I get out of here before I do something stupid.* "How about we have our own jazz festival? You've got a good half mile of wire on your speakers. Let's set up out here, play a little music for Trent."

"They're not UL listed for outdoor use."

Lee glanced up. The sun hovered at the edge of the clear sky. "I'll bring them in if it rains."

"I wouldn't want to disturb the neighbors."

"The Godards went to the lake, the Srokas went to Branson, the Buffums to St. Louis."

"You know my neighbors better than I do."

"House-sitting, dog-sitting."

"What about..." She finger-spelled *Bryan.*

"All quiet when we walked Bear." He leaned back in the patio chair, surveying the adjoining yards. Was Caroline really worried about Bryan's P.I. taking more pictures? Naw, changes threw her off. Or maybe she didn't want him to stay, smart girl. *If I had any smarts at all, I'd go.* "Trent, help your mom clear the table, I'll take care of things out here."

Lee spread out the blanket they had used at the fireworks. He found a jazz station on the stereo and set up the speakers outside the sliding door. Using the empty tree buckets and Caroline's emergency candles, he rigged flambeaux around the patio. Anything short of a military night vision camera would shoot all black. Playing with fire, he thought, setting a match to the wicks. He turned off the outdoor lights and the overhead in the rec room. Trent joined him, pointing at each flame.

"Hot," Lee cautioned. "Don't touch." *Now take your own advice, bubba.*

They stretched out on the blanket, the boy mirroring the man's propped on one elbow position. A trumpet riff filled the night air. Caroline slipped outside with a scrape of the patio screen door. She hesitated by the candles.

"Hot!" Trent warned, helping her find them in the dark.

The grass had vanished in the night. Caroline floated toward them on the melody. "Your nephews seemed to enjoy my brownies."

"Not as much as I do." Lee took the tray she offered and passed one of the cut squares to Trent.

Caroline knelt on the other side of her son. "I'm sorry your family couldn't make it."

I'm not. "Thanks for dinner. You're a good cook."

She looked around the backyard. "It's the least I could do after sticking you with the tree planting job."

"Come here, Trent, I'll show you some pictures in the sky." Lee lay down, propping the boy's head on his shoulder, and pointed out Orion and the Big Dipper.

The music faded into an ad for the Missouri lottery. "What would you do if you won all those millions?" The stars outlined Caroline, sitting bolt upright.

"Can't win, 'cause I don't play." Lee flipped the lottery motto on its back.

"All things are possible. What if some long-lost uncle named you in his will?"

"If any of my kin knew how to write, and owned a piece of paper, the best I'd get would be a gator gun, or a pirogue with a bad leak. And that'd be gone before the body got cold."

"If they discovered oil..."

"Mineral rights were sold off in the '30's, shortly after Grandma dug up the yard and didn't find Jean Lafitte's pirate treasure."

Airplane, Trent pointed out the flashing lights crossing the sky.

"Airplane," Lee confirmed. Her questions hit a bruise deep inside him. "Okay, so what would you do with your millions?"

"Well, after I paid taxes and set most of it aside for Trent, I'd like to travel, maybe go some place warm in the winter."

"No fair. You can do all that now. You just have to save up. Me getting money? No chance."

The ads and station identification ended. "Going to Kansas City" beat from the speakers. Trent skipped to the patio.

Lee sat up. "Caroline, the odds are about the same as finding a cure for Down's. Impossible." He felt her tense and knew he owed them both an apology.

Trent danced across the patio. He moonwalked to one corner, then karate kicked to the other. Michael Jackson meets the Ninja Turtles. Boogie melted into tap, and tap into ballet's pirouettes and leaps. Keeping perfect time, the boy combined steps and styles into his own celebration. Candlelight outlined his graceful motions. He lifted his face to the stars in an expression of pure joy. The song ended. Feet together, hands at his side, he bowed. His mother burst into applause.

You beautiful, Lee signed because he couldn't talk over the lump in his throat. He opened his arms. Trent returned his hug, grabbing with arms and legs like a monkey. "You are beautiful," he whispered into the boy's ear. Then louder, so Caroline could hear, "And perfect just the way you are." He held the child through the next song, swaying with him in his lap. "All things are possible, eh?" he said to Caroline. "You've been reading the Bible?"

"Well you said it, I wouldn't drive a vehicle without reading the owner's manual."

He stared at her dark silhouette. She heard what he said after church last week, and didn't turn it into a sparring match. *All things are possible...*

Another song started in the same slow tempo as the crickets. Trent brushed fingertips over the palm of his left hand. Dance.

"Go ahead." He lifted the boy onto his feet.

"No. Lee, Ma," *dance.*

Lee rubbed his mustache, glad the dark hid his blush. He hadn't showered after all that digging. He hadn't danced since Auguste Broussard's third wedding. He had no right touching Caroline. And if he didn't stop thinking of excuses, this slow song would be over. He stood and opened his hand to the woman sitting cross-legged on the edge of the blanket. "Miss Caroline, may I have this dance?" She hesitated and Lee knew she had her own excuses. "It's not in your schedule," he teased. She reached to swat him and he pulled her standing. A shiver ran down the arm tucked under his. "Cold? Your sweatshirt's sitting on the dryer."

She stepped into his arms. He held her hand, trying to stiff-arm a space between them. But she shivered again and somehow he ended up wrapping both arms around her. They swayed in a tight circle, surrounded by an alto sax solo. Caroline rested her head on his chest. Her back muscles rippled warm and firm through her thin cotton top. He wondered if she could hear the music over his heart. They could keep dancing on and on, through the commercials, the fast songs. Hope this is one of those stations that plays music all night.

Let now be forever, Caroline...

She stopped, tilting her face toward his. "The song's over."

This is where the hero gets to kiss the girl, if he's slain a dragon, or gotten a job or something.

"Yea!" Trent applauded.

"He's eating the brownies." Caroline pulled out of his arms and dashed to the blanket.

Smooth move, Trent. Save your mom from the bum. "He only ate one. Bedtime, you. Go on."

The boy trotted into the house. His mom picked up the blanket. Lee grabbed a corner, helping her shake off the grass.

"Caroline…" *I'm going to lay you down on this…* He cleared his throat. "Do you have a nickname? Nothing wrong with your name, but you call your brother Chip, and I wondered what he calls you."

She finished folding the blanket and took the tray from him. "No, I don't have a nickname." She stopped at the screen door and looked back over her shoulder. "I have a friend who calls me *chère.*"

"Nothing to do with Sonny Bono's old singing partner. It's just something Cajuns say." It means expensive in French.

"I know. It means 'dear' in French." She smiled. "Thanks for making my little dream come true. I wish I could do the same for you."

Lee blew out the candles. How many times would she thank him for those silly trees?

CAROLINE POINTED her flashlight into the grimy cavern of the broken ventilation unit. What a mess, she groaned, referring to the weekend more than the equipment. Lee probably felt coerced into planting those trees. He won't visit any more. That remark about the dog guarantees it. He didn't volunteer to help with the obedience training. He didn't ask if her offer of a room was still open. He just agreed she didn't have time for a pet and buttered another ear of corn.

Analyze it. She braced her feet on the ladder and leaned into the machine. Instead of diagraming the flow of air, her mind formed another equation. Given these starting materials: a boy, a man, and a woman. First, the boy. Caroline plotted a mental graph. The line went up: improved behavior, helping around the house, better communication.

Second, the man. Caroline remembered the questions he'd

asked about Trent's health, the way he'd opened her kitchen cabinets. Invasive. On the positive side, he was patient, always teaching, ever gentle. The graph showed a steady line.

Third, the woman. She'd been suspicious, defensive, then relieved when the man took charge of Trent during her Florida trip. And now, her reaction to him? The line curved up, then oscillated off into a high frequency sine wave.

The product of the reaction? Memories flashed in her head: his handshake, their private karate lesson, dancing with him this weekend. Heat. Consistently. Every time man and woman touch. Why? The reaction occurs independent of sunlight; rule out photosynthesis. Maybe thermal conduction, heat flowing from high to low temperatures when bodies are in direct physical contact. That wouldn't explain the heat generated when the woman thought of the man. Combustion produces large quantities of heat, but—

"Hey, Jameson, how's it look?" the senior engineer's voice crackled over the radio.

Caroline startled, almost dropping her flashlight into the unit. "Fine. I see the problem." *And if you believe that, I'll sell you the Chevette that won the Indianapolis 500.*

Chapter Seventeen

The phone rang just as Caroline and Trent finished dinner.

"Mrs. Jameson? This is Gemma Aquino. I'm a nurse at Children's Mercy."

"Yes, I remember you."

"I just heard from a friend at Liberty Hospital. One of their newborns has Down syndrome. Of course they won't know for sure until the genetics report comes back, but she has epicanthic folds on her inner eyes, simian creases on her palms, small ears, other signs of Down's."

"Is the baby healthy?"

"Oh, yes, or they would have transferred her to our NICU. I'm calling to ask if you would visit the mother."

"Is she ready for that?"

"Oh, yes. She is asking many questions. Please take Trent with you. It would help her so much to see how wonderful he is."

"But he's not, I mean, there are probably other families who handle this much better."

"That is not what I hear from Lee." The nurse hesitated, her voice dropping several decibels. "Mrs. Jameson, when the doctor told parents the diagnosis, the father walked out."

"We're on our way."

Caroline gave Trent a swipe with a damp washcloth and a brief explanation. On their way through the rec room, he dove into his toy box.

"No, it's not time to play. It's time to go." Caroline tugged on his arm, but he squirmed away.

"Baby." He pulled out the device that had hung on his crib. It played music and lit up with swimming fish.

"You want to give your toy to the baby?"

He nodded.

"That's a great idea." Caroline gave him a hug, then hurried him into the truck. What could she bring? She thought back to those lonely hours in the hospital. After hearing the diagnosis, Bryan had bolted. Her in-laws never showed. Her parents were weathered in, waiting for a flight out of Detroit. All the other rooms on the maternity wing were full of happy visitors and flowers... Caroline pulled into the grocery.

Trent took her hand and walked with her to the floral department. Rows of breakables greeted them—glass vases, ceramics shaped like cradles and lambs. No parents were consulted on these designs.

"Ma? Doh." Trent patted his leg, then pointed to a dog made of white carnations perched in a willow basket.

Not breakable. "Perfect." She paid for the arrangement, then kissed his head. "You know how to pick presents."

Thank you, he signed.

And, she thought as they climbed back into the truck, he knows how to behave in a store. Now for the next challenge...

"This is a hospital. Do you remember when you were in the hospital? You had a cough. You slept a lot." She did talk too much—Lee was right. "Quiet voice. Hold my hand."

A trickle of sweat ran down Caroline's back. What if Trent terrorized the mother into putting her baby up for adoption? *Please, Lord, let him have a little more good behavior left this evening.*

"I'm sorry, but children aren't—" The receptionist did a double take at Trent, then let out a big breath. She gave her the room number and buzzed them into the maternity wing. "We're so glad you came to visit Melanie."

She hoped they wouldn't be even happier when she and Trent left.

The new mother sat in a rocker by the window, her face hidden by a tumble of caramel-colored waves.

"Melanie?" Caroline introduced herself and Trent.

The woman took one look at them and burst into tears. Not a good sign. Trent passed her a tissue box and patted her back.

"I have to give up my earrings." Melanie tugged on her hoops.

Caroline sat across from her. "I work at the Ford plant, so I don't wear jewelry. Just like any other mom, you'll put your earrings away when your little girl starts reaching. You can wear them again when she's old enough to understand not to pull."

Melanie wiped her eyes and tried not to stare at Trent. "Sorry I'm such a mess."

"Hormones." Caroline set the flower basket on the windowsill.

Trent held up the crib toy. "Baby?"

"You brought gifts, our first. Thank you." She gulped, trying to stop crying.

"So what did you name your little girl?"

"We were going to name her after his grandmother Virginia, but..." The sniffles increased to a sob. "Poor baby doesn't even have a name."

"I understand. Trent wouldn't have his father's name if we'd gotten the diagnosis before the birth certificate." Caroline touched her knee. "What would you think about calling her Ginny for now?"

"Ginny. I like that."

"Baby?" Trent looked around the room. "Baby?"

"Could we see her?"

"I'll have to ask the nurse." Melanie stood.

Trent slipped his hand into hers. Caroline held her breath, hoping her son wouldn't go into arm-yanking mode, but he seemed to realize the new mother needed a gentle touch. They shuffled down the hall to the nursery. In the back of the room a nurse measured a newborn as her coworker entered the numbers in the computer. One infant slept in a bassinet by the window.

"Oh she's all alone. Poor Ginny. All the other babies are rooming in, but mine..." The tears increased.

The nurse left the computer and wheeled Ginny to the door. "She's been asleep a couple hours. Probably ready to wake up and greet her adoring fans."

Trent raised up on tiptoes, peered into the bassinet, and blew a kiss. "Baby? Hello!"

Caroline captured his hands. "Be careful."

Two dark eyes opened, giving Trent a glance before focusing her on mother.

"She knows you. She recognizes your voice." Caroline said, digging deep to remember anything helpful, anything positive, anything that made her feel better in those early days. "Let's go back so you can sit."

Leaning on the bassinet, Melanie made it to her room and collapsed into the rocker. Caroline refilled the water glass and passed it to her. With all her crying and no family here to encourage her, she had probably become dehydrated.

Trent held up the toy and showed Ginny how to work it. The baby studied it. She waved her arms, opened her mouth, then let out a "mew."

"You are just as beautiful as your mother." Caroline unwrapped the blanket, setting off a flurry of kicking. "Such perfect skin."

The mewing increased in volume.

"When did she eat last?" Caroline picked the baby up. The new mother wore a nursing gown. "She's probably hungry."

"Are you allowed to—I mean, is it all right?" The tears resumed. "I don't know anything about taking care of a baby with..."

"They're not letting you hold her?"

"I nursed her right after birth, but then they took her away and said she had..." Melanie glanced at Trent.

Caroline positioned the bundle in her mother's arms. "Right now she needs the same things as every other baby–milk, cuddling, dry diapers, love."

The tiny head rooted in the mother's gown and clamped on. The new mother settled back in the rocker with a deep sigh.

"Ginny knows what to do." Caroline pulled Trent onto her lap, missing those quiet moments. She whispered in his ear, "I fed you like that when you were a baby."

"I bi bo," Trent signed *big boy*. "I eat." His hands listed a dozen foods.

Melanie blinked. "He signs. One of my friends gave me a baby sign language kit at my shower."

"You're way ahead of me. I just started a few months ago." When a deliciously devious karate instructor tricked her into learning.

"What else? What else do I need to know?"

"Relax and enjoy Gorgeous Ginny. Take care of yourself–nap when you can, eat healthy, drink lots of water."

The weeping resumed. "How did you manage, all by yourself without your husband?"

"I moved closer to my parents. Do you have family nearby?"

"My mom lives near St. Louis. She'll be here tomorrow."

"Good. And you've got us." Caroline wrote down her phone number.

"Trent's wonderful. You're wonderful."

Trent raised his arms overhead and pushed up, no doubt the sign for *wonderful*, then gave a giant yawn.

"Bedtime. Sorry, I clock in early." Caroline hugged the young mom. "Melanie, you're doing fine. Call any time. You and Ginny are going to be okay."

The sun slid behind the hills as they left the hospital. Trent walked beside her, speaking in a quiet voice, then climbed into the truck and buckled his seatbelt. No tantrums, no running, no screaming. Whew. Trent *was* wonderful.

Thanks to God and His gift of a big-hearted karate instructor.

CAROLINE DRAGGED the dirty laundry out of the linen closet. The hospital visit last night had put her a load behind. She'd have to squeeze two loads in tonight.

"Heh." Trent placed his right fist on his left palm and raised his arms. *Help*, he signed.

"What do you need help with?"

Concentration creased his forehead. *Help you.*

"Yes, I'll help you. What do you want?" She stood and reached for his hand, so he could lead her to his problem.

Go. Motioning her out of the way, Trent plopped down in front of the closet. Whites, darks, mediums. *I help you.*

Caroline blinked away a tear. "Thank you," she signed, the motion reminding her of blowing a kiss. The phone rang.

"Mrs. Jameson?"

Another call from school. Warning lights blinked in Caroline's brain. "Yes?"

"This is Mrs. Wenger, Trent's resource teacher. As you know, I retest everyone at the beginning of the school year, to confirm placement. Trent did exceptionally well on the reading portion of the assessment. His sight-word vocabulary is on the beginning second grade level. He needs a lot of work on decoding and phonics, but I can't justify keeping him in resource for reading. We'd like to try him in the regular second grade class group. I can't promise success, but I'd like to give it try."

"Sure," Caroline said, too surprised to put together a complete sentence for the teacher.

"Whatever you're doing at home, keep up the good work."

He's reading! Caroline set the phone down.

It rang again.

"Mrs. Jameson? This is Laurie Wisniewski, down the street. My son Joe is in second grade with your son Trent. We're starting a Cub Scout den here in the neighborhood, and Joe wanted Trent to join."

Caroline wrote down the meeting time and agreed to bring Trent over Saturday to show Laurie his sign language. *Lee, where are you when we have so much to celebrate?* She should buy him a cellphone.

Wait a minute. He had written out his schedule after Bryan

switched airports. Caroline found it taped to the inside of the spice cabinet. Sections showed eraser marks and corrections; he must have updated it when he was here for the jazz festival. Her heart went into rough idle at the thought of their dance. No, that wasn't why she raced across town to William Jewell College's Mabee Center when she should be doing laundry. She wanted to share Trent's good news, that's all. He might be too busy. His schedule probably changed again. She braced for disappointment. Taking her son in hand, Caroline entered the field house. A half-dozen boys dribbled basketballs around the gym, slow and lazy in the late summer heat. Caroline followed the track around and peered into an open door.

"Hello, Trent! Hello, Trent's mom." Dusty, the car salesman's brother, greeted them from the weight room. "I work out!"

"Lee?" Trent asked, cutting off his loquacious friend before he could get started.

"That way." Dusty pointed across the gym and continued bench pressing. "Racquetball court."

Caroline heard Lee's deep voice before she saw him.

"Right roundhouse. Block. Side-kick. Stop. Let's try that again in slow motion."

"Ssh," she told Trent. She steered him up the stairs to the shadowy balcony, then lifted him to peek over the wall.

Lee and a young man sparred in the middle of the brightly-lit court. The instructor shot his foot toward the student's ear. The boy raised his arm, blocking the kick. He stepped toward Lee, directing a punch to his chest. Lee kicked, but the student jumped and returned the attack. Moving with the grace and tight choreography of ballet, they continued several minutes.

"Reverse punch. Good move. Backfist strike. Tighter fist. Side snap kick. Higher, higher. Again. Knife hand strike."

"Oops! I almost stepped on you, here in the dark." A man with a neatly trimmed beard joined Caroline and Trent on the balcony. "That's my son, the redhead." He pointed down at the sparring pair. The straight angle of the boy's nose and the widely spaced eyes matched his father's.

"He's doing very well," she whispered.

226

"Now he is. A year ago I would have said Ryan was looking forward to a career as a plasma donor." The man's chin dropped toward his shoulder. "He got himself fired from his bagger job for stealing cigarettes. We took away his car, got some family counseling, had his teachers send home weekly reports. But what really made the difference was karate. Lee took him on, taught him discipline, respect for others, setting goals. He made the honor roll, started attending church. These days, he's actually fun to have around the house."

"You got it." Lee stepped away. "Real time. Ready?"

The student groaned and wiped his face on the sleeve of his uniform.

"Don't let an old man wear you out."

With a quick smile, the boy moved into ready stance. They shifted into overdrive. Arms and legs flashed. Kicks and punches blended into a whirl of motion. Caroline watched, mesmerized by power and precision. The student breathed loudly, grunting on each high kick. Lee continued his words of instruction and encouragement.

The pair finished sparring and bowed to each other. Lee directed cool-down stretches with a quiet voice.

Trent squirmed out of his mom's grasp and darted down the stairs. The bearded man followed. Caroline blinked, realizing she'd been crying. She dried her face and blew her nose.

"My Trent, my favorite little *karateka*." Lee tossed him up in the air. "How'd you get here?"

"Ma."

Ryan's father handed Lee an envelope. "Looks good."

"He's ready for the tournament, yeah. Have him drink a quart of water when he gets home. He's worked up a sweat."

Three teenagers, gym bags slung over their shoulders, filed into the room.

"Duncan, lead the warm-ups, please," Lee told a compactly built boy. "I'll be right back."

Still carrying Trent, Lee stepped into the corridor. "Caroline? What's wrong?"

"Nothing. We have some good news." She motioned toward the court. "I didn't realize you'd be so busy."

"Let's get some air." He led them to a side door overlooking the farmland northeast of Liberty, now cast in deep purple shadows. Caroline related the calls from school and Cub Scouts, and their visit to the hospital last night.

Trent gave a proud grin and raised his arm for a high five. The man's large hand swallowed the tiny palm.

"Great news! You deserve a hug!" The boy seemed to disappear in the folds of Lee's karate uniform. "I'm so proud of you."

Caroline put the brakes on her wish for a hug and leaned against the blue door. "All your work with the flash cards paid off."

I help Ma, Trent signed.

"Yes, he helped sort the laundry. Did you teach him that, too?"

"Back in April." Lee stared down his nose at the boy. "And you waited until today to help Mom? Grr." He tossed the boy over his shoulder, holding him upside down with one arm. The other hand floated to Caroline's cheek. A finger stroked her temple. "You'd think 10W-30 wouldn't run when you cry."

She swallowed. "Your teaching, the karate..."

"Yeah, if I can't fight off my opponents, I try to get them blubbering."

"Lee, I am sorry. Offering to get you an application for the plant was an insult. This," a turn of her wrist indicated the classroom, "is what you should be doing. Your profession, your art."

A warm palm pressed her cheek. He leaned toward her, holding her gaze. "I'm glad you stopped by."

"*Sensai!*" a voice echoed from inside. "We're done with warm-ups."

Long fingers brushed the hair behind her ears. "I've got to teach."

"Yes, you do." She smiled and he backed away.

Lee stepped over the threshold, then stopped. Trent still hung on his back. The man hauled up the giggling wiggler up for another hug, then passed him to her. He paused, mouth open as if he had something else to say, then smiled and jogged back into the building.

Another tear rolled down Caroline's face. She scrubbed it off and walked Trent to the car. If only Stop-Leak worked on people...

LEE CIRCLED HIS CLASS, paired up for sparing. Just give them something to do besides flunking eighth grade, setting fire to the middle school boys locker room, and tattooing themselves with pencil lead, and they're a great bunch of kids.

"Rising block. Center punch. You got it. Lower block. Pick up the speed, Duncan. Backfist to head. Front kick. Block it, Sergio. Left punch. Right punch. Good job, all of you." He strode to the front of the room and began the cool-down sequence. "This week practice your *kata*. Testing for orange belts next week. Work on those kicks."

"Mom took down my Styrofoam block. Said it got in the way of her vacuuming."

Lee stepped forward into a lunge, palms braced on one knee. "Mom's vacuuming your room?" He gave each boy the raised eyebrow. "All of you need work on upper body strength. This week's good deed: vacuum the entire house."

"My room's so bad, I can't even find the floor," Duncan snorted.

Lee switched legs. "The whole house. If you have to pick up first, not my problem."

"Aw, *Sensai*..."

"I know where you live." *And I'll probably drop by about dinner time.* Lee moved to the "attention position" and bowed. "See you next week. Happy housecleaning!"

The kids filed out, except Mike. Lee walked him up the stairs to the west door. The boy seemed fine, no longer a runaway risk, but he could see his folks' point of view - the kid had been trolling the Paseo. Police found him before trouble did.

Mais, yeah, kids just want an adventure. That's all Lee had in mind when his fifteen-year-old thumb got him out of town. Two blocks from the French Quarter, Aunt Jeanette caught up with him. A crawfish pinch on his ear dragged him into her pointy-finned Cadillac. Bosom rising like a storm surge, she recounted his sins, the worst of which was worrying Grand-mère. The possibility of catching a social disease, getting mugged or stabbed, were mentioned only as something that would shame the family. Not wanting to be the cause of anyone's heart attack, he stayed away from New Orleans for six years, well after Grand-mère's passing.

A blue minivan pulled up. Lee made the hand-off to Mike's mom, then headed back into the field house.

"There he is!" Dusty's hoarse voice hailed.

"Just the man I need to see. Buy you a cold one?" Dusty and Jerry's dad jabbed his thumb toward the pop machine.

"Thank you, sir. Juice'd be fine."

Mr. Drewer handed him the cold can of apple-cranberry, then nodded toward the lounge area. "Take a load off."

Lee collapsed into the upholstered chair, then levered himself into a more upright position. Dusty's dad had been in the Navy. The retired officer's straight posture, buttoned-down shirts, and buzz cut always made Lee feel like a slob. "Sir?"

"At ease, Marivaux. This isn't a court martial, merely an informal inquiry." He sat directly opposite Lee. "I'm just trying to figure out why you set Jerry up with..." His index finger tapped the arm of the chair.

"Trent's mom," Dusty chimed in.

Lee took a couple swallows of juice. He'd thought that mess was over and done with weeks ago. What brought it up now? Jerry call Caroline? She wouldn't go out with him a second time, he'd bet his ashtray of laundry quarters on that. "They're both interested in cars. Caroline works at the Ford..."

"Works at? Lee, she's an engineer. What were you thinking?" Mr. Drewer leaned forward, his lips a tight line. "Jerry can't keep waitresses interested long enough to take his order."

Dusty twisted his finger beside his nose, the sign for boring.

"Trent's one of my students. His mom said she doesn't go out because guys are put off by the boy's Down syndrome. So I thought of Jerry."

"Are you one of those guys put off by Down's?"

"No, sir. Trent's a great kid."

"Just like me!" Dusty raised his arms overhead in a victory salute.

"At ease, son." Mr. Drewer flicked the young man in the stomach without looking away from Lee. "Do I know this family? Have they been to any ARC functions?"

"No, sir." The Association for Retarded Citizens would be a great support for Caroline, but she didn't have time.

Dusty bounced in his chair. "Trent and his mom come see you tonight."

Lee nodded. "Trent's getting mainstreamed for reading. She wanted to tell me the good news."

Dusty arched an eyebrow. "She likes you."

"Naw, she's a nice lady."

Now both eyebrows came up. "She wants to kiss you."

Heat flared in Lee's face. "You taking up spying?"

Now all of Mr. Drewer's fingers tapped the chair. "Ever since Dusty started dating, he thinks he's an expert on women."

Ah, a change of subject. He wiped the sweat off the back of his neck and asked, "Anyone I know?"

"Angie." Dusty whipped out his wallet and passed him a Glamour Shots photo of a blond in a sequined cowboy hat.

"Hey, I've seen her before. She works at the Walmart in Gladstone."

"Yeah. I met her at Maple Valley. We go to prom."

Mr. Drewer leaned forward. "You have any questions about being the father of a kid with Down's?"

"No sir," Lee stammered.

"You disqualify yourself from this mission because…"

"Oh man, I can barely keep myself in red beans and rice."

"I understand she already has a house."

"Nice house," Dusty added.

"And a car."

"A truck, Dad, a nice truck."

Knuckles rapping the arm of the chair, Mr. Drewer launched into a pep talk. "It's a challenging job, Lee, one that will keep you up late nights. But no other job is as rewarding, as enjoyable, as worth-while. No other..."

While his dad expounded on service to God, country, and Trent Jameson, Dusty slipped the picture from Lee's fingers. "Soon as I save enough money for a big bed, I ask Angie marry me. Trent's mom have a big bed?"

Lee figured he'd turned as red as the juice.

With enough patriotic noise to merit raising the flag, Mr. Drewer wound his speech to a close. "Glad we had this talk, son. Clear the air. Call me if you have any questions. That's what I'm here for. Dusty?"

Too stunned to move, Lee watched the Mr. Drewer march out the door, Dusty lockstepping behind. The glass door closed, reflecting a large Cajun in a shabby *gi,* overdue for a haircut, tired from a full day teaching.

He was a man who'd never take advantage of a woman.

CAROLINE PADDED THROUGH THE HOUSE, turning off lights, checking the two-by-four in the sliding door track. In the living room she latched and locked the storm door, then the oak door, promising herself a good night's sleep. Moonlight outlined the idle piano. All right, just one piece. She slid onto the bench, wishing for a lamp. She only knew a few songs by heart. Her right hand found two notes, then another pair. The left hand felt out the chords. "Tonight" from *West Side Story.*

Where is Lee tonight?

Think of something else, she chided, but her hands kept playing. So much keeps people apart: race, family, geography. Her mind added the lyrics, and the words connected to Lee. Perhaps that dance under the stars was their only "Tonight."

The phone rang. Desire skidded and hit the ditch. She picked up the receiver. "Hello?"

"What a disappointment. I was hoping to wake you up."

So much for a good night's sleep. "What do you want, Bryan?"

Chapter Eighteen

L ee's students lined up and punched the red foam pad their
instructor held.

Caroline's eyes glazed over. For the past twenty minutes, she'd
been staring at the third page of the National Highway Traffic
Safety Administration crash testing report. She folded the article
back into her purse.

"Hello? Chicken! Hello!"

A second word. Caroline mustered a smile for Andie's foster
mother.

Lee dismissed the class with a bow. "Next week, you'll break a
board with your fist."

Caroline's heart torqued in her chest like a Wankel engine. She
had to tell him or he'd be checking the hospitals. She waited until
Trent had his sneakers on, then tossed over her shoulder, "We'll be
out of town next week." She took the boy's hand and hurried toward
the exit.

"Vacation, eh? Well you deserve it. I'll save a board for when
you get back, Trent. Have a good time." A swish of nylon. Lee
picked up his gym bag.

Her hand reached for the bar on the door. She'd almost made it.

"Wait a minute. You're pulling Trent out of school when he's doing so well? How'd you get another week off? Where're you going?"

"Boston." The door slammed behind her.

SPEND *enough years in karate and you take a swift kick in the gut. First, you feel the impact. Then panic because you can't breathe. Then pain as your insides catch fire.*

Bracing his gut with one arm, Lee staggered outside. "Caroline!" His voice sounded hoarse without any air behind it.

She helped Trent into the truck and shut the passenger door. One hand covering her throat, the other braced on the hood, she edged forward. "If you need a place to stay, you can house sit."

"You weren't going to tell me." He stepped toward her and she scooted around the front bumper. "You were going to leave town without saying anything."

"I knew you'd be mad."

"Mad?" Oh man, oh man. He gave the parking lot a once-over, then crouched down, sitting on the curb between their vehicles. Speaking just above a whisper, he said, "I'm mad, yeah. At Bryan. For making you afraid."

Large, dark eyes blinked at him.

"Don't you know..." he swallowed and had to start again. "Don't you know I... I'd never hurt you? Never." He touched the concrete beside him. "Come. Sit. Tell me what happened."

Five minutes must have passed before she pushed off from the fender, wobbled over, and sat beside him. Her hand inched away from her neck, trembling down to her lap. Before he could take hold of it, she laced her fingers and clamped them between her knees. He hesitated, his arm raised in the space between them. Oh why not. He let it fall across her shoulders and pull her shaking body close. "You're the smartest person I know, Caroline," he told her, his lips brushing the top of her head. "You must have good reason for going to Boston."

"Bryan asked me to bring Trent up for some campaign appearances."

"Asked? You mean blackmailed." Stay loose. Focus. "He's got more pictures of me? Something from Trent's school records?"

"No. Payroll records from July downtime." She blinked at the rust on the VW's hatch, then her shoes. A medley of vacation Bible school songs warbled from the truck's cab. "Wilson-deGrazia, my lawyer, says there's precedent for him to be awarded custody, based on my work hours and his wife staying home. Even though my parents were providing care."

If Bryan gets custody, Caroline will move back to Massachusetts. This gut punch hadn't caught him completely by surprise, but it still hurt. He tightened his grip on her shoulder. "And if you quit Ford's, go on welfare, they'll say he can provide a better environment. Man, that stinks."

"He could take Trent..." She inhaled with a series of jerking gasps. He tucked her in closer and felt a tear drop inside his collar. Good thing he was wearing one of his old *gi*: softer against her face, better at soaking it up.

"Easy, *chère*, all right. I'm not mad at you. No. You've got to keep custody. Just wish I could help you out of this." Like putting Bryan out of our misery. No, don't think of that. Steady now. He loosened his hold, moving his fingers in light, slow circles down her sleeve. "Don't suppose anyone has an eleven dollar airfare to Boston?"

She shook her head.

"If someone ever came after you while you're putting Trent in the truck, jump in behind him. Hit the locks and lean on the horn. You don't have time to run around and fumble with your keys in the other door."

She nodded.

Trent cranked open the window and tossed out a paper airplane.

"Hey you, no littering," Snatching the glider, Lee frowned the boy back into the cab. "Hope this isn't anything important."

She struggled to her feet and fished a tissue out of her slacks' pocket. "Employee benefits form. I'll pick up another at work tomorrow."

He followed her around to the driver's side. "When's your flight?"

"Sunday afternoon."

He stood in her way until she looked up at him. "I'll be there."

"Miss Pearl?" Lee stuck his head in the doorway of the tiny office.

"Lee! Just the excuse I need to take a break from the paperwork." Pushing back from the computer, the woman waved him into the wooden chair.

"Bernie sent some more plants for you." Lee held the cardboard box in one hand.

"Let me see," Pearl pulled open the flaps and rattled off several Latin names. "Wildflowers. Herbs. Sprouts. Your sister is an angel."

"An angel? Miss Pearl, if you knew her like I do...." Lee reached for her elbow. "What's this?"

"They're trying to take my blood, but I'm not letting them have it." She crossed her arms, covering the purplish black bruises, and lowered her voice to a whisper. "Lee, what do you know about the medical uses of marijuana?"

"Not much. I'll see what I can find out." Marijuana? It's that bad? He'd better keep his problems to himself. He studied the woman, trying to see if she'd lost any more weight. "Do you need a source, a supplier?"

She gave a tiny shake of her head. An sly smile lit her face.

"Miss Pearl!" He flipped open Bernie's plant box and inspected the cuttings.

"Jeopardize your work with the children and the police departments? Heavens, no."

He jumped to his feet, peering out the window into the garden.

"Dear boy," she giggled. "I'd never compromise the shelter with illegal activity. Lee, the less you know about this..."

"Take the brownies out of the oven and leave before dessert."

"Brownies? Oh, that sounds so much more fun than smoking. I wouldn't have to worry about running into some patron when I buy rolling papers." She checked the watch pinned to her sweater. "You're early."

"Wondering if you've heard anything about that grant."

"We were turned down." Her knuckles wrapped a file folder. "Try, try again."

Lee collapsed back in the chair with a loud creak. He couldn't tell Miss Pearl why he needed the funds—she'd try to give him the money. Maybe Bernie would loan him a couple hundred. When gators do the two-step.

"I'm sorry, dear. Volunteer banquets just don't pay the bills. I'll understand if you have to cut back on your time here."

"No, this is important. I'll keep teaching."

"All our other volunteers have spouses with good salaries."

"All your other volunteers are women."

"As the kids say, 'so?'"

Lee's face heated. "Aw, come on, Miss Pearl. What would you think of me marrying money?"

"Dear boy, if it weren't for Henry, I'd snatch you up in a minute. Now what would cause more comment, the difference in our ages or our incomes?"

"My hair's almost as white as yours. People probably think we're the same age."

Pearl's laughter turned to coughing. Lee made a hurried trip to the kitchen for a glass of orange juice. She got her breath back, then turned her violet eyes on him. "Lee, I don't want to lose my number one volunteer. If you've fallen in love with someone who has money, I'm breaking out the champagne."

TRENT DODGED and squirmed past the waiting passengers to reach the window overlooking the Kansas City airport's ramp. Lee followed, telling the boy to watch for his suitcase. Caroline checked her tickets again, her feelings tangled like wires in a junction box. What could she say? He knew all about trash pick-up, watering the new trees, the emergency money under the M&M's. She had changed the oil on the truck last weekend—it shouldn't need any maintenance.

Come with me, please. Bryan makes my skin crawl. He'll be worse than ever on his own turf, surrounded by his cronies and trophy wife. I need someone on my side, an ally, a friend. I need you. If you weren't so stubborn about money...

Nothing to worry about. Bryan would never try anything this close to the election. Besides, what would Marnie say if she brought Lee? And Bryan? He'd explode. But if she had to... She looked back up at Lee. If she didn't come back with Trent, would he ever forgive her?

The large man leaned on the window frame, keeping an eye on Trent. His thumb and index finger smoothed down his mustache. "What did Ford say about you taking another week off?"

"I'm out of vacation, so I had to buy my time off."

"Ouch. That's a lot, as much as you make."

"It's a good week to miss. We finished rebalances, adjusting assignments so no one's over- or under-worked. The superintendent says one of my line workers has to be laid off. I hate that. I went to school for machine problems, not people problems." Caroline locked her knees, trying not to pace. "And you? How's your schedule this week?"

"The usual. Anything you want done around the house?"

"After planting all those trees, I couldn't ask you for one more thing."

He gave her a sidelong glance, one brown eye under a raised eyebrow. "I guess we should have talked about this earlier, before I took Trent to church. I asked the brothers and sisters to pray for you two while you're in Boston."

"Thank you." She looked at Lee now, memorizing the angle of his jaw, the spot of peeled skin on his nose where he'd gotten sunburned, the wide brow over his dark brown eyes. Chocolate brown. Chocolate...

Her son barreled into Lee's legs.

Lee gathered Trent in a hug. "Quiet voice. No kicking. No

punching. Listen to the music Sharon gave you." The boy wrapped his arms and legs around him. Eyes closed, Lee rocked back and forth for a moment. Then he set the child on his feet, putting his small, square hand in Caroline's.

What if...

What if one of Bryan's corrupt judges has already awarded him custody? What if she couldn't bring Trent home?

"Call every night. Stay safe. Hurry home." Lee opened his arms to her. A smile twitched under his mustache.

What if she never get a chance to tell him...

She stepped into his embrace, pressing her cheek to his. Her body ignited like an acetylene torch.

"How much weight have you lost?" His fingers traced her ribs down her spine.

She pulled away from him. "Downtime. The heat, the hours."

His hand lingered at her waist. "No. You've lost more since then. All they've got to eat in Boston is baked beans."

She smiled at the old joke. He was trying to break the tension, ease the parting. She supplied the punch line. "Boston cream pie, too."

"*Mais*, yeah, chocolate you'll eat. You'd better go." Lee watched Caroline and Trent step through security. His heart felt like he'd just started down the first descent on Worlds of Fun's tallest roller coaster. Dragging his feet across the bowling alley style floor, he wandered to the deserted baggage claim area. Through the tall double-pane glass, he watched a guy carrying a tool box hurry under the jet. The mechanic engaged a second uniformed worker in an arm-waving discussion. What if the plane was broken, the flight canceled? Something wrong with the plane? The second vertical drop on this roller coaster scared him worse than the first. No, he prayed, let the plane work perfectly. The jet pushed back to join the flock of departing airliners. He should have asked Caroline which side they were sitting on. Pressing close to the glass, Lee swung his arm overhead in an arc. His middle and ring fingers bent down, forming the sign for "I love you."

Chicken.

Lee staggered away from the window and out to the truck, Caroline's truck, thankful he didn't run into anyone he knew. The rear view mirror flashed his frown back at him. What a mess. Concentrate. Center. Just like a preparing for competition. Mental picture. Focus. He closed his eyes, seeing Caroline and Trent buckled into their seats. Throughout the cabin he saw angels. Angels in every empty seat, standing in the aisle, hovering by the ceiling. Angels in the cockpit, on the wings, straddling the engines. Big angels wearing white *gi* with black belts. The little boy put on his headphones and watched the clouds flash by the window. Caroline's shoulders drooped. Her face relaxed just like the night he massaged—

Quit before you really get into trouble.

Lee headed back to Liberty. His heart's roller coaster ran level until he pulled into the garage. Then it looped, flipping upside down. Empty homes are bread and butter for house sitters. At best he had a family pet or two for company, if they didn't take him for a burglar and go into attack mode. But he'd been in this one when the owners were home. It seemed more lonely than usual. Even the VW, parked in the other stall, looked forlorn. And knowing Trent and Caroline were on their way to Boston... He crossed his hands on the steering wheel and laid his head down.

The passenger door clicked open. The seat shifted with the weight of another person. He inhaled the aroma of fried pork chops. Sharon. "Lee?"

He didn't look up, not wanting her to see how bad he hurt. "My heart just flew to Boston."

Sharon patted his shoulder the way she'd consoled her own children and the hordes of kids she baby-sat. "Remember you don't have to be with them to fight the power of darkness."

"Yeah, but maybe I could get her to eat. She won't say how much weight she's lost."

"I know." Sharon sighed. "Last week, I came over to borrow sour cream and they were having toasted cheese sandwiches for dinner. I'm not too worried about Trent—we feed him a big breakfast at our house, and he eats hot lunch at school. But Caroline..." She sighed, a weary mother's sound. "I did get her to eat three brownies the other day."

"I'll freeze some casseroles for her this week." Lee got down from the truck.

Sharon met him at the tailgate. She nodded across the street where her little girl chalked designs on the driveway. "It's easier now that I have kids of my own to love."

Lee picked a leaf out of the pickup bed. "Guess it will always be hard for me." He plodded to the VW for his sack of clothes. "*Regardez donc.* New wiper blades." He yanked the lid off the trash can and found three yellow and blue Anco boxes. "Caroline put new wiper blades on my car. I can't let her do that." He tugged the old blade from the package. The rubber crumbled into chunks, none longer than a car key.

"You are an idiot, Lee Marivaux."

"Lots of things crawl out of the bayou," he muttered. "Genius ain't one of them."

Sharon jabbed herself with her thumb. "Do I work?"

Lee squinted. "Yeah. Harder than anyone I know. Garden, home school, church, Vacation Bible School, take care of every stray cat and freeloader in Liberty."

"Plus run a household and raise kids. Other than child care, I never see a penny for my work. No Social Security, no sick days, nothing. I bet I make less per hour than you. That doesn't mean my work isn't important. It just isn't well reimbursed in a capitalist society. Same as your work."

Lee rubbed his mustache. "Yeah, but you're a woman. Pete's the breadwinner."

"What is the authority for your life? You've read Proverbs 31, the last chapter?"

"The virtuous woman."

"One point, Mr. Marivaux." Sharon made a vertical line in the air. "Who works outside the home in that chapter? The woman. Traditionally in ancient Israel, the woman brought home the bacon." She dope-slapped herself. "Bacon in Israel. You've got me so riled up. The Bible does not say the husband has to make more than the wife."

If God gave the okay, would Caroline? "*Mais...*"

Sharon headed home. "Pray about it."

"*Tout le temps.* All the time."

Chapter Nineteen

A yellow-grey band of humidity and air pollution domed the Boston metropolitan area. The jet descended over the Harbor. Caroline pointed out barges and a lighthouse to her son. Trent had been reasonably well behaved. His excited comments about the flight, from the clouds to the toilet, drew a smile from the bored business traveler across the aisle. The flight attendant brought him a set of wings and responded "you're welcome, darling" to the boy's "thank you." He ate the deli sandwich served for lunch. The only disaster occurred when he opened the condiment packet, splattering himself with creamy Italian. A couple pats with a damp napkin blended the salad dressing into the pattern on his polo shirt.

The jet squeaked onto the runway, then trundled to the terminal. Caroline sent a text to Marnie, letting her know they'd landed. The other passengers gathered their carryons and unlatched their seat belts. Let them race off, she thought, we're in no hurry.

Caroline guided Trent to the restroom, hoping he learned to be independent before he got too old for the Ladies'. Searching through a bank of beige stalls scratched with rusty graffiti, she found an unclogged toilet with the necessary paper. At least Trent didn't have to sit down. Wait a minute. When did he learn that?

They retrieved their suitcase from the baggage carousel and exited. A crush of import cars burrowed through the underground roadway. Exhaust and humidity choked every breath. Caroline's eyes watered from the fumes. She should have consulted Trent's pulmonary doctor to see if there were medical grounds for refusing to return to Boston.

"Look for Marnie!" Caroline boosted Trent to stand on her suitcase. Seven years. Would her girlfriend recognize them? She should have asked what she was driving these days.

A silver BMW screeched to a halt at the curb. "Caroline?"

"Marnie! Thank God. I was afraid we'd asphyxiate."

"Nonsense. No air pollution alerts today. Hi there, handsome. Hop in." Marnie settled Trent in the back seat.

Caroline threw the suitcase in the trunk and joined her friend in the air-conditioned car. They inched into the traffic.

"What, no pointy-toed boots, Stetson hat?"

"People in Kansas City don't dress like cowboys, most of them anyway. You look great." Marnie's hair had been lightened and sculpted into a wedge. Beneath the haircut dangled gold earrings reminiscent of spark plugs. Caroline tugged on the sleeve of her friend's chalk-striped navy blue suit. "Sophisticated."

"Filene's basement." Marnie grinned. "Hope the old grouch will let you go shopping while you're here."

"He suggested it, but I don't want him alone with..." She tipped her head in Trent's direction. "Wilson-deGrazia thinks he may try for custody."

"Custody? What judge in his right mind..." Her hands tightened on the steering wheel. "Stupid question." She sighed. "You should see his campaign ads. No wonder he wants pictures of Trent. He's the only positive. Everything else is a smear against his opponent."

"Any chance of him winning?"

"None I can see." Marnie leaned on the horn, cutting in front of a Porsche. "He's not far enough behind to give up, though. Pouring big bucks into TV time."

The car squeezed into the bumper-to-bumper jam crawling from the airport.

"Ah-ah! Ah-ah!" Too soon Trent lost his shyness. He pointed out planes to Marnie. Half an hour later, they were still within sight of the airport.

Caroline stretched. "How can anyone stand to live here? Move to Kansas City, Marnie."

"And leave the Celtics, Boston Pops, James Taylor? No way. You move back here. We could rent a beach house at the Cape together, ski the Berkshires..."

"Admit it. You never do any of those things, no concerts, no sporting events, no museums, because you can't find a parking space."

Marnie laughed. "Well, Toto, we're not in Kansas anymore."

Four lanes of traffic converged into two. The station wagon in front of them squeezed ahead, its fender scraping along the concrete barrier. Hordes of cars inched down into the Sumner Tunnel. Trent kicked the back of the seat. Caroline reached around and grabbed his leg. Trapped under the Charles River with a bored child.

"Do I get to meet your latest boyfriend?" Caroline asked around the constriction in her throat.

"John Hancock? Soon as we come out of the tunnel, there he'll be standing proud." Marnie referred to her employer and its office tower. "How about you? Meet any handsome farmers, Royals players, auto executives?"

Marnie knew her dating situation. "I turn down six or seven proposals every week."

"Ma!" A fist with a thumb between the first two fingers shot up between the bucket seats.

"Trent, you've got to wait. Where's the nearest bathroom?"

Marnie looked frantically in the rearview mirror. "Not on my leather seats, Trent. Just four more miles."

It had been seven minutes since the traffic last moved. "Four miles? That could be hours. Is there an accident, construction?"

"Rush hour."

Caroline hesitated. If Bryan found out...but, chances of that were slim compared to the certainty of damage to Marnie's upholstery. She leaned over the back of the seat, helping Trent to unbuckle and unzip.

"Caroline, you're not..."

"All this white tile is inspiring." And cleaner than the airport restrooms.

And so Trent Jameson anointed the Sumner Tunnel.

"GREAT CLASS, Lee. Be sure to call the youth minister about setting up a session for the middle school girls." The coordinator waved to the last of the ladies filing out of the church gym, then handed him an envelope, thick with cash.

"Thanks." It had been his largest self-defense class ever, over fifty women, all with plenty of questions and comments. Even though they kept him busy, worries about Caroline and Trent circled his head. *Keep them safe, Jesus.*

Lee ran his thumb over the cash. God provided airfare. Next stop, the airport and a plane to Boston. He pushed through the door and found Bernie perched on the hood of his VW.

"What's wrong?" His sister had plenty to do without chasing him all over Kansas City. "The boys? Louis?"

She raised her head slowly and looked at him through wet eyelashes. "It's Miss Pearl."

"She was fine Wednesday, when I delivered your plants. Is she..." Back in the hospital? Please say she's back in the hospital.

Bernie pushed to her feet and gathered him in a hug. "Yesterday morning. She didn't wake up. I'm sorry, Bear."

No. Yes. No more suffering, needle pokes, drug side effects. Lee wrapped his arms around his sister and leaned into her. "That's what she prayed for—falling asleep at home and waking up in heaven."

She patted his back. "You okay?"

"I'll miss her wisdom and—" He tensed as he recalled their last conversation. "When is the funeral?"

"Tomorrow afternoon."

"I've gotta go to Boston." He held up the envelope. "Miss Pearl would understand."

Bernie pulled a folded sheet of linen stationery from her jeans pocket. "You're doing the eulogy."

"*Mais*, yeah, I've been working on it. Didn't think I'd need it so soon." He leaned against his car and opened the paper. The instructions were addressed, "To Lee, my favorite volunteer." She asked him to tell the story of the women's shelter, from the birth of the idea when they met during a self-defense class at her church, through all the lives changed since. At the bottom, the ink color changed and the handwriting grew shakier. After the date, last Wednesday, she quoted 2 Timothy 1:7, "For God hath not given us the spirit of fear; but of power, and of love, and a sound mind."

"Power and love you've got. Sound mind might be a lost cause." Bernie asked. "So what are you afraid of?"

"Good quote for the shelter." He tucked the page into his gym bag. "I'll finish the speech, but if Caroline's in any danger, the new director will have to give it."

She grabbed his chin and gave him her big sister version of a death glare. He never could hide anything from those eyes. "What are you afraid of?"

He pushed off the car and stomped across the parking lot and back. "I'm afraid...I'll lose Trent...if I tell Caroline how I feel." He stopped in front of Bernie, breathing hard. "*Merde.* I've already lost them, haven't I?"

"When God answers your prayer for their safe return, will you let go of your fear?"

He looked down at the duct tape holding his shoe together. Was it possible that God wanted to provide a family for him, that Caroline would accept him as her husband? Could he muster the courage to ask her? Grand-mère would say he needed a serious dose of moxie. *Mais, yeah, Lord, I'm going to need moxie, courage,and the perfect proposal.*

"I'll pick you up at noon for the funeral." Bernie gave him a noogie and headed home in her minivan.

And one more thing, Lord, a eulogy for a great lady.

"Caroline!" Marnie called. "Your phone rang." She muffled the phone with her hand and whispered, "It's a man, but not Czar Bryan the Terrible."

"Probably one of his accomplices."

"I don't think so. He's way too down-home friendly. Said not to interrupt you if you're eating."

"I know who it is." She took the phone. "Lee?"

"Caroline. I was starting to worry." The man's deep voice echoed in the phone lines.

"I just got Trent into bed. I was going to call."

"Your dime either way. How's it going?"

"Fine."

"You sound tired."

Before she could stop herself, the story of the airport spilled out. "I could use one of your back rubs," she concluded.

"I can be there tomorrow." He paused and she heard paper flipping in the background. "Hear that? Figure that's enough for a ticket. I got paid today. Big class, lots of students."

Oh, yes! Caroline hesitated. *No.* Airfares ran over half his monthly income. He needed that money for other things, like snow tires. What would Marnie read into Lee's arrival? And Bryan? He'd explode. "Thank you, but... that's too much to ask. You'd have to cancel your classes for the week."

"You sure? If you change your mind, Bryan tries anything, call. I may just show up. This whole mess stinks like a swamp full of dead nutria." His voice lowered. "When do you have to see, what does your friend call him, the Czar?"

"The campaign bus picks us up at nine. I'm not sure when we'll get back. It could be an all day ordeal."

Lee groaned. "Remind him Trent's bedtime is eight. What have you eaten today?"

"We brought home D'Angelos, like a sub in pita bread."

"Sounds healthy. I'll let you go, then. Call me tomorrow."

"I will. Good night." Caroline hung up and wandered into the kitchen. "What can I do?"

Marnie pointed her glass of White Zinfandel toward the dining room table. "Tell me all about him. Who's been giving you back rubs?"

Caroline's face heated. "Lee, Trent's karate instructor. He's house sitting."

"House sitting?" Marnie unwrapped her sandwich. "I thought Liberty was a low crime area."

"Since Jesse James left town." Caroline pushed stray shreds of lettuce back into the pocket bread. "No, Lee just needed a place to stay."

Marnie gaped over her wine glass. "He's living with you?"

"Only when I'm not there." Caroline thought back to two conversations with Sharon. In the first, the sitter said Lee wanted to move in, under his own terms. In the last, she indicated Lee wasn't sexually attracted to her. She'd have to ponder the contradiction when she wasn't so tired. "He's not interested in me, just Trent, the truck, my tools."

"But you're interested in him."

"Marnie, I work with men all day. I'm rational, objective, production oriented. But when it comes to Lee, I'm..." Hours and miles later, her mental image of Lee at the airport, the warmth of his hug, accelerated her pulse. "I'm silly."

Marnie belted out, "I can't stop falling in love with..."

"Please, I'm too tired for Elvis."

"So what's the problem? Is he married, gay, Pee-Wee Herman's double?"

"No, he's a hunk. Muscles, chest hair, the usual." Embarrassed at her foolish description, she attacked her sandwich.

"Caroline Jameson! I never heard you talk about Bryan like this. Of course the old grouch has all the sex appeal of a credit report." She refilled their wine glasses. "Hope you brought a photo."

"Mother took pictures of him in a swimsuit."

Marnie grinned. "I just love your mother."

CAROLINE LEANED in the doorway of the bus, watching the umpteenth campaign stop of the day. Holding himself stiffly, Bryan delivered his speech over the heads of the crowd, with only an occasional glance down his nose at the unwashed masses. Caroline closed her eyes, picturing Lee moving through the congregation after church. He rested a hand on Bob Highfield's shoulder, lowering his head to the shorter man's eye level while they discussed a junior high student they had in common. A tiny monkey of a girl, recently adopted from Vietnam, climbed Lee's leg in search of a hug. Down on one knee, he greeted Miss McNamara, asking about the wheelchair ramp he'd built for her. Youth group members got high-fives and congratulations for making honor roll. Wanting to introduce her to the pastor, Lee's palm touched the small of her back, gently, protectively. No demands, no coercion. Unlike some people...

Impeccable gestures accented the highest quality political rhetoric the candidate's money could buy. Caroline fiddled with her phone, scrolling through the sign language app in search of appropriate insults. If Bryan caught her reading, though, he'd have one more thing to snipe about. Toward the rest of his entourage, he spread the praise thickly: rally the troops, victory is at hand. He seemed energized, running on high octane. Then he'd see Caroline and all his tension would backfire in her face.

The driver returned from his trip to the back of the bus, accompanied by the distinct odor of beer. At each stop he made a withdraw and a deposit. He adjusted his pants and resumed his seat. Caroline hoped he'd be sober enough to navigate Boston's narrow streets when the speeches ended.

Time for the candidate to introduce his "family". The new Mrs. Ashcroft, blonde hair sprayed into a curled helmet, stepped forward. Gina dabbed Trent's chin with a tissue, then passed him to Bryan. The candidate lifted the boy. As instructed, Trent waved to the crowd. His natural ham tendency blossomed with each stop. Here he blew a kiss to the Channel 3 camera. The lukewarm crowd erupted in applause. Caroline retreated to her back-of-the-bus seat.

"What a kid! I bet we make the six and the eleven news!" Karanda hurried inside, arms overhead. Someone ought to tell him his antiperspirant quit working.

"Ma! Ma!" Trent raced down the aisle and jumped in her lap.

"Good work." She signed the "toilet" question. He shook his head.

The rest of the team filed in. The campaign staff didn't include acquaintances from their married days. Most seemed to be related to the new Mrs. Ashcroft. Perhaps they were all her family. It would be just like Bryan to marry for political connections.

The bus lurched into the ever-present traffic. Gina balanced with a hand on the back of Bryan's seat. "Bry, Bry," she struggled to break into the conversation between her husband and his campaign manager.

"Later, babe."

Caroline cringed. He still didn't know anything about being a husband.

Gina persisted. "Campaigning is hard on the boy. Let me take him someplace fun tomorrow, the zoo, maybe."

"Ridiculous. You know we've got a full schedule now through the election. We don't have time for nonsense. He seemed happy enough today. The crowds ate him up."

"Wait a minute. Gina, you may be onto something. Tomorrow, Trent will be yesterday's news. Let me work on it. Maybe there's a game at Fenway." Karanda scanned the bus, spotting Caroline. "Who would he root for if the Red Sox play the Royals?"

Bryan sneered over his shoulder. "Caroline doesn't know who the Royals are."

"I'll tell George Brett you said that, next time he's over to grill out." Her worn self-control skidded on Bryan's icy regard. Other conversations screeched to a halt to rubberneck their collision.

"As bad as you cook..."

"Bryan!" Karanda reigned in his candidate. "Our next stop..."

· · ·

THE MERCEDES PULLED to the curb in front of Marnie's apartment building. This year's model, Caroline noted. New car for the new wife. Mrs. Ashcroft pushed open the passenger door. "Sorry I'm late. Bryan had me answering his phone messages."

Rough life. "We haven't been waiting long." Caroline and Trent climbed in. She had chosen casual clothes, chinos and a Madras shirt, for their day as tourists. Gina looked like an ad for Joseph A. Banks Clothiers in an elegant burgundy suit, ivory silk blouse, and an antique garnet necklace. Caroline wondered if the woman owned anything comfortable.

"Hi, Trent! You're going to love the aquarium." Gina headed into the city. Trent responded with a string of babble.

Caroline focused on the apartments passing by the windows. What rules governed conversations with the ex's new wife? *Has his mother driven you crazy? Is he planning to seek custody? Has he strangled you yet? Miss Manners, Dear Abby, I need some help here.*

Gina took the lead. "Have you been to the aquarium?"

"No. School kept me busy when I lived here."

"MIT." She nodded.

"Bryan told you." What else did he say about her?

"I'm sorry he's so," deep red ovals fluttered over the steering wheel, "so disagreeable to you. He's tense about the election. We really appreciate your letting Trent campaign. I hope he can come for a real visit after the election."

Caroline blinked at the woman. She had no idea how Bryan got Trent here. Blinders or loyalty? Either way she wouldn't believe the truth. "He can't miss more school."

"I'd love to have him come for Christmas."

During their marriage, Bryan spent the holidays in a continuous round of parties for his business contacts. Politics wouldn't convert him to family-oriented celebrations. His party schedule might grow even more frantic. Caroline rested her hand on her son's smooth knee. "What does Bryan say about that?"

"We haven't had time to talk about it. Everything depends on the election."

Caroline held her breath. The plant shut down between Christmas and New Year's. Engineers spent long hours on equipment maintenance. Her parents gave Trent his holiday. If Bryan found out... "Please don't ask him. Trent's all I have. I'd be alone at Christmas."

Gina pulled into a parking garage. "How thoughtless of me. He can visit another time. Would you like that, Trent?"

Still agreeable this early in the day, the boy nodded. He grabbed both women's hands and swung his legs up. Gina winced.

"Trent, no." Caroline disconnected her rowdy son from the small-boned woman. Directing their conversation to the boy, they stumbled over red brick sidewalks the two blocks to the New England Aquarium. Gina paid their admission and checked the schedule of shows. Trent raced to the first display, a dozen penguins. He called to them with a squawking sound. In unison, the birds turned to him and flapped their wings. Trent raised his hands overhead and applauded.

"He's adorable," Gina cooed. "You shouldn't be apart at Christmas."

"It's too bad you don't have children of your own." Then Bryan would leave Trent alone.

"We've tried." The perfectly coiffed woman wandered to the base of the enormous central tank. "The doctors say it's not me. Bryan refuses to be tested. Trent is evidence enough of his... ability." She paused to show the boy a moray eel grinning open-mouthed from his cave. "I'd like to try artificial insemination. We could choose a donor who looks like Bryan, but..."

"The Ashcroft family line."

Gina looked her in the eye. "Exactly." Beneath the pads of the tailored jacket, her shoulders relaxed, just for a moment. She turned back at the coral reef. "I shouldn't have said anything."

Trent called from the level above them. The two women met him around the next curve. He waved his hands from side to side.

"Fish," Caroline explained.

"He signs! That's wonderful. I'll take a sign language class as soon as the election's over."

Easier with each other, they finished touring the aquarium, then boarded the Discovery barge for the sea lion and dolphin show.

Here's a safe, neutral topic of conversation. "Trent got to feed the dolphins at Worlds of Fun," Caroline told Gina while they waited on the bleachers.

"How exciting!"

Trent pantomimed his performance, acting out not only himself, but the dolphins, Lee, and his grandparents.

"I hope you got a picture of that."

"My father did." Caroline turned to dig in her purse. A movement out of the corner of her eye caught her attention. When she lifted her head, she didn't see anything out of the ordinary. She held her phone for Gina. Trent wiggled between the women, adding his commentary and scrolling through the photos.

"This must be your mother. I can see the family resemblance. But this man is too young to be your father."

"He's younger than me. That's Trent's karate instructor."

"Oh, your live-in. I can see why Bryan got so upset."

Caroline sighed. "He's not my live-in. He just takes care of Trent sometimes."

"Oh?" Two perfectly arched brows drew together into a frown. "I must have misunderstood..." She held up the Ferris wheel shot. "Looks like he and Trent are quite fond of each other. If only Bryan would..."

The last picture showed Trent on Lee's lap. The boy looked up at his instructor. Chocolate ice cream dripped from his chin and cone onto the big man's rumpled shirt and shorts. Lee's head tilted toward the child's. His face glowed with a gentle smile.

"Bryan wouldn't." Gina returned her phone.

When Caroline reached for her purse, she saw someone raise a camera in their direction. "Gina." She used the woman's name for the first time. "Look behind my shoulder. Someone's taking pictures of us."

All expression, all traces of sadness, disappeared from the woman's face. "Maybe... you're right. The political goldfish bowl. Ignore it."

Caroline tried to enjoy the performance, but part of her mind stayed on the photographer. Probably someone who recognized Gina. Trent reveled in the show, signing instructions to the animals, and applauding their every move. He gave them a standing ovation at the end.

Gina laughed. "Trent, I give you a standing ovation. Let's go have lunch."

Most of the crowd wandered back to the aquarium. Caroline took Trent to the rest room. Gina purchased a T-shirt for him in the gift shop. The three pushed through the glass doors into the sticky Boston afternoon.

A Channel 3 van stood at the curb. A reporter and a cameraman jumped out. Caroline expected them to go into the aquarium. Maybe one of the lobsters had babies. Or do they lay eggs? The Channel 3 team focused on Gina.

"We'll meet you on the other side of the street." The armor of the candidate's wife reappeared: the plastic smile, erect posture, and contrived gestures.

"Trent, stay with Gina." Caroline slipped around the end of the van.

"Mrs. Ashcroft, Trent. How did you enjoy the aquarium?" The reporter pivoted for the best lighting.

"We had a wonderful time." Gina bent to lift Trent to camera level. She wobbled on her two inch heels. Forty pounds was a lot if you weren't used to it, if you hadn't been lifting the child since he weighed in at seven pounds, six ounces.

"What was your favorite part?"

With wild motions, Trent reviewed the dolphin and sea lion show for the camera.

"That's sign language for fish," Gina explained. "Nice seeing you again, Ms. Stainer." She set the boy down and took his hand to cross the street in front of the van.

"Ma!" Trent called.

The cameraman returned to the van. The reporter chased after them.

"You're Trent's mother, the first Mrs. Ashcroft. Why did you abduct the boy?"

"I don't give interviews."

"I gather you're not on friendly terms with Bryan Ashcroft. Why did you come? What is your custody agreement?"

"Please, no."

The reporter pulled a business card from her pocket. "I'd like to hear your side of the story."

Gina slipped the card from the reporter's fingers. "How would you like an exclusive tour of the candidate's home? I'll call you next week to arrange it. Now if you'll excuse us, Ms. Stainer, we have a hungry little boy to feed."

GINA PARKED the Mercedes in the alley behind the office building. She had been cordial during lunch, centering the conversation on Trent. Only the tapping of her fingernails on the saucer of her coffee cup showed her agitation. Now she slammed the door harder than required by German engineering.

Turning to the boy, she asked, "Want to try out your dad's bathroom?" He skipped around the car to take her hand.

Traditional red, white, and blue posters pitched Bryan Ashcroft for State House. Clusters of people working the phones and stuffing envelopes paused to wave and call hello. Gina responded with a tight nod, then directed Trent to the appropriate facility. Gazes shifted from the boy to his mother. Frowns and whispers ricocheted through the ranks. Caroline raised her chin. *I've faced down the plant's UAW rep—you can't scare me.*

A door opened in the back.

"Gina, you made the Channel 3 noon news. Good job." Darrell Karanda reached for her hand.

She linked arms with him, steering him into the office. Caroline followed, her pulse racing with the wicked anticipation of a demolition derby spectator.

Gina turned on Karanda. "Don't you ever do that to me again. When I ask for time off, that means no reporters."

Bryan looked up from his cluttered desk. "What are you complaining about, honey? You looked great. Show her, Darrell."

Gina's lipsticked mouth thinned. "After the camera was off, the reporter came after Caroline."

"What?" Bryan shot out from his desk. "If you'd stayed back in Kansas City like I told you." His hand formed a claw. Caroline took a backwards step toward the door.

Karanda moved in front of the candidate. "What happened?"

Gina answered, "Caroline refused the interview. I can't protect her privacy unless I know when to expect the press. Someone took pictures of us at the aquarium, too."

Karanda shrugged. "If Caroline wants privacy, she can stay home."

Gina's fists clenched at her side. There goes the manicure. "She can't stay home. Trent communicates in sign language, which none of us knows."

"He needs to learn how to talk."

"Bryan!" Gina's shoulders shook with an all too familiar frustration. "This is exploitation, bordering on child abuse."

"No it's not. He's enjoying himself. Darrell, show her what you got for tonight's game."

Karanda held up a boy-sized Red Sox uniform. "He'll love it. The games starts at 7:05; we'll pick him up at six."

"Caroline!" Red-purple blotches started to show under Gina's makeup. "Why do you let him do this to Trent?"

She crossed her arms. "Would you like to answer that, Bryan?"

"That's none of your business, Gina."

She spit out a swear word, startling the outer room into silence. "I'm the one holding his hand while you campaign. I'm the one holding his hand when Channel 3 shows up. Trent has become my business."

"I'll thank you not to corrupt my wife's mind with your trash, Caroline." Bryan lunged for her again.

"You do that all by yourself." She pressed two fingers to his throat. It worked like a charm. Bryan retreated, coughing. "Could you give me a ride back to Jamaica Plain, Gina? I'd like Trent to get a nap before the game."

Gina snatched the Red Sox uniform from Karanda. "If you'll teach me how to do whatever you just did."

Caroline looked over her shoulder at her ex. "I'd be glad to teach you all kinds of things."

THE CHEVY BOUNCED through the potholes on the roads out of Fenway Park. At the seventh inning stretch, Bryan had ordered her to take Trent back to Jamaica Plain on the T. Gina countermanded him: it wasn't safe to ride public transportation this late at night. The campaign staff caucused, nominating Rico. His car had vinyl seats.

"Whoa, baby," Rico pumped the brakes as they approached the light.

The car stalled in the middle of the intersection. Rico cranked the starter. Nothing. The driver behind them leaned on the horn, then pulled around with a squeal of tires. Caroline glanced at Trent, stretched out in the back seat. He stirred, but didn't wake up.

"Do you have any tools?"

"I have a set of those miniature screwdrivers for fixing cameras."

"That'll do." She held out her hand.

"They're at home."

Caroline took a deep breath. The sharp smell of gasoline overrode the pine cleaner-scented air freshener dangling from the rearview mirror. A search of her purse unearthed a ballpoint pen. "Pop it." She climbed out of the car, raised the hood, and removed the air cleaner lid. A stuck choke butterfly. It flipped open with a poke from the pen. "Do you have any carburetor cleaner?" She glanced around the dirt encrusted engine compartment. Why did she bother to ask?

"No. Should I get some?"

"Among other things." She closed the hood and returned to the car.

The Chevy started again and wheezed to the next light.

Clunk. Caroline wondered if it would be safer to trust their fate to the Metropolitan Transit Authority. She cocked her head, listening to the ticking of the lifters. The light turned green. Clunk.

"You've got a broken engine mount."

"Huh?" Rico frowned.

"You need an oil change," Caroline continued. Bryan always said she wasn't good at small talk. "And new shocks."

Caroline glanced over her shoulder. Clouds of white smoke obscured the view behind them. Trent had conked out before they left Fenway. In the pulsing light of the streetlights, his face looked pale, his eye sockets dark. He's low on his fluids, too.

The engine died. Caroline held her breath. This neighborhood, bustling during the day, looked like a slum at night. The few pedestrians loitered like drug pushers, prostitutes, muggers. She should have hired Lee as their bodyguard.

Rico mumbled a long string of profanity. With a scream that made her teeth ache, the starter caught. The Chevy lurched deeper into the squalor. Caroline peeked at the driver. Maybe Bryan told him to dump her here to get rid of her. The man seemed totally absorbed in the car, white-knuckling the steering wheel, pulsing the gas pedal. They turned the corner and hiccupped to a stop in front of Marnie's building.

"Thank you, Rico." *Thank you, God.* Caroline threw Trent over her shoulder and raced for the door.

A half-dozen locks later, they were safe in Marnie's apartment. Caroline fastened the security chain and carried Trent to the guest room. He didn't wake up when she pulled off his mustard and relish stained baseball uniform. She dumped the filthy clothes in the bathtub.

Her phone rang. "Lee?"

"Caroline. How did it go at the game?"

"It started out okay. The campaign manager found a Red Sox uniform for Trent, which he enjoyed. He conducted the National Anthem. It embarrassed Bryan, but his handler was ecstatic about the free TV coverage."

"He conducted the 'Star Spangled Banner'? Did he sing along? I'd have loved to see that."

"Yeah, it was fun. But then Trent got restless as the game dragged on. The staffers bought him junk food to keep him happy and..."

"Let me guess. He threw up, hopefully all over Bryan."

Caroline chuckled. "Over his slacks and wingtips. Hot dogs, nachos, and orange soda. He won't wear that suit again."

"His Terribleness wore a suit to a ball game? What a pervert."

"How did you know Trent was sick?"

"He almost got me at Worlds of Fun. Hamburgers and lemonade before one of those tilt and spin rides. Pretty dumb of me."

"You never mentioned it." Bryan had gone ballistic, turning red and nearly hyperventilating.

"No big deal. He looked a little wobbly, so I ran him into the bathroom. He did his thing and was fine the rest of the day. How's he now?"

"Asleep, but I'm wondering if I should wake him up to give him fluids."

"If he only arfed once, he shouldn't be dehydrated. Probably better off without all that salt and artificial coloring. You may want to start off easy tomorrow morning, dry toast, clear liquids."

"Dr. Lee to the rescue."

"Dr. Lee wants to know what you've been eating, hopefully not ball park food."

"I had an interesting lunch today with the second Mrs. Ashcroft. We spent the afternoon practicing self-defense techniques."

"No kidding? If you can get her on your side in this custody battle..."

"He won't try anything," she interrupted, "not with all these reporters shadowing him."

"Sure hope not. Thought I got a lot of money, but it's not enough for a plane ticket. You're on your own unless another job drops in my lap."

"I've got your prayers. So how's life in Kansas City?"

"Quiet." She heard him shift positions. Hamstring stretch again. "Nice sofa bed."

"Oh, thanks. I got it for my parents' visit. The waterbed makes them seasick. Is the mattress long enough for you?"

"Diagonally."

"The waterbed's longer. Why don't you try it?"

He made a strangled sound. "Get something to eat. Call me tomorrow."

"Yes, sir."

Chapter Twenty

Lee stared into the night, watching dawn form a ceiling and walls out of blackness. What had he been dreaming about? Boston? No, St. Louis. A teacher he'd met at the competition. Who? What was the name of that school? Concentrate. *Nogare* breathing. Let the answer come to you. *Lord Jesus, please help my tired head...*

Toshi! He'd remember! Lee rolled out of the sofa bed and jumped down the stairs into the kitchen. He punched the numbers on the phone.

"Huh."

"Toshi, this is Lee."

"Lee?" he yawned. "This better be an emergency. I didn't get home until—"

"Sorry." He glanced at the clock and flinched. "Do you remember the name of that Japanese guy we met in St. Louis who runs a *dojo* in Boston?"

"You're asking me a question before I've had my coffee. My alarm goes off at seven, that's an hour and half from now. You try back around seven-thirty."

"Those people I had with me at your playground, Caroline and Trent..."

"Pretty face I remember."

"They're in Boston." Restless fingers tugged at his mustache.

"And want to take karate lessons at sunrise."

"Domestic violence situation."

"Oh." Toshi cleared his throat. "The *sensei* from Okinawa."

"Come on, man. I can't call every *dojo* in Massachusetts and ask if they have a teacher from Okinawa."

"Does Caroline know you're this much fun in the morning? I saved the program. It's around here somewhere."

"Find it. I'll wait." *Got nothing but time.*

CAROLINE FINISHED her morning to-go coffee as the campaign bus arrived at a gray-shingled building. *Crippled Children's Center* the sign read. She winced. Lee would hate that name. The Channel 3 van pulled up behind them. Reporter Allison Stainer seemed to have embraced Trent as her cause célèbre. Largely due to her stories, CCC invited Trent and his candidate father for a visit.

The principal wore a Chanel suit in Ford emblem blue. "Good morning, Mr. Ashcroft. Welcome. Mrs. Ashcroft, a pleasure. And this is Trent. You're going to love it here."

A Freon-cold chill doused Caroline. Is Bryan considering placing Trent in this school? Shivering, she joined the fringe of the group.

The older woman addressed the cameraman. "Not all of our students have photo releases. I'm afraid you're limited to pictures of Trent Ashcroft only."

Turning back to the candidate, she began a well-rehearsed spiel. "CCC opened in 1963, well before federal law required education of children with special needs. Local school districts now take some of the more able students, but those with severe handicaps come here for our expertise. We also serve children with complicated medical needs. We have a registered nurse on duty every school day."

Trent pushed past the group into the first classroom. He had been so excited when Caroline told him they were visiting a school today. School, unlike aquarium or ball park, was a word he recognized. He raced up to each student and waved hi. The children, positioned in a variety of equipment, responded with puzzled looks or shy smiles. Gina followed at his heels. But Bryan, after a cursory glance around the room, fixed his stare on the principal as if her presentation held the secret of life.

"Some of our students are on a field trip to the pumpkin patch today, so it's pretty quiet..."

Trent squatted in front of a girl lying prone on a foam wedge. He pressed a red saucer sized pad, activating a toy fire truck. A tiny fireman climbed the extension ladder. Sirens and bells sounded.

"Trent, no!" The color drained from Bryan's face. A thin string of drool spilled from the student's lower lip.

"Good work, Trent." The teacher sat on the floor with the children. "You're showing India how to make the truck go."

Following a jerk of Bryan's head, Gina took Trent in hand. The group moved to the next classroom. Here a suspended platform caught the boy's attention. He jumped on, sending the device swinging across the room.

"Trent seems familiar with our equipment. His school in Kansas must be well supplied." The principal searched the crowd.

"Missouri," Caroline corrected, earning a scathing look from Bryan.

"Oh. I thought Mr. Ashcroft said Kansas City." Fluttering her hands in confusion, she led them to the next room.

Trent dived into a ball bath, disappearing under a sea of blue, red, and green spheres.

"These bright colors will make a good shot," the cameraman suggested.

The reporter glided into position next to the principal. While she did an interview on sensory stimulation, Trent demonstrated a variety of swimming strokes. He started throwing balls around the room. Caroline found a plastic pail and handed it to Gina.

"Give him a target," she whispered.

Their next stop resembled a home ec class. Trent worked the

room, greeting each student, while his father waited by the door. Bryan won't waste a handshake on people who can't vote.

The kitchen timer dinged. An older boy with Down syndrome turned off the oven.

"You like cookies?" He asked Trent. The little boy licked his lips and nodded. "I make. Be careful. Hot." He motioned for Trent to back up. Gina held him by the shoulders. The older boy slid a sheet of chocolate chip cookies from the oven, filling the kitchen with a heavenly fragrance.

The principal bent over, eye level with Trent. "The cookies are hot. Hurt your tongue. When they cool, we'll come back and eat."

"I save one for you. Two, maybe," the older boy promised.

Caroline braced for a tantrum, but Trent allowed the woman to guide him into the gym. His face lit up at the sight of the equipment. The PE teacher, a curly haired woman in sweatpants and T-shirt, offered to take Trent on the trampoline. She fastened the boy into the harness, and recruited Gina and Karanda to serve as spotters. Trent bounced and yelled, "yahoo!" The principal explained the importance of physical activity to the reporter while the camera rolled.

Caroline leaned against the wall, blindsided by crushing loneliness for Lee. He would have enjoyed watching Trent jump on the tramp and play in the ball bath. He'll be proud to hear Trent greeted people. The boy climbed through the play structure, guided by the PE teacher. This is the kind of job Lee should have.

A student glided down the hall. A frame held his body upright between two large bicycle tires. He propelled himself by pushing forward on the wheels, the wide base of support compensating for high center of gravity. A surprising amount of engineering went into making these children's lives better.

The next room contained a computer. The speech therapist demonstrated a variety of switches and software. Trent played music, changed the pictures on the screen, and typed his name on an adaptive keyboard. Even Bryan seemed impressed. Caroline squeezed into the tiny room. She had debated buying a home computer for Trent. Perhaps it would be worth the investment.

Ms. Stainer directed the group into the empty cafeteria for a concluding interview.

Bryan launched into his specially tailored speech. "...advocate in the legislature for these," Bryan lifted Trent, "Massachusetts' special citizens..."

Trent twisted in the man's arms. Making eye contact with his mother, he waved his fist. *Toilet.*

Wait, Caroline signed, working her way through the traffic jam of campaign staff and school personnel. Trent signed again. The principal saw it and reached for the boy, but hesitated. The camera was still running. The third time he signed, several teachers recognized the motion. Whispers ricocheted through the group.

Bryan spit out a curse word and dropped Trent. Only the quick catch by the principal kept the boy's head from hitting the floor. Caroline forced her way to the front of the room. "Another suit ruined!" Bryan's face turned purple. "You did that on purpose, you little—"

"Bryan." Karanda grabbed his candidate by the shoulders. "The camera."

The principal hurried Trent out of the room.

"Caroline!" He screamed. She recognized his tone. He had lost it, completely lost it. Pulse racing, she jockeyed for position between the raging man and her son. *I'll stop him. I'll keep you safe.*

"Go!" she signed to the principal, still holding the boy. The woman looked up and down the hall, trying to decided where. "Run!"

Bryan twisted out of the campaign manager's grasp. Arms stretched in front of him, he came at Caroline like some B-movie Frankenstein. "You! You planned this! You ruin everything you touch! It's all your fault!" His hand closed around her neck. Her head hit the cinder block wall with a loud crack. Pain burst in her skull. Her fingers dug into his wrist bones. Instead of prying him loose, he tightened his grip. The world went black. Fighting for air, her straight hand swung at the place she guessed his nose would be. Nothing. His arms must be a foot longer than hers. Her head felt like it would explode. *Dear Jesus, help!* Through the roar in her head, Lee said, *A woman's strength is in her legs.* Desperate for air, she kicked. Contact! Bryan yowled. The hands left her neck. She gasped. Air, sweet air. She crumpled to the floor.

"Turn off those cameras!" Karanda yelled.

Caroline's vision cleared just as Bryan started crawling toward her. Trent thundered down the hall. His flying front kick landed on the man's ribs. Bryan shrieked and thudded to the floor. One of the school janitors grabbed her ex under the arms and dragged him toward the front door. The PE teacher led Trent in the other direction.

Ms. Stainer had the campaign manager in an head lock. "Shall I let him go?"

"Yeah," the camera man swung in her direction. "We've got the story."

"Please," Karanda sobbed. "You can't televise this. I'll... make a donation to the school, a sizable donation."

"The tour is over." The grim-faced principal took his arm. "The police are on their way. I'll escort you to the door."

A young woman with a ponytail knelt beside Caroline. "How many fingers am I holding up?"

"Two," she answered. "I'm okay." Thanks to God and Lee Marivaux.

"I'm the school nurse. I'm going to check the back of your head." She leaned Caroline forward and gently parted her hair. "You're going to have quite the bruise. Let's get some ice on that. Can you walk? My office is just around the corner."

Stepping in rhythm with the throbbing pain, Caroline wobbled down the hall. The PE teacher and Trent met her inside the door. She collapsed onto a cot.

"Ma! Ma!" He threw himself on her.

"Hi, sweetheart." Caroline returned his hug.

The older student dropped off a plate of cookies. "You okay? You scared? Me, too. Mom okay? Here Mom, have a cookie."

"Thank you," She accepted the soothing confection.

Gina stormed in, carrying the plastic bag with Trent's change of clothes. "Caroline! Are you all right?"

Nodding reignited the pain.

Gina plopped into a vinyl chair. Her fingers ran through her hair, destroying its salon perfection. After a few minutes staring at the ceiling, the young woman turned to Caroline. "Could you recommend a good divorce lawyer?"

Chapter Twenty-One

"D o you need another copy?" The flight attendant handed her Section A of the *Boston Globe*.

"Thank you." Caroline folded the paper into her purse. She had read the headlines this morning at Marnie's. "Candidate Announces Resignation." The still photos taken from videotape showed Bryan's Dr. Jekyll/Mr. Hyde transformation. They looked like something out of *The National Enquirer*, not the conservative *Globe*.

The flight attendant returned with pillows and blankets. She folded up the armrests on the seats across the aisle. "We're light this afternoon. If you'd like to stretch out..."

Caroline nodded her appreciation. Her injuries weren't serious, just uncomfortable. All this special attention. This morning a limo brought a trio of Lee's friends from the nearest *dojo*. The instructors had escorted her and Trent from Marnie's to the airport. They presented the boy with an honorary orange belt. Caroline settled her son with his music player, then curled up across the aisle.

Kansas City here I come...

Lee... What did Marnie say about his phone calls? "He refers to you as 'my Caroline'. I'd say his interest extends beyond your truck."

"Ladies and gentlemen, we're beginning our approach into Kansas City International..."

Caroline ran a brush through her hair, a mess after her nap. She made a sweep over Trent's head, fighting static electricity for control. Her hands shook when she reached for her purse. Too much stress, too little chocolate.

"Lee!" The boy dodged through the deplaning passengers. The big man pulled Trent into his arms. The child clung to his neck. Lee lifted his head, scanning the crowd until he found Caroline. She felt a physical jolt, like improper handling of battery cables. She couldn't look away, couldn't blink, couldn't even breathe. Greek god, Marnie had said, but Caroline thought he looked like an angel. Certainly his shoulders were wide enough for a heavy duty set of wings.

He shifted Trent to one arm and drew Caroline to him with the other. She closed her eyes and sank into his embrace.

Home. Safe.

He let Trent down. "Are you..." His voice sounded hoarse. His index finger slid under her jaw, tilting her head up. He tugged at the scarf Marnie had loaned her, parting the silk. His eyes blinked. A muscle twitched in his jaw. "My Caroline," he breathed. He pulled her close, both arms this time. A coarse vibration shook his frame. Caroline tightened her hold, dampening his shudders with her body.

Hold me forever.

"I should never have let you go without me," he whispered into her hair.

"I shouldn't have gone without you." If he didn't let her go soon, she'd kiss that place under the open buttons of his white henley.

"Not going to argue. Must be a concussion."

"Ma! Eat!" Trent pounded her on the leg.

Lee ran his hands down her ribs, gauging her weight. "Can you wait until we get home?" he asked the child. "I've got chicken marinating for the grill, corn on the cob, s'mores for dessert." Lee pulled away, leaving Caroline with an out-of-control feeling like her shocks had failed. "Are you dizzy? Do you need to sit down?" His hand braced the small of her back.

I just need you. "I'm fine," she smiled up into his worried dark brown eyes. "Let's go home."

THE CLOSER THE truck brought them to Liberty, the sweatier the steering wheel got. Lee wiped his palms on his jeans. Again. Earlier in the week, building a privacy fence around the patio seemed like a good idea. With the community college between semesters, he had too much time on his hands, time to worry about Caroline and Trent. He needed to pound something, preferably something constructive like nails into wood. His friend Dale had given him left-over slats and posts from one of those new mansions off Broadway. A fence would hold back the sun from fading Caroline's furniture, stop the wind from blowing out the fire in the grill. It might even give her a little protection from spying photographers sent by her snake of an ex. The roof part would keep the cement cool. Then yesterday, his hammering brought Sharon over. His reasons didn't seem quite so logical under her piercing gaze.

Lee glanced over at Caroline. Her hand, delicate and graceful, rested on Trent's leg. Don't touch, he told himself, tightening his hold on the clammy steering wheel. His little building project prob-ably overstepped his bounds. Well, if she didn't like it, he'd take it down. Sharon and Pete's kids could build a treehouse with it.

"It's so beautiful here. Pastoral. Clean."

"Naw. After Boston, Kansas City must look like the set of *Green Acres*." He sang the first four lines of the theme song. Trent reprised his conductor role from the ball game.

Caroline grinned. "That's exactly how I feel about Boston—keep it. I'm so glad to be home."

Lee parked the truck. Here goes nothing. Caroline and Trent went inside. He trailed behind with the suitcase.

"What's this?" She crossed the family room and opened the sliding glass door. "Lee?"

"Some fancy Italian word."

"Pergola." The setting sun glowed pink on Caroline's face. "Thank you. This is a wonderful surprise." She reached for him. For a split second Lee thought she intended to give him another one of her blood-rushing hugs. He braced, his self-control slipping worse than the steering wheel. Instead she touched the back of his wrist. "I've been wanting to make this patio habitable. I'd considered a trellis with some sort of vine, but that might attract bees. This is absolutely perfect."

"Glad you like it." Tonight when he was alone, he'd bask in her happiness. Now he caught Trent's attention. "Look." He lit the grill. "Hot. Fire. No touch." The boy nodded. "Wash your hands, then come eat."

"I should unpack."

"Change, too, get comfortable. Your clean clothes are on the dryer." He saw her stiffen. "You didn't want me to do laundry?"

"No, that's fine. Thank you."

After the week she'd been through, a little prickliness shouldn't surprise him. He'd have to watch what he said.

Lee set out a bowl of fruit and Trent's snack plate, fresh vegetables from Sharon's garden. The boy raced out the door, hands dripping. He stuffed his cheeks with cherry tomatoes, then put the fence to good use playing peekaboo through the slats.

Caroline joined them, wearing shorts that revealed more legs than her skirt had. *Keep an eye on the food.*

"What can I help with?"

Lee surveyed the table: silverware, plates, iced tea, napkins, citronella candle. "Nothing. Just take it easy."

She whirled back into the house. He shook his head. Did it again. Like walking through the swamp in the dark. Like sparring blindfolded.

Trent shoved an orange into his hand and signed *help.*

"For me? Thank you."

"No. My oh." *Help.*

"You want me to peel your orange. No."

Please? He tilted his head and drooped his bottom lip.

Lee eased himself into the lawn chair. "No, I won't peel it for you, but I will teach you how to peel it." He pulled the boy onto his lap, noticing how much he'd grown in the last month. "See this end?

It looks like a bellybutton." He tickled Trent's stomach, sending him into squirmy giggles. "Take your thumb and stick it into the orange's bellybutton."

The stubby finger poked the fruit. Lee grabbed the hand, frowning first at one thumb then the other. "Men don't chew their nails. We don't paint 'em, don't keep a whole lot of dirt under 'em, and we don't chew 'em." He picked up a spoon from the table. "Until yours grow out, use this." He helped Trent pry off the thick skin.

While he worked with the boy, Caroline slipped back to the patio. She gave the privacy fence and pergola an engineer's inspection, but the air around her vibrated with tension. *Don't fight it. I'll hold you while you cry. Don't mind at all.* But he figured, clumsy as he was, he'd better not say anything. At least until after dinner.

Lee made it through the meal without any noticeable blunders. Insisting she clean up, Caroline carried the dishes inside. Gathering Trent, he moved over to the lounge chair. "Tell me about your trip."

The boy began a long involved story. Lee recognized a few signs and words: airplane, talk, ball, school. Wiggling down, the *karateka* demonstrated the kick he'd used on his father.

"You used karate to help your mom. Good. Don't kick other people unless they are hurting Mom. Don't kick kids at school. Don't kick kids at Sharon's."

Trent looked hurt, puzzled. He'd been expecting praise. But if praise was all he got, the boy might think fighting was the solution for every problem. "Good job, Trent. You did the right thing, helped Mom. I'm proud of you." Lee pulled Trent back onto his lap. The boy curled up with his head on Lee's shoulder. "*Do-do.* Say your prayers and I'll take you up to bed." Trent mumbled sleepily through his requests, mentioning a couple new names, maybe people in Boston. The crickets sang their quiet chorus. Temperatures dropped into a zone where holding a warm little boy body felt comfortable. Trent went limp. His breathing slowed. Overhead the stars came awake and the moon peeked over the roof.

Caroline stepped out onto the patio. Lee watched for stress. He saw more caution than anger in her hesitation.

"Join us." Lee pulled a lawn chair closer.

"Is Trent asleep? I'll take him upstairs."

"No rush. I've missed him."

Caroline perched on the edge of the seat. He wished he'd moved the chair to his other side so he could see more than her profile. She cleared her throat. "Won't that spoil him? Holding him while he goes to sleep?"

"Not unless it's the only way he can fall asleep." Sometimes victory in a karate meet hinged on a surprise maneuver, taking a risk. "Bet Bryan gave you that advice."

"His mother."

"Bet she thought you should put him on formula, quit nursing him."

He earned a quick glare, more shock than anger. "How did you know?"

"No pictures of baby Trent dragging on a bottle. He's got straight teeth." Lee looked her in the eye. "Caroline, you always choose the best for your son."

"What about all your criticism, like..." She scooped her hand in the air, trying to pull in a stray memory. "...like the clothes I buy?"

"Sometimes we disagree on what's best. For you, Trent's got to look sharp. For me, he's got to get dressed by himself." He wanted to stroke Caroline's hair, to smooth out all her rough feelings. Instead he worked on Trent's flyaways. "We had a talk about what happened. He's handling it. Not pulled apart like kids at the shelter who've seen their mom and dad fight."

"Thank you." She watched Trent a few minutes. The light from the full moon outlined her in silver. "We Jamesons seem to have a bad habit of falling asleep on you."

"A gift." He reached for the back of her neck, finding a line of hot tension spots. "It's a gift of trust from you both to me."

"Lee..." She tried to move away from him.

He pressed her shoulder, keeping her in the lawn chair. "Let me give you this. I wasn't there to stop Bryan, but maybe I can stop the hurt. Some of it anyway."

She stayed quiet for a minute, then, "How's that song go, something about 'it's good to be back home again'."

"Yeah. Johnny Cash, John Denver, someone." Humming a few bars, he circled his fingertips into the knots around her shoulder blades. Still on guard, this woman. But too tired and too late tonight to run her by the gym so she can beat up the punching bag. What worked before, at the hospital and that night she came home from working too hard? Ah..."Yeah, it's good to be home," he started in a quiet voice. "You made a fine home here. Safe place to raise your son, quiet, neighbors watch out for each other." *Mais*, yeah, there she goes. He stroked down her spine. Just keep talking. "Life is good. Maybe I'm the worst poverty case you've ever met, but, man, I feel rich. I can hold this little boy in my lap while he falls asleep. I can enjoy the night stars. I've got friends like you, and Pete and Sharon, to pass a good time with. Don't have to worry about getting bit by a gator." He wiggled his bare toes.

"The guys I went to high school with..." he continued, low and quiet. "Lost some to accidents, driving through the swamp after a night of moonshining, falling off an oil rig. Couple of them disappeared to keep from paying child support. Half dozen or so still living with their mom or grandma, pooling welfare and social security checks to buy smokes." Naw, that sounded awful grim. "Mostlikely-to-succeed's got the world's largest collection of Styrofoam peanuts: pink ones, green ones, and, of course, classic white." A small laugh rippled under his hand, like a slow current under a pirogue. He rolled his fingers up her vertebrae, enjoying the silk of her hair on the back of his hand. "Life is good, real good."

"Be careful. There's a bruise where I hit my head against the wall."

"Where Bryan hit your head against the wall," Lee corrected. "Nightmare of a vacation."

She turned toward him, her earlobe soft against the pad of his thumb. "My vacation is having you around. Everything goes better with you. We eat healthier. The house is cleaner. Trent..."

"*Mais*, yeah, he walks the straight and narrow whenever there's an extra pair of eyes watching."

"Not just any pair of eyes. When my parents are here, with Mother's arthritis... How can I explain this?" She paused for a moment and he resumed slow stroking the back of her neck. "With my parents and Bryan, I had to be the shock absorber—justifying, apologizing for Trent's behavior. But I don't have to worry about you. You take care of yourself. You take care of me."

He gulped a deep breath, hoping for the right words before he could chicken out. *God hath not given us a spirit of fear.* "Caroline, do you suppose, I mean, if you ever—"

The phone rang. She jumped up.

Lee groaned. "Guess it's time to call it a night." He levered himself out of the lounge chair. Ought to make heavy duty models for big guys, he thought. The fabric sagged, almost touching the ground. Carrying Trent on his shoulder, Lee followed Caroline into the house. Passing through the main level, he overheard her conversation.

"I didn't... Bryan, you've been drinking."

Lee signed *no*, but she ignored him. Moving as fast as he could without waking the boy, he set him in bed and closed the door. He jumped down the stairs, his loud thud startling Caroline into looking at him.

Stop talking, he signed with fast, angry chops.

"But Bryan, you..."

Give me phone! Now! Lee loomed over her. She retreated into the corner of the kitchen. He followed, reaching for the handset. The expression that intimidated hundreds of disobedient students formed on his face. She dropped the phone into his hand.

"Ashcroft," Lee growled.

"Lover-boy? Sh-still hanging around waiting for the iche prinshesh to thaw. Better be shoon. I'm coming to get her, finice her off."

Not if I get to you first. "Where are you?"

He belched. "Not telling."

"You listen real good," Lee lowered his voice, "I'll tell you a secret."

"About Caroline?"

"Yeah. This time you beat up on Caroline, you lost the election. The time before, you lost your son."

"Not mush of a shon."

I'm going to crush every bone in your sorry carcass. "The next time, you're going to lose again. You don't want to spend the rest of your life in prison. Get some help." A tremor spread from Lee's phone arm through the rest of his body. He hung up.

Peace. Nogare breathing.

I'm going to rip him to shreds.

Again. Don't let anger control you. Peace.

He slouched, trying to make himself look less threatening, then faced Caroline. With effort, his voice stayed quiet, just above a whisper. "Didn't mean to scare you."

She leaned against the cabinets, hands resting behind her on the counter. "I know you won't hurt me."

It took a moment for her words to sneak into his thick skull. "*Mais,* yeah. About time," he said softly. He allowed himself a quick grin. "Arguing with a drunk is like trying to teach a gator the two-step. Did he say where he was?"

She shook her head.

"He's probably too sloshed to come after you, even if he was next door. I didn't hear any background noise: that rules out a bar."

"And his jet." She stepped toward him. "He doesn't get drunk in public. He's home."

"What's the number?"

Caroline scrolled through her cellphone to Bryan's number. Lee hit the call button.

"Busy signal. Do you have a picture of him?"

She flipped open the paper, today's *Boston Globe*. His mouth went dry. Front page, center. A man gone around the bend. His face twisted with rage. His hand on Caroline's neck. More pictures. Scowling at Trent. Being dragged out by the police. Mouth wide like he's yelling. Lee closed his eyes.

Focus. Breathe.

"You may want to keep this, in case he brings up custody again."

"I have another copy."

"They let him run around loose..." Shaking his head, Lee punched in the number of Liberty's police department. "Hey, Christy. Lee Marivaux here. Max working tonight?"

The dispatcher grunted. "If you call hanging out at Perkins Restaurant work."

He gave her Caroline's address. "I'll be out front. Thanks." He hung up the phone. His gaze caught on the photo of Caroline being strangled. "Oh, man, I should've been there for you."

"It was like you were there." She turned to the back page, the continuation of the article and another photo. "I could hear you coaching me. I felt God's peace."

He studied Caroline's kick. "Wow. Good form. Nice elevation. His Terribleness won't be using that leg for a while." *My very own superwoman. Wait... Mine?* "You go on, get some sleep. I'll lock up."

She reached across him to off the phone's ringer. Some soft woman-part brushed against his arm. "I wish you'd stay."

"I'll be close." Lee nodded in the direction of Buffum's house. "I'll keep you safe."

She paused, one foot on the first step. "That's what I promised Trent. Lee... thank you."

Chapter Twenty-Two

"Ma! Ma!" Trent jumped on the bed. Caroline moaned and rolled over. This was her last day to sleep in, and she intended to stay in bed until at least six. "Ssh. Mom's asleep."

"Ma! Ma!" Small fingers, sticky and smelling of fresh oranges, patted her cheek. "Lee!" He pointed toward the back of the house.

Caroline shot to her feet. The boy scampered to his bedroom window and pointed down to the patio.

The man slept stretched out on the chaise lounge. His feet hung off the end from beneath his forest green sleeping bag.

"That looks uncomfortable." Caroline hurried to her room, and slipped into the shorts and T-shirt from the night before. Trent raced through the house. He tried the sliding glass door, but couldn't dislodge the security bar. With a whoop, he dashed out the front door.

"Well, let's just wake up the whole neighborhood." Caroline slipped into her sandals. On the way downstairs, she paused to pour herself a Diet Coke and turn on the phone's ringer. The answering machine light glowed red, no messages. She joined the two guys on the patio.

Lee knelt on the concrete, teaching Trent how to roll up a sleeping bag. "Good morning. Any more phone calls?"

"All's quiet." She perched on a lawn chair, watching the ripple of thigh muscles below the man's sky blue running shorts. The back seam had been repaired with X's of green thread, emphasizing the curves of his buttocks. She pressed the cold glass to her face. "Sharon throw you out?"

"I most certainly did not!" Sharon Buffum stomped around the corner of the house. One hand on her hip, she waved a zucchini. "I have tried to be patient and stay out of your business, but this has gone on long enough." She frowned at Caroline. "Just how hard did you hit your head that you're letting this man sleep out here? Trent, go get your church clothes. You're coming to my house for pancakes."

"Pancakes?" Lee stood.

"Not you. In fact, get on in the house, both of you."

"Your teacher hat is showing," Lee told the sitter as she chased them into the kitchen.

"Then you better have your student hat on, because today's lesson is about to begin." She directed them to chairs at either end of the table and sat between them. Lee set out bowls and cereal. "We're waiting on you, Mr. Marivaux." He swatted her with the Raisin Bran box. She parried the blow with a thrust of the zucchini. "I'm going to take Trent to church with us. You two are staying here. When I get back, I want to see some progress in this relationship."

"What relationship?" Caroline asked. "We're just friends."

"You know I don't date." Lee poured a glass of milk for Caroline.

"I'm not talking about..." Sharon growled with frustration. "What is the purpose of dating?"

"Do I have to raise my hand?" Lee asked.

"No, you don't. This is home school." Sharon crossed her arms. "Do you know the answer or are you stalling for time?"

He sat up straight in the chair, hands folded in front of him. "The purpose of dating is to get to know someone."

"You know each other pretty well, wouldn't you say?"

"He does my laundry," Caroline volunteered.

"I know where she hides her M&M's," Lee added. "She knows when my oil needs changing."

"This morning, you need to talk about what you don't know." Sharon grabbed a memo pad from the counter by the phone. "You can't talk about Trent."

"But I wanted to ask if Lee would attend his IEP."

He looked up from his cereal. "Just tell me when."

"No Trent and no truck," Sharon wrote.

"No truck? But I wanted to ask Caroline about the new one she's ordering."

Caroline raised her eyebrows at the man across the table. "I suppose you want to pick out the color."

He laughed, choking on his cereal.

Sharon gaveled the zucchini on the table. "Let's get serious here."

"Sounds like it bothers her..." Caroline began.

"More than it bothers us," Lee finished with a laugh. "Sorry. We can't talk about Trent and trucks, because they begin with T?"

"No, because Caroline thinks those two things are the only reason you hang out here."

"She does?" Brown eyes turned back to her.

Caroline studied the fluid dynamics of the milk in her cereal bowl. "The kitchen, too."

"And if I were a gambler," the zucchini waved in time with her words, "I'd bet she hasn't told you how she really feels about you. So, that's what you need to talk about." Sharon wrote "relationship" on the paper.

"How you really feel about me..." The big man leaned back in his chair. Caroline crushed the flakes into smaller and smaller pieces. She couldn't eat while he stared at her.

"Wait until Trent and I leave." Sharon glanced from Caroline to Lee. "Get out the chocolate if she gives you any trouble. Always works for me."

He craned his neck to see the next word. His large hand dropped over the memo pad. "Can't."

"What?" Caroline gave up on breakfast. She slid the memo pad from under Sharon's hand. "Wedding? You want us to talk about getting married? But he won't even move in with me."

"And do you know why? No. You need to ask him, find out what needs to happen before he moves in. And you," she swung the zucchini on the man. "You're always testifying about God providing for your needs. He's trying to provide you with a family and you don't see it. Pay attention!" Sharon thundered up to Trent's room. "Can't find your slacks? I bet Luke and Paul have something you can wear." She came down with the pajama-clad boy in tow. "Set a wedding date by the time we get back from church, or else."

"Or else, what?" Lee called after her.

"I'll pack that Volkswagen of yours with zucchini."

The front door slammed. Lee put the breakfast dishes into the dishwasher. "Can I fix you something else? Omelet? Biscuits and gravy?"

"No, thank you. I'm not hungry."

Their voices echoed in the empty house. Lee tromped downstairs. Caroline rubbed her queasy middle. Well, that's the way he wants to deal with this mess. They were supposed to talk, so he disappears. Hopeless. Not that she had anything as respectable as marriage in mind anyway. Marriage? Why did Sharon have to bring that up? That kind of talk could ruin a decent friendship. It's a wonder Lee hadn't gone full throttled out of here already. Intending to roll their "relationship" back, Caroline started down the stairs. The big man lay on the floor, knees bent, eyes closed. He looked up when the bottom step creaked.

"You couldn't have been comfortable last night."

"My back's a little stiff, yeah." He stretched. "I was praying."

"Did you get an answer?"

"Not yet." He patted the cushion of the couch. "I'd like to ask you about something."

Caroline didn't want to be near him, but taking the recliner seemed rude. She sat as far away as possible, folding her legs beneath her.

"What is Sharon talking about, how you feel about me?"

She felt her face grow warm. "I'd rather not say."

Lee propped his hands behind his head. "Sounds bad. When did you and Sharon have this conversation?"

"The day you borrowed the truck to move Rapunzel."

"Who?" He frowned, then gave a slow blink of recollection. "Oh, yeah. All that work hauling her junk around, what does she do but goes back to her husband. I called their minister, asked her to do some counseling. Hope it works out for them."

"If she hadn't gone back to him, would you be with her now?"

A vertical line appeared between his eyebrows. "No. Why would you think that?"

"She's feminine. I know you like long hair, and the dress. I must look like a bum, an old shop rat." She dropped her chin into her palm.

"I understand why you keep your hair short. After all the sleepless nights I've had over you, the last thing I need is to worry about your hair getting caught in some machine." He rolled into sitting and touched a strand, letting it slide down his finger. "Caroline, even if you were bald, you'd be the classiest lady I've ever met."

The phone rang.

Lee levered her to her feet. "That's your dad."

"He never calls." She ran upstairs and picked up the phone. "Hello?"

"Caroline. You're back from Boston."

She leaned down the stairway to give Lee a puzzled look. "Father?"

"Are you and Trent all right? The Sunday paper has a picture of Bryan..."

"The school nurse checked us over. We're fine."

"Honey, I hate to second-guess you, but why didn't you take Lee with you?"

"Lee?"

The man in question braced his wide shoulder against the frame of the sliding glass door, looking out over the backyard.

"Yes. Every father wants his little girl taken care of. I don't want you to pinch pennies, sweat mortgage payments. Your mother and I thought you had financial security with Bryan. We should have looked at the man's priorities."

"Priorities?"

"Yes. Lee puts God ahead of money and power. That's real security. Ask your lawyer, Wilson-whatever..."

"Wilson-deGrazia."

"Ask Wilson-deGrazia if she can get Bryan to relinquish parental rights. Get him out of your life. Then Lee can adopt Trent."

"Father, are you all right? Are you talking about..."

"Much better, now that I know you're safe." He rattled the paper. "Well, maybe there is justice in this world. Says here Bryan's bail was revoked late last night, on a complaint from his second wife. Oops, there's Mother back with the bagels. I've got to hide the paper. We'll talk later."

Hands shaking, Caroline refilled her Diet Coke, then wandered back to her spot. "If you were praying about Bryan, he's back in custody."

Lee nodded.

"How did you know my father would call?"

"Answered prayer." Turning from the window, he rubbed the corner of his eye with a knuckle. "When they visited, I could tell your dad wasn't impressed with my finances."

"He wants you to adopt Trent." She traced the diamond pattern of the upholstery, afraid to look at him. "He hung up before I could tell him you want kids of your own, normal kids."

He reached over the sofa, hooking his index finger around hers. "First of all, I'd be proud to call Trent my son." He captured her middle finger. "Second, odds of your having another baby with Down's are about the same as anyone else's." They linked ring fingers. "Third, with babies you've got to take what you get: boy, girl, handicapped, healthy. There's lots of things worse than Down's. Anyone who's not prepared to take that risk, to love whatever child they're given, isn't ready to be a parent." He snagged her pinkie. "Much as I'd like to have a big family, I don't know if I can ask that of you. Your job is so tough, the long hours, the heat."

"I could put in for light duty, take a leave of absence," she said, spellbound by the growing softness of his expression. "We'd need an extended cab..." Finally hearing her own words, she jerked her hand from his. "Wait a minute. Are you okay with me making more than you?"

Lee stood and paced the room. "Well, like Bernie pointed out, it'd be hard to find a woman who makes less than me. All those big decisions: shall we live in your car or mine?" he asked an imaginary penniless wife.

"And your family? Your sister canceled our plans for the Jesse James play and the Spirit Fest. She had me dress up for that car salesman."

"Naw," Lee chuckled. "That was all for my benefit. She knew exactly what would get my attention." He raised his arms, palms against the ceiling, to stretch. "Ever since Fourth of July, she's been fussing about you. All this 'plan stuff then get sick', is her way of throwing us together, making us go out." He shook out his arms, rolling his broad shoulders. "She made a good point the last time I was down there: I'm no dumb-as-dirt redneck. You're not some stuck up debutante. Maybe somehow in leaving Massachusetts and Louisiana, we've found a middle ground here in Kansas City. Well, the way she said it made sense."

"No, I understand. We've both changed."

"Louis said something about chemicals reacting only in certain environments. I should have him explain it—too profound for me." He waved his hand over his head.

"A chemical reaction." Caroline nodded.

"These feelings about me..." He sat cross-legged on the carpet in front of her. His brown eyes seemed to hypnotize, to hold her in place. "Sick to your stomach, claustrophobic, positive, negative, what?"

"No, they're positive, I guess. A shock to Sharon, though." She stripped the Coke glass of its condensation, then touched her cold, wet finger to her neck.

"Marnie said she'd never heard you talk about other men the way you talk about me. Physical or mental?"

She rolled the glass between the insides of her wrists. "Physical. Hormones, I think. Because I haven't..." she swallowed, "...been with a man since before Trent was born."

"Caroline Jameson has the hots for me?" A smile grew behind the thumb circling his mustache. "You're sitting here giving yourself a cold shower."

Heat rising in her face again, she set the glass on the end table and tucked her hands under her knees. "This will kill our friendship. Sharon shouldn't have brought it up. She said you don't reciprocate."

"I don't know where Sharon gets that idea, but she's wrong. Way wrong." He leaned his wide forehead into the palm of his hand. "I thought karate had taught me everything there was to know about self-control, but I have to fight to keep my hands off you. That night, July downtime, when I carried you up to bed, you don't know how close I came to joining you."

"I wouldn't have objected," she whispered, hoping he didn't shock easily.

"You were just this side of comatose. Your father would have killed me when he got back. Talk about justifiable homicide." He tilted his head close, forcing her to look at him. "I don't do one night stands."

"You're welcome to stay as long as you want."

"You'd rather shack up than get married? So you can throw me out when I drip boudin grease on the carpet?"

"No, I'd never... You wouldn't..." She ran her fingernail along the cushion's seam. "I didn't think anyone would want to marry me. I have a handicapped child."

"Who needs to know the people in his life are in for the long haul. You, too." He slid his hand around hers. "God knows I couldn't handle leaving you. Caroline, when I take you to bed, it's permanent, forever, married. I want you wide awake. Maybe wearing that lacy nightgown."

A fine vibration hummed through her frame. "If you'll wear your silk *gi*."

His jaw dropped. "That was months ago. You were so flustered, I thought Chevy'd announced they're making six-pack coolers standard equipment."

A spike of common sense pierced her inflated libido. "This is totally illogical." She shifted away from him, leaning her cheek on the back of the sofa. "I can't think straight around you. Doesn't it take more than physical desire to make a marriage?"

He nodded. "Let's see: respect, admiration, happiness, love..."

"What does love feel like?" *Please let this be love.*

"It's like... thinking about the other person all the time, no matter what you're doing. Is she okay? What's she doing now? When she hurts, I hurt, too. I want to build fences around her," he waved toward the patio, "to keep her safe. I want to make her life easier."

"Fill all the potholes to make his road smooth."

"Thanks for the wiper blades."

Caroline watched his jaw clench around the words, "you shouldn't have," to which she would answer, "Yes, I should have, months ago." Instead she said, "You're welcome."

Her insides felt like they were being power wrenched. She pressed her middle to dampen the oscillation. "Lee, you're counting on Trent someday getting a job and moving out. But what if he doesn't? Some kids with Down's develop Alzheimer's or heart trouble. What if he never moves out?"

"Then we'll deal with it. Just like other parents deal with car accidents, drug abuse, teenage pregnancies. I'll help you keep him healthy, keep him out of trouble. I'll stick by you, no matter what. That's the 'for better or worse' part of the deal."

Her eyes closed against the hope. "I thought I'd be alone, raise Trent alone, the rest of my life." She peeked at him. "Lee, are you sure?"

"Sure about what? Sure that I'd like to have a roof over my head, food on a regular basis. Sure that I'm ready to have a family, go to IEPs and PTAs and Cub Scouts. Sure that I love you. Yeah." He rubbed his palm across his chin stubble. "I'll shave. I'll make your breakfast, pack your lunch, get Trent ready for school. Maybe he'll do better if he gets a little more sleep in the morning. I can start a load of laundry before I go to work, fix dinner before my evening classes..."

Caroline touched her fingertips to his forearm. "Lee, stop. This isn't one of your trades. Just be yourself. that's more than enough, more than I ever imagined." A tear formed at the corner of her eye. Before she could find a tissue, Lee caught it on the tip of his calloused finger. All her important thoughts skittered away like ball bearings on the loose. Caroline pressed her hands together and took a deep breath. "Last night you said I had given you a gift of trust. Yes, I trust you'll never hurt me or Trent. Lee, please trust me about money. I'll never use it against you."

"You want me to change my name to Mr. Jameson?"

Seeing the struggle in his face, she slid her fingers into his palm. "If you're going to adopt Trent, would you mind if I took your name, too?"

"*Ca c'est bon,*" he murmured, worry wrinkles curving into smile lines.

"And your work. It's a waste of your time, your gift, to do anything other than teach karate."

"No more house-sitting, that's for sure." His slow grin sent her heart pulsing like an anti-lock braking system. "I'd like to know what else has been going on in your head."

"I have been thinking about one of the self-defense moves you showed me."

"Does this have something to do with our assignment?"

She nodded. "Lie down again."

"Be gentle with me."

"Always." She sat next to him and pinned his wrists to the floor.

"And your question?"

"Is your mustache as soft as it looks?" She leaned over, running her tongue over his fringed upper lip. Better than chocolate...

Lee groaned. He slipped out of her grip. One hand on her shoulder, the other on her waist, he rolled her across his chest onto the carpet. His lips pinned her down. High octane. The ignition of a thousand spark plugs. Zero to sixty in 3.2.

With a gasp, he pulled away, flopping onto his back.

"I have another question."

He moaned. "No more questions."

"If you can reach the minister by phone, can we get married right now?"

"We need a license." He rose up on one elbow. "You're saying yes, you'll marry me?"

"If you promise to kiss me like that every day for the rest of your life."

He grinned. "You're going to blow away the stereotype of engineers having no passion. Maybe you're really Cajun. Maybe some Acadian stopped by New England on his way to Louisiana." Keeping an eye on her, he sat up. "Oh man, this is dangerous, being alone with you."

She nodded. "We should do it more often."

"After we're married." His face glowed transmission fluid pink. "Let's grab Trent and go celebrate."

"After a cold shower." She flapped the lower edge of her T-shirt. "Have you ever been to Stroud's? Their chicken, cinnamon rolls..."

Lee reached for his wallet. "Maybe a picnic, since it's so nice out."

Beyond the sliding glass door, heat waves shimmered across the backyard.

Caroline slid her hand into his. "Lee, no more 'mine' and 'yours'. Everything, the money, the house, the truck, Trent, has to be 'ours'."

Lee rubbed his mustache with his thumb and index finger, studying her through half-opened eyes. "Hurry and take your shower before I decide that's 'ours' just now."

WAITING for a break in the traffic, Lee glanced at the woman seated on the passenger side of the truck. His Caroline. "So much to talk about."

"Hopefully not china and silver patterns."

"Naw. I eat with my fingers."

Caroline snapped the air conditioner to high.

"Red in the face, like that night at the playground. What are you thinking about?" The front right tire slipped off onto the shoulder.

Lee yanked the pickup back into the lane. "No, don't tell me when I'm driving. After we're married."

"And alone."

"*Laissez les bon temps roulez*," he breathed and pulled onto the highway leading into Kansas City. "We have to talk about... Oh, yeah, holidays. Halloween? You want to give out candy or walk Trent around?"

"You can take him trick-or-treating. You know the neighbors better."

"Then you can eat all the chocolate."

"That's my plan." She grinned.

And his plan was to get her happy like this every day. "Now, Thanksgiving. Bet you've never had your turkey deep-fried, then blackened on the grill."

"At Bernadette's? Sounds great. What will she want me to bring?"

"We'll bring dessert. You can shingle roofs with Bernie's pie crust. Although she does a nice pumpkin pone." He moved into the left lane to pass a yellow Dodge. "Christmas?"

"I usually have to work. Mother and Father do all the baking and decorating."

"The tree, natural or fake?"

"I have an artificial one in the basement."

"Mind if Trent and I cut one? Seems like a waste to own a truck and not use it to drag home a real Christmas tree."

"He'd like that."

Lee took the North Oak Street exit. "New Years?"

"I'm still cleaning up from Christmas."

"That's gotta change. Big party time for Cajuns. Crank up some Beausoleil, Buckwheat Zydeco. Neville Brothers for the slow songs."

"Do you mean have people over?"

He shook his head. "Just you and me. Dancing on the, probably be too cold on the patio, in the family room." He turned into the church lot, parked in the fire lane, then jogged around to open the door for Caroline. She wore a knee-length dress, some clingy dark blue material with little white flowers, and sandals with narrow straps. How could she think she wasn't feminine? No comparison. Rapunzel would flip her wig. "Celebrate on through Mardi Gras, you and me."

"Don't look at me like that. You're making me overheat."

"I have to stare. You are..." His chest tightened, making his voice come out in a whisper. "...more than I ever imagined, my Caroline."

Her mouth turned in a little smile, the kind of smile that made Lee think about kissing. "When I asked, prayed, for help, I had a vague idea about a foster grandmother, the fairy godmother from Disney's Cinderella."

He chuckled. "Got the white hair right." He lifted her hand to his lips. She slipped out of his grasp, running her fingers along his jaw, behind his ear. His scalp and several other body parts tingled. Any moment the congregation would march out and find them doing something that shouldn't be done in public, especially not in a church parking lot. He took her hand and steered her into the building.

"*Chère*, I wish I had something to give you. A ring. But I have nothing."

"Nothing but love. And that's more than I've ever had."

"Is this real?" he asked. "Can I tell people?"

"If anyone's interested."

"I figure Sharon and Pete..."

The sanctuary doors had been left open. The minister began the altar call. "With every eye closed and every head bowed..." He stopped. His collar microphone picked up the whispered comment to Sharon, "They're holding hands. I'd say that's a good sign."

The congregation turned in the pews. Lee's face burned. Caroline's hand squirmed in his.

Sharon stood up. "Have you completed your assignment?"

"Yes, ma'am." Lee pulled Caroline into the sanctuary.

"And?"

"She said yes!"

The congregation erupted in cheers. The organist belted out a hockey rink version of the "Hallelujah Chorus."

"Well, get on up here. This is an altar call for the record books."

Lee tucked Caroline in closer. They pushed through the crowd of well wishers.

Sharon plopped a large appointment book on the lectern.

"Sister Buffum, did you break into my office?"

"No, Pastor. You left your door unlocked." Sharon turned to the couple, giving them a wink and a grin. "What date did you decide?"

"Valentine's Day is open," the pastor suggested.

"That's six months away. I can't wait that long."

The pastor's microphone picked up Caroline's response. Giggles broke out in the congregation.

No wait, Lee signed.

"Darn right you can't wait." Sharon snatched back the appointment book. "He'll freeze to death on her patio. Not to mention what his sleeping bag smells like when it rains." More giggles and whispers. "What time do you get done with work Saturday?"

"Four." His mustache brushed the crest of Caroline's ear. "Saturday. Will that give you enough time to plan, to get your folks and Marnie out here?"

She murmured, "That's six days away. I don't know if I can wait that long."

He gave into impulse and blew a kiss into her ear. "*Mi aime jou.*"

Sharon grabbed the pastor's pen, ignoring her lovestruck neighbor's mumbling. "Schedule the wedding for five on Saturday, then. It won't take you long to shower and get dressed."

"I don't own a suit."

"That's all right. I don't have a white dress." Caroline leaned her cheek against his shoulder.

"You can wear the dress you've got on. Lee, you can borrow one of Pete's suits."

A hearty guffaw erupted in the back pews. Lee flinched, knowing they were imagining him trying to squeeze into bean-pole Pete's clothes.

An extra-large man in the third row, left, lumbered to his feet. The tips of his handlebar mustache twitched with nervousness. "Lee."

"Yes, Eldon."

"I've got a suit."

"Eldon, I don't believe I've ever seen you in anything but jeans and a Harley T-shirt." Today he wore the latest Sturgis Rally commemorative.

The man fidgeted with the chain running from his belt to his back pocket. "Mama made me buy a suit when she got married last summer. White shirt and fancy tie, too. I don't recollect the size, but you're welcome to it."

"He wears size 38 Fruit of the Looms," volunteered his wife, a candidate for *Truckin'* magazine cover girl.

"Stacy!" Groaning, Eldon collapsed into the pew.

"I'm sure it will do just fine," Lee said, trying not to laugh.

A woman on the right stood. "Caroline could wear my wedding dress."

"I don't think so, Laura, she looks smaller than you." This from a woman way in the back. "More my size."

"Well, I was slim before I had kids."

A third woman entered the fray. "My dress says ten, but it's really a twelve."

Caroline tugged on Lee's arm. "I shouldn't be wearing white."

He circled his flat hand over his heart. *Please.*

Sharon whistled over the erupting discussion. "My house, today, one-thirty, everyone with dresses and veils for a try-on party. I've got sewing supplies, so don't worry if you need repairs." She noted the time on the appointment book. "Let's move along. Reception to follow. Last names A through K, main dish. L through Z, side dish."

"What about dessert?" someone yelled from the back.

"Wedding cake. I'm making it. Chocolate." She winked at Caroline. "Set up for the reception and decorating the church, three-thirty. Everyone who has a garden, and I know who you are, brings flowers. Photographer?"

Three people raised hands.

"See the pastor for instructions. Organist?"

The first four bars of Lohengrin's "Wedding March" blared double time over the speakers.

"Kenny, I sure hope you come up with something better than that. Call..." Lee flashed a look at Caroline, then back to the man with the coke bottle glasses. "Call my fiancée for some suggestions. She's a piano player."

One of the ushers strode to the front of the church. He pulled a jam-packed key ring from his suit pocket. "All those times you escorted me and my couriers through the airport..." He sorted through the sizers until one fit Lee's ring finger. "Finally, I can express my appreciation." He turned to Caroline. "Hmn, nice hands. Have you considered a career in watch repair?"

"Good guess, Jim. Those hands build America's finest pickup trucks." Lee grinned, enjoying the surprise rippling through the congregation.

Sharon cleared her throat. "Premarital counseling. This is going to be tough to schedule, Pastor. Caroline gets off work at three-thirty. What time are your evening classes, Lee?"

"Six, except Friday."

"Four to five at Caroline's, then. I'll watch Trent." She turned to the pastor. "Start with money."

He grabbed the appointment book. "Thank you, Sister Buffum. May I schedule the rest of the sessions as I deem necessary?"

She shrugged. "You're the pastor."

He checked his watch. "Until the nursery staff get ahold of me. Please stand for the benediction. May the love of God, which we have seen here today," he smiled at the couple, "strengthen us to complete the work which we have been assigned."

The organist pounded out the chorus of "Victory in Jesus."

Lee started to turn down the aisle, but he felt a hand over his pounding heart. Caroline's eyes shone. He took her wrist, raising her hand so he could kiss it. The middle and ring fingers bent, the thumb and other fingers stayed straight.

I love you.

Acknowledgments

With thanks to Nebraska Novelists critique group, especially Katherine Barnett and Angela Kroeger, Ami and Ellee for the TLC and carriage house, and Josephine Flahive and Shari Hubble for research.

Also by Catherine Richmond

Spring for Susannah

Through Rushing Water

Gilding the Waters

Off the Ground

Two Hearts One Piano

The Shelter of Each Other

I love to hear from readers! Please write to me through my website CatherineRichmond.com or Facebook.com/CatherineRichmondFans.

If you enjoyed *Third Strand of the Cord*, a review would help other readers find this book. Thank you so much - I'll celebrate with chocolate!